WAR RI

BATT

Transmitted by . . .

Katherine Kurtz
BATTLE OFFERING

Decimated by genocide, no race could have sacrificed more for the Alliance.
Or could they?

David Drake
FAILURE MODE

All the battle cruisers in the galaxy can't match the lethal power
of this newest—and most ancient—weapon . . .

Christopher Stasheff
HEARING

A space refugee's peacetime defect is a deadly asset in war and espionage . . .

Esther M. Friesner
YOU CAN'T MAKE AN OMELET

This recipe for revenge may not be appetizing to Fleet command—
but it is food for thought!

AND MANY OTHERS!

Ace Books Edited by David Drake and Bill Fawcett

THE FLEET
THE FLEET: COUNTERATTACK
THE FLEET: BREAKTHROUGH
THE FLEET: SWORN ALLIES
THE FLEET: TOTAL WAR
THE FLEET: CRISIS

BATTLESTATION
BATTLESTATION: VANGUARD

BATTLESTATION

BOOK TWO

VANGUARD

EDITED BY **DAVID DRAKE** AND **BILL FAWCETT**

ACE BOOKS, NEW YORK

This book is an Ace original edition,
and has never been previously published.

BATTLESTATION: VANGUARD

An Ace Book / published by arrangement with
Bill Fawcett & Associates

PRINTING HISTORY
Ace edition / March 1993

ISBN: 0-441-86032-X

Ace Books are published by The Berkley Publishing Group,
200 Madison Avenue, New York, NY 10016.
The name "ACE" and the "A" logo
are trademarks belonging to Charter Communications, Inc.

PRINTED IN THE UNITED STATES OF AMERICA

10 9 8 7 6 5 4 3 2 1

Dedicated with thanks to
Jim Baen
who used to work with the Fleet,
and our newest crewperson, Katherine

CONTENTS

PROLOGUE

FLEET BATTLESTATION *Stephen Hawking* had been in action close to three years, fighting a lonely battle against the predatory Ichtons. It had lost nearly half the warships assigned to it—destroyed or too badly damaged to carry on the fight. Morale had taken a severe blow right at the start, when the battlestation had arrived only a few weeks too late to prevent the annihilation of one of the races they were supporting. Then, the allies' defeat in the Battle of Gerson, and the subsequent loss of the Gerson home world, had shown them just how overwhelming the task ahead of *Hawking* was.

Fleeing from Gerson and gathering her resources, the *Hawking* prowled between the stars, avoiding contact with the major Ichton fleets. The damage inflicted in the Battle of Gerson had made it clear to everyone on board just how vulnerable their position was at the far end of a supply line two hundred thousand light-years long. While the Fleet personnel had volunteered for the mission of saving the three worlds of the races whose representatives had traveled so far to ask for help, not everyone shared their sense of dedication to the mission. Even the surviving races in the Core preferred to spend their limited resources defending their own planets, rather than rallying around the battlestation.

Likewise, many of the merchants whose companies had subsidized the building of the *Hawking* were preparing reports recommending that they cut their losses. In practice, this meant abandoning the battlestation and fleeing for safety, even though the journey to the nearest Alliance world, three months away at top speed, was nearly as risky as staying to face the Ichtons.

Already a few of the more timid Indie merchant ships had been gone suspiciously long without returning for fuel or repairs. It was a toss-up whether they had fallen prey to the enemy, or were burning up the parsecs in a headlong flight back to the Alliance.

The survivors manning the *Hawking* had good reason to feel vulnerable. Skirmishing with the Ichtons went on constantly. The buglike enemy had come close to destroying the *Hawking* once already. None of the promised reinforcements had appeared; they could be months away, if indeed the notoriously stingy Alliance Senate hadn't already decided to withdraw support from an apparently failing campaign so far from home.

With morale so low, it was no surprise that a few of those who had been attracted to the mission by the promise of quick riches turned elsewhere in hopes of guaranteeing their own survival.

DEADFALL

by Scott MacMillan

"PAYDAY," HARVEY GRUMBLED to himself. "You line up for almost a half hour, then you stick your pay card in a slot in the wall, and guess what?" He pressed a button marked "Adjust" to the right of the small screen. "After this thing gets through deducting what you've spent, you're lucky if you've got enough credits left for a six-pack."

The small screen went blank for a moment, then flashed Harvey's ID on the screen.

KIMMELMAN, HARVEY JOHN.

Harvey pressed the button marked "Yes."

ENTER PERSONAL IDENTIFICATION NUMBER.

Harvey tapped in his six-digit number, waited a few seconds, and pressed the button marked "Enter."

ONE MOMENT PLEASE.

Although the liquid circuitry of the machine rendered it totally silent, Harvey liked to imagine that from somewhere behind the polished stainless-steel walls he could hear the whir and click of small gears meshing in engagement as the central banking and finance computer debited his Earned Credits Account.

KIMMELMAN, HARVEY JOHN. The screen seemed to darken slightly as if it were scowling at some sort of economic malefactor.

ECA AUDIT SHOWS SIGNIFICANT DEFICIT.

"Great," Harvey snorted. "Just great."

PAY CARD RESTRICTED TO ESSENTIAL PURCHASES ONLY FOR NEXT 24 PAY PERIODS.

Twenty-four pay periods . . . "Jeez," Harvey groaned, "that can't be right."

"Got a problem, amigo?" The man in the dark blue boiler suit standing behind Harvey sounded mildly concerned.

"I'll say I've got a problem," Harvey answered. "This machine is all screwed up. It says I'm two years over my credit limit."

"Well, are you?" the man asked.

"Hell, no. I couldn't be more than maybe two or three days over at the most." Harvey scowled at the small screen.

PLEASE REMOVE YOUR CARD.

"You haven't loaned anybody your card, have you?" the man asked.

"No," Harvey lied. "I haven't." *Except for that bimbo up on Dark Green Ten,* he thought. *If she . . .*

"Well then, it's probably this pay station," the man in the boiler suit said, derailing Harvey's train of thought. "All kinds of crap contaminating the circuitry down here in Violet One and Two." He put his own card in the machine and tapped in his code as he spoke. "Look," he said, pointing to the screen. "The damn thing shows me having way more pay credits than I should."

"That's great for you," Harvey said. "But I'm still busted until I can get up to Twelve deck next month and sort this out with someone in Finance."

The man in the boiler suit gave Harvey a wicked grin. "How much you need to hold you over till then?"

"Huh?" Harvey asked, a little slow on the uptake.

"Look. I've got more than enough 'extra' pay credits here to cover anything I'll need for the next month. So why don't I just transfer some of them into your Additional Credit Account? You can then transfer them to some of the clubs on Dark Green Ten and enjoy yourself next time you're heading up north." He gestured toward the overhead deck with his index finger. "Come on"—he gave Harvey a conspiratorial grin—"my treat."

Harvey thought it over for about two tenths of a second. Since it was a simple transfer from one account to another, there was no way he could get into any trouble with Finance or the Internal Security Unit.

"Thanks," Harvey said, slipping his pay card into the slot marked "Transfers" on the wall next to the screen.

"Okay . . . now we press a couple of magic buttons"—the man's fingers tapped out a coded response on the keypad—"and your card gets credited with an extra two pay periods." The Pay Link machine began digesting both cards.

"So, what do you do down here in the T decks?" the man asked as the machine transferred the funds.

"I'm a ballastician," Harvey said with a serious look.

"Ballistician?" the man asked, not sure that he'd heard correctly.

"Yeah." Harvey grinned. "I move ballast around to keep the station trimmed. It's important to keep everything evenly dispersed down here in the south pole, otherwise the *Hawking* would wobble on its axis. That'd screw up the gravity, mess up the gunners' aim, and spill that high-priced booze up in the Green Zone."

The man in the boiler suit laughed at Harvey's joke as he withdrew both cards from the slots in the wall.

"Careful where you point this, amigo. It's loaded," he said, handing back Harvey's card. "See you around."

With a brief wave he turned away from the machine and headed down the gangway to a freight belt. Grabbing one of the handles he stepped onto the freight platform and rode the belt up to an intermediate freight deck and vanished between the rows of neatly stacked containers.

Harvey turned back to the Pay Link and inserted his card in the slot.

"Jesus!" he half gasped. "This is a small fortune." The two pay periods that had been logged into the credit memory of his card represented more than eight of his own pay periods. Whatever the guy in the blue boiler suit did, it sure paid a hell of a lot better than running a forklift down at the south pole.

Harvey took his pay card out of the machine and stood there for a few minutes, absentmindedly tapping it on his thumbnail. In less than five minutes he'd gone from busted to flush, courtesy of . . .

Harvey realized that he didn't know his benefactor's name. He put the plastic card back in his wallet and headed over to his forklift, wondering if maybe he shouldn't have followed his mother's advice: "Never take money from strangers." Shrugging then, he stuffed his wallet into his back pocket and climbed aboard his forklift.

Pressing the starter button, he made a series of mechanical growling noises as the unit rose silently from the polished floor on its pale violet tractor beam. Then he made a sound that he imagined resembled the crunch of shifting gears as he headed back to the freight bays on Violet Four deck.

The *Stephen Hawking* carried several thousand megatons of cargo in her holds on Nineteen and Twenty decks. Foodstuffs, toilet paper, and a host of other nondurable items were stacked and racked beside trade goods from other planets, surplus military hardware, and contraband items confiscated from the occasional tramp freighter that had been unsuccessful in running the Alliance trade monopoly blockade. As the nondurables were consumed by the ten thousand–strong crew, Harvey Kimmelman and his forklift raced around the hold, constantly shifting containers from one side of the ship to the other in order to keep the giant man-made planet rotating smoothly around its central axis. The work was not particularly demanding, but Harvey enjoyed it.

Harvey spent the next three or four days in silent apprehension as he waited for the Central Finance Records Division to discover their error and track down all of the extra pay credits that had been downloaded onto his pay card. But as the days slid into weeks and no one from Internal Security came to question Harvey, he began to realize (or at any rate believe, which in his case was just as good) that somehow the computer that did the continuous credit audit somewhere up on one of the L decks hadn't discovered the error. When a month had passed and still no security men came to drag him away in the dead of night, Harvey was convinced that he'd avoided detection.

To Harvey, that meant only one thing. In ten days, when his periodic recreational leave came up, he was going to Green One and have a real blowout. And if at all possible, he was going to find Frosty Hooters and ask her to explain how the six-pack of joy juice she used his card to buy ended up costing him two years' pay. Once he'd settled things with Frosty, he might even treat himself to a few days in one of the orgasmatrons. . . .

The digital readout on the control panel of Harvey's forklift interrupted his idle speculation concerning auto-erotic stimulation on Green Seven: *15MK: T7.021.690.*

"Okay," he said through clenched teeth. "Fifteen thousand kilos to shift. All in a day's work for"—his voice produced an instant echo effect—"Harvey Kimmelman-man-man-man, Space Ranger!" He provided a few more sound effects as his forklift silently glided between the neatly stacked rows of color-coded freight containers.

As he reached sector 021.690 on T7 deck, Harvey lowered his infrared scan shield, focusing its laser beam on the bar coded manifest that occupied the lower right-hand corner of the nearest container.

OWNER: Griewe Galactic Novelties
CONTENTS: Entertainment Chips
PRODUCT COUNT: 192K Gross
BALLAST WEIGHT: .0175M ton

Turning the control on the dash of the forklift, Harvey adjusted his scanner to read only ballast weights as he cruised along looking for a heavier container.

"Come on," he said as he moved along the aisles. "Gimme a nice heavy combat vehicle or maybe a bunch of heat-shield tiles. Something *real* heavy." His voice dropped two octaves on the word "heavy." "Anything," he said, "as long as we find it before the cargo computer tells me what to start moving."

The cargo computer was faster, and inside of ten minutes had not only located the precise items to be moved but had told Harvey where to put them. Sixteen hours later Harvey made his way back to the work sector to get the last of the containers. As he positioned the forklift to make maximum use of his tractor beam, he heard giggling coming from behind him.

Swiveling around in his seat, Harvey saw the silhouette of a woman standing on one of the containers, her figure a seductive dark shape in front of the high-intensity work lights. Her hands rested on her hips, and her shapely legs were spread wide, the intense backlighting filtering through her gossamer dress.

Harvey tried to shield his eyes, to get a better look at the girl. She giggled again.

"Harvey Kimmelman!" the voice was warm and inviting. "Imagine seeing you here!"

Squinting into the light Harvey couldn't make out her face, but he did recognize the voice.

"Frosty?" he asked in a tentative tone. "Is that you up there?"

"You remembered!" she cooed, jumping down onto the deck. "How sweet."

Standing next to his forklift, Harvey could see the delicate features of her face, the gentle curve of her throat, and the firm roundness of . . .

"Sure I remembered," he said, forcing himself to look into her eyes. "A man's not apt to forget a beautiful girl like you. Especially after the time we had up on Green Ten," and he thought, *Especially after you took my pay card and ran up two years' worth of credits buying a six-pack.* Harvey suppressed an overwhelming urge to climb off the forklift and throttle her.

"So, did you come to visit?" Frosty asked, puckering her cherubic lips into a delicious smile.

"No," another voice said. "He's working. Isn't that right, Harvey?"

Harvey turned and saw a man in a blue boiler suit step from the shadows of the stacked freight containers.

"Long time, no see, huh?" he said as he walked over to where Frosty Hooters stood, still smiling vacantly up at Harvey.

"Yeah, I guess so," Harvey said, slowly recognizing the man in the boiler suit as his benefactor at the Pay Link machine.

The man slid his arm around Frosty's waist and gave her a little kiss on the cheek. "Frosty, could you leave us alone for a few minutes? I've got something I want to discuss with Harvey," he said.

"Sure, Forsythe," she said, kissing him on the lips. "Bye, Harvey." She waved. "Hope to see you again sometime." Turning, she vanished into one of the aisles between the stacked freight containers.

Despite his anger toward her, Harvey felt a twinge of jealousy tug at him somewhere behind his belt buckle. Forsythe watched Frosty vanish between the containers and, when he was sure she was out of earshot, turned back to Harvey.

"Well, amigo, I suppose you're more than just a little curious about what's going on." He gave Harvey the same grin he had used back at the Pay Link more than a month ago.

"Yeah, you could say I'm curious," Harvey replied. "I don't get too many visitors down here in the cargo hold."

"Harvey," Forsythe said through a public-relations smile, "I know I can trust you, so I'm going to let you in on a little secret." He walked over to the side of the forklift. "Can you switch that thing off for, say, half an hour?"

Something told Harvey he shouldn't do it, but he said, "Sure," and almost involuntarily switched off his machine.

"Good. Now, hop down and come with me," Forsythe said with a conspiratorial grin.

Harvey did as he was told and followed Forsythe between two rows of neatly stacked containers.

"If you don't mind, do you suppose you could fill me in on what you and Frosty are doing down here?" Harvey said before they had gone more than a few meters into the labyrinth of stacked freight.

"Not at all," Forsythe said. "We work down here."

"Bullshit! You don't work cargo." Harvey stopped in his tracks and grabbed Forsythe by the arm. "So what are you doing here?"

"Easy, amigo." Forsythe brushed Harvey's hand off his arm. "I didn't say I worked in cargo."

"Oh, yeah? Then what do you do?" Harvey asked in a voice like old leather.

"I guess you could call me a packager. I take ideas, people, concepts, and put them together in such a way everybody walks away smiling." He grinned at Harvey. "Even you, amigo. I'll have a smile on your face in five minutes flat."

"How so?" Harvey asked, not sure whether to follow along with Forsythe or head back to the forklift.

"Simple. Just walk down to the end of this row of containers and turn left. You'll like it. I promise." Forsythe gestured down the corridor formed by the dully gleaming containers.

Harvey shrugged, and walked the hundred or so meters to the end of the stack of containers. When he reached the end he stopped and looked back at Forsythe, who waved.

"Go on," he shouted. "Go on."

Harvey turned left and froze in his tracks. There, not more than ten feet in front of him, was Frosty Hooters, in all of her pagan, transgalactic, naked glory.

"Hi, Harvey," she said. Then crooking her finger, she beckoned him to follow her as she turned and scampered down the narrow aisle between the containers.

"I told you I'd make you smile."

Forsythe's voice made Harvey jump.

"Holy crocodiles!" Harvey exclaimed. "What's going on here?"

"Come on." Forsythe sounded like he was speaking to a confused child. "I'll show you." Taking Harvey by the arm he led him down the aisle to a dark green container. As the two men approached the end of the container it swung inward, revealing a hidden entrance.

"In here," Forsythe said.

"Why?"

"Trust me. I put a smile on your face, didn't I?" Forsythe gently tugged Harvey toward the opening, and Harvey reluctantly followed him in.

The door of the container hissed shut with a metallic click, and for a few moments the men were wrapped in total darkness. Then a soft blue light slowly filled the interior, changing in hue from a pale azure to a rich warm violet. Harvey could feel his skin prickle as the light increased in intensity.

"What the hell?" Harvey said as his skin began to tingle.

"Relax," Forsythe said. "Just a little decontamination, that's all." He nudged Harvey in the ribs with his elbow. "Gotta be clean for the ladies."

The door at the other end of the container opened and Forsythe led Harvey into the chrome-plated lobby of a deep-space sin bin.

For a moment Harvey was stunned by the gleaming black walls, the white tables, and the red patent-leather divans. Jaw slack and eyes wide with amazement, he tried to take it all in: the hot, glowing colors of the neon lights, the soft-as-moss carpet beneath his feet, and the almost-sensual musky smell of the air.

Forsythe threw himself down on one of the divans and signaled to one of the girls at the bar.

"Drink?"

Forsythe's voice brought Harvey back to semiconsciousness.

"Huh? Yeah, yeah, sure. A beer."

Harvey gawked as a well-muscled Telluran at the bar smoothed her delicate pink fur while the bartender poured out their drinks.

Picking up a small tray with the beer and Forsythe's lemon vodka on it, she walked over to where the two men sat.

"Here you are, boys," she said with a voice that sounded like the purr of a satin cat. Her fur stood out provocatively as she handed Harvey his drink. "Just let me know if you want anything else."

Harvey thought he was going to faint.

"Calm down, amigo," Forsythe said over the rim of his glass. "She only serves drinks. You know the law."

"Yeah. They can only, uh, mate with their own kind."

"Species," Forsythe corrected him. "Otherwise it's fatal for their partner. Complete sensory overload."

Harvey grinned. "I hope that wasn't what you had in mind when you said you'd put a smile on my face."

Forsythe laughed. "No, but that's good, amigo. Real good."

Harvey set down his beer, pleased that Forsythe had laughed at his joke—although he had been only half joking when he said it. "Forsythe, I don't want to sound naive but just what kind of place is this?"

"I guess you could call it a very special nightclub," Forsythe said, tossing back the last of his lemon vodka. He watched Harvey's reaction out of the corner of his eye. "It's very discreet, caters to some very special clients, and is more or less legal."

"What do you mean, 'more or less' legal?" Harvey asked.

"Well, I have an entertainment license for a small bar up on Green One. Packed, it can serve maybe twenty people. All very intimate." He signaled for another round of drinks.

"One day about three years ago"—the Telluran brought the drinks and Harvey felt his blood pressure begin to rise—"we were remodeling after a couple of Indies did a fair amount of damage to the place during a private party. That's when I discovered that there was an old service elevator that ran right through my club to the cargo decks." He sipped his lemon vodka before continuing. "So, I decided to expand. Down here.

"I had a company Earth-side design a modular nightclub and finessed a permit that gives me permission to operate anywhere in the Alliance, provided I stay at least one thousand meters from any of their clubs." He gave Harvey a quick grin. "That's what I mean by semilegal. I'm only 980 meters from their nearest beer bar."

"So, who comes here?" Harvey asked. "I've been pushing cargo for two years, and I've never seen anyone down here before today."

"That's because we're careful. Our customers are very important people," Forsythe said, finishing his drink. "They can't go slumming in the Green Light district or be seen crawling out of some sleazy orgasmatron at four in the morning. That's why they come here, amigo. They have a good time, they go home, and nobody knows."

"Well, that's all very interesting," Harvey said, setting down his half-empty glass. "Maybe someday I'll be rich enough, or important enough, to be one of your customers. But for now I've got some cargo to shift." He stood up to leave. "How do I get outta here?"

"Same way you came in, amigo. Only before you go, I'd like to offer you a job." Forsythe gave Harvey a long, sincere look. "I think you're just the man I need down here."

Harvey's new job was simplicity in itself. Forsythe had a specially constructed container that served as the shuttle between the access elevator and his private club. Harvey would move the container to the door of the elevator at the end of his shift and then, after dinner and a beer, he'd wander back to the freight deck and, climbing on board his trusty forklift, return the container to the front of the club.

Harvey had been shuttling the container back and forth for nearly six weeks when a strange thought hit him. Every night he took a container full of people to the club. Who, he wondered, was taking them back to the elevator? Two days later, at the Pay Link machine, Harvey raised the question with Forsythe.

"I've got another driver on the payroll who works the graveyard shift," Forsythe said as he downloaded a stack of credits onto Harvey's pay card. "Not that it's any of your concern."

"Sorry I asked," Harvey said as Forsythe withdrew his pay card from the Pay Link machine.

"No problem, amigo," Forsythe said. "Look, I'm going to be closed for the next few days, so why don't you go topside and enjoy yourself. Take Frosty with you. God knows, with what I'm paying you, the two of you can have quite a blowout." He regarded Harvey for several long seconds. "I'll set it up. You two can stay in one of the hotels on Green Two. Well? What do you say?"

Harvey could only think of one thing to say.

"Great. When do we leave?"

"You can leave tonight, after the customers arrive." Forsythe handed back Harvey's pay card. "Frosty will join you tomorrow at the hotel."

"I can't go tonight," Harvey lied. "I have to cover for a pal on the morning shift."

"Okay, amigo. Then blast off tomorrow." Forsythe smiled. "You're rich, do what you like."

That evening Harvey collected his passengers as usual and transported them to Forsythe's club. Before he lowered the container to the floor, he hopped out of the forklift and stuck a wad of gum that he had been chewing to the underside of the container. Climbing back into his forklift, he lowered the container into place, and then went back to his quarters.

The next morning Harvey gunned his forklift to life while producing a cacophony of mechanical sounds, including the squeal of rubber on concrete at he pulled away from the loading dock. Soon he was easing the forklift between the rows of containers to approach Forsythe's club. He glanced around casually as he stopped it and hopped off, bending down to examine the edge of the container he had placed on the floor the night before. Oozing out from under the edge of the dark green container was a wad of pink bubble gum.

Quietly, and without any sound effects, Harvey drove back to the loading docks. He didn't know what was going on in the club, but one thing was certain. The container he had dropped off the night before hadn't been moved. On the way back to his quarters he tried to decide what he should do.

In the shower he toyed with the idea of going to Internal Security, but decided against it. If Forsythe's operation was legitimate, his visit to Internal Security would cost him his job—a job, he reflected as he toweled himself dry, that had paid him nearly a year's salary in less than two months.

Harvey finished dressing and tossed a few things in an overnight bag. No, he decided, he wouldn't go to Security. Not until he'd had a chance to talk to Frosty about what really went on in Forsythe's club. Switching off the lights, he left his quarters and took the express elevator to Green Two.

The lobby of the Hilton Hotel exuded an aura of expensive elegance that made Harvey feel slightly ill at ease as he waited for the desk clerk to confirm his reservation.

"Ah, here it is," the balding man said as Harvey's name came up on the screen. "Suite 1121 . . . Mr. Kimmelman and Ms. Hooters." He looked up from the CRT and gave Harvey a smile that looked as if it had been pickled in alum. "Just follow the guide to your room, sir."

A small robot glided to a stop next to the desk. Harvey set his bag on it and then followed it across the lobby and down a series of well-carpeted corridors until at last they came to suite 1121. The robot opened the door, allowing Harvey to enter first before it followed along with his bag.

By the standards of accommodation on the *Stephen Hawking,* the hotel suite was big. Harvey figured it to be at least four or five times the size of his quarters down in the south pole. There was a small video room with several comfortable-looking chairs opposite the three-dimensional video wall, and next to that was a bedroom with a huge bed. Beyond the bedroom was a bathroom, and through the open door Harvey could see Frosty reclining in a deep bath filled with the most wonderful-looking suds.

"Hi, Harvey," she called the moment she saw him. "Come on in, the water's fine!"

Harvey didn't bother to undress, but simply stepped into the tub and slid down next to Frosty.

The next thirty-six hours blurred into a nonstop orgy of indulgence. For the first time in his life Harvey was rich, and he was enjoying it. He and Frosty went shopping, took in a concert, ate in the best restaurants, and made love. It was after a particularly satisfying bout of lovemaking in zero-gravity mode that he had almost decided to forgive Frosty for having scammed two years' worth of pay credits, and was seriously thinking about marrying her, when she managed to break the spell.

"Gee," Frosty said, "it's a shame about the Club, isn't it?"

"What do you mean?" Harvey replied, trying not to think about her long fingernails as they slowly dragged their way across his belly.

"Well, just that Forsythe may have to close it down," Frosty said.

"Close it down? Why?" In his mind's eye Harvey could see little pay credits with wings flying out the windows of his dreams.

"Well," Frosty said coyly, "it's because business hasn't been all that good."

"Well, I sure seem to bring a lot of people there every night." Harvey reached down and took Frosty's hand in his own. "What do you mean that business hasn't been good?"

"Just that we don't get very many customers. Sometimes only one or two show up, and most of those leave early." Frosty's other hand was teasing the inside of Harvey's thigh.

"What do you mean they leave early?" Harvey moved closer to Frosty, forcing himself to concentrate. "How could they?"

"Well, I don't know how they leave, but they do. I've even asked Forsythe about it, and he just shrugs and says, 'They've gone.'" Frosty laid her head on Harvey's chest. "I thought maybe you took them back."

"How many came last night?" Harvey asked.

"Silly," Frosty replied. "It was just you and me. . . ."

"Not last night then," Harvey said with some exasperation, "but the last night you worked at the Club. Before we came up here?"

"Oh, that's easy," Frosty cooed. "Four. Two regulars and two new guys. But the new guys didn't stay long; they left after about an hour."

"How did they leave?" Harvey asked, afraid of what the answer might be.

"Well, Forsythe said you took them back to the elevator." Frosty lifted the covers on the bed and looked down toward their feet. "You're not paying attention," she said.

But all Harvey could think of was the wad of bubble gum oozing out from under the container. It hadn't moved all night, and if the two new customers had left, then someone else had taken them.

"Frosty," Harvey asked, "is there a back entrance to the Club?"

"I don't think so, Harvey," she said. "There's the bar and the casino, then the playrooms, a kitchen, and the dorms." Frosty pulled her face into a cherubic pout. "I've been everywhere in the Club, but I've never seen any other entrance except the one you came through when Forsythe hired you." Her face brightened suddenly. "Unless there's another entrance in the hen house!"

"The 'hen house'?" Harvey asked.

"I think that's what it's called. At least that's what one of the regulars called it. I remember that Forsythe actually got upset and told the man he'd have to leave." She smiled at Harvey. "Can we . . ."

"What do they do in the hen house?" Harvey asked, interrupting Frosty's playful request.

"I don't know," she said. "But I'll show you what we do in the playrooms." She pressed against Harvey as she reached across to turn off the lights. "Oooo," she cooed in the darkness. "Now you're really paying attention!"

The next morning Harvey went down to the desk to check out of the hotel.

"How much do I owe you?" he asked when he finally managed to attract the desk clerk's attention.

"Name, please?" The overhead lighting gleamed on his bald head.

"Kimmelman. Harvey Kimmelman." Harvey tossed his pay card on the polished desk, secretly hoping he still had enough credits to pay the bill.

The bald head bent over the CRT and tapped away furiously at the keys. "Ah, here you are," he said without bothering to look up. "Three nights with Ms. Hooters . . ."

The desk clerk stopped in midsentence. "Yes, Mr. Kimmelman, everything is in order." His tone of voice had become very deferential, and Harvey wondered if the man was about to transform into a toad right before his eyes.

"So, what do I owe?" Harvey asked, a slight edge to his voice.

"Why, nothing, Mr. Kimmelman. Your stay has been with the compliments of Hilton Hotels." Slight beads of perspiration glistened on the desk clerk's sandy-colored forehead. "I hope that everything was to your satisfaction?"

"Sure. Just fine," Harvey said, picking up his pay card. "See you again in a couple of weeks."

Picking up his overnight bag, he headed out the doors of the hotel and across the bustling mall on Green Two. As he stood waiting for the express elevator to take him back to the south pole, he mulled over what he knew of the Club and what he had learned from Frosty. By the time he was strapped in to a deceleration seat, he had reached a simple conclusion: Things didn't add up.

It didn't take a tech level one propulsion engineer to know that the Club wasn't raking in enough to pay him the sort of cash Forsythe was splashing around. That meant that the money had to come from some other source.

Forsythe's Club on Green One? Maybe, but Harvey doubted it. Blackmail? Frosty had said something about regulars, but it was doubtful that they would be able to come up with enough credits to cover his salary week after week, let alone take care of Forsythe's operating expenses.

The express elevator hit four g's on stopping at the south pole, and despite the gaseous suspension of the seat, Harvey still felt like he'd left his stomach up around Seventeen deck. Untangling himself from the harness, he left the elevator and went straight to his quarters.

After the opulence of the Hilton, Harvey's quarters seemed almost claustrophobic. With his bed folded into the wall the room measured not quite three meters by four. It contained the regulation folding chairs, a small video screen, a bookshelf, a closet, and a mini-galley where Harvey could reheat a meal purchased from the vending machine in the corridor if he didn't feel like dining in the chow hall.

The soft plastic walls were teal-blue with stainless-steel trim, and the self-cleaning carpet a ubiquitous gray. A door next to the bookshelves led to a small bathroom that contained the one luxury that made the small apartment worth every credit it cost: a genuine liquid shower complete with hot and cold taps.

Harvey surveyed his domain, wondering if it would still be his when he finished poking around the Club. The thought surprised him. Without realizing it, he had devised a plan and now he was putting it into action. He tossed his bag onto one of the chairs and headed out to the cargo decks.

On board his forklift, Harvey snapped down the safety visor on his helmet.

"Rig for silent running." His voice had the harsh metallic crackle of an old P.A. system.

Easing the machine out of the loading docks, Harvey made a series of sonar pings until he was sailing down the wide aisles of Violet Two. Navigating his way through the islands of stacked containers, Harvey finally sighted his first port of call.

He eased his forklift into the docking bay accompanied by the sound of tugboat engines thrashing the briny sea into foam. The central cargo computer had less memory than all the inhabitants of the *Stephen Hawking* combined, but it did serve one very useful purpose: It kept track of every piece of freight, every bit of cargo, and every single container on Violet One and Two.

Leaning over, Harvey took one of the mainframe cables and plugged it into the bayonet socket on the side of his machine. Keying in the coordinates of Forsythe's Club, he asked for a profile of freight distribution on the deck. Within a matter of seconds, his on-board display lit with a schematic of the containers, a virtual floor plan of the Club. Harvey entered the information into the memory of the forklift's computer and then disconnected from the central cargo terminal. Without a sound he glided down the freight corridor, headed for Forsythe's Club.

Taking a printout of the area as a map, Harvey parked his forklift twenty meters from the Club and proceeded on foot to Forsythe's container complex. Easing himself between the tightly packed rows of containers, he slowly made his way toward the front. Finally, at the end of one of the narrow corridors, he dropped down onto his stomach and carefully peered around the corner.

The dark green container that Harvey had placed in front of the Club four days earlier was still anchored to the floor by a wad of pink bubble gum. Harvey pulled back and stood up, hesitating for only a moment before he began backtracking to a point where he could circle around to the back of the Club.

The rear approach was going to be more difficult. Here the containers were stacked three deep, and it was obvious to Harvey that he wasn't going to be able to climb on top of them without some sort of assistance. Trotting back to the forklift, he hopped on board and, accompanied by the sound of squealing tires, drove the machine around to the back of the Club.

Harvey pointed his scanner at the bar code on the top container.

ALLIANCE MORTUARY STORAGE
HUMAN REMAINS

The next two containers were the same.

So that's how he avoided having his containers moved, Harvey thought. *He's running his Club in the middle of a graveyard.*

A shudder ran up his spine. Alliance regulations were crystal clear about the remains of the dead. Once placed in storage they were not to be moved or tampered with. Some species had unusual notions about proper respect for their dead. Harvey couldn't remember what the penalty was for "mortuary disturbance," as the regulations called it, but he was sure of one thing: It ranked with murder, arson, and treason in Category A crimes.

Taking a deep breath, Harvey locked his tractor beam onto the topmost container and lowered it gently to the ground, followed by the next one. Then, locking on the bottommost container, he moved it slightly to the left, opening a gap of about forty-five centimeters. He replaced the top two containers, then drove back around to the front of the Club.

Climbing down from his forklift, Harvey made his way past the dead of the *Stephen Hawking* and squeezed his way into the complex of containers that housed the Club. Inside the walls of cargo that surrounded the Club, Harvey was surprised to discover that Forsythe's containers were packed in a tight cluster that left a clear three-meter path around most of its perimeter. At one corner of the cluster one of the containers was moved forward to where it butted up against the wall. This, Harvey surmised, was the entrance to the Club.

Working back from the entrance, Harvey mentally ticked off each of the containers. The bar and casino in one; the playrooms in another; the dorms for the girls and the kitchen. And behind the kitchen, the hen house.

Harvey leaned against one of the containers, trying to get his bearings. Behind him, coming from inside the container, he thought he could hear a high-pitched whine. Pressing his ear against the smooth green container, he strained to catch the sound again. Faintly, over the pounding of his own pulse, he finally heard it.

Instinctively he tried to mimic it, the way he reproduced the sounds of everything from a crash-diving submarine to an FTL engine with warp failure. The whining sound grew louder, as if whatever was making the noise were drawn nearer the wall of the container by Harvey's mimicking sound. Stepping back from the container, Harvey was convinced that he'd located the hen house. Whatever Forsythe was up to, the answer was in that container.

Two sides of the container were flush against the others, while the third side left a gap of slightly more than half a meter between it and its neighbor. Harvey slid into the gap and pressed his back against the container, wedging himself in place. Slowly, hand over hand, he crawled up the side of the container like a mountaineer moving up the crevasse of a stone face. When he reached the top, he spread his arms across the opening and pushed himself onto the top of the container.

From this vantage point he could see the layout of the containers and the small courtyard that separated the hen house from the rest. Crouching low, Harvey trotted along the top of the container until he reached a point above the courtyard. Lying flat on the roof, he lowered himself over the edge until he was hanging down the side with his arms fully extended. Pushing away from the container with his feet, he let go and dropped the last three meters to the deck.

The courtyard wasn't more than five meters on a side and, to Harvey's immeasurable relief, there were two doors that opened onto it. One led into the hen house and the other, if Frosty's description was to be relied on, led into the kitchen.

Harvey pulled back the kitchen door just wide enough to look inside. The stainless-steel galley seemed deserted, and he quietly closed the door.

Harvey pushed the hen house door open and slowly eased his way into the container. He found himself in a small, empty room lit only by a pale green work light. Closing the outside door behind him, he stepped across the room to another door. Before he could reach the door latch, the light began to change color and Harvey felt a prickling sensation all over his body as the by-now ultraviolet light completed its process of decontamination.

As the light level slowly faded back to a pale lime-green Harvey opened the inner container door. A thick, musty smell rolled out and filled the small room, reminding him of the odor he had noticed when Forsythe had brought him into the Club nearly two months before. Stepping through the door he found himself in a room racked with shelves from floor to ceiling, each shelf holding something about the size of a man contained in a black plastic bag closed with a heavy zipper.

At first Harvey thought that he was in one of the mortuary containers, and for a moment a wave of pure panic crashed over him, threatening to drag him under in a sea of terror. He took several deep breaths with his eyes screwed shut against what he had seen. Then, as he felt himself calming down, he opened his eyes once again.

The body bags were still there, but even in the dim light of the container Harvey could tell from their shapes that they didn't contain bodies. Carefully he unzipped one of them. Inside he found a set of Fleet battle armor, complete with helmet and plasma gun. He opened two more bags and found more armor and weapons. In the semidarkness of the container he managed a quick count. Enough equipment to outfit a hundred men.

It didn't make sense. What would Forsythe want with all this gear? A hundred men in battle armor could take over a ship. . . .

The realization of what he was looking at hit Harvey between the eyes with the force of a hard ball coming off a Major League bat. Forsythe was planning a mutiny.

For just a moment Harvey's knees seemed about to buckle under him, and the room seemed to sway around him. He reached out to steady himself against the shelves when he heard the noise. It was a high-pitched whine that warbled up and down, much clearer than when he had first heard it outside on the cargo deck. With a deep breath, Harvey walked past the body bags filled with weapons and stopped in front of the steel door at the far end of the container.

Unzipping one of the bags, Harvey eased out a plasma gun and checked its charge level. The small needle in the dial set into the stock swung up to the top of the green band. Even on maximum power, he had a hundred shots before he'd have to replace the magazine. He set the firing selector to three-round burst, switched off the safety, and opened the door.

The smell was overpowering, a rotten, fetid, decaying stench that caused Harvey to double over in a retching spasm that sprayed his lunch across the floor of the container. Struggling to stand up, he dragged his sleeve across his tear-filled eyes, blinking hard to see what was in the room.

The room was filled with long, narrow tables about chest height, covered with plastic trays filled with rotting compost. Floating in the semiliquid slime were hundreds of rusty ivory-colored oblongs, bobbing gently up and down in the decaying filth.

Skulls, Harvey thought. *Probably all that's left of the bodies of the Fleet Marines who owned the gear in the other room.*

Just then one of the skulls floated to the surface of the liquid compost and slowly rotated toward Harvey, a trail of black slime wrapping itself around its forehead. Harvey watched in morbid fascination, at any moment expecting the empty eye sockets to fix him with their hollow stare. The skull slowly turned and then sank back into the ooze. It took Harvey a full minute to realize that the skull didn't have a face. It couldn't. It was an egg.

For some reason, the realization that he was looking at an egg didn't surprise Harvey in the least. He had come to the hen house to find—

The high-pitched whining started again, interrupting his thoughts. Rising and falling, it seemed to be calling something, as if it expected an answer.

Harvey moved forward in the semidarkness, edging his way toward the keening sound. As he moved between the tables he saw the eggs rising and falling to the tempo of the whining sound, almost as if they were children responding to a lullaby. The whining increased, and from the tables Harvey could hear a clicking sound as the eggs tapped against one another.

And lower, beneath the sound of the whining and the tapping, there was a scratching sound. The sound a cat makes when it is scratching at the door to be let out.

Crack.

Harvey spun around at the sound, ready to blast anyone behind him.

Crack.

This time it was next to Harvey, and as he continued to back down the aisle he watched the eggs on the table next to him rise and fall, rise and fall, in time to the whining sound that seemed to be filling the room.

Crack.

A dark fissure appeared on one of the eggs, a musty red fluid seeping out.

Crack. Another fissure appeared, and a tiny hand with three opposed digits poked its way through the crack, picking at the shell, trying to get out.

The crooning stopped, and for a moment the only sound was the tapping and cracking of the eggs. Then a shrill scream exploded behind Harvey. Instantly he spun around and found himself less than three meters from a female Ichton.

Instinctively Harvey pulled the trigger, and three rounds slammed into the Ichton's chest, sending it staggering back against the wall. Harvey turned to run and knocked over one of the tables, sending the eggs crashing to the floor in a welter of liquid compost. The female reared on her hind legs, screaming furiously at Harvey, and launched herself at him.

Diving under a table, Harvey slipped in a gooey mass of compost and Ichton hatchlings and slid into another table. Giving a might heave against the leg of the table he sent it tumbling down, its precious eggs smashing as they hit the floor of the container. The hatchlings squirmed on the floor, squeaking in agony as they tried to burrow into the compost for warmth.

The female Ichton bent down and moved forward, trying to scoop up as many hatchlings as she could and place them in the compost trays between the still intact eggs. Harvey watched her through the targeting system of his plasma weapon. He could see three closely spaced wounds on her upper thorax, one of which seemed to be suppurating, the result of having partially penetrated the Ichton's exoskeleton.

Harvey lay perfectly still, waiting for a clear shot at one of the Ichton's powerful legs. On the targeting system the room seemed as bright as the cargo decks outside, and Harvey was just squeezing off his shot when he felt something jab into his leg.

His shot went wide, with only one round even grazing the Ichton's leg. Looking down as he scuttled closer to the door, Harvey saw a hatchling hanging on to his pants leg, trying to stab him with a shard of eggshell. He scraped it off with his boot, its still-soft exoskeleton popping as he crushed it against the wall.

The female continued to busy herself rescuing hatchlings, and seemed to be ignoring Harvey, despite the injury to her leg. Propping himself up into a crouch, Harvey brought his weapon up to his shoulder. Scanning over the female Ichton, he tried to decide where he was the most apt to kill her with his next shot when he heard a faint whining sound behind him.

Jerking around, Harvey fired in the direction of the sound, just a heartbeat before the second Ichton let loose a blast from its weapon. The three slugs struck the Ichton under the chin, throwing her own aim wildly off. The spray of micro-slugs from her weapon ricocheted off the wall of the container and flew around the inside of the hen house like a swarm of angry hornets. As she fell forward, her lifeless hulk crashed into two more of the tables, smashing more of the eggs onto the floor.

Leaping to his feet, Harvey dashed to the door, firing over his shoulder in blind panic as he went. Behind him the remaining Ichton screamed as it bounded on in pursuit, apparently oblivious to its wounds. Harvey slipped and fell as he ran past the body bags filled with weapons, sprawling full-length on the floor of the container. The Ichton became tangled in its own legs trying to squeeze through the narrow doorway, giving Harvey barely enough time to scramble to his feet and stumble into the courtyard.

For a brief moment Harvey considered shooting the Ichton as it came out of the container, but a voice at the kitchen door changed his mind.

"Harvey!" Frosty shouted. "This way!"

Bounding to the door, Harvey grabbed Frosty by the arm and dragged her across the kitchen.

"We've gotta get out of here! Which way to the door?" he demanded.

"Ooo, Harvey," Frosty cooed. "You're so forceful!"

"The door!" Harvey barked. "Where the hell is it?"

"There." Frosty pointed to a thick-necked Telluran who stood blocking the door to the Club. "Behind him."

"Move it, pygmy!" Harvey yelled, covering the seven-foot-tall tower of muscle that blocked his way.

"You're bug meat, pal," the Telluran said, drawing a slug gun from under his cook's apron. "You and—"

Harvey fired twice, the six slugs from his weapon blasting a hole in the Telluran big enough to step through.

"Come on," he shouted, dragging Frosty over the smoldering remains of the Telluran. "We've—"

Harvey's voice was drowned out by Frosty's scream as the Ichton pushed its way into the kitchen.

"Go, go, go!" he shouted, pushing Frosty through the door and into the Club. "I'll cover you!"

He swung the muzzle of his weapon up and fired three quick bursts from the hip.

The Ichton slowed slightly in its advance and looked around the kitchen, blinking its honeycombed eyes. Unable to distinguish the exact shapes of Harvey and Frosty, the Ichton sprayed the room with a burst of automatic fire, unleashing a torrent of micro-slugs that ripped through the kitchen like a buzz saw. Harvey dived clear, and rolling behind the bar for cover got off another burst at the Ichton.

Two of the plasma slugs grazed past the Ichton, but the third slammed into its left front leg, shattering the insectoid's knee. The Ichton reared up in pain, its finger still on the trigger sending a full-auto burst into the ceiling of the kitchen. Bellowing in agony, the Ichton came forward on three legs, scuttling sideways like a wounded crab.

Harvey dashed across the Club and made a dive for the door, rolling onto his shoulder as he hit the floor, coming up with his weapon blazing as the Ichton leaped toward him.

"This way!" Frosty shouted, holding open the door that led from the container to the cargo deck.

Firing a burst over his shoulder, Harvey raced out of the container and onto the deck. There, not twenty meters away, was his forklift.

Harvey sprinted past Frosty as he raced to the forklift. "Go get Security!" he shouted as he climbed into the cabin of his machine.

Hitting the starter, he swung the forklift around to face the container that had been used as a shuttle for the Club. Running forward, he hit the tractor beam and locked in on the container. He was just about to hoist it aloft when a slug crashed into the frame next to his head.

Diving for cover, Harvey threw himself off the forklift and onto the cargo deck. Bone cracked as he hit the ground, and a blinding pain seared up his arm. Struggling to get up, his broken arm dangling at his side, Harvey heard Forsythe's voice coming from near the entrance of the Club.

"Harvey, you blew it!" Forsythe was angry, and his voice edged on the hysterical. "You were one of the chosen, amigo, but you blew it. You could have been a survivor, one of the kings. The Ichtons would have let you live, it was part of the deal. But not now, amigo. Not now."

A shot rang out and another slug slammed into the forklift. Harvey raised his head above the edge of the cab just enough to see Forsythe moving toward the forklift, a small pistol in his hand.

Harvey weighed up his chances of surviving where he was and decided that Forsythe would kill him before Frosty returned with Security. He raised his head slightly to see if he could reach his gun where it had fallen on the floor of the forklift's cab.

Another shot rang out, and Harvey ducked back down and then half stood up, darting into the forklift to grab his gun.

Forsythe fired twice, but missed. Crouched next to his machine, Harvey fumbled his weapon to his shoulder and, with his good hand, switched it from "Burst" to "Full Auto." Moving around the back of the forklift, he took a deep breath, then dashed toward the nearest stack of containers, blindly spraying a burst at Forsythe as he ran.

It worked. Forsythe flattened himself on the deck as Harvey's shots passed harmlessly overhead. Recovering, he rolled into a kneeling position and let loose a string of shots in Harvey's direction.

The Ichton cautiously stepped out of the shuttle container and onto the cargo deck. She held her shattered foreleg folded up tight against her abdomen, and a thick mustard-yellow fluid continued to ooze from the wound on her thorax. Using the container for cover she cautiously peered around its edge, her multifaceted eyes picking up the patterns on the cargo deck as a mosaic of shapes, colored only by their infrared heat values.

She could detect some movement in front of her, and the fine fibers in the joints of her elbows tingled to the bark of Forsythe's pistol. Cocking her head, she tried to decide if the moving heat pattern crouched on the deck in front of her was friendly or not. Unable to decide, she brought up her weapon. The eggs, the hatchlings, had to be protected. The thing in front of her wasn't an Ichton, wasn't important to the swarm. She pulled the trigger.

A thousand plasteel fléchettes spun out of the barrel of the Ichton's gun, separating from one another until they reached the outer limits of their static charge adhesion and formed a pattern precisely ninety millimeters in diameter. Each fléchette had three stabilizing fins that wound themselves in a spiral the length of the shaft, imparting a 1500 rpm spin to the projectile that turned it into a lethal drill no thicker than a hypodermic needle.

The first blast caught Forsythe in the back and drove him to the ground. Within three tenths of a second, another two thousand fléchettes bored into the pulped flesh and bounced crazily off the deck, rattling into the stacked containers around the Club. Forsythe's legs jerked spasmodically against the deck for a few moments and then went still.

Harvey was frozen in place by the awesome destructive power of the Ichton weapon. Staring at what was left of Forsythe's body, unable to make his legs obey the command to run, to get the hell as far away as possible from the Ichton, the only thought he had was that he was next—that in a matter of seconds, he'd be reduced to a pile of quivering pulp like Forsythe.

Fear saved Harvey's life.

The Ichton leaned out farther from the container, looking for the enemy that had destroyed the eggs and killed so many hatchlings. Her eyes picked up a mosaic of shapes and colors, but nothing that she could identify at the distance. There was no movement, and the dull orange heat shape ten meters away was identifiable as a machine. Satisfied that there was no living threat in front of it, the Ichton stepped back behind the container to continue looking elsewhere.

Harvey's legs came back to life. Running to the forklift, he climbed into the cab and grabbed the tractor beam joystick. Pushing it forward, he began raising the container.

The wounded Ichton sensed movement behind her and turned and fired wildly into the side of the container, sending a shower of fléchettes ricocheting in all directions. Limping back from the container, she brought her weapon up, ready to fire at the first sign of movement.

Hunched down in the cab of the forklift, Harvey slowly brought the microphone of his bullhorn to his mouth.

The Ichton thought she detected movement of some sort on the dull orange heat shape. Slowly she rotated her head, hoping to detect some movement on the facets of her eyes. In the upper periphery of her vision she saw the container overhead as if it were some sort of dark rectangular cloud. Around her she saw the smooth green walls of the containers, the dull gray flooring of the cargo deck, and the slowly cooling remains of Forsythe.

The Ichton concentrated on the dull orange heat shape of the forklift. Inside the container she had left were eggs and hatchlings that needed her, while outside was danger to her brood. Better safe than sorry. She raised her weapon to her shoulder.

There was a metallic chirruping. The Ichton cocked her head to one side and moved her elbows outward to trap more of the sound. The chirrup came again, this time followed by a low whining sound, much like the lullaby she had crooned to the hatchlings as they struggled to be free of their eggs.

She made a high-pitched warbling whine, cocking her head and elbows to catch any sound of an answer.

The chirrup struggled to duplicate the sound, but couldn't.

It had to be a hatchling, one that had somehow been dragged or carried out of the nest. If they were to continue to avoid detection, she had to rescue it.

It chirruped again, and she took a hesitant step forward.

Harvey watched as the Ichton stepped into the shadow of the container held in the tractor beam of his forklift. He chirruped into the microphone—and then turned off the tractor beam.

From nearly eight meters up, the sixteen-ton container dropped onto the deck with a deafening bang, crushing the Ichton to a yellow smear.

Harvey smiled to himself and clipped the microphone back onto the dash of the forklift. Switching on his computer, he accessed the mainframe on Twelve deck and typed in a brief coded message.

Then, swinging down from the cab of the forklift, he headed toward the Club. As he passed the spreading pool of mustard-yellow slime that oozed from under the container, he made a popping sound, like someone stepping on a bug. Bending down, he picked up the Ichton's gun in his good hand and headed back into the Club.

When Internal Security arrived with Frosty, they found Harvey in the hen house, ankle deep in broken eggshells and rotting compost and dead hatchlings. Security set up a command post in the bar, and while the security officers helped themselves to free drinks and a medic worked on Harvey's arm, their commander interrogated him.

"So let me get this straight," the security commander said. "You were moving an empty container when this guy, er . . ." He turned to one of the security men. "You got a make on the meat pie outside?"

The security man shook his head.

"No? Okay." He turned back to Harvey. "So you saw this guy come running out of here with the Ichton hot on his tail. The Ichton shoots the guy, and you drop the container on the bug. Right?"

"Yup, amigo. That's exactly how it went down." Harvey smiled at his interrogator. "Any more questions?"

"No, not right now." The security commander stood up. "You can go. We'll call you if anything else comes up."

"Sorry," Harvey said, "but I'm not leaving."

"What do you mean, *you're* not leaving? This is a security matter, and I'm sealing off all of these containers." He signaled for the two security men at the bar. "You're going. Understand?"

"What I understand is that under the Alliance Salvage Laws, these containers were unrecorded enemy possessions. It doesn't say anywhere that they have to be outside the ship, just not in the memory banks already. Only that mess in the back has any intelligence value. As the sole surviving combatant they are now mine. Even the permits for the bar up on Green will take weeks to revoke." Harvey held up a printout from the computer in his forklift, mimicking a trumpet as he presented it. "If you'd care to read this, you'll see that I filed for salvage eleven minutes and twenty-one seconds before you arrived."

The security commander snatched the printout from Harvey's hand. His scowl turned to a frown as he examined the document. It would take months, maybe years to sort this one out and there was a rumor of imminent combat. Legal technicalities weren't his problem and the Ichtons were dead. And there was no way to guess how the upper command would react to the incident. No use rankling a potential hero, and he might want to come back here when he was off duty. He waved the two approaching security officers off with a shrug.

"Now, unless you want to start paying for your drinks, I'm going to have to ask you all to leave." Harvey's smile was hard enough to cut diamonds. "Okay, amigo?"

The security man glared at Harvey, tried to smile, then handed back his deed to the containers.

"Okay, Kimmelman." He turned to the two security men who were now standing next to Harvey. "Come on, men, we're outta here."

The two men followed their chief to the door, where he turned and gave Harvey a last glowering look.

"I'll be back for the bug box, Kimmelman," he said, then turned and left the Club.

Frosty came over from behind the bar and sat down next to Harvey. "Are you going to be all right?" she asked, stroking the back of his neck.

Harvey stretched his injured arm. The medic had done a good job repairing the broken bone, and aside from the tickle of the current and a twinge of pain as he pulled Frosty closer to him, Harvey could tell that he'd be fine in a few hours.

"Better than ever," he said, giving Frosty a smile and a little squeeze. "Now, why don't you show your partner-to-be the playroom?"

Frosty cooed with delight.

OLD GRUDGES

ELSEWHERE ON THE *Stephen Hawking* there were the sectors owned by those corporations rich enough to have purchased their own floor or wing. Along with the megamerchants were a number of companies financed by the governments of their respective worlds. Among them perhaps the most unusual, and certainly the most flamboyant, was that of the Baratarians.

Barataria was actually a group of asteroids that had originally harbored fugitive Khalians who had refused to accept their defeat by the Fleet. Eventually, like most Khalians, they realized that the Families, and the Schlein family in particular, had used them, and used them badly. This led to a grudge that was passed on undiminished to the next generation of Baratarians. Like the pirates of Earth, many of the Khalian pirates found legitimate or somewhat legitimate ways to invest the wealth taken from both Fleet and Family ships. This wealth gave them considerable leverage in the chaotic period after the war when the Khalian and Family economies were in shambles. As a result the Baratarians became prosperous merchants and dubious, but valued, members of the Alliance.

Their leader had been a misshapen human known to them only as Globin. His warped exterior hid one of the best minds in all humanity. Globin's decision to retire after almost seventy years came as a relief to the Fleet sector commander. There is nothing like having an only mildly socialized genius and ex-pirate under your command to keep things lively. Globin's decision to spend his "retirement" as the head of the Baratarian mission on the *Hawking* presented the battlestation's commander, Anton Brand, with some perplexing problems.

HEARING

by Christopher Stasheff

SELENA SCHLEIN DREAMED. She lay in cold sleep, very cold and very deep, so cold that her mind had the illusion of warmth, so cold that the stream of life had ebbed to a trickle—and as she slept, she dreamed a nightmare.

For she dreamed of the Fleet, whose ships chased those of her family over the sky—which couldn't be; they didn't know of the Schlein family. At least, so far as anyone knew, they didn't know of the Families—but there was no telling what their spies had ferreted out, and in her dream, the Fleet had found them, and had chased Selena's exploration ship to the center of the galaxy, even though they couldn't have, even though part of her shouted silently, No! It wasn't that horrible Fleet, it was those implacable insects!

But in the nightmare, the pursuing ship loomed larger and larger in their viewscreen, and her husband Hans was shouting, "Get the women into the lifeboats!" but she was protesting that, no, she would rather remain there by him, to die with him if it was necessary, but the whole ship shuddered as the Fleet vessel grappled it, one of the bulkheads fractured and split open like an egg, and an alien form slipped through, but it wasn't the dreaded Fleet uniform, nor one of those horrible bugs, it was even more horrible, it was one of those vicious, savage Weasels, the Khalians, whom the Families' agents had so successfully suborned into attacking the Alliance, but now it was a Khalian, but Dobie and Harl who were carrying her away to stuff her into the life-pod, strapping the tubes with the needles to her wrists, and she was screaming, "No!

I can fight, too!" but the drugs were taking effect, the world was growing dim, then vague and fuzzy, then totally dark, and she relaxed with a flood of relief, safe in the darkness even as her heart ached for Hans, frantic with worry for him, but her fear and worry were distanced somehow by the darkness. . . .

But the blackness was lightening, her eyelids trembling, trying to open. She fought to keep them closed, keep the safe warm darkness wrapped about her, but it wasn't warm anymore, it was chilly, and she shivered, it was cold, so cold, and her eyelids opened all by themselves, to look for warmth. . . .

And the nightmare slammed back, her two worst fears coupled together, for there, not two feet from her face, hung the monstrous Khalian face under the Fleet uniform cap, its furry snout split in an evil, gloating grin, and Selena screamed, thrashing about, trying to escape, but horrible soft arms held her imprisoned, and she screamed and screamed and screamed, until the warm fuzzy darkness came back to shield her, and free her from the responsibility of wakefulness.

Globin looked up at his secretary. "But how would it be if the Gersons had been a sentient race that had nothing in common with us, Plasma? If they had been, let us say, thinking plants—or living stones?"

"Speak only of what is possible, Globin," Plasma said with a rare show of real anger. "This we know: Giant bugs seek to destroy beings like us, with warm blood, and that is all we need to know."

"So it comes down to like and unlike," Globin sighed. "Is there no more to Right and Wrong than that?"

"Of course not, Globin! The Ichtons seek to slay the folk of other races and take their planets, as they slew the Gersons and laid waste their home!"

"That is true," Globin said, nodding, "and surely it is wrong to steal and murder—but right to defend, and kill in defense of others' lives."

He was quite well aware that the Ichtons must surely believe—if they were truly thinking beings, rather than mere biological calculators evolved to solve technological problems of slaughter—believe that their own conquests and genocides were right, and that men of his own species had once believed the same. It did not make the Ichtons any more morally sound, but it did make Globin wonder.

He wondered even more that he should wonder. Who was he to ponder questions of right and wrong—he, Globin, traitor to his own kind, pirate king, space-thief, and murderer, responsible for the deaths of many who had been killed when their ships had been taken by his men—more accidentally than intentionally, true. His orders had always been to take without killing if possible, but to kill if it was necessary, but responsible nonetheless. So he was a murderer, yes, and could not deny it. His only justification was loyalty to the Khalian pirates who had adopted him when men of his own kind sought to slay him, and that had always sufficed—till now.

Why did it suddenly bother him? he wondered. Now, when he had lived one hundred years out of a probable hundred thirty—now, when he had turned his pirates into legal merchants and made their peace with the Alliance; now, when he had resigned his place among the Baratarian Khalians and taken a horde of young and eager volunteers to help defend the weaker races at the Core of the galaxy, against a marauder who annihilated all in its path, without reason or cause save its own greed. Surely there could not be a cause more right, nor a moral issue less ambiguous!

But Globin was keenly aware that the Ichtons, more alien than any species he had yet encountered, could hardly be said to think as human beings did, nor even as mammals did—and he was also aware that learning how they thought was the only real path to stopping them. Defeating them completely was improbable—there were simply too many of them, too many ships, too many conquered planets, and more disappearing into their collective maw all the time. It would be as much a feat of diplomacy as of war to make them stop, as it had always been—as MacArthur had helped the Japanese to realize that commerce was a more certain path to dominion than military conquest, and Gorbachev had played peacemaker between the United States and China.

But when he began to try to learn how the Ichtons thought, he began to wonder about their own ideas of morality—and thus, so late in life, had begun to ponder the issues that had for so long been clear. Oh, they still were—clear for him, clear in terms of what he must immediately do; but on the cosmic scale?

The viewscreen on the wall lit, and an excited Khalian looked out at him, tense with the enthusiasm of youth. "Globin! Plasma, tell Globin at once! There is a life-pod! Our scoutship has caught it!"

Globin was on his feet. He would have to move fast; any such detritus brought in was common property of the whole ship, and the humans of the Fleet would have overheard Platelet's message. "What is in the life-pod, Platelet?"

"Terrans! Females! Globin, come and see!"

Globin stood stunned. "Terrans? Here? So far from home, from any Terran home? How could they have come? None are being sought by the *Hawking*."

"Ask it of them yourself!" Plasma was already halfway to the door. "Globin, come quickly!"

The life-pod was clamped to the underside of the Khalian scoutship, seamed and cratered with the impacts of space junk. But its cargo had already been transferred to the Khalian ship, and were now being carried through the airlock—

On stretchers.

"They screamed when they saw us, Globin." Platelet looked up, his eyes huge, for a Khalian. "Screamed, and called us monsters, and begged for mercy. They would not be quiet no matter how much we reassured them, so we sedated them. It is best if they see you first, when they waken."

But one last Terran woman came walking, behind the stretchers of her mates. Globin caught his breath; she was beautiful, even under the dirt and caked sweat of a long sojourn in the life-pod, even with the strain ravaging her face, and her golden hair dulled by dirt. But her eyes were huge, and frightened.

Plasma nudged him, and Globin came out of his reverie. He stepped over to her. She looked up, terrified, like a doe about to run at sight of the hunter—then saw a human face, and relaxed.

Almost collapsed.

She sagged against Globin's chest. It was unexpected, and he fell back a step, then braced himself and took her in his arms, making soothing sounds. "There now, the ordeal is over, you have come to safe harbor, you will be all right. . . ."

She seemed to melt against him, but made no reply.

Emboldened, he held her away just a little, and said gravely, "But you must tell me, child. How did you come to be here, so far from human space?"

The girl watched his face intently, with a little frown. There was something odd about that gaze, something troubling, but Globin set it aside for later analysis and said again, "How did you come to be here?"

"Speak more slowly," the girl said in an odd flat voice. Globin would have interpreted that as sarcasm, but the intentness of her gaze made him realize that it wasn't.

"How . . . did . . . you . . . come . . . to . . . be . . . here?" he asked. "What . . . happened . . . to . . . your . . . ship?"

Then he realized, with a shock, what was odd about her gaze. She wasn't making eye contact. Her gaze was lower, watching his lips. A strange feeling went through Globin, a shivering thrill at the strangeness of it.

"We came to study the Core," she said. "Men and women, many married."

"The *Dunholme* Expedition," Globin breathed. He remembered the story, discovered in the Schlein family archives after the surrender, and released to the media. Even in the Alliance's triumph, the expedition had been heralded as an example of devotion to science. A dozen couples had embarked on a virtual suicide mission, for the Core was so far away, at the speeds attainable a century and a half before, that there was very little chance the people would come back alive. The ship would, but they would not. It was a monumental case of self-sacrifice, choosing to spend virtually their whole lives cooped up in a single ship—never mind that the ship was so large as to be a tiny world in itself—and forswearing having children, for they had no right to commit unborn people to such an existence.

Of course, some of the critics had noted, these were people to whom science was so important, so thrilling, that what they were giving up was balanced by the opportunities they were gaining. Others had noted the psychological profiles of the people aboard: they were mostly misanthropes, who had felt rejected by others, and rejected society in turn (How well Globin had understood that!), though they got along well enough with one another, enjoying the society of fellow rejects; and none of them really wanted to have children. The two qualities seemed to go together, somehow.

But they had never come back. Oh, they hadn't been expected to, not for a hundred years—but they had set out a hundred fifty years before, sent by the wealthy and ambitious Schlein family, striving for more wealth and greater power among the Merchant Families, sent to find some secret of Nature that would give them a huge edge over their rivals. But the long-delayed war had come to the Schleins, and cut them away, and Globin had grown old waiting for the *Dunholme* to come back, grown to the age of eighty yearning for the knowledge they would bring, had set off with the *Hawking* for the very core to which they had gone, fuming at them for not having sent back their data.

But when they had confronted the Ichtons, he knew what had happened to them—or guessed. Now he had merely to confirm it.

"The *Dunholme* Expedition?" he asked the girl again, then remembered to say it a third time, slowly. He was beginning to realize what was wrong with her.

She nodded. "We were attacked by the insects, but we escaped—and the FTL drive was damaged. We fled for months, fleeing at light speed, but their pursuit ship finally caught us and disabled our engines completely. The men put all the women in a cryogenic chamber, this life-pod in which you found us, while they worked to make the ship come alive again, knowing they would probably die trying. The last one alive was to release the pod, so that we at least would have some hope of rescue—and praise Heaven it has come!"

"But they were all mature men and women on that expedition," Globin protested, "in their thirties or forties, and you are scarcely twenty, if that."

The girl nodded, her eyes huge and luminous—and Globin felt his heart twist. He berated it silently, and himself for an old fool, and made a conscious effort to focus on her words, not her face alone.

"They had agreed not to reproduce," the girl said, "but had not forsworn lovemaking, and most of them were married. What went wrong with the contraceptives, I do not know—but there was an accident, and I was born."

Globin frowned. "That was dangerous. With so little space, if others had followed your mother's example . . ."

"But they did not," the young woman said firmly. "Everyone deplored the bad luck, my mother most of all—but with every breath of condemnation, she smiled with secret delight. At least, that is what my father said, as well as all my aunts, with a touch of envy. You see, they had all reared families already, but they tell me that nothing raises the desire for one last child so much as seeing someone else pregnant."

"So you grew up aboard ship," Globin said, frowning, "and never knew what it was to live on a planet."

"Never," she said, "until now."

Globin resisted the smile of amusement that pushed at his lips. "This is no planet, child, but only a ship, albeit a very large one."

"And I am no child," she said firmly, "albeit I am much younger than you."

Globin gazed at her a moment, then inclined his head. "Your pardon, fair lady."

"Of course." She smiled, and her face was a sun.

Globin held his gaze on her while he waited for his blood to stop effervescing. Then he said, "So you never knew of the Khalian War."

"They have told me of it," she said evenly, "and have showed me the holocines shot during the worst of the battles. The Khalians looked terrible, then. They do not look so monstrous now."

"You are not seeing them in combat," Globin pointed out. "Did your parents not tell you of the horrible things they had done?"

"Yes, but I could understand only the broad outline." The girl tapped her ear with a forefinger. "I am deaf, you see."

She said it matter-of-factly, as though it were the most natural thing in the world. Globin sat immobile as his hardened old heart softened amazingly with pity; she had adjusted admirably, or developed iron-hard emotional defenses.

Unless . . .

Unless it *were* the most natural thing in the world.

"Deaf from birth?" he asked.

The young woman nodded. "Cosmic radiation, we think—the ship was not entirely proof against it. Though Heaven knows, there were enough other sources available. It took them a year to understand why I did not respond to sounds, but only moved my lips. Then, slowly and painfully, they taught me to speak—but by the time I could understand a large enough vocabulary to comprehend the accounts of Khalian atrocities, I was old enough to be skeptical, too, and to think that no living being is inherently evil."

So that was why she had been afraid, but not terrified. What the other women knew as contemporary terror, she had known only as history—and could not have been raised with species hatred, for she had not comprehended the gory details.

"I would have said so, too, at one time," Globin said grimly. He was thinking of some of the more unpleasant examples of his own species.

The young woman misunderstood. She frowned. "Do you speak of the insects?"

Globin had to consider that before he answered. "I do not think they are evil in their own minds," he said, "assuming they have minds, as we know them. But as a species, they are as evil as a cancer."

"But no more than a cancer," she pointed out. "After all, a cancer has no mind, no will; it does not intend to cause pain."

Admiration for her mind kindled in Globin now, and he warned himself to beware. "Exactly. It *does* evil, but it may not *be* evil. As with the Ichtons—that is what we call these marauding insectoids. For now, though, we must fight them."

"Of course," she said with perfect composure.

"And that is all you knew of your parents' universe?" Globin asked. "Only the broad outlines of the war?"

"Oh, I learned the details when I was in my teens," she said. "It all seems like a story in a book, though, for that is what it was."

Globin held her gaze while something shriveled inside him, at the thought that he was history to her. "What of the Khalians after their war with the Fleet?"

"I was told that the war was ended," she said, studying his face, "ended many years ago, and that most of the Khalians had joined with the Alliance. Some, though, would not be appeased, would not stop fighting, but became pirates, so that they could continue to prey upon the ships of the Alliance. They told me also that a human renegade had clawed his way to command of all the pirates—a misshapen creature called the Globin." She shrugged. "Surely he could not have endured long—a lone human among his blood enemies."

Globin took a deep breath, turning away, then remembered that he had to face her while he talked, or she would not be able to understand him. "One human did—a Captain Goodheart. His ship was blown up by a Family squadron."

She frowned. "They told me of Captain Goodheart—scary tales for darkness. Was not this 'Globin' his assistant?"

Globin nodded. "Globin led the search for Goodheart's killers. He found them, though it took years—and all the Families with them."

She stood rod-still, galvanized, eyes wide. "What happened then?"

"War," Globin told her, "between the Alliance and the Families. The Khalians, learning that they had been used as the Families' tool, screamed betrayal and allied with the Fleet, seeking revenge."

Her face was ashen; she had to moisten her lips with her tongue. "And the end of that war?"

"The Fleet and its Khalian allies defeated the Families. Their worlds were occupied; they paid reparations."

"They were conquered," she whispered. "All because this Globin found them?"

He could see from her face that she knew the fate of those who were conquered, but he found he could not lie. He nodded, and felt his heart plummet.

But it revived at her next words. "I cannot believe that he was so thorough a villain—that he must have had reasons for what he did, other than money."

Globin nodded, with relief. "You are right." But he was annoyed with himself, too; her opinion of him should not matter so much. "What is your name?"

"Lusanne," she said. "What is yours?"

"People call me 'Globin,' " he answered.

She would not scare. No matter what he told her, no matter how much of the gritty truth, she would not scare. She was only interested—perhaps "fascinated" would be a better word—for she was confronting a living legend, a character from the pages of history.

And she was very curious. Globin decided she must be a natural historian.

But while he discussed history with her, he had to manage the present, with an eye to the future. Both were summed up in one name: Brand.

Commander Brand had raised the roof, or at least the ceiling; his voice almost shook the speaker off the wall. "Globin, what the hell do you think you're doing holding human prisoners?"

"None more human than I, Commander," Globin told the image on the screen, "though you may find that hard to believe."

"Any prisoners taken are under the authority of the Fleet, Chairman! Any shipwreck survivors rescued are under my jurisdiction!"

"With the commander's pardon," Globin said, his old tone of authority reasserting itself, "the survivors were rescued by a Baratarian corporate vessel, taken to the Baratarian sector, and are currently the guests of the Baratarian Corporation."

"Damn it, Globin, they're Schleins!"

"And very sick ones, too," Globin said, authority turning into iron. He reflected that Brand's intelligence network was, as always, excellent. "It would be very dangerous for them to be moved just now, Commander. With all due respect, in consideration of the survivors' welfare, I must respectfully decline to allow them to leave the Baratarian sickbay until they are restored to full health."

"They're human *women,* Globin! And you've got 'em being nursemaided by a bunch of Wea . . . Khalians!"

"Khalian doctors," Globin snapped, the iron transmuting into steel, "under the direction of my personal physician, Dr. Arterial—who is a graduate of Camford University on Terra, I might remind you, as well as of the College of Physicians of Khalia."

"But he's not human, Globin!" Brand took a long breath, then said, "My quarters. Chairman. Right away—if you please." The last was very grudging, but Brand knew the contract—and the laws to which he would answer if the *Hawking* returned to Terra—and, moreover, knew that Globin knew them, too.

"It is always a pleasure to accept your kind invitations, Commander," Globin returned evenly, then rose with a satisfied smile. "Plasma, if you would join me?"

The *Hawking* was a huge ship, so by the time Globin and Plasma arrived at the commander's office, Brand had had enough time to both calm down and think things through—so, as Globin came through the door, he was all sweetness and light. "Now see here, Globin. I think we can both agree that the ladies' welfare is foremost."

Globin breathed a secret sigh of relief. He was more than halfway home free. "Yes, Commander, I can agree with that."

"Well, these women are Schlein family. How do you think they're going to feel if the first thing they see when they wake up is a Khalian muzzle?"

Globin remembered how the one woman had reacted already, and said slowly, "You point is well taken, Commander." Of course, Brand knew just exactly how well taken it was; Globin didn't doubt for a second that the commander knew about the one woman who had half waked, screamed, and lapsed back into unconsciousness.

"Well, that's all I'm asking—just to have Terran doctors treat them." Brand held up a hand. "No, I'm not asking for your Dr. Arterial to be excluded from his own sickbay, or for any of his assistants to be kicked out—I'm just asking that human doctors be allowed in there, too."

"And that they be the first one the revivees see." Globin nodded slowly. "I'm afraid I cannot disagree with you in any degree, Commander—as long as we are only speaking of five or six doctors, and they are coming to our sickbay, not the other way around."

"Done!" Brand grinned like a shark. "I'll have them down there in five minutes, Chairman!"

Globin decided that Brand would pay for that grin.

But it would take time to decide how to exact that penalty. Oh, Globin knew what it would be—he would keep the women in the Baratarian Quarter. But how to achieve it would take long days of thought, and nights of letting the elements of the problem link themselves up while he slept.

While the problem stirred itself around in the back of his mind, and the physicians labored over the other survivors, Globin allowed himself the luxury of the company of the youngest Schlein.

And a pleasure it was, for she showed not the slightest distaste at his presence. He took her for a tour of his domain, the Baratarian Quarter of the ship. They visited the workshops, the mess hall, the lounge, and ended by strolling through the park. Lusanne looked about her with bright and eager interest in all the strange sights. "So vast," she whispered.

It was only five hundred meters in diameter, and fifty high, but the walls and ceiling were painted to give the illusion of a limitless expanse of plain rolling away to an imaginary horizon, to fulfill the need of shipbound creatures for open spaces. Globin realized with a shock that the poor child had never seen open fields or sky, any sky but the star-strewn night of the Core. She might have been afraid, but instead she was eager, and his admiration for her, already high due to the courage he perceived in her, rose still more.

She would far more likely have been afraid of the Khalians who rose from the long grass now and then, bounding away in frenetic joy at escaping the close confinement of their quarters for a few hours, or strolling slowly by, chatting. Always Khalians, always fur and leather, never human skin and clothing. Raised to fear Khalians as other children feared bogeymen, Lusanne might have shrunk gibbering in terror—but she greeted every encounter with the fresh enthusiasm of a child let loose to discover its world—or a scientist given free rein to examine whatever she wished.

"So I am a pirates' prisoner?" she asked in her oddly uninflected diction.

"Scarcely!" Globin stifled a chuckle. "You are a guest, Lusanne, and we are no longer pirates. I guided the Khalians of Barataria into legitimate commerce forty years ago. They are a legal merchant corporation now and obey all laws."

"Forty?" She looked up, startled. "But our ship departed on its expedition only thirty years ago!"

Globin stared at her, amazed, realizing just how long she and her shipmates must have been drifting in that capsule. He said gently, "It has been one hundred fifty years since your parents began their quest, Lusanne."

She stared. "Can we have been in that life-pod for so long?"

"Perhaps not," Globin said slowly. "You said that the Ichtons—excuse me; that is what we call the insectoid race that attacked the *Dunholme*—you said that your ship fled for several weeks, at nearly the speed of light?" She nodded, and Globin said, his suspicion strengthened, "There is a time-squeeze effect; for each week that passes near the speed of light, years pass on the surface of a planet. So you may not have been in the capsule longer than a decade or so—but between your long sleep and your long escape, twelve decades have passed."

Tears formed at the corners of her eyes. "Alas! For my father and the brave men who died with him! For even if they escaped the Ichtons, they must be dead by now!"

Globin remembered that she had said the last man alive had released the pod, and knew that the men for whom she mourned had almost certainly died. "They died that you might live, Lusanne," he said softly. "Surely there can be no greater mark of a man's love than that. Let the tears flow, Lusanne, for they must fall sometime. Let them fall."

Her face reddened, her fists clenched, but the tears began to flow in earnest.

Globin felt his heart twist, and held out his arms. Lusanne came into them like a child to be comforted. He folded his arms around her and patted her back gently as the sobs racked her body and she clung to him as though to a life ring in a turbulent sea. Globin rested his cheek against her head, savoring the warmth and the sensation of her body pressed against his, concentrating on every touch, every pressure, to be sure he would remember every detail, for he had never held a woman in his arms before and knew he probably never would again.

Finally, the tears slackened, and Lusanne pulled away from him, eyes downcast. Globin's handkerchief was instantly in her hand; she dabbed at her eyes, then blinked up at him with a tremulous smile, and he felt his vitals turn to water. "Thank you," she said. "I had not known . . ." Her voice trailed off.

"Emotional shock," Globin explained, and wondered if it was true of himself, too. "You've had a traumatic experience"—he managed a sardonic smile—"culminating in rescue by a pirate."

"But you said you are no longer a pirate." Her eyes were wide and very blue.

"I am not," he told her. "The Khalians elected me their leader, and over a decade, I managed to move them more and more into legitimate trade. Finally, our commercial ties were so strong that the Alliance virtually had to offer us membership, or lose too much gold to us in trade. As part of the treaty, and to save their collective face, we agreed to cease piracy, which we had almost eliminated anyway."

She stared, horrified. "You are of the Alliance now?"

"We are," he said gently, "and the war with the Families is over."

She began to tremble. "Yes—the war with the Families. Will not your Khalians hate we Schleins?"

Globin bit his lip. He said gently, "The Khalians realized they had been used by the Syndicate, betrayed, so they joined with the Alliance. The result was foregone, but tedious."

Her face was pale. "What is left of our homeland?"

"Your homeland is intact." Globin was terse. "But its armaments, and the factories that built them, are gone."

"They are defenseless, then," she whispered.

"The reparations are paid," Globin told her, "and they have nothing more to fear from the Fleet. Oh, there were atrocities, yes, but as few as the command could manage. Your countrymen are humbled, and many died in the war, but they are by and large intact. They could have fared much worse—and the Fleet that fought them now protects them."

Lusanne watched out of the corners of her eyes, uncertain. "Will the Fleet not seek to revenge itself on us women, if they find us?"

"They have," Globin said gently, and waited for it to sink in.

It did, and she pulled back with a gasp. "Not you!"

"Not really," Globin said. "In Barataria's decks, there are few Fleet personnel—but those decks are leased from a Fleet battlestation, and the overall command of the ship is Fleet."

"Then we are lost," she whispered.

"No," Globin said, "you are saved. The men of the Fleet might still harbor hatred for the Schlein family, but even they will certainly be courteous to civilians—which you are, especially since the war is long gone."

"Only courtesy," she whispered.

"Only that," he agreed. "But you are in the midst of Khalians here, and young Khalians at that, to whom your government's treachery is only a tale from a history book, and whose fathers' desire for revenge has been slaked, and forgotten—for that is how the Khalians are. You are safe among these, my adopted children."

She darted a curious glance at him, but all she said was, "I must tell all my aunts about this."

Globin nodded. "Come—let us see how well they have recovered."

Behind the glass wall, the women were sitting, still dazed and groggy. The Fleet doctors moved among them, their faces masks of impervious politeness—though now and again, one slipped, and the contempt showed through.

Lusanne shuddered. "Must we be left to the cold care of such strangers as these?"

"Only until your aunts are restored to full consciousness and mobility," Globin assured her. "That has been the subject of some spirited discussion between the commander of this battlestation and myself."

That was a huge understatement, he reflected as he thought of Brand's fury over the intercom, and the hatred that still seemed to echo in his voice when he said the name "Schlein." So now, as Globin stood with Lusanne gazing at the groggy women sitting upright in their flimsy hospital gowns, supported by their raised mattresses, watching their human and Khalian physicians with fearful eyes, Globin deliberated about the next phase in his campaign against Brand.

He was certain that he was right to want to keep the Schlein women in his own bailiwick. These were not women who had undergone the defeat of their home planet, and been chastened by it and come to be grateful for Alliance clemency, but women who were still mentally at the height of deceptive war, regarding the

Fleet doctors as their captors and hated enemies, and the Khalians as their despised but lethal pawns. In Brand's territory, the best they could expect would be ostracism; at worst, they would be targets for the long-buried vengefulness that they themselves would reawaken.

Globin's recruits, on the other hand, were all young Khalians, who would not really think about the Schleins having been traitors to either race, for to them, the war was only a tale told by their elders, albeit a very vivid one. Like Lusanne, they would be more curious than vengeful, and willing to be patient, coaxing their prisoners ahead into the modern day, and waiting patiently for friendship.

There was no question—the women had to stay in Barataria.

But how?

"Let us go in," Lusanne said. "I can see what they are saying to one another, when the doctors' backs are turned."

See what they say? Globin frowned down at her, then remembered that she was reading lips. "Yes, of course. Let us go in."

They came into the recovery room, and every woman instantly locked her gaze on to Globin, apprehension deepening at the sight of one more strange male. Then Lusanne's presence beside him registered, and they relaxed—a little.

"Thank heavens, child!" Selena croaked. "We were afraid you were dead!"

"Very much alive, Aunt Selena," Lusanne assured her. "Our rescuers have been very courteous and gentle with me. I would like to introduce you to our host, the chief executive of the Baratarian Corporation."

"Thank Heaven!" breathed the tallest, a woman in her fifties with tousled, auburn hair, still beautiful even though she was drawn and wan with the strain of her long coma. "A man who isn't a Fleet officer!"

"Be quite, you fool!" snapped an aging matron. "That's not a man, it's the Globin!"

The auburn woman stared, horror coming into her eyes.

The women all shrank back against their mattresses in alarm. "The Globin!"

"Am I so notorious as that?" Globin blinked around at them in mild amusement. "I had not thought that my reputation would reach all the way to your home world!"

"We have heard," Selena said, her mouth dry. "We have also heard that you treat your captives well, because you expect their governments to ransom them."

Globin nodded gravely. "But I am no longer a pirate, madam, nor are my Khalians—and Barataria is no longer a pirates' nest, but the home world of a commercial conglomerate."

There was a stir among the women, and Selena glanced at Lusanne for confirmation. Lusanne nodded ever so slightly, and hope lighted Selena's face. "You have become legitimate, then!"

"We have," Globin acknowledged. "But we will still extend every courtesy to our guests. Indeed, the Distressed Spacefarer's Law allows no less."

"It does not require 'every courtesy,' " Selena said with irony, "but we are grateful for all that you have given us thus far." She had rallied; pirates might be dangerous, but businessmen would strike a deal, and Selena, scientist or not, had been raised to business. "We are, then, aboard one of your Baratarian ships?"

"I fear not, madam. You are aboard the *Stephen Hawking,* an Alliance battlestation operated by the Fleet."

Instant consternation spread throughout the recovery room—consternation verging on panic. "So that is why those doctors were so cold, so hostile!" the auburn woman cried, and Selena snapped, "You cannot surrender us to them, sir! You must not!"

"Peace, peace, Aunt," Lusanne said. "The war has been over for years!"

The women stilled, staring at her, huge-eyed.

"What war?" Selena whispered. "The Khalians were defeated three years before we left!"

"The war between the Fleet and our Families." To Lusanne, a whisper was as good as a shout. "The war is history, and the wounds have healed."

"But how can so much have happened in so short a time! You were not even born when we left! Only twenty-six years ago! Could our home world have fallen so quickly?"

"Madam," said the Globin, "how old am I?"

Selena turned and stared, suddenly registering the lines, the wrinkles. "I had thought it was only space tan," she whispered.

"I fear it is more," the Globin said. "In fact, I have been told that I am uncommonly well preserved for my years, especially in view of the strains of my life in administration."

Selena's lips parted, but her voice was a bare whisper. "How . . . how long?"

"You have been in cold sleep for several decades," Globin said gently.

"Several?" Selena licked dry lips, swallowed, and asked, "How long?"

"Many years," Globin answered, and Lusanne said, "We have been on our journey for a hundred fifty years, Aunt."

Selena reeled, squeezing her eyes shut. Lusanne was at her side in a second.

"No, no, child, I am not going to faint," Selena muttered. She recovered her poise, pushed Lusanne away, and said, "So the battle is lost, and the rancor has cooled—but not completely, as we have seen from our doctors." She glanced nervously at the medical team who hovered behind Globin. "All in all, I think we might be safer here."

"You are my guests for as long as you wish to remain." Globin inclined his head graciously. "Or at least for as long as I can stall off Commander Brand."

"And how long will that be?"

"At the least, until you are completely restored to fitness and peak physical condition. How did you say you felt, madam?"

The Klaxon sounded.

Throughout the Baratarian Quarter, Khalians scrambled for battlestations. The Klaxon's braying modulated into words: "Enemy approaching! Enemy penetrating screens! Enemy attack on south pole!"

The quarter rocked at a sudden blast that rang through the hull into every cubicle. The Khalian crewmen stumbled, throwing themselves against walls for support; a few fell to the floor. Then they were up again and running as the Klaxon yammered, "Hull penetrated at cargo hold South 24!"

South 24! Globin had a momentary vision of trade goods spilling out into space by the gross, trade goods fired by energy weapons within the hull, trade goods trampled under . . . Then he shook it off—if they didn't manage to repel the Ichtons, all the trade goods in the galaxy wouldn't do them a bit of good. He yanked open the cabinet on the wall and pulled out his rifle, then hauled the door open and went into the corridor. At his age, he knew better than to run, and his crew knew better than to let him near danger—but Plasma had dashed off after the attackers, gray muzzle or no, and no one would see the Globin coming out to the fight. . . .

He was amazed at himself; his self-image was still fixed at twenty, when he would have shied away from any combat in sheer terror. But a lifetime with Khalian pirates, and Goodheart's careful instruction in unarmed combat, had given him back the courage the boyhood bullies had stolen, and he went toward the sound of battle, not away from it.

Then the deck lifted against his feet, and the walls shuddered. He lurched against a bulkhead, but kept his feet while a chorus of screams broke out ahead. Globin stared, then ran. It was only a few steps to the sickbay. . . .

"Hull holed in Khalian sickbay!" the Klaxon blatted. "Infantry to sickbay!"

Globin swerved into the doorway, remembering to leap aside so other defenders could come in—and they did, in a stream; but a fireball blossomed in the doorway. Khalian screams shrilled; Globin shrank back, turning his face to the wall while the light faded. Then he turned and saw dead Khalians on the floor. His heart wrenched at the sight, but more of his young Weasels were leaping in and dodging to the sides, and there was no time for grief. Globin turned ahead and saw the huge insectoid shapes grabbing at the Family women. They shrank back shrieking, looking about them wildly, clawing at the walls. The oldest one had found a plasma holder and was beating at a carapace; the Ichton tore it out of her hands and turned its rifle toward her, but younger women jammed chairs between them, and their screaming was beginning to be as much in anger as in fear. Lusanne had a bit more presence of mind than he would have expected—she had found a pole lamp and was stabbing the glowing tube at the Ichton's eyes.

It was valiant, but would do no good. Globin steadied himself, resting his barrel on a bedstead. He aimed for the insect's eyes and waited for a split second when there would be no human head in the way. Auburn hair swung aside; Globin pressed the trigger. The energy bolt flashed. Women screamed as they leaped aside, giving Globin a clear field of fire. He shot again and again.

The Ichton's shrilling was at the upper edge of his hearing, tearing through his head, and the monster swung its firearm about, blasting blindly. The women hit the deck. Globin realized, with satisfaction, that he had burned its eyes out. He lowered his aim to the thorax and fired. His bolt smashed in; three more of the Khalian crew joined in, focusing on the thorax. The monster bucked, then fell dead.

Globin looked up and saw that his crew had seen what he had done, and were imitating. Bolts flared at Ichton eyes; bug rifles spewed in every direction, but hit only the walls. Khalian fire focused on thoraxes and burned through.

Then Plasma leaped in front of him, chittering in rage. "Globin! If you die, we are all lost! Get back, get away!"

A dozen young Khalians leaped in, a living wall between them and the Ichtons—but the living bugs were retreating, firing as they went back out through the hole they had blasted in.

"That is a long tunnel," Globin said to Plasma. "We are nowhere near the hull."

"But there is vacuum somewhere at the other end," Plasma snapped. "They are fainting from loss of air!"

And indeed, the women who had thrown themselves down were not rising. Here and there, a few Khalians were falling, clawing at their throats. The air being sucked in from the rest of the quarter had sustained them thus far, but it was almost exhausted.

"Lusanne!" Globin cried. "Quickly, Plasma! The oxygen!"

Plasma moved more quickly than his chief, and a few of the youngsters saw what he was up to as he cracked the valve on the oxygen cylinder in the clinic. Some leaped to help him, finding other green cylinders; others caught up blankets and sheets and slapped up a quick barrier over the hole.

Moving more slowly, Globin brought an oxygen mask to Lusanne—but she was already working her way to her feet, and pushed the mask away. "Selena—my other aunts—they need it more than I."

Globin sighed and turned to help the Schleins who knew from personal memory what had caused the animosity between them.

"All told, we got off very lightly," Brand told the hastily assembled conference. "It was just a raid by a couple of destroyers, backed up by a battlewagon. The big ship sat back and helped pour fire into one point on our shield until it overloaded, causing a sector to collapse. Then they sat back and provided covering fire while the destroyers broke in and started shooting their way toward the sickbay. When they found out they were dying faster than we were, they pulled out. All told, we lost four of the Schlein women and six of our own crew, plus thirty wounded. All things considered, it could have been much worse."

"Let's hope they don't think to try it with a larger force," someone said grimly.

"We know they will, now," Brand said, his face heavy. "We'll just have to start shooting if they come anywhere near. That's pretty obvious, though. The real question is, why?"

Everyone was silent, avoiding one another's eyes. It was the question they'd been hoping not to have to think about.

Brand turned to Globin, pointing at the cross-sectional map of the ship. "They attacked your quarter, Chairman. That might have been accident, but coming into the hold and blowing their way through wall after wall until they came to the sickbay—that was deliberate, very deliberate. Why?"

He turned back to the assembled officers. They all frowned, looking back; then one voiced the thought that all were thinking: "The women."

Brand sighed. "Good. Then I'm not the only one who sees it. But . . . why?"

The officers exchanged puzzled glances. Then one said, with an apologetic half laugh, "Because they're beautiful, of course."

The reaction was out of all proportion to the joke—if it was a joke. Everyone took it as such, though, laughing till the tears came. Brand took it well, grinning as he looked about them, stifling a chuckle of his own. After all, it *was* hilarious—giant insectoids thinking human women attractive. It was almost as funny as the notion of one of the bug queens exciting desire in a human male—and every one of them must have thought of that, too, for when the laughter had begun to slacken, it suddenly redoubled in a new wave. When the noise had subsided, though, Brand frowned, serious again. "Okay. What possible interest could they be to the bugs? And how could the swarm have found out about them, anyway?"

There was only muttering for a while; then Globin had a sudden inspiration. "Commander! They could never have seen the women before, or the Schleins would not have lived for us to find them!"

The conversation stilled; everyone turned, amazed. "Why, that's very true, Chairman," Brand said slowly. "They could only have seen the Schlein vessel."

"But they destroyed the ship," someone else pointed out, "and all the male Schleins aboard."

"Yes, Commander, that tallies with what the women have told us," Globin corroborated. "The men ejected them in a life capsule and stayed to fight."

Someone else said slowly, "Why did the men stay?"

It was a good question, and the apparent answer was so obvious that no one had ever thought of it. They looked at one another in surprise.

"Yes," Brand said slowly. "Once the women were safe, why didn't the men escape in the same fashion? Obviously, because they couldn't."

"Of course!" cried a captain. "If they all ejected in a life-pod, the bugs would have blasted them out of this space-time! The men had to keep the fight going long enough for the women to get lost in the depths!"

The room was very quiet for a few minutes, as each man contemplated the courage of those Schlein men, fighting to certain death, knowing they stood no chance of winning, but also knowing that each second they bought would give their loved ones a little longer to recede into the dark and cold of interstellar space. Even here near the Core, there was enough room between stars so that one tiny, hundred-foot-long life-pod would be indistinguishable by radar from a thousand other asteroids—if it were beyond the reach of telescopes.

"So the bugs knew someone had escaped," Brand summarized, "but they couldn't find them. Why would they be so fanatical about killing them, though, once they'd been found?"

"The Ichtons are fanatical about everything," someone said.

"Sheer cussedness," someone else suggested. "They hate not finishing something they've started."

"No." Brand shook his head. "They've always been very logical—we've seen the records, we know they've gone past hard targets to find easy ones, and not come back until they had so much strength massed that the hard targets had become pushovers. It's not like them to take a risk of any kind, let alone what amounts to a commando action against overwhelming odds. They had something to gain from this, more than just a sixty-year-old grudge."

"More to the point," someone else said, "they must have had something to lose."

"Of course!" Globin was on his feet, eyes wide with sudden understanding. "That's been bothering me for a while—why would they have taken the trouble to eliminate a single ship, one that didn't even bear enough armament to be a military vessel? Why bother swatting a fly?"

"Unless," Brand said slowly, "the fly has come too close to your lunch."

"Or your heart," Globin said grimly.

Brand's eyes glowed. "Yes! They saw something, Chairman. They saw something on their viewscreens that they shouldn't have seen—and the bugs have to make sure they don't tell anybody. When your men found the life-pod, the bugs must have picked up the radio transmissions—we know they have some kind of intelligence service. They wouldn't have had to understand very much to know that your people had found something. A little thought, and a bit of record-checking, could have told them what."

"Seems kind of farfetched," an officer said slowly, "for them to find out that much just from some half-understood radio transmissions."

"I don't like to think of the alternative," Brand said grimly.

Neither did anyone else—that there was a traitor aboard or some kind of listening device. The atmosphere grew strained; they knew that Brand couldn't discount the possibility, now that he'd thought of it, and that Internal Intelligence would be very alert for any signs of treachery from now on.

"Still, it seems possible," Globin said slowly. "A lone picket who picks up a sudden flurry of language-noise, then gets close enough for his long-range sensors to see something heavy being towed in. . . . Of course, he wouldn't attack himself, not if there was a chance he'd be shot down instead of bringing back important information. No, I don't think it requires a spy."

"Maybe not," Brand conceded, "but it does require the Schlein women being a lot more important than we thought they were. Chairman, I really must insist they be moved into the Fleet sickbay, where they can be guarded more securely."

Globin bridled, but kept his tone soft. "I beg to differ, Commander. This incident has set back their convalescence by several weeks; it is very important that they not be moved."

"But your sickbay's shot to pieces, Globin! You can't take care of them anymore!"

"Repairs on the sickbay are almost complete," Globin demurred. "The survivors are comfortable in the recreation room in the meantime—and your counselors are helping them to cope with the shock of the invasion."

"We must have them submit to hypnosis and memory scan, Chairman! It's absolutely vital!"

"Agreed," Globin said easily, "but they cannot be subjected to any such exertion until they are fully recovered. You know that, Commander. Ask your own physicians. What good is a dead source? How much water can you draw from a dry well?"

Brand was still a moment; his eyes narrowed. "There is one among them who is fully recovered, Chairman. I have seen her walking in your company."

"What, Lusanne?" Globin shrugged impatiently. "She is scarcely more than a child, Commander. What could she know? What could she have understood from what she had seen?"

"Her information is vital, Chairman!"

"But it cannot be gained without her consent," Globin said, his voice iron. "Hypnosis will not work on an unwilling subject. There is no point in the scan unless it is voluntary."

"Then ask her, Chairman!"

Globin sighed. "Very well, Commander. I shall ask."

• • •

Lusanne drew in upon herself, her eyes wide. "Must I, Globin?" Then she answered herself. "Yes, of course I must. If it might save lives . . ."

"But you are afraid," Globin interpreted. "It will do no good if you are afraid, Lusanne. You would be too tense to achieve the trance. Even if you did, it could not be deep enough."

"What could I have seen that the Ichtons would care about?"

"Nothing, probably," Globin said, "unless everyone on your ship saw it, too. But in all probability, they did not—only those who were on duty on the bridge at the time would have had the chance."

Lusanne nodded slowly, frowning. "That would make sense. . . ."

"Who was on the bridge?" Globin asked softly.

"Of my aunts? Only Selena, and Maude and Mirabile—they were the only ones of command rank. The rest of us couldn't have cared less. There were only a few of the men, too—no one wanted to take time away from their experiments, to do it. Someone said it was like having to be chairman of a mathematics department."

"Perfect irony," Globin said, and reported it that way to Brand. "They may be trying to kill people who do not have the information they fear, Commander. The ones who did know, they have done in already."

"It's possible," Brand admitted, "but we must be sure. Can't you persuade her, Chairman?"

"I probably could," Globin said slowly, "but she is afraid of the Fleet, Commander. Your doctors have not hidden their hostility very well."

"And the scan would be unsuccessful, if she's so fearful," Brand sighed, sitting back. "Very well, Globin. We'll work at creating an atmosphere of trust. Let's just hope that the Ichtons don't manage to rob us of all atmosphere of any kind, first."

But Brand couldn't be stalled forever. A good long time, true—his own doctors admitted that the women were thoroughly depleted by their long sleep; muscle tone was gone, digestion was delicate, and nervous systems were recovering rather slowly from thirty years of dormancy. Still, even Globin couldn't delay physical therapy with any good conscience—the women's lives depended as much on their physical fitness, as on their dwelling place. So the day came when Brand invited Globin to a conference again, and demanded, "They are restored to health. We want them."

And Globin, with the utmost courtesy, replied, "Your pardon, Commander, but they wish to remain my guests."

"The war may be over, Globin, but those women were not residing on any of the planets that surrendered and are not yet included under the terms of that treaty. They may have information about the Core that we need, and may not wish to accept the armistice."

Globin stood rigid, hoping he was mistaken about what the commander had not said. "Just how strong an interrogation do you intend?"

"What?" Brand stared, taken aback as much by the iron tone as by the words themselves. Then he realized Globin's meaning and leaned back with a long whistle. "Oh, no, Globin, what do you take me for? Of course we don't intend torture! But the women are human, and must reside among their own kind!"

Globin relaxed, but only a little. "I would send them in an instant if they wished to go, Commander, but they are . . . apprehensive."

"Apprehensive? About what?"

"About their reception among Fleet personnel, Commander. Even their doctors treated them with a contempt that was only slightly veiled."

"We are only human, Globin. You can't be surprised if the presence of Schlein family members straight from the middle of the war brings back old . . . antagonisms."

"Not surprised at all," Globin said dryly. "Under those circumstances, *you* should not be surprised if they find the company of my young warriors more congenial."

"We must have them, Globin!"

"They are my guests, Commander. I shall not ask them to leave."

Brand slammed a fist down on his desk like a gavel. "You are bound by the regulations of the *Hawking*!"

"As you are bound by the terms of our contract," Globin returned.

Brand's face turned stony. "I will convene a formal hearing. The arbitrators shall decide the issue, and their judgment shall be binding upon both parties—as is stipulated in your contract!"

"To arbitration I shall submit." Globin's tone made it quite clear that he would not submit to Brand.

The hearing chamber, somewhat ominously, was also the room intended for courts-martial and any other legal proceedings that might have arisen during the voyage. However, its architecture didn't suggest the majesty of the law—more the boardroom of a corporation. There were three tables, joined to form an "I"; the stem, the longest table, was taken up by a double row of officers, corporation executives, and a few high-ranking civilians, such as scientists and doctors. Two of the faces there were Khalian; only one was Baratarian.

At the head of the "I" were Brand and his counselors; it was the head because that was where Brand was sitting. However, an enlargement of the Alliance seal took up most of the wall behind him, whereas the wall at the foot was blank, with a paleness that suggested the holotank it truly was—invaluable for the conferences for which this room doubled. Even in so large a ship as the *Hawking,* every space had to be used for at least two functions.

Globin sat at the foot of the table, with Selena Schlein, Lusanne, and Plasma, who was surrounded by a reader and its record-spheres.

Brand brought down a gavel. "This hearing may begin. Let the record show that on this date, the Fleet invoked its authority to take into its care any distressed space travelers taken aboard the *Stephen Hawking,* and that the Baratarian Corporation has refused to surrender its prisoners."

"We are not prisoners," Selena Schlein snapped.

"Objection," said the military attorney next to Brand, and the commander said, "Sustained." Then, to Selena, "Please do not speak unless you are recognized. For the record, please tell us your name and—"

The alarm blared.

Everyone sat bolt upright.

"Battlestations!" a voice snapped over the sound of the Klaxon. "Ichton ship has penetrated inner defenses! Commander Brand to the bridge, please! All personnel to battlestations! Enemy is within range, but his shields are holding, and his fire is concentrated on a single zone of ours! All personnel to battlestations! Conflict is imminent!"

"Adjourned!" Brand struck the gavel down one more time, even as he rose and turned from his seat.

"Back to our quarters," Globin snapped, and they rose, he and Plasma to either side of the ladies. Dr. Arterial stepped up from the witnesses' seats to stand in front of them, and the single Baratarian officer fell in behind. In formation, they went out the door and toward the drop tube.

"They cannot really manage to board so huge a ship as this!" Selena protested.

"The *Hawking* is big, but that only gives it a greater area to defend," Globin returned, "and the Ichton ships are big, hard, and mean. They have probably spent a dozen ships and all the lives on them, to bring a single cruiser so close—but there are as likely to be three as one, and—"

The floor lurched out from under them.

Howls of anger split the air, and smoke filled the hallway. A huge insectoid form came looming out of that smoke, fire spearing from it.

Their little formation wheeled about; the young Khalian who had been the rear guard was suddenly the point. He drew his weapon in a single clean motion. . . .

A piercing, high-pitched tone stabbed their ears, so loud that it sent a singing pain right through their brains. The young Khalian dropped his weapon, clutching his ears and rolling on the floor in agony. So did Globin, Selena, Dr. Arterial; Globin fought to pull his hands away from his ears, but found he couldn't bear the shriek emanating from the Ichton.

Lusanne scooped up the young Khalian's fallen weapon, aimed, and fired. A small box on the Ichton's front blew into bits.

The shrieking tone stopped.

Lusanne's fire tore at the Ichton. Terran shouts and Khalian shrilling echoed down the hall, triumphant; a fallen weapon came skidding toward them. Selena pounced on it and opened fire on the Ichton, but it kept coming, looming closer and closer. The fire from its weapon was a mad spray now, tearing at the walls and the floor, battering all about them, but not hitting.

Globin finally managed to draw and fire.

The addition of his weapon was enough; the Ichton dropped. Its body jerked as fire tore it apart. Finally, the pieces lay still.

Another loomed through the smoke behind it.

Their fire tore it to shreds.

That wasn't all there was to the fight, of course. It raged on for hours, and for the first time in decades, Globin was in the thick of it, trying desperately to protect the women, who were trying desperately to protect him. The other Schlein women caught up discarded weapons and remembered childhood training; they became a battle unit. Decades of daily exercise paid off; Globin's old heart labored, but it did not fail him. Lusanne, Selena, and the other Schleins fought on by his side with their scavenged weapons, snatching up charge packs from dead soldiers as they came upon them.

The new noise boxes were in constant use; it was an experiment, but more than a dozen Ichtons had them. Globin would hear the shrill screech and urge his little squadron toward it—after all, any direction was as likely to bring the ladies to safety as any other. As they came closer, they were disabled by the piercing tone, but Lusanne, with unerring accuracy, exploded box after box. Globin began to wonder about her hobbies.

Finally they linked up with a squadron of Marines, who formed a circle around them, and Globin and Plasma gratefully let the younger generation take the brunt of the fighting. His young Khalian fell, and until another squadron of soldiers joined them, Lusanne filled his place in the circle, side by side with a young blond giant who fought like a very demon and cheered her on to victory. "After them, woman! Oh, what a lass! Kill every last one of the stinking bugs! Don't even *think* about mercy—'cause *they* won't! By the stars, I've never seen such a woman as you!"

He couldn't know that the object of his admiration couldn't hear his praises; she fought shoulder to shoulder, and could not see his lips. She could only sneak quick glances at him as he fought—but that she did often, her glances became longer and longer, almost gazes of awe.

When the battle was over, and the amplified voice of Brand told them that surviving enemies had retreated, that all other hostiles were dead, and that the hull was sealed—then, finally, Lusanne could look up in admiration at the big soldier who towered over her—and was amazed to see him gazing raptly down at her and breathing, "You are the most remarkable woman who ever lived!"

"But—I am deaf," she protested.

That rocked him for a second, but only a second. Then he said, "Thank Heaven you are, or we'd all be dead this minute!" And he seized her and kissed her.

They froze, lip to lip, for what seemed an unconscionably long time, and something seemed to unknot and flow inside Globin's chest as he watched—but he smiled sadly, and nodded, for yes, this was how it should be, youth to youth, without some dried-up old misshapen man in between.

Love inspires trust—and Lusanne was willing to undergo the memory scan, if her Sergeant Barkis was there to hold her hand. Of course, the psychiatrist and the interrogation specialist were much warmer toward her now, and made no secret of their admiration for her courage under fire; that did no harm, either.

Her three aunts who had been on the bridge were interrogated, too, about the few days preceding the attack sixty years before. All their testimony agreed they had discovered a new planet; everyone on the ship had been very excited about it, so the bridge had relayed the pictures from the visual sensors to the big screen in the lounge. They had gone considerably closer to try to determine if the planet could support life. It could; they had come too close, and Ichton ships had boiled out into space to attack them.

That was all the three aunts remembered. But Lusanne's memory held an extremely clear picture of the viewscreen when the planet was first identified—and the astronomers were able to identify the stars at the outer edge of the screen. From that, they could make an excellent guess at the location of the planet.

"A home world," Brand said with immense satisfaction. "Maybe not *the* Ichton home world, but certainly an Ichton home world. Young lady, you have done us an invaluable service."

"But how?" Lusanne protested, eyes wide in bewilderment. "How can I, when all of us saw it on the big viewscreen in the lounge? Why could I, when my aunts couldn't?"

"Because they use all theirs senses, Lusanne," her sergeant said. He pressed her hand, and she turned to watch his lips. "They don't emphasize what they see as much as you do," he explained, "so your visual memories are much sharper, much more detailed."

Lusanne stared at him, startled. "I held the clue *because* I'm deaf?"

"Sergeant Barkis may have found the answer," the psychiatrist agreed.

Globin could see the fear in her eyes, so he hastened to reassure her. "Yes, I know—that makes you an even more vital target for them, you, and you alone. But not if they or their spies discover that your secret is out, and that we all know of the home world now."

"How can we tell them that, though?" she asked in consternation.

"By the most direct message possible," Brand said, and keyed his intercom. "Bridge! Astronomy is sending up a set of coordinates they got from Psych. Set a course for the Ichton home world!"

"Aye, Commander," the bridge responded.

Brand sat back, gaze glittering. "Now the Ichtons really will attack!"

They did.

WEAPON OF WAR

WITH ONLY LIMITED space available there were no ships larger than a cruiser brought to the center of the *Hawking*. The fact that all the warships and dozens of merchants had to be carried within the *Hawking*'s hull on the six-month journey to the galactic center had mitigated toward the *Hawking* carrying a larger number of smaller ships. Many of these were the almost-unarmed scouts, specially equipped to find and warn the races threatened by the Ichtons.

The smallest of the combat aircraft were the Fleet SBs. Designed to serve as patrol ships among the shipping lanes inside the Alliance, the SBs were the smallest ships capable of warp drive. Too small to carry engines capable of powering laser turrets that were effective at anything but near point-blank range, the SBs' sting came from the two dozen missiles jammed into launchers that occupied nearly half the ship's length. Individually the SB was little threat to any larger combat ship as both sides protected them by antimissile laser banks. A squad of six to ten SBs could launch enough missiles simultaneously to overwhelm even a small cruiser's defenses. The cost was often two or three of their number destroyed in the attack. Needless to add, the SBs attracted only the most reckless, and often creative, pilots.

In the six months after the fall of Gerson, the *Hawking* fought a series of delaying actions against three large Ichton fleets that were moving on parallel courses around the galactic center. The Fleet warships were slowly losing this battle of attrition when two of the Ichton fleets simply disappeared. After a week, Anton Brand ordered all the remaining ships to concentrate on the remaining large fleet. In a number of sharp actions, the Fleet forces joined with those of nearby allied races to shatter this third Ichton force. This victory gave a needed boost to everyone's morale. Everyone except Anton Brand and those of his staff, who realized that there had been virtually none of the dozen of mother ships normally found at the center of any Ichton formation. The Ichton fleet they had destroyed had obviously been meant as a distraction, one that had succeeded and further bled the remaining Fleet forces as well.

While the larger Fleet ships had engaged the Ichtons, the smaller SBs continued to patrol at the edges of the area of conflict. It was one of these forces that discovered not the new combined Ichton fleet but one of the many supply convoys needed to maintain it.

CHARITY
by S. N. Lewitt

Charity is incumbent on each person every day. Charity is assisting anyone, lifting provisions, saying a good word . . . Removal from the way of that which is harmful is charity.

—**Hadith of the Prophet Muhammad**

"DAWN LEADER, WE have bogers four o'clock, axis Z. Repeat, four o'clock, axis Z."

Dawn Leader didn't say anything at all. He spun the heavily armed SB as hard around as he could up the axis Z, bringing guns to bear on the enemy. The computer blinked into targeting and then fired the volley on autoselect. Slow, so screamingly slow, he thought. The best they could rig in the limited space and energy requirements of the SBs, but the smart controls weren't near the reflexes in any true ship of the line.

And it was too late. The SB *Dawn Walker* exploded in a million colors across ten klicks of raw space. And the shards of that explosion tore up the smart missile he had launched only nanoseconds ago.

Shards that should have torn through the enemy fighter, but instead were directed harmlessly around it. An energy shield, up and in place. Made no sense for the Imps of Shaitan. What did they care for an individual to live or die? They had no concept of Paradise. No, it was all to insult their human prey, to throw a challenge across the battle lines instead of fighting like honest men.

Group leader Hassan Ibn Abdullah was furious, and he knew that was exactly where the enemy wanted him. Angry and ready to make mistakes. He could hear their laughter in his head, if the Ickies laughed at all. And he knew better than to imagine it. The thought only led to mistakes.

"Dawn team, report," he ordered briskly.

Element one was in good shape; element two was a little too far from the group. Hassan ordered them back. And three, three was gone. *Dawn Walker* and *Dawn Singer* both.

The four SBs, even armed as they were, were not the ideal craft in which to fight the Ichtons. SBs had never been designed as primary fighters. They were only scoutships for transport and exploration, and rigging them with the heaviest guns they could carry was not going to make them a match for the Ichtons' protecting horde.

And Dawn Group hadn't been on a combat mission. At least they hadn't thought it was a combat mission when the assistant head of Planetary Astronomy had briefed them. In fact, Hassan had been upset at that briefing. He had wanted to be in the attack group, not given some Cub Scout assignment.

"We've got some readings that indicate there may be a habitable planet in this system," Rhys Davies had said softly. Dr. Davies always talked as if he were lecturing undergraduates in the intro class he didn't really want to teach. "And my department has been asked to find a place to settle the Gerson survivors." This was said with distinct distaste.

Not that anyone, even Davies, could possibly want not to help the few remaining Gersons. He merely resented being forced to be application-oriented when there was obviously so much more important theoretical work to do. Hassan had come to expect this attitude whenever he had to deal with the Science staff. Which meant that he dealt with them as little as possible.

"In any event, it is well out of the heavily trafficked areas and the military advisors have said it is not in the general thrust direction of the swarm. There is no reason to believe that the Ichtons have ever found this sector, and hopefully they will be eliminated before they do."

For the first time Hassan found himself agreeing wholeheartedly with Davies. If not with the assignment. He wanted to be out there doing some damage, not playing human probe.

That was an uncharitable thought, he knew. The Gersons had already lost so much, their home world, their people. The few survivors were not particularly happy aboard the *Hawking,* no matter how comfortable the civilians tried to make them. So Hassan tried not to protest, to hold it in his mind that this was a great service.

Maybe it wasn't killing bugs, but there were lots of bugs out there. More than enough to go around. Plenty left for him and the rest of Dawn Group to kill. They could spare a few hours for an act of charity.

Still, Loe Sebeng had their SBs fully armed and loaded and in top shape. "Never know what you might find out there," Sebeng had muttered, shaking her head. "Never know. Too damned much garbage around this place anyway. Want to dump some garbage while you're out?"

"We might be on routine," he protested. "But we're not the garbage scow."

Sebeng had given him one of her rare smiles. "Well, you're armed as far as I can make you. The only ammunition you're not carrying is what won't fit."

Hassan had been pleased by that much, but resigned to one more routine patrol. If they found a place for the Gersons, well and good. If not, well, there were plenty of bogers to go around.

Which was why the convoy out here was such a surprise. No one had anticipated it. And Astronomy should have been able to pick up on all that leaky radiation from primitive drives. They should have spotted this from the other side of the big black donut it was so bright. And he and Dawn Group had just blundered into it.

A single scout group shouldn't be alone with a four-freighter enemy convoy. No, a destroyer should be out in this mess, sweeping up handfuls of those little Ichton fighters that protected the big ships, sweeping them up and cracking them open. Even the Ickies couldn't live in hard vacuum.

Why wasn't there any cover? Why hadn't Astronomy picked up that bright red-hot trail when they did the survey routine? The questions flew through Hassan's mind and he dismissed them. No time to think about that now. Just time to do what was necessary.

Get the four survivors back to the *Hawking.* Better to let the brass know about the little convoy over in this sector, ready to pull out and invade disputed space. Which by Ichton standards wasn't disputed at all. They didn't believe in disputed space, weren't genetically capable of recognizing any claims other than their own.

"Break hard around the rock, kids," Hassan said. The casual ease of his voice masked his tension. The tiny moon ahead of them was really no more than a glorified asteroid caught in orbit around an inhospitable planet. Puny for a moon, but big enough to give the Dawn Group a little shelter. They split, two elements going in opposite directions and jinking hard against their expected trajectories. That would confuse anything but a real smart-read missile, and would be hard to follow even if it could be read.

The moon seemed enormous this close. Hassan skimmed his SB down so close he could feel the drag of the flying lunar dust, barely a meter above the surface. Let them follow that, he thought in fury. His signature IR should be lost in the background reflection of the surface itself. Even a smart missile couldn't take him there.

As he rounded the lunar curve, his stomach clenched again. There was a moment of terror, thinking that the rest of the group had not made it. And then he saw them, each one planing the horizon and appearing in the shadow of the only shelter they had.

"No one followed us, boss," said *Dawn Breaker.* That would be Solange des Salles. There was a question at the edge of her voice that came through even on the private line.

"There seems to be a pattern here," Hassan said. "Did any of you note when pursuit dropped off?"

"At about two klicks from their destroyer, looked like to me," Martin Hong answered. "But that's an approx., boss. I was too busy taking care of business to get their exact address, if you know what I mean."

Hassan thanked him and sighed. Marty always did manage to embellish even a simple report. But Hong's observation coincided with his own, and with Bradley in *Dawn Tiger* and des Salles again. So. That should mean they were safe enough behind this rock for the time being, until they could slip away after the convoy had passed.

Hassan was not about to bet that there wasn't going to be any pursuit at all. Good Muslims didn't gamble, and a serious stint in Tactical School had shown him why. So far, it was the one taboo he hadn't broken. Yet. Besides which, he didn't like the idea of sitting still like a convenient target while there were enemy nearby. It made his skin crawl.

Part of Hassan Ibn Abdullah wanted to stay, to keep on blasting ammunition until the entire load Sebeng had stocked was gone. He knew better. They needed some bigger guns out here. More important, Intelligence had to know about these movements. There was something brewing in the Ickie strategy that they had not anticipated, and it was worth all their lives, let alone their kill ratios, to get the news back.

"So it's time for all good Dawn Riders to get back to Mama," he muttered. Then his voice became louder and more distinct. "Let's take it in slow formation, ride this shadow down, and use the radiation background cover of the planet to slip around. Then we can head straight home. Those Ickies are going in the other direction, and they'll be there when we get back with some reinforcements."

"Ah, boss, c'mon," Marty Hong half teased and half pleaded. "You wanna share all the glory? I could win my Silver Cluster out there."

"You think the taxpayers got nothing better to do than buy you new boats?" Hassan clipped him short. "Let's get back to base and tell the tech toys all about this convoy."

One by one, in a stepped formation, the Dawn Group departed. Their single SBs drifted down toward the dead planet below and disappeared against the background radiation. Which was very high. This place had more radioactive elements than the *Hawking*'s drive. It would be a major find for whoever could exploit it, but deadly to live on. Even the Ichtons, it seemed, had decided to pass it by.

Hassan, in *Dawn Leader,* came around last. On the far side of the planet the team regrouped for their jump back to the *Hawking.* Far enough from any gravity well to slip free, they disappeared into speed where the enemy could not follow.

But Hassan Ibn Abdullah did not feel any relief even when he saw the battlestar before them, larger than the moon he had used as a shield. Which made no sense. Here he was safe. The enemy possessed nothing, nothing at all that could damage the battlestation. It was like trying to blow a minor star. The great docking bays around the north pole were cavernous black, beckoning. He herded in his little group, smaller by two than when they had gone out. But the sense of well-being, the break in tension that had always signaled homecoming before, did not touch Hassan. Not even when the airlock had cycled through and he was standing on solid deck in his "indoor" blues.

"We weren't expecting a convoy out in this direction," Hassan said, debriefing to the tack officer of the watch. "We were just on an exploratory patrol since this wasn't a sector we'd done more than survey. We were under orders from the Science section, to be honest. But after we took a look at the rock, which would be real interesting to a merchant and absolutely no good to resettle our Gerson survivors, we came around to take a quick peek at the rest of the system. And we ran into what had to be a major column movement. I didn't see anything I could identify as an egg ship, so I don't think they were moving to take possession of a new place. At least not right now. But there may well be another population under attack out there that we don't know about."

The tack officer's face remained completely unreadable. "Thank you, Group Leader," the tack officer said. "You can go now."

Hassan knew better than to try to make his case more strongly. Instead he rose and left the debriefing room with all its glow maps and screen charts. The misery that pressed down on him didn't leave, even though he was off duty now for twelve hours.

Solange des Salles had waited for him outside the briefing room. She settled into a long stride that matched his as they moved away from the offices. "Tanya and Lee are on duty now," she said casually, naming her roommates. "My place?"

Hassan grinned. "How about a little later?" he asked. "It was a stretch. I want to unwind a little first."

Solange nodded, shrugged, and left. Much as he and des Salles had a useful arrangement, he already had other plans. He had a serious date with the rack.

But even as exhausted as he was, Hassan couldn't sleep. Instead he lay awake in the dark haunted by his last year at home, the year he had made the decision to join the Fleet. To become a warrior, a protector, one of God's Chosen.

A warrior earned Paradise, if he fought in defense of Muslim people and for God. There was no reason to worry about death, though Hassan had worried often before formulating his application on his father's ornate writing desk. His worries had been normal boy fears. What if he died in a fire, or crossing a street, or got kicked in the head in a soccer game like Sa'ad Ibn Ibrahim? Then he would surely go to Hell, since God saw into his heart and knew all the times he had missed prayers and had broken fast during Ramadan. All the times he had the opportunity to give charity but passed them by, or, worse, did not even recognize them. No matter how many times Mr. Ali in Religion class tried to quiet their fears and remind them of how God had promised Muhammad to count each believer's good deeds as ten and each of his sins as one, Hassan was quite sure that his total was in danger.

There had been only the normal boy things until Rashid's older brother Farid had been killed in the vacuum accident. Farid had been a fixture in Hassan's life, the counterpoint to Mr. Ali. Farid had taught them all to be bad.

Farid had been out working on the communications software, doing the overhaul that Sho-Co promised would bring in all the new Omni transmissions on full-time broadcast. Al-Shabir was on its way to becoming one of the mainline worlds, not a secondary franchise consumer. So when the stress points on the ancient Maktab orbiter went critical during a crew visit, there was very little left to bury. Sho-Co took the blame and paid indemnities to all the families. It controlled the Omni in seventy-three systems.

Hassan had gone out with Rashid and his brother Farid the week before Farid had died. He was the first young person Hassan had known who had died, excepting Sa'ad in the soccer game. But Sa'ad had been seven years old and the imam had assured everyone in school that he was in Paradise now and didn't have to study quadratics or memorize the Koran anymore. Farid was different. Hassan was older and he knew that Farid had been very far from Paradise.

Farid Ibn Salah had enjoyed what he could in his short life, and what he enjoyed most was horrifying his elders. He had done a good job of it, introducing Rashid and Hassan to home-brewed whiskey and "hard" tobacco in the bubble pipe. He never said his prayers, even proclaimed himself an atheist. Though once he did say to Rashid that he wasn't, really. Just that he was young and he thought the mullahs didn't understand that and hated all the techs who didn't adhere to the old ways. That was all. And after all, Farid was young. He could make up for all the mistakes later, when he was older. Once he had made his point.

He hadn't gotten the chance. Hassan had heard about the accident and gone to Rashid's home, miserable and afraid. That Farid could die and go to Hell, Farid who was always so full of life, so ready with a joke, that frightened him. It had frightened Rashid, too, and the two friends had finished off the last of Farid's imported stash of Johnnie Walker. The next morning, hung over, he couldn't go to school. He could barely move. At least his parents believed it was only grief over Farid's tragedy and let him stay home from school while they went to work. He had turned on the Omni and there had been the ad screens.

They had said that the Fleet was once again looking for young fighters to seek out the evildoers who would annihilate sentient species. The Fleet was the defender of all humanity, and so by extension was the defender of the Holy Places and the Peoples of the Book. There had been marching music in the background and holos of great warrior heroes from the earliest days of Islam, Abu Bakr and Ali, Akbar the Great and Salah-El-Din. There were glittering machines and uniforms glittering even more from decorations.

Despite the splitting headache of his hangover, Hassan Ibn Abdullah had immediately gone to the interactive and requested the application and filled it out then and there. His father would be proud of him he was sure. And his mother would not be too disappointed about his not graduating from Caliph Umar University and sitting in the Majlis. She would understand that he would have a better chance to get elected if he was a war hero, and she would be sad but not object.

The acceptance had come by the next morning. And Hassan Ibn Abdullah was duly inducted into the defense of Mankind, and incidentally his own hope of salvation.

He had never questioned the rightness of that decision. Indeed, as he had progressed through training, winning more opportunities to advance, to become a fighter and then a group leader, he had only had his first impression confirmed. This was where he belonged. God had placed him in this Fleet for a true purpose.

And it had been easy for him, too. There was something poetic and whole about the way groups moved in combat, patterns of victory and defeat that came as clear before his eyes as the fanciful flowers and birds on the carpets in his parents' home. He had enjoyed the physical training, more demanding than soccer practice. And most of all he had loved learning to fly.

Piloting an SB was like becoming a bird, one of the great hunting hawks his grandfather had showed him when he was small. He felt like them, strong and fast and utterly unafraid, swooping and skimming over the surface of a planet, free and utterly alive in space.

Talent, his instructors had called it. He had been promoted and given more opportunities to take classes and advance. Things that were never taught at home became his daily work. And people who were not like those at home became his closest friends.

It was not that he left the faith of his people. It was merely that he wanted to be liked by these people, his new peers. He wanted to spend time with them, to fit in. He had been very young and felt very alone. There wasn't anyone else from Al-Shabir in his training group. He wasn't sure if there was anyone else from Al-Shabir in the entire Fleet.

And certain of the restrictions wore down slowly. After refusing too many times he couldn't stand being alone anymore and had joined the rest of his group in the bar. And he really hadn't intended to drink alcohol, truly he hadn't. The image of Farid in Hell haunted him. But when the group ordered pitchers and Solange des Salles had poured him out a glass and put it down in front of him with a wink, he hadn't wanted to refuse. Al-Shabir seemed very far away, and these people were his group. It wasn't like he had never drunk alcohol before. It wasn't like anyone else he knew was worried about going to Hell. After a few times it seemed very silly, very old-fashioned, to stand off from his friends. He couldn't deny it.

Not the beer, not the wink either. He hadn't been wrong. And while Solange was too strong, too insolent, too independent to be the kind of girl he had dreamed about, she had thick blond hair and a wide engaging smile and freckles on her nose. She was exotic, tempting, drunk.

Being a bad Muslim didn't mean that he didn't believe. It only meant that he knew he had guaranteed his own safe conduct after death. He didn't have to worry anymore and he wanted to enjoy all the advantages. He never doubted that war was the one path he had to salvation.

As he had never doubted victory. There was no other possibility. A believer was always victorious. He had been raised on the history of the Battle of Badr and the conquest of North Africa. The only time they failed was when they fought those who were also People of the Book whose faith was stronger, who were more committed in their duty and their prayers.

Hassan Ibn Abdullah had always thought that obvious. And working with the men and women of the Fleet, with his group and even the Marines on board, he had never had a moment of doubt. That the Ichtons were completely godless was a proven fact. And if many of his colleagues and associates were not of the best moral character, there were plenty of others who made up for them. Among the Muslims aboard the *Hawking,* the small chapel was always filled to capacity and many worshipers were stuck in the hallway during the Friday noon service.

There were better Muslims than Hassan on the *Hawking*. But Hassan Ibn Abdullah of Al-Shabir had never minded. They weren't warriors. They weren't guaranteed. Some of them weren't with the Fleet at all. One of the civilian technicians, Ahmed Al-Dookhi, had seen him going into the Emerald Isle with Solange des Salles and Marty Hong and the rest of his group, and had tried to talk him out of it. Reminded him of his obligations and what was forbidden.

It didn't matter that things were forbidden. They were the Elect, there was no question in his mind. So he spent more time with Solange, sampling other pleasures that were normally outside the realm permitted on Al-Shabir. After beer came the whiskey and the rum, which he never really liked.

Solange introduced him to the sausages she enjoyed from her own home, not telling him at first they were made from pig.

He had been horrified when he discovered it and Solange had laughed. She had been sitting naked on his bed, glasses of wine balanced on the floor, a plate of cheese and crackers and sausages between them.

"Really, this is so much worse than all the rest?" she had asked in honest confusion.

And Hassan, after careful consideration, had to agree that it was not. And that he didn't belong to Al-Shabir properly anymore. He was all Fleet now. Just like the others, his friends, his lover. He told himself that again and again over the next days until he didn't have to say it anymore. The words appeared in his head along with the beer and the sausage and Solange.

But in the dark, trying to sleep, Hassan Ibn Abdullah found the source of his unease. The idea of that convoy, so far from the fronts, disturbed him on more than a professional level. He could see them, imagine all the space between the millions of stars, all filled with the Ichton swarm. Nothing stopped them, nothing could turn them from their purpose. And their purpose was an evil one.

The legion of Shaitan advanced through the darkness a planet at a time. There were billions of them who had no par in the fighting, who didn't even know or care it was going on. The devil had won. And Hassan's faith was shaken down to the core.

He could be a bad Muslim. He could violate every stricture in the Koran. But he could not accept that God would give those, those bugs a victory over men. That was beyond comprehension. That was a bad dream.

He gave up on sleep, got up and washed and put on the civilian dress of his home. The plain white robe and headdress were exotic on the *Hawking,* but it still was more comfortable to Hassan than the dark trousers and shirts that felt like just one more uniform. The long white *dishdasha* made him feel connected to the person he used to be, not the amalgamation of characters he found himself playing now.

He left the military levels and wandered down onto Green Three where some of the more affordable shops were clustered. He wanted to look at the people more than the goods, at the relaxed cheer that pretended normalcy. As if anything here was normal. As if it was normal to be shopping quite securely in the middle of a war zone where people were running out and dying.

"Hey, Hassan, I owe you a drink, boss." Marty Hong came over, clapped Hassan on the shoulder, and tried to steer him in the direction of the Emerald Isle, Marty's favorite watering hole, the only Irish pub on the battlestation.

But something had snapped inside Hassan. He felt isolated, outside Marty's camaraderie. Suddenly it seemed like everything here was as alien as what he found on the planets of the Core. The corridor of Green looked dirty, full of the refuse and detritus of another culture. Alien, not for him. He shook his head. Marty shrugged and went off, confusion on his face at Hassan's refusal. For the smallest fragment of time Hassan wanted to run after Marty, say it was just a joke, and join whoever was off duty down at the watering hole.

Something held him back. From the very depths of his mind came a word he had not heard in a very long time. A word he had not heard since he had joined the Fleet. *Haram.* Forbidden.

It made him think of the clean places back home, the expanses of shoreline rippling pristine in the sun. Or not so clean. There had been bright filth all over Al-Shabir, hard glints from the litter, the beverage cans and food tins strewn over the sand reflecting in the moonlight. That night he had gotten drunk with Farid and Rashid they had sat out on the rocks and watched the warm ocean tide, emptied the bottle of imported whiskey that Farid had brought back. *Haram.* Emptied it and thrown it out into the sea where it had floated and glittered in the dark water. It had been ugly and small and unclean, just like everything in his life.

He turned sharply and went directly back to the hull elevators, muttered "Orange Four" at them, and waited. The doors opened silently and he was back on the barracks level again. He was only glad that being a group leader, he had private quarters even though his rank didn't rate the luxury.

It was thought that group leaders might need some privacy to talk to members of their groups, and they surely didn't rate private offices. The one overcrowded space they shared to do the required records work and sign in for their briefings was never quiet enough for a serious discussion, let alone secluded enough for one that would go better without others present.

Now he was glad only that he had a place to go to be alone. Completely alone. He walked the nearly half klick of corridor around to his door and sealed it shut behind him. The panel would have the privacy indicator lit so no one would interrupt.

It had been a long time since Hassan Ibn Abdullah had said the required prayers, had found that need in himself. He had spent too many years trying too hard to be the proper Fleet group leader. On Fridays he went for public services at noon, but otherwise was more concerned with fighting than with other obligations. After all, he was a warrior. He was guaranteed Paradise.

Now, however, he felt overwhelmed. He had not come to terms with the enemy before, with their enormity and the strength of their drive. They could not be the Chosen of God, the ones assured of victory. And yet, and yet . . .

He could not clear the vision from his mind. Hundreds, thousands of the tiny fighters. Each one armed better than the SBs. All of them swarming together around a nucleus of destroyers and frigates marching out under orders. Marching across the sky, marching in the dark masked by the myriad planets and stars of the galactic core.

He tried to drive the image from his mind and concentrate only on the words that flowed from him. Verses of the Koran came unbidden, the language rippling like flowers in a breeze. Like the enemy convoy stealing around in secret.

And it all came together, a single inspiration. He rose from his prayer rug with a more grateful heart than he had ever experienced. The vision was complete, perfect, and it encompassed him. Hassan knew the keen pleasure of it even though the image was hideous, frightful. He could see the beauty because he could see past it and into what it meant.

God had spoken to him, directly. He had no doubt. Now he only had to get the tracking from Astronomy.

Not even bothering to change out of the white *dishdasha* and headdress, he ran out of his private quarters and to the lift as if he were on first assault and they were under attack.

He got down to Astronomy in the Civ sections and started banging on the indigo door with Rhys Davies's name lit on the plate. He slammed his fist against the steel until his hand ached.

Davies opened the door. "Why can't you use the bell like a normal person?" the scientist groused. "Did you find anything useful?"

Hassan shook his head. "What happened?" he asked Davies as if the other understood everything that had gone on in the past sixteen hours. "Why didn't you find the convoy in your data?"

"What convoy?" Davies asked, then turned his back on the pilot without inviting him into the office.

Hassan didn't bother waiting for the invitation, but pushed his way through the closing door and after the planetary specialist. "There's an Ichton column moving through that system," he informed Davies hotly. "Bleeding radiation all over the place. You should have been able to spot them in your observations. You do make observations, right?"

Davies turned suddenly and cocked his head. "A column movement that we didn't see?" he asked, ignoring Hassan's anger. "Let me pull the records."

He touched a keypad on his desk and the wall display lit with a bright orange backdrop, then dissolved into star fields Hassan didn't recognize. In fact, they changed and became something else entirely, graphic plots of color that didn't make particular sense to the pilot.

"These are the spectrographic prints," Davies said. "Now, let's try again. You said that the convoy was coming around LLR-1182?" The display shimmered and changed again. Now hot yellow filled the screen with streaks of blue and green and pink smudges across the face of it.

Davies ignored him. "Hmmmm. Yes. Yes." The astronomer's face glowed with excitement.

"Yes what?" Hassan demanded. He couldn't make any sense of the display.

"I'll have to do some more looking," Davies said.

Hassan was so curious and frustrated that he wanted to shake the heavyset older man. "What? What is it? What do you see?"

Rhys Davies licked his lips. "I never thought it would be a practical application. Of course, I'm not in stellar architecture. We'll really have to do a full departmental study to get the complete picture. I'm not sure really . . ."

"Please, please tell me," Hassan begged. This man was going to make him crazy.

"We may have a signature for the Ichton drive," Davies said simply. "It's dirty, you're right. But against LLR-1182 the element signature is hidden under the star's own element band. Every star has a spectrographic signature. Elements exist in different proportions everywhere, and each one has its own color. But against that signature the drive emissions are masked. Wait."

The screen became more yellow and the green, blue, and pink moved around. The colors started to flash. Hassan felt a little dizzy. The scientist said nothing but "Hmmmm." And then Davies smiled.

"I can see it," he said finally. "They're using the stellar radiation to mask their movements. You wouldn't think they'd be able to. And they don't do it all the time. I wonder . . . Only certain stars would be suitable. It wouldn't be hard to check."

Hassan thanked Davies emphatically and then hurried out. He understood. There was more and no doubt the astronomers and the intelligence analysts aboard would create a detailed picture. Maybe it would even indicate something far different from what Hassan saw in his own moment of inspiration. But he didn't think so.

The Ichtons had a camouflaged route. Possibly it could even be traced back to their home planet. Even if it wasn't quite that direct, they had worked out this area to keep their movements hidden. Secret.

Hassan could barely keep from dancing in the corridor. The idea overwhelmed him. There were indeed more than enough bugs to go around. It would be a charity to them to remove them from the universe. From harming decent species' lives and homes. Surely this was the greatest charity of all.

In the sudden extreme clarity that surrounded his thoughts, Hassan Ibn Adbullah realized perfectly why the warrior merited Paradise. It was not fearlessness or commitment or any of the things that he had thought. It was charity. In the truly just, war was the highest expression of charity to others. And everyone in Mr. Ali's class knew that God loved charity above all other virtues.

Hassan managed to get back to his own quarters and change into his working blues. He didn't think he would impress the tactical staff in his native dress. And this had to be done right. He was anxious and excited, but to hurry wouldn't help.

So he made a proper appointment through the proper channels, filed the paperwork with more routings than strictly necessary, and changed. The duty roster on his screen rippled as the new appointment came through. He had a meeting in twenty minutes with the division's tactical superior and staff. But Hassan Ibn Abdullah was perfectly calm as he took the lift from Orange down to a Briefing Red on the operational front.

"This could be part of an overall assault plan," the tack said softly. There was no denying the interest in his face. Hassan felt more than vindicated.

"I would expect it is, sir," he agreed. "It seems that they are trying to bring in more ships and fighters behind cover and converge on us without us expecting them. I think we've got them a little frightened."

The tack smiled without humor. "Very possibly. That would be the way we would do it. Only the Ichtons aren't us. And I'm not sure we have any idea of what they would do or why. Although that's my best guess. Astronomy promised they'd have the readings up to us as soon as they'd isolated the pattern. But that could take days."

Hassan nodded. "I realize that, sir. Dr. Davies briefed us. But maybe in the meantime we could make life a little less comfortable for the bugs."

"Ichtons, Mr. Ibn Abdullah. Our enemies are sentients, not bugs, and the minute we forget that we're in trouble," the tack repeated by rote.

Hassan ignored the routine warning and went on. Only the high tacks ever bothered with those fine distinctions. He knew perfectly well what he meant and he wasn't about to underestimate the enemy even if he used the wrong terminology. "Well, sir, they were sticking pretty tight in formation. They wouldn't even follow us out to the moon we hid behind. They're avoiding the rocks and keeping to empty space. And staying between the orbits and the sun, for camouflage I'd guess. But they aren't expecting to be hit out there. They're just sitting begging for an ambush there."

The senior tack shook his head. "That convoy will be nearly through by now," he said. "And since you already engaged with them they know that we know. . . . And, honestly, we can't afford the forces to sit and wait until another convoy tries to come through using the same trick. We don't have enough manpower as it is, and we're short on armed SBs. Which you should know. Hell, we could hardly spare the garbage scow."

Hassan had known and ignored the fact. Sebeng always managed to make sure the Dawn Riders were equipped to the teeth. He had been so certain, so clear about what needed to be done.

In his mind he could hear the voice of Mr. Ali chanting over and over again, *It is charity to remove something harmful from the way.* The garbage scow. The empty Johnnie Walker bottle floating in the tide, reflecting light like a beacon to the thing that was unclean. And Hassan Ibn Abdullah began to laugh.

"Sir, could I take the garbage scow out for a run?" he asked when he got his breath back.

The tack officer's eyebrows went up abruptly. "Why, Group Leader?"

But Hassan Ibn Abdullah was laughing so hard that it took several moments to catch his breath to explain.

There was a convoy. Maybe not the same one. Hassan Ibn Abdullah couldn't be sure. But there were Ichtons out there, using the masking radiation of this star to keep their movements out of sight.

Only now Astronomy knew what to look for. Astronomy even found a fun problem in the tracking, something that could interest theorists like Rhys Davies.

Not that Hassan cared. He only cared about what he was doing, about this moment. The garbage scow was large and unwieldy. It had not been made for a human driver in general, but the calculations were too intuitive to be left to a machine. Hassan didn't even know how to explain it properly.

The dark folded around him. He took the tug out slowly, dragging it around the column from the orbital side. And he opened the hatches. Refuse from the *Hawking* spewed into space. Beer cans and bottles from the bars, bits of meal covers and shiny wrapping paper from the rich inhabitants of the south pole. He guided the barge gently forward, running it out as fast as he could, trying to outdistance the column.

There were fighters after him. He tried to jink but the scow balked and bucked under him. Damn. He pushed on ahead, continuing to spray the entire sector with debris, waiting for the hit.

Only it didn't come. He saw them in the scan between the slivers of bright garbage, saw them coming straight in on him and then fluttering around, lost. A few feeble attempts to fire and a single smart missile dropped into the dump and was unable to fix on a target. Was unable to find a target.

He pushed forward, hoping there would be enough. That Sebeng had packed the hauler as full as she did the SBs' holds. Already his plan was working, was beautiful. So beautiful that he could barely contain his pleasure.

He came around full and cut off the front of the convoy. Here they had better shots at him as he upped the pressure in the refuse chamber. Pieces shredded finer with the higher energy surge and the whole segment of his own position between the planet and the star had blotted into garbled haze.

The garbage was all reflective. And it was shining all that energy back at the enemy. The radiation from the star and the nearby planet, the power leaking from the Ichton drives, the communications bands and all the scanners, everything was being broken and bounced among a billion billion crushed fragments of landfill. Like grains of sand, each one a mirror on the shore, the chaff drifted into eddies and rifts, spread and spun insanely through the Ichton convoy.

The enemy tried to fight back. They fired energy weapons that were immediately dissipated by the chaff. They tried smart missiles whose targeting devices were completely stymied. Even their navigation and orientation were affected and what had once been a neatly purposeful convoy through camouflaged space started to resemble the kiddies' bumper car ride at the Eid Al-Fitr fair.

Hassan could appreciate the view only through the windows in front of him. This was no fighter, it wasn't even a patrol SB and so his own screens were as confused as the enemy's. And so he never saw the large Ichton destroyer that was on his tail and that ripped the garbage scow neatly in two down the keel, adding even more to the confusing backwash.

• • •

"Dawn Riders, open fire," Dawn Leader commanded. They came from behind a chunk of moon, something irregular that had most likely been an asteroid captured by the planet's gravity. They had ridden this way before.

Solange des Salles, acting group leader, read out the coordinates. That was unnecessary. The attackers could see targets strewn across the environment like loose cut gems on a jeweler's velvet. Targets that lay drifting helplessly, surrounded by chaff, unable to navigate or fire. Blind.

"It's almost a pity to just pick them off," Marty Hong said.

Three SBs, even loaded with all the ammunition Sebeng could pack into their holds, could only account for three quarters of the disabled Ichton column. The Dawn Riders didn't protest when the frigate *Viceroy* arrived on the scene and began mopping up the remains.

That night the Dawn Riders bought all the drinks in the Emerald Isle in the name of Hassan Ibn Abdullah. They drank and threw the glasses against the wall to commemorate his victory. And his death. Credit for the full column, by popular demand, was given to him alone.

"And he can't enjoy it," Marty said, trying to keep sentimental and drunken tears from his eyes. "He's dead."

"I don't think so," said a stranger in a white robe. "But he wouldn't enjoy the beer. He died properly, and in Paradise no one is ever drunk."

Des Salles listened, and then ordered another round. "Here's to you, Hassan," she said as the rest of the Dawn Riders raised their final round. "Looks like we're gonna have to do all your drinking for you now. Looks like you got to be a good Muslim in the end anyway."

RX

A MASSIVE ICHTON force had gotten between the *Hawking* and their strongest ally, the Emry. Anton Brand reacted by attempting to call all the Fleet and the allied race's ships back to the station, a difficult task considering how thinly they were spread. As the *Hawking* gathered its strength, it began to edge slowly toward Emry. Isolated and outmaneuvered, the crew of the Battlestation *Stephen Hawking* fought two battles. The first was against hundreds of small and large Ichton units. The other battle was against themselves.

The level of stress, already considered unbearable, increased geometrically as the *Hawking* crept toward Emry and a confrontation with far superior Ichton forces. Occasionally a small Ichton force would discover the *Hawking,* forcing yet another change of course to avoid ambush. Those fighting on the ships or inside the station had nowhere to run and only the prospect of greater danger to look forward to. Under this burden any psychological problem became severe. It was the responsibility of a few members of the medical staff to assist those who need their help the most. Repairing their minds as well as their bodies. But who watches the watchers?

MEDIC

by Mercedes Lackey and Mark Shepherd

DR. ALTHEA MORGAN paused in the hatchway to her office, leaned against the cold metal, and sighed. This job was not something she was looking forward to, but it was better than the alternative.

Thinking.

Although being cramped in that tiny cell of an office was almost as bad as thinking.

It's a good thing they don't allow claustrophobes in space.

Her so-called "office" was about the size of a supply closet, and had just enough room for her desk, chair, and terminal—and, if the visitor happened to be the size of your average ballet dancer, room for one other person as well. At least she had a chair. Visitors got to perch on a narrow metal flap that folded down from the desk.

Why did I ever agree to be staff administrator, anyway?

She squeezed past the end of the desk and settled into her chair, steeled herself, and reached for the computer terminal to turn the Cyclopean monster on.

It immediately chided her for not touching it since the *Elizabeth Blackwell II* hit norm-space by beeping at her. *Angrily,* she thought. Then it presented her with a flood of memos about how crowded her message-queues were, followed by a directive from the Admiralty about saving queue-memory.

I know, I know. She hadn't turned the damned thing on because she hadn't *seen* the damn office since they hit norm. She hadn't seen anything except the surgery, the prep room, *her* room (damn little of that), and the corridor between her room and surgery.

Nominally, she was the director of the medical personnel aboard the *Elizabeth Blackwell II.* In actuality, she did as much hands-on work as any of her staff, right down to holding bedpans if it came to it. And during the last few weeks, there'd been a lot of hands-on. She'd taken all of the Neuros, most of the Neuro-musculars, all of the Spinals, and even a couple Thoracics.

Or, in the jargon of the no-nonsense first-in surgeons of the Fleet—the Heads, the Hunks, the Backs, and the Chests.

For a moment, she buried her head in her hands, overwhelmed not so much with memories but with a flood of *impressions.* Things had happened too quickly for memories. The *Blackwell* served the same function as the old MASH units had for ground-based troops; she was only one of many, but sometimes it seemed as if *Blackwell* was the only one of her kind out here. All alone, except for the Big Ship, the *Stephen Hawking.* That was what *she* called it, the Big Ship; she had not set foot on it for weeks, and to her it was a great deal like returning to Heaven. She had never been there, and probably wouldn't go there until she died—she sent a lot of people there, though, and none of them ever came back.

Or if they did, she didn't recognize them.

Blood; that was the primary memory. Blood, lots of it, in all the variations of red. And internal organs. Many kinds, often not human. Sometimes fluids she didn't even recognize as blood, forms she had never seen before, organs with functions she couldn't even guess. The medicomp knew, though, good old many-eyed Argus; and the replicator could reproduce the fluids, the organs, from a cubic mil of clean tissue. Nothing fancy; that was for the *Hawkins.* She just saved them, patched them, and got those all-important clean samples; the Big Ship made them whole again, grew them new lungs and spleens and *feshetti,* carved them faces that looked like faces and not nightmare-horrors. Whoever had said that combat in the modern world was clean had never been on the *Blackwell.*

More memories. Operating with one eye on the comp screen and one on the patient. Comp over the table, Eye of God, beloved Argus, that told her and every other surgeon everything she needed to know about her patient, including where her hands were in the welter of blood and God knew what. The comp that guided her hands.

Not the same comp that was bitching at her now, beeping at her, chiding her for her inattention. *That* was Admin. Cyclops. The Eye she hated.

Well, there was one advantage to not logging on for weeks, even months. There was a lot of crap she wasn't going to have to deal with. Computer-sent messages have a short life span. Administrative crap had an even shorter half-life.

She typed slowly, cursing the ancient, outmoded keyboard. Anyone over the rank of CPO in the military side had a Voice-Response-System. Anyone with any kind of rank had a VRS. If she had had a secretary, the *secretary* would have been issued a VRS. But, in the usual FUBAR of the military, because she was an administrative head and *should* have had a secretary to deal with all this garbage, she didn't need a VRS.

Never mind irreparable nerve damage that made her hands shake so much that she could stand in for the drink mixer in the ship's lounge. Never mind that her secretary had been co-opted to man guns somewhere on the Big Ship. Never mind that *somewhere,* without a shadow of a doubt, there was a friggin' *closet* full of VRSs doing nothing on the Big Ship. There might even be one hidden somewhere on the *Blackwell.* No VRS for Admin personnel. End of story.

Thank the Deity-of-Your-Choice for mass queue-purges.

First mass purge: all social notes. Not that there were a lot, but there was no point. Somewhere there was a reg that said that on so-called noncombat ships there must be regularly scheduled social events for the purpose of crew morale. So Cyclops scheduled them and reminded everyone to attend; probably even programmed the ship's mess for refreshments that no one came to eat, then sent bitchy notices about food wastage.

Second purge: all ship-to-ship general notices older than yesterday.

That freed up a lot of queue-space, and mollified the damn Cyclops enough so that it stopped *beep*ing at her. Now all it was doing was issuing reminders ever five minutes or so.

Now selective purges. Anything personal older than a week ago. Most of the personal notes were stupid; residue of interstaff quarrels and infighting, reminders of things that she would never have forgotten anyway, and if she didn't remember them, they hadn't been worth remembering. Requisition orders older than a month; if someone hadn't chased her down for her thumbprint in person, they'd found a creative way of solving the shortage.

In general, that was how things got taken care of on the *Elizabeth Blackwell,* you either chased Morgan down for the print, found something else that would do, or did without. There were some ingenious jury-rigs on the *Blackwell.*

That took care of the nonsense. Now came the work.

The only part that she cared for were the personnel files of new staff. Not that she hadn't met them all by now, but buried in the files were the little things that made a face into a person. That Trauma Spec Jharwat Singh Rai was a near concert-level violinist. Or Sanders, the head ward nurse, was the champion Swords and Spellcast player in the Fleet. Or that Orthopedic Surgeon Ledith Alsserth from the Indies collected old Earth jazz recordings, even though his people had never so much as seen a saxophone. She wasn't even certain one of his race could *play* a saxophone.

So she left those until last, as a reward for good behavior. It was amazing how much paperwork accumulated whenever they docked with the Big Ship; the transfer orders were enough to fill twenty megabytes alone, and that was in compressed mode. *Why* do the stuff in triplicate, when "paperwork" didn't exist in hard copy anymore?

Never mind. She could fill them out. It didn't matter. As long as she kept busy, she wouldn't have to think. Think about how the ultimate weapon the Fleet had built, the *Stephen Hawking,* the *battlestation* that was never supposed to see close combat, had just been through the trash-masher. How there was an even bigger enemy armada than the one that had trashed them coming down the Throat right now. Straight for them.

How the cavalry was not coming over the hill. Not out here, back of beyond of anywhere. Not when they already *had* all of their eggs in one basket.

No. Better not to think. She would take care of her job; let the ones in charge try to think of a solution. She had plenty to do. If work on the *Blackwell* ran out, she could volunteer for reconstructive surgery on the Big Ship. There was plenty of that. There was always plenty of that.

More crap to wade through; complaints. The *Blackwell* had taken some scrapes and minor hits, and systems were cranky. Very cranky. Minor malfunctions all over the ship—including, predictably, the mess hall, reducing the already minimal palatability of the food down to the flavor of flour paste. Not that *she* could do anything about that, but she got the complaints from her staff anyway.

Just hope nothing major breaks loose before the overhaul crew can get to us.

By the time she had waded through the last of the muck, her trembling hands and wrists ached, and she was only too glad to be able to simply page through the files without having to type anything.

It would be nice if she could have a pair of StediGloves in here—but those required the medicomp to operate.

And of course, since there were no requirements to extend Argus's all-seeing Eye into the office, there was no way to get the Eye in here. Administrators had no need for the Eye—what, was she going to do surgery on the desk?—and neither did secretaries.

So, Eye, no gloves, no steadying influence on her hands. Have a nice day.

"Hell, even *chaplains* have VRSs," she muttered, and called up the first of the files.

Working from bottom rank up; nursing staff first. As always, she heard the voice of her mentor in her mind's ear. Good old Doc Glock. "Nurses. Get to know them *well,* girl—they're your lifeline, your extra hands, your other eyes. Got three things going wrong at once; put your ops nurses on two of 'em. Chances are they'll do as well as you. Need a third eye, put your nurse on the comp and have her read the damn thing back at you. *Let* 'em close when you're done if there's another on the table waiting for you, let 'em do what they can. Let 'em do any damn thing if they're capable, and to hell with regs. This won't be Saint Simeon's; there won't be anyone looking to book them for practicing medicine without a license, or to sue you for malpractice. *Let 'em work right up to the limits of their capabilities, and thank 'em afterward.* You won't be any less a doctor. Those boys and girls and whatevers are gonna be damn glad they're still alive when you're done with 'em, and they won't care who or what did the work. . . ."

As she called up pictures, file (usually from graduation) and current, she didn't get many surprises. Other than the usual—how the trim and ultra-proper loosened up; the young and shiny and eager got some of the shine rubbed off. How the ones so sure they were God Almighty you could see it in their eyes learned they were mortal after all.

Nothing like getting the shit scared out of you a dozen or so times to get rid of those anal-retentive tendencies. The *Blackwell* had gotten a fair share of close calls, and even a few minor hits. That's why the *Blackwell* was armed—and had the best legs in the Service.

Now Althea was well into the smaller corps of surgical doctors and trauma specialists. New chest-man; that was good. Even better that his specialty was Xeno. That was probably why she'd only seen him over coffee in the lounge. She was human Neuro; for Xenos, even with neurological damage, a chest-man with Xeno specialty was a better choice than a human with no Xeno experience. She tagged him mentally for call-up when the time came; two sets of experiences sometimes saved a "kid" of whatever race that one alone couldn't. Not if, *when.* For the time would come that she would need him, as night followed day.

There were no surprises until she came to the last file, highest rank. The new Chief of Surgery. File image; bright, cheerful, new-and-shiny. Laughing eyes. Nice girl.

Whom she did not recognize.

What the hell?

She called up a recent image; it was like seeing images of two different people, and *this* one she knew. Except that she'd had no idea this was her CoS. For a moment she toyed with the idea of a ringer—though *why* anyone would try and place a ringer on the *Blackwell* she couldn't imagine—but the tissue typing done just last week matched the one in the file that went with the graduation image.

Two different people. And the second one was a nonentity. No expression. Hair cut to a short little fuzz. Nothing in the eyes.

That was why she hadn't thought the woman was even a full doctor. There was *nothing* about Celia Stratford that was remarkable. The file was a blank. No hobbies. No interests. No friends. . . .

Fifteen transfers in fourteen years.

What?

Her first thought was that the woman was a major trouble-maker—or attracter. But there were no discipline hash marks against her in the records; nothing, in fact, but glowing commendation after commendation. All the transfers were voluntary. *Requested.*

The longest she'd stayed in any one place was two years; the shortest, six months. She'd been on the Big Ship until the hookup before this one; she'd requested transfer again, and she'd gotten it. Then the fluke—because she had an outstanding record, and because Althea's old CoS had gotten conscripted elsewhere, the computer threw her into the CoS slot with an automatic upgrade.

Fifteen transfers in fourteen years. A nonentity. A mystery. A puzzle to solve, to stave off thinking.

Just what the doctor ordered.

She ordered a copy of the file—and any others that Celia was mentioned in—transferred to her Pers area. Later, she could warm up the terminal in her cabin and look it over lying flat on her bunk.

She gazed once more into the eyes of the nonentity on the screen, before dismissing the image. There was a person in there, with a reason for all those transfers. And Althea Morgan was going to find her.

Ready or not, Celia, here I come.

Still groggy from the jump, Celia wove her way through the breakfast crowd in the mess hall. She shrugged and stood in line, wishing she could be invisible. Over the years, through trial and error, she perfected her body language to effectively broadcast, to a wide area, *stay away.* All except the most imperceptive individuals could read her posture, the folded arms, the hostile look, the stance that turned slightly inward. She was more comfortable being by herself, and made no secret of it to the world.

It's better this way, she thought, waiting in the incredibly slow line. *It's better to have no friends than lose the ones you have to those damned intelligent grasshoppers. If I never see another insect again, it will be too soon.*

The cafeteria, if one could call it that, was small and cramped, like everything else on the ship. There were perhaps thirty people in here, mostly medical staff in their traditional whites, with a few ship's support in green coveralls thrown in to keep the eye from going snow-blind. The ship's captain, whom she had met briefly when transferring from the *Stephen Hawking,* along with the higher ranking doctors, would probably be taking meals in the officer's mess. She couldn't help but laugh, remembering the XO orderly's expression when he told her she had that option, and she had declined it. Apparently nobody ever did that.

I'll be more invisible with the larger numbers, she told herself. *If I mix with a group of senior staff, I'll be expected to make small talk. Here, I can be quiet without raising eyebrows* or *questions.*

As she had expected, breakfast was the usual dull military fare. All reconstructed soy made to resemble, if you had a vivid imagination, eggs, bacon, and ham. Or for those of other persuasions, oatmeal, bagels, and cream cheese. The coffee more than made up for the pseudomeal; somewhere in the brew's distant ancestry, there must have been at least one or two real honest-to-God coffee beans. That, or the replicating equipment on this ship was more advanced than the mess on the *Stephen Hawking.* Not likely, given the rest of the meal.

It doesn't matter, she thought, selecting a table (thank God) that was sitting off by itself. *As long as I don't know a soul, I'll be happy with bread and water.* Checking her watch, she saw that she had two hours before her shift officially began. *Of course, they'll expect me there an hour early. Good thing I came when I did. If this is slow for this place, I'd hate to see what it looks like during a rush.*

Everyone around her seemed to be in the advanced stages of waking up and not particularly looking for company.

For all intents and purposes, just like her.

Another trick she learned a while back; early breakfasts usually insured privacy.

How long has it been, anyway? she thought, playing with her make-believe bacon. *Ten, eleven years?* She added the years, surprising herself with how long it had *really* been. *Great Good God,* Celia thought, dropping her fork. Fourteen years. *My, how time flies when you're having* fun.

She remembered the way it had been, in the early days, shortly after graduation. *I was so young, so fresh, so . . . stupid.* Janet Walter had been her roommate all through med school and her best friend since their freshman year, so it was natural that they should ship out together, to the same ship's hospital. Janet could make a good joke out of just about any bad situation, and acted as the perfect counter to Celia's own unpredictable mood swings, made worse by the nasty little border war they were cleaning up after.

Being a doctor seemed so very heroic then. Working near a war was even more so. Or so all the holos, the books, the newsvids said. Her teachers told them that they were going out to bring life amid death. That they were special. Important.

And it certainly felt important. She had been prepared for the horrors of battlefield surgery; she had spent her internship in a charity-hospital trauma unit. She had been prepared for the chaos, the constant stress.

What she hadn't been prepared for was that the medical personnel might be a target.

She didn't even remember who they were fighting. Or where. It could have been any battle in any conflict. It might not even have been the enemy; it might have even been an accident, so-called "friendly fire." The details were not important; what was important was that up until that moment she had no idea what it was like to lose someone important, someone close.

She closed her eyes and bent her head over her pseudo-eggs as the memory overwhelmed her.

She'd been asleep, off-shift. The ship rocked; that woke her up. She grabbed for the light switch; her overhead died, and emergency services went on-line, the red lights, the wheeze of the ventilators. She didn't even remember dressing or running down the corridor to the surgery. Just being there, as body after body came under her hands. Waiting for Janet to come pounding in from her room.

The last person she expected to see come in on a stretcher was Janet.

And she was the last person Celia expected to see *die.*

Curdled, blackened burns covered her body, and Janet's screams still haunted her sleep. Her best friend was so racked with pain that she didn't even recognize Celia.

Celia had not lost control of her emotions, at least not during the procedure. She had calmly and coolly applied the plastic flesh that would hold Janet together until a burn specialist could see her, until someone from Rad could see how much of a dose she had gotten.

Triage; minor, major, grave. Janet got the red band—grave—but there were lots of red bands. Too many; the ship had taken a major hit to the crew quarters. She had learned later that Janet had been with that young ensign she'd met in the mess. The young ensign's body had shielded hers from the worst of the blast.

Too many red bands, and not enough doctors to see to them. Celia had lacerated spines to put back together; heads with the brain laid bare. Everyone was busy, there were too many bodies, too many seriously injured.

The red band wasn't enough. She had wanted to shout, to drag the burn man over to Janet, to point out that this was another *doctor,* one of the fraternity. But her professional etiquette prevented her.

Janet's screams had stopped suddenly.

Even in the tumult of the overfilled trauma ward, the other moans of agony, the shouts of doctors and nurses, the wheeze of machines, Celia heard that horrible silence.

She had whirled, staring across the room, patient forgotten. Janet gazed upward, eyes open, mouth frozen forever in a silent scream.

Dead. In a room full of doctors and nurses, of lifesaving machinery, she was dead. Even after the training, the years of schooling, Celia still hadn't a clear idea back then of how fragile life really was.

We had breakfast together. She was laughing, talking about her new boyfriend, about how wonderful working in a war zone was. Why were we hit? We were a hospital ship, damn it! Where were the people who were supposed to be protecting us?

To this day, a million questions hammered at her. They had then, and none of them had ever been answered. The answers, she knew deep down inside, wouldn't bring Janet back.

Nothing would; not technology, equipment, or training. Janet would not come back.

The rest was a blur. She had a dim recollection of turning back to the table, of turning back to her work, with tears streaming down her face; more burn victims, some worse than Janet was, some not as bad. Not for her; hers were the shrapnel recipients, the fractured skulls and broken bones. Somewhere in there was the first time she had seen the results of decompression, though why anyone had thought the ER could actually *do* anything with the mess on the gurney escaped her.

She went to bed; when she woke, there was nothing inside.

When Janet died, Celia decided later, her emotions died with her friend. A hidden gear, a thrown switch, put her in a detached, unfeeling, mechanical mode.

She remembered the next few weeks, the vague sense of moving with a purpose, with no real sense of joy or pain. No sense, really, of anything. *Nothing.* She got through each day, just barely. When she went to her room to cry, nothing happened. The tears wouldn't come.

And they never did, Celia thought. *Will they ever?* She shook her head. *Probably not. After fourteen years, what would be left?*

She had requested an immediate transfer then. She wasn't sure why, not at the time. All she knew was that like a wounded creature crawling away to lick its injuries in private, she needed off that ship, since leaving her profession altogether was out of the question.

But when she made the request, they had denied it!

Only then did some kind of emotion wake; rage. She barely restrained her anger when she had her conference with the Chief of Surgery, a large, aggressive bitch of an old woman who refused to listen to her.

Her supervisor informed her in no uncertain terms that she was needed on that particular ship in that particular slot. She had no experience in combat medicine, and she was lucky to have a chance to gain some of it where she was.

The CoS made working in that nightmare that had killed Janet sound like a *privilege.*

And one more thing; regs. She didn't really have a choice. She wouldn't be allowed a transfer for another year. Only senior staff were allowed transfers.

Celia could have strangled her then.

She returned to her cabin in a state of barely controlled rage. But somehow, in the interval between the end of the interview and the beginning of her shift, she came to the startling realization that she was only a working part of a larger machine, the workings of which were decided by other, more important people.

What, Celia had asked, *would I have to do to get transferred?*

Become the best damned medic we have, the supervisor informed her with a self-serving sneer. *That is your only ticket out of here.*

Then I had better get back to work, Celia replied, and proceeded to *become* the best damned doctor, the best damned surgeon, the Fleet had ever seen.

Then she went a step further; she went back to the books for further surgery specialization. She surprised everybody by picking up the old manual skills, the kind used in the most primitive of field conditions; old-fashioned surgery with scalpel and sutures. Except for a few who kept their hands in because they were assigned to ground-based MASH units, most surgeons didn't even bother picking up a metal scalpel once during their whole careers.

With every patient that came past her, she remembered Janet, and put as much energy into saving that person as she would her best friend.

It became a challenge, to be the best so that she could have the most freedom.

In the end, she had the freedom of the Fleet. Not only did she have a ticket off that particular ship, she discovered that she could write her ticket to wherever she wanted.

And she discovered something else. There would never be another Janet. There had been too much pain in losing the first one. So she started running away, whenever people began coming too close.

For a while each change of location helped keep her isolated, but inevitably she began forming acquaintances. Acquaintances had the potential to become friends.

There must never be friends.

She was never sure what criteria she went by, or if there was anything specific that went on in her head. But at some point in every assignment, she realized that her time was up.

Time for a transfer. Before I get too close to these people.

She sensed something distantly wrong with her attitude, as well as her lack of feelings, and like a good little professional, she sought confidential help from a psychiatrist. She was a little hesitant about seeing a man, but she didn't have a lot to pick from. Dr. Reynolds was the only shrink on the ship. It was him, or the chaplain, and she had long ago lost any faith in a higher power of any kind.

Dr. Reynolds soon became "Walter," then "Walt." With each session, some grueling, she relived Janet's death, and bit by bit Walt peeled away the layers of her psyche, like the skin of an onion. She didn't like what she found there, but Walt didn't give her a choice. He forced her to face herself, and learn to deal with what was there.

Slowly, the feelings began to return. But not the kind of feelings she expected, or even *wanted.*

Textbook case, Celia. Like so many fools before her, she was falling in love with her shrink. And he was happily married.

She never told him why she stopped seeing him, but she somehow never had time to schedule another session, and after a while, the comp stopped reminding her. Celia avoided him fairly easily; her schedule and his didn't exactly mesh. She went back to repressing her feelings, which she did with relative ease. She was pretty good at it by now.

Then the mine struck the ship. Weeks later, the technicians couldn't quite figure out what race had made the bomb, but whoever made it knew what they were doing.

It might even have been from a race centuries extinct, made for a conflict that someone had won or lost when man was still fumbling about in his own solar system with sublight spacecraft. It might have been something from their current enemy. Wherever it came from, the device had drifted through several layers of security, deftly evading them all before it impacted on the hull.

Celia was on duty when it happened this time. A quarter of the ship had decompressed, killing large numbers of crew before automatic doors sealed off the damaged sector. Those who weren't killed probably wished they had been, in the few minutes that were left to them.

Decompression is such a nasty business, Celia remembered thinking. Of the thirty patients brought in, they lost twenty. Before she went off duty, they brought in one last survivor.

Walt Reynolds. He was gasping for air with ruined lungs when the stretcher floated past. Celia stood there, frozen, for several moments, before she realized she was the only surgeon who wasn't busy with someone right then.

He looked at her with frightened, bloodshot eyes as she put the oxygen mask over his face, checking his skin for the instant frost-bite that often accompanied decompression and vacuum exposure. She looked in those ruined eyes, laced with scarlet ruptures, remembering how reassuring they had once been, after gently exposing her mental wounds.

Triage. Minor, major, grave.

She knew before she got started that Walt was going to die, but her training stepped in, seized control of her body.

I'm the best damned doctor on this ship, she thought, wondering why that was important then.

But even the best damned doctor in the universe couldn't save someone with no lung tissue left to breathe with. Not when all the mech-lungs they had were plugged into other people.

When Walt died, she felt nothing, nothing at all.

After that, her career became a series of transfers, initiated whenever she thought she was getting too close to someone. There were many ships in the Fleet, but not all of them had—or were—medic units.

Then there was only one option left open to her. The *Stephen Hawking*. Heading out near the Core, facing yet another brand-new enemy, where the fighting was the heaviest.

The *Stephen Hawking* was a huge ship—but not big enough. Only too soon, she had to run again.

They were losing more ships than ever now, and even medical craft like the *Blackwell* weren't immune to fire, friendly or otherwise.

As she knew.

The Ichtons didn't care what they destroyed. To transfer would mean suicide, sooner or later.

Celia transferred.

And now—now none of it mattered, really. When the huge Ichton fleet had been detected days before, she remembered thinking not so much that she was going to die, but that the running, finally, was over. Instead of the understated fear that those around her were showing, she felt calm, almost serene. In a way she was grateful for the approaching fleet; her heart welcomed them.

The running is finally over.

She would have gone on, wallowing in these cheery thoughts a little longer. But a sudden lull in conversation made her look up, and she noticed the staff administrator had just entered the mess hall. An older gal, she had that seasoned look of someone who had been in medicine a long, long time. *What was her name? Dr. Morgan. Althea Morgan. Neurosurgery and Personnel.*

She had a searching look, a little frown on her face as she scanned the mess. *Who is she looking for?* Celia wondered.

Althea's eyes passed over everyone in the mess hall, then settled on Celia. A smile swept over the mature features, leaving no doubt that she had found who she was looking for.

Celia panicked. *Oh,* shit. *She's looking for* me.

A hunch told Althea that Celia would be hiding out in the mess hall, and as usual her hunch proved to be correct.

There she was, huddled over her plastic tray, sitting alone, eating by herself.

No big surprise here, after reading her file.

When their eyes met, Althea could almost feel the panic she saw there.

Celia's file said she was forty-two, but she looked much, much older. *Well, she has seen a lot of action—but that much action?*

Even from where she stood she could see stress lines in Celia's face, and she wasn't close. On the other hand—the woman wasn't taking any pains to look attractive, either. Not even close.

Forty-two and a veteran. Did I look like that when I was her age? she wondered. Well, it really didn't matter, did it? What was important was what was going on inside that head, not outside it.

She put on her friendliest smile and approached her table, hoping the woman wouldn't flee before she got there.

"Well, hel*lo,*" Althea said, flashing that all-important smile. "I'm Althea Morgan. You must be our new Chief of Surgery, Celia Stratford."

Celia stood still for a moment, then offered a weak smile. Slowly, like a caged animal reaching uncertainly for food, she extended her hand. "Very pleased to meet you," Celia said, but Althea was far from convinced that she was. "What, ah, can I do for you this morning?"

Althea looked down, at where Celia had put her hands after the tentative handshake. They were gripping the table sides, and the knuckles were turning white. Had she met Celia before seeing what she could do in a surgery, this tense display would have been alarming. But apparently she left the strain and discomfort behind when she went to work; her work, so far, had been exemplary.

Good thing, Althea thought. *Or this girl would never have made it past the first day!*

"Please don't think of this as business, per se," Althea said soothingly. Oh, it was business, all right, but not the kind Celia would think of. *If there's a neurotic working for us, it's my business to find out.* "I was just going over the new personnel files and saw yours, and realized we hadn't actually met."

"I see," Celia said.

That fits. Monosyllables. Not unfriendly, but there's nothing there to make anyone want to continue a conversation, Althea thought, and consciously turned off the frown that started to form on her own face. *Well, let's see if I can't get past the first barrier and see what your next line of defense is.*

Althea chuckled, hoping it didn't sound as artificial as it felt. "You know, in the good ole days of medicine, or anywhere else for that matter, the medical director would be the first person the new transfer would meet. But now, with all our computers . . . well, you know how it is. There's not enough human contact, in my not-so-humble opinion. Especially in our profession. Machines do enough as it is; we shouldn't let them take over our whole lives."

"My mentor made the same observation," Celia said icily. "But at the same time he pointed out that the technical advances in our field have made it possible for the surgeon to concentrate entirely on his specialty and not on extraneous nonsense."

"What, like doctor-patient relations, and bedside manner?" Althea grinned. She'd gotten a response, a negative one, but a response. *Let's jab the needle in a little deeper.* "Frankly, my dear, you can call me old-fashioned, but I think that kind of attitude sucks."

She had deliberately chosen the single most offensive way to phrase her reply, short of marine-class obscenity. She hoped fervently for anger.

Something to show that the personality was only buried, not amputated. She had a shrewd idea, now that she'd had a look through Celia's files, of where the problem was, and at least part of the cause. She'd left old Cyclops on a search-and-categorize mission that ought to keep him from pestering her with any foolishness for a while. He was looking for something specific; people with whom Celia had either extended professional or social contacts who had died violently—on the same ship where she was stationed. Good chance that she would have been in the trauma center when they came in.

Meanwhile, she was going to stick some pins in the girl and wake her up.

She got her response. "Battlefield conditions are no place for bedside manner, Doctor," Celia said with a spark of anger in her eyes.

"Oh, I beg to differ." Althea raised one eyebrow. "A little personal attention just before the anesthetic hits can make all the difference between someone fighting for his life and giving up. I've seen it happen too many times to discount. And it doesn't take any time at all—I mean, you have to read Ar—I mean, the medicomp screen anyway. You just pay attention to what it says about that kid on the table, lean down while your nurse is spraying your hands, and say, 'Hey, soldier, we're gonna get you back to that pretty little bundle of fur in no time, with a fancy scar to prove you're a hero.' Or maybe, 'Don't sweat your boyfriend, honey.

The *Hawking* crew is warming up a brand-new face for you right now. Want to pick out cheekbones when you wake up?' Or even, 'Show these humans what you're made of, soldier. You're worth a dozen puny bareskins!' "

Celia's hands were shaking as badly as Althea's. "You're making them into people—not patients—"

She shook her head. "Not at all. They already *are* people, and their lives are mechanical enough. I just remind them that other folks know they're people, too. Let them know that somebody cares that they were there, that they live through their injuries. I even talk to them while they're under."

"You *what?*" Celia was properly horrified. Actually, Althea had disturbed quite a few medics with her little eccentricity before they saw the results. "That's insane! How could—"

"That's good medicine," Althea corrected. "Or haven't you read your studies of the effects of anesthetics on the conscious mind? Most species listen to and understand *and are affected* by what they hear when they're under. In fact, you've got a pipeline straight to the raw psyche right then, bypassing all the usual protections we put on what we hear. Tell a patient something while he's on the table and he'll take it as from the mouth of the Deity-of-His-Choice. So I tell them they're doing fine, make jokes about the mess they got themselves in, tell them that the staff on the *Hawking* is going to put in some improvements that'll wow the extremities off their mates. Lots of times I get kids pulling through that had no right to."

The rest of the staff had recognized that she was having *one of those conferences* with a new doctor; the mess had mysteriously cleared of personnel. *Good. Because I'm getting to her, and she won't perform with an audience.*

"I—didn't know—" Celia whispered, her eyes dark with *some* kind of emotion. "But—what if they don't—pull through? You've made them into people for you, and what if—"

"What if they aren't faceless simulacra anymore?" Althea gentled her voice; there was an edge of hysteria in Celia's words that she didn't want to push just yet. "What if they die?"

There was no doubt what the emotion was in Celia's eyes now. It was pain. She didn't say anything, she didn't even nod. She just sat there in frozen silence. But her eyes begged for an answer.

"Celia, that is the price that we pay for being mortal. People die—of *stupid* things. I lost my mother when a house fell on her." She shook her head, her mouth twisting in remembered pain, but still able to see the absurdity. "Some idiot was moving a living-unit with an inadequate lifter; he dropped it, it went through the pedwalk and crushed my mother in a shoe store two levels below. Imagine how I felt the first time some poor innocent reacted to a bad mood I was in by asking sarcastically, 'What's the matter, did a house fall on your sister?' Shit happens. You work through it, and live."

Celia shook her head, and to Althea's joy, there were signs of tears in her eyes.

"We pay doubly, because we are physicians as well as mortals," she continued. "We have the skills to save lives—"

"But sometimes we can't—" Celia choked, and then shut her mouth tightly.

"Sometimes we can't," Althea agreed. "That doesn't mean we should cut ourselves off from feeling. Not even pain. Pain lets us know we're alive; so does love. Maybe that's why we've come running out here to get ourselves killed, trying to keep them from turning the rest of the universe into their private lunch counter. I don't know. I *do* know that no matter how much *feeling* costs, I'm not going to stop—because when you stop feeling, you're dead."

Okay, wrap it up, quick. Get out of here so she can recover from what you just shot at her. Althea glanced at her watch and swore. "Damn! I'm in surgery in an hour. I'd better grab a bagel and get out of here." She reached over and patted Celia's icy hand. "It was good meeting with you, Celia. I expect we'll be seeing a lot more of each other, now that I know who you are."

She made a quick exit, snatching a bagel for form's sake, and headed for her cabin, restraining her feeling of triumph.

Good work, there. Got some real emotion out of her. She palmed the lock on her door with anticipation. *Now to see what Cyclops has for me, and see how close to the bone I came.*

She hit the Enter key on her terminal before she even sat down on her bunk, and to her immense satisfaction, Cyclops had found not one, but two possibilities.

The first . . .

Omigod. Med school roomie; best friend. Requested assignment to same ship. And, yes, Celia had been in the trauma room when her roommate came in. The hospital ship itself had taken a hit, and every skilled hand on board had been summoned to duty.

Probably watched the poor thing die. Althea looked over the old records with a professional eye. *God. Gamma rays just sheeted through that compartment. Those weren't blast burns, not entirely. The girl was dead before they took her to the trauma room, just nobody knew it. Not even Jesus Christ himself could have done anything. But I'll bet Celia never knew that.*

Then two years later—

Her shrink. Shit, doesn't it figure. And he would *be a classical Freudian, too, which means he encouraged her to fall in love with him as part of the therapy and I'd be willing to pin my job on the fact that she didn't know he was Freudian. She'd have been better off going to the chaplain, at least he had Gestalt training.*

She lay back on her bed and laced her hands under her head. *Celia, Celia, what am I going to do with you? Are you bright enough to actually* listen *to what I'm telling you? I hope so. Because I can't have you on my staff, otherwise. You'll wind up killing people and never know you were doing it. But you're ready to rejoin the world. I can sense it.*

Or else you'll crack, when we need you most.

And if it comes to a choice between helping you out of your morass slowly, or getting you out of the way, I'll commit you on a Psych charge, girl.

Because while I have compassion for you, I have no pity. I have no time for pity. None of us does.

Stunned, Celia watched Althea get her bagel and leave the cafeteria. They had spoken maybe four minutes, five tops, but it felt like she had just gone through one of those grueling hour-long sessions with Walt: like a glass of ice water had just been thrown in her face.

Like she'd just been peeled bare, right down to the bone, then casually put back together.

What is she? she wondered. How did a paper pusher in administration, a surgeon, get to be so good at getting inside people? During their brief discussion Althea neatly dissected her as if she were some kind of frog, or if she were psychic, or both. *She's in Personnel. She must know everything about me. Janet, my transfers, Walt, the transfers.* Celia had never felt more exposed in her life, and it was *not* a feeling she was comfortable with.

Her cold breakfast sat untouched in front of her as she wavered between anger and revelation. The ice Althea had just chipped away revealed wounds, not flesh, and she wasn't certain what she should feel just then.

Some of the things Althea said were just plain crazy—

Or were they? She *had* heard some of them before, like the part about talking to the patients who were under. All the times when she might have done such a thing in surgery, she remembered being so busy with the technicalities of the operation to even consider it.

Still, it sounded a little wacky, even with evidence to support it.

Or did it sound wacky because *she* didn't want to believe it? Didn't want to think that some muttered remark, some unthought curse, might have pushed one of her own patients over the edge of survival?

She sure knew the right buttons to push. Celia shuddered. *Who does she think she is, anyway?* She reached for the anger, and found that it wasn't there. *Damn it, where did it go?* she thought. *I have to be angry about this . . . don't I? If I'm not angry, then what does that mean?*

That I believe what she's trying to tell me. The exchange rolled over and over in her mind, and Celia tried to analyze it further, looking for the hidden meaning that must have been there. But wasn't.

"When you stop feeling, you're dead," she whispered. *That's what she said. And damned if that's not how I've been feeling all along.*

Her soul seemed to decompress. A feeling of release filled the void that she had willed all these years; sense that a burden had gone, a feeling of light and weightlessness.

I can be a doctor and be human, too, she thought. *They're people, not patients. Let them know it.*

Then, another thought; the recollection of Althea's face, the graying hair. The lines of care and pain that not all the laugh and smile creases could erase.

She's lost people, too, and not just her mother. And she lived. She can laugh. She has friends, I know she does—

Then, greatly daring, trying the thought to see if it hurt; *I'd like to be her friend.*

She looked up, feeling silly that she was the only one left in the mess hall. She got up and consigned her breakfast to the disposal; she felt strange, as if she'd been hit with some kind of psychotropic drug, and had no idea what it was going to do to her. But even that was better than the emptiness that had been her constant companion all these years.

Leaving the cafeteria, she entered a triangular hallway of bare steel girders; pretty Spartan for a medical ship, but she knew that the paneling had been stripped earlier for more important sections of the *Blackwell.* Only a few crew and medical staff wandered the halls. The day for most had begun. Celia glanced at her watch, and, seeing she was late for her shift, walked a little faster.

From somewhere beneath her came a loud *whump.*

It rocked the floor and walls so hard she stumbled and went to her knees. Simultaneously a red alert alarm began wailing in the hall, followed by the flashing red light near every intercom.

What the hell? she thought madly. But her battelfield training took over and she kept her head low in case something else might explode or fly through the air, working her way over to the wall to clutch at an exposed girder.

Is this finally it? she wondered, calculating the proximity of the Ichton fleet, which should still be quite far away. *Must be something else, but what?* The red alert sounded only if a life-threatening situation occurred *on* the ship, or if the ship itself was in danger.

Considering the intensity of the explosion, and the fact that they were still docked with the *Hawking,* it was probably the former. She found a rude laugh somewhere inside her. *Ironic, if I die now. At least,* she thought whimsically, *I'll have some peace of mind if I do.*

A sharp pain in her right leg hindered her as she tried to get up. Blood had soaked the leg of her uniform, vivid against the white fabric. She swore softly and rolled the leg of her pants up; she found it was a long and shallow gash, bleeding messily, but not immediately threatening. A special patch in the ER would stop the bleeding. Fine and dandy. That's where she was going anyway. She'd probably cut it when she fell; there was certainly enough crud lying around in the halls because of the repairs going on.

"Shit happens," she said to the ship as she hobbled toward the ER. Now, behind her, she heard shouts, and some other ominous, unidentifiable sound. One of the shouts became a scream; she quickened her pace.

Here we go again, she thought, going into surgeon mode. *This isn't just a job. It's a fucking adventure!*

When she got to the lifts, she discovered that whatever exploded had apparently taken them out as well. *Great,* she thought. *It's only two flights. Not bad, even with the artificial gravity. Here's hoping* that *stays up.*

It took several more minutes than usual to get to ER. When she finally got there, all hell had broken loose.

Most alarming was the group of doctors huddled around the medicomp CPU, as if it were a patient, not the marvelous tool the staff had come to depend on. The main screen was blank; one of the doctors slapped the monitor on its side, as if to urge it to life. Nothing happened.

There were no patients there yet, but she had a sickening feeling there soon would be.

"She's here," someone said. The room became silent, and one by one all heads turned to her.

One of the doctors, an older surgeon just months away from retirement, hung up a phone. Dr. Powers's expression was grave. He saw her, and slowly padded his way through the others. The crowd parted, letting him pass.

"Dr. Stratford," he said, glancing briefly at the leg wound. "We should get a patch on that."

"In a moment. What *happened,* Doctor?"

"It appears," he began, addressing all present, "that a water boiler in the crew section has exploded, due to residual damage from the last battle. It's a nasty situation down there, and it's taken out the airlock along with a few other goodies. We won't be able to transfer patients to the *Hawking* until the dock crews get a temporary lock set up, and cut through the old one. Until then, we're on our own. Ladies and gentlemen, get ready for a long night."

Celia knew there was more; Dr. Powers didn't disappoint her.

"The explosion created a power surge—and repairs had taken the breakers and power cleaners off-line. The surge took the medicomp and a lot of our electronics out as well." Powers took a deep breath. "Here's what we're faced with. We have some telltales, the ones built into the tables. EKG, EEG, body temperature. We have stand-alone equipment, like the oxygen, blood replacement, and suction devices. No laser scalpels; they were slaved to the medicomp, and until we get a tech up here to get them unhooked, they're useless. No StediGloves."

"How're we going to know where our hands are?" someone wailed.

Powers gave him a look. "Eyeball. This is going to be metal scalpel and suture time, kids. Nurse Ki'ilee?"

An odd-looking anthropoid with arms far too long for its uniform stepped to the front of the group. "Thir," it lisped.

"Find the autoclave and all the manual gear. I think it's in one of the holds with the spare IV equipment. Requisition whoever you need to trot it up here and get it set up. On the double."

"Thir!" The nurse saluted sharply and ran off. Powers turned to Celia.

"According to your records, you spec'd in field surgery." He looked at her as if he expected her to deny it.

"I did," she replied.

A tiny bit of relief crept into his expression. "Then you're the best CoS we could have right now. What do we do?"

She froze for a moment—then her mind went into high gear.

"We'll be getting patients in here in a moment—" She examined the room. "Triage in the hall; there won't be room in here. God forbid it happens, but if there are any medical personnel hurt, they get priority. You, you, and you—" She pointed to three nurses. "You're triage and hall prep. If you spot any paramedics out there, put them on triage and get back in here."

She turned her attention back to the huddle of doctors, as a secondary—explosion? Or the crew of the *Hawking* trying to get in to them?—shook the floor. "Each one of you pick three nurses to help you; you'll need them. One holds clean instruments, one assists, and one operates the breathing equipment. Put a bucket or a pan under the table for dirty instruments." She thought quickly as the nurses and doctors together started setting up what they could; even as she thought, the anthropoid nurse arrived with a bulky container on wheels and a line of ships' personnel with boxes.

"You sailors!" she snapped—and the men and women came as close to snapping to attention as they could. "You stay here. Nurse, these people are yours for the duration. You set up the autoclave and start sterilizing instruments. You sailors, you take clean instruments to the doctors and take the used ones away, back to the nurse. *Spray your hands every time you touch something that isn't clean.* Nurse, tell them what you want."

The nurse stood up taller with the new increase in status, and began issuing orders in its soft lisp. Celia surveyed the room, and noted the dismay and despair on some faces.

"Stop thinking about this as an impossibility," she said gently. "I've done this hands-on. Scalpels are the same, they just don't cauterize, so there'll be more blood. Nurses, if you're assisting, keep the suction going and blot delicate areas with sponges. Doctors—how many of you have done real suturing?"

Only two. "Nurses?" A couple more. "All right, has anyone ever done needle-and-thread sewing? Handwork or embroidery?" Three, including a paramedic who had just wandered in. "Fine. You six are the closure specialists. Doctors, you do internals, nurses, muscle tissue and major vessels, hand workers, final closure. We'll run this like an assembly line."

She got them set up; patients would come in the door to the nearest empty table. Anyone *not* working on someone would prep them, then keep them going until the first available surgery team could take them. Then surgery, then closure, then out the door and the anthropoid nurse's team would clean the table for the next.

"Get them patched together and keep them alive," she ordered, and did a quick mental reckoning. "I don't think it'll take the *Hawking* more than a few hours to get to us. Give them that much time, and we're home free. It doesn't have to be pretty or neat; it *does* have to be good."

"Doctor?" One of the nurses waved her hand in the air. "What are we doing about anesthetic and blood?"

No blood analysis at all; that was the medicomp's job. "Can we get by on locals and injectables?" It was a lot easier monitoring the dosages on those.

Powers turned to the anthropoid, who nodded. "We haf jutht rethupplied," it said.

"Okay. Save the inhalants for major thoracic wounds; use your own judgment. Blood—shit."

She shook her head; the replicators were probably gone, too, or the nurse wouldn't have asked the question. "Stored where we have it, hyperoxygenated universal where we don't, and species-specific plasma or Ringers if you don't know what the reaction to universal will be. A few hours, people. That's what we need to buy them. Okay? Don't forget those clean samples; the *Hawking* will need them. Okay, on station—go—"

That was when the first wave hit.

Celia tried to be everywhere, looking over shoulders, advising, cajoling, coaxing. The first wave wasn't so bad; not nearly as bad as she had thought. No decompression; lots of burns, some pretty horrible, but nothing that needed really major surgery. Her fledglings gained confidence as they sutured their first gashes, as they cut bits of shrapnel from arms and legs. Nurse Ki'ilee *was* everywhere, turning her little corps of recruits into a real team. She lost a few in the first couple of minutes, as weak stomachs couldn't handle the gore of the OR—she gained more by sending the unsteady out to wake up the rest of the med personnel and haul them in.

It was just as well that they had that first wave to practice on, because when the second wave came in—the victims who'd been pried out of their wrecked rooms—they needed every bit of confidence that they'd gained.

Here were the major injuries that Celia had feared; yellow bands weren't coming in the door at all, just red. Severed limbs (put it on ice, stop the bleeding, kill the pain, stem the shock, let the *Hawking* handle it), torsos ripped open, spurting arterial wounds, punctured and collapsed lungs. . . .

Celia shoved doctors aside when they hesitated, taking over and scolding and swearing at her patients like some kind of cross between a first sergeant and a mother hen. "What in hell were you doing in bed, anyway? You're gonna have to get yourself back up off that bunk in double time, mister, you hear me? Making all this shit for me to do—" Encouraging? It was the closest she could come. At least she was filling those unconscious ears with the sure message that they were going to live.

They were people. They were her responsibility. And suddenly she found herself caring, caring passionately, that they would live.

"Celia!"

The urgency in that voice made her head snap up. Someone across the crowded OR waved frantically at her.

Dr. Powers. He wouldn't call her unless he needed her.

She wriggled her way between the tables, across a floor slippery with cleaning solution and much-diluted blood—Nurse Ki'ilee was making certain that the OR stayed as clean as it could be. But when she reached Powers's side and he made room for her, his white face did not prepare her for what she found on the table.

Dr. Althea Morgan.

Her mind froze; her body wanted to run—and her soul screamed.

Not again—not—again—

Powers gestured at the massive chest wound. It looked as if she must have been reading something off her terminal when the explosion occurred; shards of razor-edged plastic and glass had ripped into her body, somehow sparing her face.

I can't—I can't—

"I can't do this," Powers said numbly. "I haven't got that kind of skill."

"Nobody does—alone," she heard herself saying. "Pull Urrrlerri off whatever he's doing, and get me Nurse Merfanwy. And then take over for Urrrlerri."

She found her hands reaching for instruments; found herself going to work on the worst of the slashes, a puncture that threatened the lung.

Found tears streaming down her face and soaking her mask. "*Damn* you, Althea Morgan," she snarled as the two assistants arrived, and she put Merfanwy (incredible visual acuity and sight in the low UV) on picking out the near-invisible shards of glass, and Urrrlerri (tentaclelike fingers with incredible flexibility) to work on the abdomen while she did the lungs. "*Damn* you, you old bitch! How dare you talk to me like that and then do *this* to me? You psychotic bitch from *hell*! What did you think you were doing? You're going to come out of this, you monster, I'm going to drag you out of this by your damn *hair*! If you even *think* of dying, I'm going to pump you so full of stim you'll *dance* over to the damned *Hawking*! You hear me? You hear me?"

Oblivious to the sideways glances from the rest of her operating team, she continued to rage at Morgan under her breath, alternately cursing her and telling her that she'd better not abandon her *friend,* leaving her to face the coming Ichtons alone.

Ignoring the tears that threatened to blind her until her nurse sponged them away, her hands worked with maniacal speed; patching, suturing, making whole.

Then it was over—someone wheeled Althea out—

And there was no more time to agonize, for a sucking lung puncture was on the table in front of her, and another patient to curse back into life. Then another, and another—they had Walt's face, or Janet's or Althea's—

And she gave them all her curses, her tears, her skill—told them all they were needed, that they *would* live—or she would, by all the gods anyone ever swore by, come *after* them!

Suddenly, silence.

The OR was empty. Not even a green bracelet in sight. She blinked once, looked around at the equally weary bodies around her, and slowly pulled off her face mask.

There was someone at her elbow; someone she didn't know, but in medical white, *clean,* with a look of concern and a little name tag that said "Dr. R. S. Rai."

"I'm from the *Hawking*," he said, slowly, carefully. "We've got all your patients, Doctor. You did incredibly well, you didn't lose anyone who made it this far."

"We didn't?" she replied ingenuously.

He smiled. "Not one. Six hours on your own and not a single one."

"Oh," she said vaguely. "That's fucking wonderful." And she let him lead her off to a bed.

"So," Althea said the moment they let Celia into her room, "I'm a nasty old bitch, am I? And you were going to pump me full of so much stim I was going to dance over to the *Hawking*?"

She grinned at Celia's look of shock. "Told you that people heard what you said to them." She lowered her voice, conspiratorially. "Did you know that there's now a story going around about a foul-mouthed angel who wrestles victims right out of the hands of Death and then kicks their butts back to their bodies?"

She laughed out loud at the look on Celia's face, even though it hurt.

"I—uh—"

"I bet you didn't even know you knew those words." She reached out and took Celia's hand. "Look—I snooped into your records, so I know about your friends. I'm sorry, Celia—"

"But enough is enough," the woman said, herself. "You were right. All I was doing was—anesthetizing. As soon as it wore off, something was bound to break."

It was Althea's turn to be surprised, and Celia smiled—the first time she'd actually seen that expression on the woman's face. "I've had some time to think—and to get a little help. I found a good female shrink on the *Hawking*, and an even better chaplain. Oh, I'm still a mess, but we all are, right?"

"Right," Althea said softly, with a silent salute to her own legion of dead. "That's part of the price we pay, we survivors. Beats the hell out of the alternative."

Celia nodded, and the life in her eyes brought back a hint of that laughing girl of the graduation picture. "Speaking of beating the hell out of someone—" she said, a hint of humor starting to show— "I figured I'd snoop in *your* records while I was temporary admin head. And I found out that you fancy yourself as a *go* player." From behind her, she whisked out a board and bag of stones, and placed them on Althea's tray table. "So I thought I'd show you just where you really stand in the *go* hierarchy around here."

Althea raised an eyebrow. "Is that a threat?"

"No." Celia's smile turned wicked. "That's a promise."

"Care to make a little wager on that?"

"Sure." Celia licked her lips. "I take on the paperwork—against *you* taking on me." Her look was challenging. "You're degreed in head-shrinking. And I don't intend to lose."

Althea felt a warm rush of irrational happiness. "The game or the friend?"

"Either." A shrug. "Maybe we don't have much time. So I want to learn how to enjoy what time we have left. I figure you can do that *and* help me get my head straight."

"You're on." She selected black. "You know—I *am* the kind of person your parents warned you about. You're about to learn things they never taught you in med school."

Celia just laughed. "Why do you think I made that bet?"

REINFORCEMENTS

IT WAS CONFIRMED that, as Anton Brand had feared, the two missing Ichton fleets had united and were moving toward Emry. In their effort the invaders were bypassing a number of usable, inhabited planets. This was a change of procedure that worried all of the strategists of the races united to fight them. Beyond the Fleet's more effective warp drive, only the Ichtons' predictability had so far enabled them to be met and defeated, even locally.

One of the worlds bypassed was that inhabited by the Squarm—a young race, by local standards, that physically resembled Earth's walruses. Initially reluctant to abandon the defense of their world, when the Squarm leaders realized how easily the Ichtons that had already passed would have overwhelmed their defenses, they agreed to contribute half of their space navy to the Fleet-led effort. The other half was retained to defend the planet against the numerous smaller bands of Ichtons appearing more frequently in the Core systems. Other nearby races followed this example, almost doubling in number, if not quality, the forces based on the *Hawking*. The appearance of allies gave a boost to the nearly negligible morale of the *Hawking*'s crew. It also placed a strain on the station as it strived to support almost twice the number of ships it had been designed for.

The decision was made to intercept and divert the Ichton fleet. This would buy time for the Emry to complete the construction of new factories designed to build new orbital defenses based upon the most effective Fleet weaponry. The planet Emry was also supplying many of the resources needed to maintain and repair the *Hawking* and had to be defended if they were to continue the defense. So the battle began, but Brand had underestimated the determination of the Ichtons to punish and destroy any opposition. Rather than turn to face the new threat posed by the Fleet, the Ichtons' combined fleet continued on toward Emry at full speed. Dropping out only to navigate, re-form, or snap at their pursuers. Unable to use its superior speed without leaving all their ally's ships behind, the *Hawking* found itself in a stern chase. They followed the Ichton fleet, with individual units pushing ahead to engage their rear guard. The decisive battle Brand sought had, instead, degenerated into a running fight covering hundreds of light-years and several weeks. One in which the constantly reinforced Ichtons more than held their own.

The arrival of over a hundred destroyers of the hundred forty dispatched from Tau Ceti months earlier was a second tremendous morale boost for the crew of the *Hawking*. Their crews were exhausted from the seven-month journey to the Core, but Brand had no choice but to throw them instantly into the battle.

Along with mail, spare parts, and the latest trivid programs, the reinforcement fleet also brought a few unwanted visitors. Dealing with them proved a new challenge for even the combat veterans on the *Stephen Hawking*.

TAKEN TO THE CLEANERS

by Peter Morwood

THE LIEUTENANT RAN one finger around his tunic's high collar, as though the garment were strangling him, then set all to rights again with a quick downward tug at the hem. Despite hours of pondering over real and imagined errors, he still wasn't sure how he had pulled this particular duty; but he was fairly certain that he wasn't going to like it much. There were too many cold eyes and rattrap mouths among the budgetary fact-finding commission for that.

"If you'll all just step this way. Yes, that's right. Stand well clear of the doors, please. Mind the gap. All present and correct? Good. Now then. Welcome aboard the Battlestation *Stephen Hawking,* ladies and gentlemen, welcome aboard. I'm glad to—"

As the commission formed up in an untidy gaggle and its shortest members pushed to the front, his voice faltered. At least the blink of disbelief that had accompanied the stumble in his words had gone unnoticed. He hoped. The shrouded mike of the wall-mounted com unit beckoned. "Er, excuse me just one second." His thumb hit the Transmit button just one second after that.

"Channel five, engage privacy mute. Joe. Hey, Joe, you there?"

Course I'm here. Where else would I be?

"Hah! Where else would I be? sez you. Do you believe this guy? Don't gimme that crap. I dunno where you'd be. Just run me a translator check. Right now."

Why d'you need a trans—

"Uh, Joe, in case you haven't noticed, the why is because you didn't tell me there were Weasels in this bunch. Are the little fleabags getting a proper salutation?"

Yeah, sure they are.

"Gender and all?"

Gender, rank specifics, even line-family enhancements.

"Jeez, makes a change."

Gimme a break. We just finished a war with the furry little creeps. You think I want to start another—

"Look, just give me some warning next time, willya? Okay? Yeah, yeah, you, too. And your mother . . ."

The lieutenant let his face relax from the fixed grin it had adopted as com control came on line, Expression #27, We're Fine, We're All Fine, How Are You? and though his facial muscles wanted to go straight into #42, Sod This for a Game of Soldiers, he managed to resist the temptation. Rule One where the Civil Service was involved, never let the Buggers in the Suits know what you're thinking.

"Sorry about the interruption, ladies and gentlemen. Fleet business, security clearances, all that sh—stuff, you know how it is."

I don't think.

"My name is Neilson, Lieutenant Robert Neilson, and Commander Brand has assigned"—*ordered*—"me to look after you folks during this short guided tour of the *Hawking*. I'd like to take a few minutes before we start to advise you all of a few points—" *which shouldn't need repeating but then we're dealing with Suits and not real people, aren't we?*

"First, this station is on full active status, so military personnel will expect to have priority for use of the on-board transport net. Second, given the size of the *Hawking*, Internal Security recommends that it's in your own interests not to go wandering off by yourselves. Yes, ma'am?"

Ohshit.

The woman who spoke was of that sort who, in an earlier historical period, would have worn a tweed two-piece suit and terrifying spiky-framed spectacles. Even though she, like the rest of the commission, was wearing the name-flagged coverall issued to all visitors who might be entering a variety of shipboard environments, she still managed to suggest that indefinable air of tweediness. Neilson concentrated for just long enough to get the gist of her question, then tuned out the rest.

"Yes, ma'am," he said at last, "I understand that an economic analysis commission doesn't expect to be treated like tourists." *It's far too good for you.*

"Then, Lieutenant, since you understand, evidently your superiors also understand." Even her voice sounded tweedy, like the nightmare of a librarian. "As the representatives of the Defense Committee who financed this battlestation, why do we need a chaperon in the first place?"

"Because, ma'am, none of you know your way around." *And little fingers pushing little buttons could smoke half of this sector.*

"Are we considered incapable of asking for directions?"

"No, ma'am. Of course you could ask for directions, but as I said"—*and why weren't you listening?*—"this vessel is at active status, and—"

"Lieutenant, do you mean, ah"—the man, a classic career civil servant whose coverall should have been in pinstripe, was fumbling for the military terminology through the filing cabinets of a brain taught to work in signed triplicates—"that we are at, ah, general quarters?"

"No, sir, not general quarters. If we were at general quarters I wouldn't be here." *And neither would you.*

"But even allowing that active status is more peaceful than general quarters, surely a civilian would have less call on his or her time than a military . . . ?"

"I doubt a civilian guide would be as useful to the members of this commission as—"

"Or is the military trying to keep this commission all to itself? What is the civilian administrator's view?"

"Sir, the administrator was consulted on the matter. Both Administrator Omera and Commander Brand thought it would be simpler if a Fleet officer acted as guide. It's a matter of security." *Mine.*

The tweedy woman said something to her neighbor that Neilson couldn't quite catch, but her tone was clear enough that he could guess the content of the words. He had heard something of the sort before. "No, ma'am. Not so that the commission's access can be restricted. Quite the reverse. As Fleet personnel, I'm cleared to take you anywhere on the *Hawking.* A civilian guide would be restricted to civilian sectors only."

"And why is that, pray? The various civilian interests represented on board have put quite as much money toward the development of this station as the military."

"That's as may be, sir. It remains equally true that a civilian has no business to be in the military sectors. Yourselves excepted, of course, but then, the bureaucratic arm is a sort of honorary military." Neilson allowed himself to sink a small pin. "I believe that has to do with funding. Now, if you'll all just follow me." He cleared his throat and shifted into lecturing mode.

"The nine deck levels immediately above this location are military in function. Further, there are eleven decks below that are entirely scientific and civilian. What isn't widely understood is that, despite popular and romantic representations, the Fleet does more than just seek out new life-forms and new civilizations, and then blows them up. Unlike the Ichtons and the Khalians—excuse me, sir, it's true and a matter of historical fact, you can't deny twenty years of war—we are not aggressors. No sir, the *Jrgen Stroop* was a orbital bombardment platform purposely built for a single operation, Case White—yes, sir, economically built, from scrap parts—and never actually used. But given the existence of such aggressive species as I've already mentioned, it's hardly surprising that a vessel like the *Hawking* needs to be well-armed. . . ."

The little group had not gone very far along the corridor before a piercing scream shattered the silence and scattered the little gaggle of bored bureaucrats. Even though he knew he was safely on board an Alliance battlestation, even though he *knew* that there was nothing more dangerous behind him than a bunch of civil servants and a couple of tooth-drawn Weasels, Lieutenant Neilson was still flattened against the nearest bulkhead with his side arm drawn before he took time out to look back toward the source of the noise.

He relaxed at once and returned his gun to its holster, watching as a small shape fled meeping past him and back into the safe shadows beyond the pools of maintenance-level light.

"Shoot it! Why don't you shoot it?"

The only thing that Neilson shot was a puzzled glance back toward the party he was escorting, and most particularly at the tweedy lady, who was now giving the impression that she wanted to be standing on a chair with her skirt pulled tight around her legs. Since the regulation coveralls were—for good or, in her bony, long-shanked case, ill—fairly form-fitting, and most certainly didn't come equipped with any sort of skirt, this took some doing, but she managed all the same.

"Shoot it, ma'am? Why would I want to do that?"

"It's some sort of nasty alien!" Quite apart from the wording of the Alliance charter, simply being alien had long ceased to be any good reason to shoot something. There was a very satisfying embarrassed pause as the woman straightened herself up, brushed herself down, and generally tried to pretend that nothing untoward had ever happened. It didn't really work, but Neilson suppressed his grin and gave her the benefit of the doubt.

"No, ma'am. That's a Rover-SAC."

"A what?"

"A Rover. A Semi-Autonomous Cleaner."

"Dear God, I thought it was alive."

Lieutenant Neilson breathed out gently through his nose, so that the breath could not be used for all the comments that came simmering up inside him. Finally, he allowed himself just one. "Ma'am, Fleet sentiologists have identified more than three hundred life-forms since the *Hawking* moved coreward. They've had wings, legs, fins, tentacles, gastropodal traction, and even gaseous substructures. But so far, no wheels."

"What does it do, Lieutenant?" Neilson shifted his gaze and shrouded everything behind it with a slow blink. That sort of question could only come from a career civil servant who hadn't been listening to anything that anyone had said.

"Sir, it cleans, sir."

"Are you telling us that this facility has spent fiscal revenue on self-propelled cleaning devices?"

I just did. "Yes, sir."

"Lieutenant, have you any idea of how much such things cost?"

I'm flight crew. Why should I? "No, sir. But probably much less than the expenditure of putting FODed equipment to rights. Foreign-object damage is something you just don't want to know about, sir. Also I would guess that the Rovers cost less than maintaining a janitorial staff big enough to deal with a station of this size. Sir."

"Thank you, Lieutenant. Carry on."

Neilson knew the tone of that thank you, just as he knew the tone of the muttering that followed him down the corridor, and he was heartily glad that he was nothing more than a guide. Before this bunch left the battlestation, somebody somewhere on *Hawking* was going to be justifying the bars on their cuffs and the salary that went with it.

"Why 'semi-autonomous'?" said a dubious voice behind him.

Because autonomous units won't let their union members wash the windows, thought Neilson with a grin. "Sir, I think I could show you better than try to describe the difference. This way, please."

The control room wasn't too far from their intended route, and it was as busy with humming readouts and glowing monitors as any other on the battlestation. Even though he knew what it was all about, Neilson found the place appropriately impressive, and from the noises at his back, so did the members of the commission.

"What is this, Lieutenant? Internal security?"

"No, sir."

"That man at the control board, with the joystick, is he some sort of pilot?"

"No, ma'am. He's a janitor."

"A *what?*"

"A janitor, ma'am. He monitors the Rovers—on an intermittent basis—and makes sure that they're only doing what they've been programmed for. Hence semi-autonomous."

"All of this"—the disbelief was palpable—"just to keep an eye on a lot of self-propelled vacuum cleaners? I'm very glad you brought us here, Lieutenant Neilson. This is exactly the sort of gross overspending that our commission was—"

"Overspending, sir? Hardly. If anything, this facility's undermanned. And the Rover-SAC isn't a vacuum cleaner. At least, not just a vacuum cleaner."

"I think you'd better explain yourself, Lieutenant." The voice had one of those deceptively gentle tones, like a razor blade concealed in soap. "This, this blatant display has done very little to favorably influence the commission so far as allocations of funds from the next fiscal year are concerned."

Meaning, give us good reason to pay, or we won't.

"Ma'am, the commission was supplied with all necessary documentation—" Neilson began.

"Documentation is one thing, Lieutenant. Personal observation is another matter altogether. I know which I prefer."

Neilson took the insult—to himself, to the Fleet, to the veracity of the Service—without turning a hair. As one of the two Khalian commissioners wandered past, nosing and poking at things in a way that he would never have dreamed possible on an Alliance ship, hair was, however, much on his mind. If the commission wanted personal observation, they could have it. "Then, ma'am," he said, "it might be worth your while to question Mr. Leary."

"Mister who?"

Just the man sitting at the console. The one with Leary on his name tag. "The janitor, ma'am."

"Then bring him here."

"It would be better if the commission went to him, ma'am. He's quite busy just at the—"

"I said here, Lieutenant. And now."

"Ma'am, I really don't think—"

"Lieutenant Neilson, all this pretense of industry isn't fooling anybody. Janitor Leary, come here please. . . ."

Neilson backed hurriedly out of the cross fire as Leary, never impressed by Suits at the best of times, made it plain that he wasn't going anywhere for anybody right in the middle of his shift. For just a second Neilson thought the old man was going to say why, but he needn't have worried. In the tradition of janitors from long before man took his first faltering steps into space and left little trails of moondust that somebody had to sweep up, Leary subsided back over his controls, muttering as if they were somehow to blame.

A Rover-SAC whirred by, paused ever so briefly, then meeped to itself as Leary hit the override and trundled on. Neilson winked at it, and grinned.

"Janitor Leary," said the tweedy woman, her thin veneer of patience wearing out after several fruitless attempts at being polite, "if you value your position on this battlestation, you'll do as this commission requires, and do it now."

"Do it," said Neilson, leaning over the console and tapping it with one finger. "Just make sure you've logged a record that you left your post subject to unnecessary duress, and McCaul can't say a thing. No matter what happens." Another Rover-SAC purred into the room, and, like the first one, hesitated as if trying to make sense of conflicting signals. Halfway out of his seat, the janitor reached out to his control board, but Neilson slapped it away. "Leave be," he said briskly. "The Suits are waiting."

They weren't the only ones. The Rover-SAC ambled along a bulkhead and scooped up a few minuscule scraps of garbage, but the little machine's heart—or processor, anyway—didn't seem to be in its work. Neilson watched it thoughtfully, wondering how something that was little more than a knee-high six-wheeled box of tubes and brushes could convey such an impression of nonchalant whistling. Every few seconds it stopped while its small sensor suite ran a check on its surroundings, almost as if it was expecting something to happen.

Like, for instance, the duty janitor to explain what was and what was not genuine trash—except that the duty janitor was also trying to explain his existence to a group of unsympathetic civil servants. That meant the Rover-SAC had to make up its own tin brain, and in common with all such dim-witted machines, it reverted to default programming. Part of that default required the collection of loose fibers and particulate matter . . .

. . . And it was unfortunate that one of the Weasels was halfway through a molt.

As the Rover-SAC lunged at the Khalian's left leg and started giving the limb a vacuum-and-rotary-brush grooming the like of which the Weasel had never experienced before in all its life, the Khalian jumped half its own height off the deck and shrilled something that its translator flatly refused to handle. It didn't help matters that the Rover's suction system was strong enough to keep it firmly attached and brushing away even when the Khalian left the ground, and within only a few seconds the leg had no further problems about shedding fur.

At least, not until some grew back.

As the rest of the commission stood dumbfounded and as Neilson and Leary came close to bursting in their attempts not to laugh, three more Rovers appeared in the doorway. The attentions of the first—still attached, still brushing, but working on the fleeing Weasel's tail by now—had left enough particulate matter of one form or another that none of the cleaning machines hesitated even for an instant. With the merest hint of tire squeal, they made straight for the Khalian commissioners, chased both of them three times around the console, followed them through the door in a whirl of rotating brushes, then down the corridor and out of sight.

"Of course," said Neilson unsteadily, "we could do away with the janitor and refit the Rovers with artificial intelligence. You know, the stuff the military use. But Leary's cheaper in the long run. . . ." He broke down in helpless sniggering for a few minutes, then hauled himself back to something like composure. "Either way, you'd better make your minds up soon. There's three hundred Emry due on *Hawking* day after tomorrow, and the Rovers'll want to brush down every one of them. . . ."

IMPERATIVES

by Judith R. Conly

THE TWIN SIREN calls of duty and desire
have launched our legions of need-driven soldiers
to conquer another hatchling-fragile foe.
Their concern-rooted hold on bountiful homeland
as precarious as their biped balance
cannot muster sufficient strength to withstand
our avalanche of dominating drive to victory.

Performing devout service to instinct's compulsion
to protect and provide for potential mates
and nourish the unborn heirs to our future,
we cleanse our new nest of its erstwhile occupants
and assemble the skeleton of our civilization
to shield the female flesh that will fill it.
Then, content with a world secured,
we follow our obsession onward through the dark.

Yet, even as we strive to pour further lengths
of rainbow-blood road across the spectrum of stars,
I cannot always succeed in suppressing
vain idle speculation about the imperatives
of those children of such alien swarms.

COUNTERINTELLIGENCE

WHEN THEY CONQUERED the Syndicate of Families at the end of the Khalian War (see The Fleet volumes one to six) they had absorbed the Family-controlled worlds there into the Alliance. Now, two generations later, most former family members considered themselves patriotic Alliance citizens. Perhaps only the Schlein family had retained their antipathy for the Alliance and the Fleet. As the youngest of the major families, the Schlein had run the intelligence branch of their space navy. When the Alliance prevailed, Fleet Intelligence determined that they no longer needed the services of any part of the Schlein organization. But the Schlein refused to disband.

After so many decades the Schlein family no longer engaged in active sabotage or outright attack on Alliance officials, but even seventy years later they still maintained a shadow organization based upon their old intelligence stations. It is hardly surprising then that several Schlein descendants were ordered to join the civilian ranks on board the largest fighting station the Fleet had ever constructed. There to continue their tradition of passive resistance and dislike for the "Khalian traitors and oppressive Fleet."

Except for a distinctive success in planting a few agents among the Ichtons themselves, the Fleet intelligence branch had little success for the first two years of the defense. Driven by instinct to preserve and expand their race, captured Ichtons proved stubborn even in the face of death or mutilation. It fell to a renegade Schlein agent and embittered Gerson survivors to realize that the best way to counter instinct was with instinct.

YOU CAN'T MAKE AN OMELET

by Esther M. Friesner

"SUNDRY ALARUMS," THE drunken man muttered, "and diversions." Peter Schlein tried to get off his bed and only succeeded in rolling himself onto the floor. Outside, the chaos that was officially, emphatically not anything for anyone on Green Eleven to concern themselves about thundered on.

"Which is why they've got every last set of blunderfoot Fleetledeets in this whole godforsaken metal marble ram—ram—ram*pag*ing, that's what, through the halls so an honest man can't even have him a drink in peace without getting sort of killed. Four—four—*four,* I think, or was it five? Ah, fuck it, *four* cycles they been at it now, and still no one knows what all the whizmadoo's about. A man's got a right to know!"

He staggered to his feet and leaned against the dear, familiar wall of his cabin. "Don't you agree, O my muzzy brother?" he asked, apparently of the bulkhead. Had he been alone, he would have kissed it, glad to be safely home again, and to hell with looking like a candidate for the psychs.

But he was not alone, nor was he actually having a nice chat with the wall.

"It is not my place to say, sir," came the rumbly reply. Big, solemn, brown eyes regarded Peter Schlein with such completely nonjudgmental acceptance for the man as he was—warts and all, constructive criticism be damned—that for an instant Peter wished at least three out of his seven ex-wives had been Gersons.

That was the *djroo* speaking, of course. Only a drink as insinuating and deadly sly as *djroo* could convince Peter Schlein that he should have married a giant teddy bear. *Djroo* had an awfully strong voice. By cycle's end it would be screaming inside his skull. Schlein already owed his life to the towering, fur-covered ursinoid presently staring at him. It was this same Gerson—Iorn by name—who had, on numerous occasions previous to this, figuratively saved Peter Schlein's skin, soul, and sanity from the horde of miniature Mongols who wreaked hangover havoc every time the man crawled back under the *djroo* samovar and turned the tap open all the way.

"Urrrh . . . Iorn, when you've got a spare seccie, would you mind mixing me up a little of that *dee*-lightful little spring tonic of yours?" Schlein sounded pitiful when he wheedled, but he had found it the tone of voice most likely to obtain promptest reactions from the Gerson. Orders, however politely couched, smacked of shouting, and shouting bespoke scenes. When Iorn was—*assigned? bonded? given into Schlein's service?* Schlein couldn't say which—he was briefed that it would be the politic thing to respect the Gersons' cultural preference for not making scenes, even in private. Good advice, this, given the size of the average Gerson.

The once-bright leading light of the Schlein family might have lost much, but political savvy was bred so deeply into his DNA that it would only abandon him five minutes after he was declared clinically dead.

Which, he reflected, had almost happened.

The Gerson turned from his contemplation of *homo inebriensis* and busied himself briefly in the very compact, very efficient, very frivolous, and most certainly *very* discreet kitchen-*cum*-bar at the far end of Schlein's living quarters. A private kitchen—complete with the requisite accompanying pantry-supply channels of dubious legality—was the stuff of legend aboard the *Hawking*. It was an indulgence whose clandestine construction had required sizable "understandings" with the slickest of the Indie traders, but every time Schlein tasted Iorn's latest culinary or potable concoction, a small, *djroo*less voice inside told him it had all been worth it.

Even when the drink was going to taste as close to Khalia tailfur as this one.

The work of moments produced a thick *uberglas* beaker filled with a frothy, somewhat viscous solution the color of old cheese that was presented to Schlein on a silver tray. "Your tonic, sir."

"Uh . . . thank you, Iorn," Schlein said. He downed the concoction in three gulps and shuddered as each swallow walloped the relative circadian daylights out of his stomach. He set the beaker down with much the same sense of relief at Duty Done as Socrates must have showed the hemlock.

Freed now from the threat of alcoholic retribution, Schlein managed to add, "I mean . . . thanks for it all. Everything you did. Not just the tonic." The words sounded inadequate, even to a man who was accustomed to giving short weight in all his personal dealings. "If you hadn't come into the lounge just then, I think that nest-fouling Khalian would've done for me." He addressed the bearlike Gerson in its own tongue—linguistic ability was what had landed Peter Schlein aboard the *Hawking* instead of in a richly deserved prison cell somewhere halfway back across the galaxy—but he dealt out the insult to his absent whilom opponent in its native language. Profanity for the Gerson, Schlein had learned, went paw in paw under the selfsame shunned aegis of making a scene.

Iorn attempted to shrug his sloping, shaggy shoulders. It was not a gesture suited to Gerson anatomy, but the alien's excruciatingly precise code of behavior encouraged him to make any effort necessary to treat with others in ways familiar to them. "It was my *ghruhn,* sir Schlein," he replied. "My . . . pleasure." He retired to the kitchen.

The translation was even more inadequate than Schlein's watery thanks, and the family man knew it. *Ghruhn* was more duty than pleasure, backed by the Gerson convention of doing what you had to do amiably, like it or not; but if you were Gerson you had damn well better *make* yourself like it. *Ghruhn* was how obligations—however unpleasant, distasteful, or downright revolting—were forcibly given both the mask and the substance of something the bounden party had wanted to do all along. As Schlein watched Iorn potter around with some mysterious new cookery project he reflected that next to the *ghruhn*-burdened Gerson, Old Earth samurai came off looking like a pack of whiny, self-indulgent shirkers.

Which was why Schlein's—*servant? batman? bearman? aide-de-drunk?*—Iorn had waded into a battle that was none of his instigation or concern and rescued him. Schlein had an abstruse sense of what was funny to say to a half-seas-over Khalian, the Khalian had a knife—surprising that was all it had—and Iorn had an unasked-for field day wiping up the floor of The Emerald with the weasely creature.

"It doesn't go with the job description, you know," Schlein called at Iorn's back as the Gerson popped a pan into the oven. An exotic, somewhat disturbing smell permeated the air until the recyclers kicked on and sucked it out. "Saving my neck. How's the—uh—arm?"

"It's nothing." Again Iorn attempted a shrug. He returned from the kitchen area and extended his hairy paw, the better to show off the expert job the medics had done. The shaved patch was almost unnoticeable, the stitches hidden by the same thick pelt that had thwarted or deflected much of the Khalian's wild, drunken slashings.

An uneasy silence fell between master and "man."

Then: "Will there be anything else you require of me, sir Schlein?" It was Iorn's way of quitting for the day, as if this day had been no different from any other.

"Hm? What?" Peter Schlein shook his head a little clearer. Iorn's tonic prevented hangovers but didn't do a damned thing toward diluting the immediate effects of strong waters. "You're going?"

"If there is nothing further required of me. Tomorrow is my day parted from you." The Gerson phrased it so that his day off sounded like the saddest cycle of his life. Which was impossible, if you knew what the Ichtons had done to his home world. "May I be forgiven tomorrow's service?"

"But wait. Not so fast. How 'bout a re—re—re*ward,* yes?"

"It was my *ghruhn,*" Iorn repeated, and shambled for the door.

In vino veritas, but Truth sometimes boots Common Sense clean out of the picture. Peter Schlein flung himself after the hulking Gerson and latched on to the creature's left paw. "Hold on a seccie, friend. I mean—family honor, you know. My life—much or little as they care for it back home—it's still—I'm *Schlein,* dammit! I've got to give you *something*!"

"Kitchen privileges," said the Gerson levelly, "such as I presently enjoy are quite sufficient, sir Schlein." Iorn gave his nominal master a hard stare, a gaze with enough ice water in it to shock the family man into near sobriety. Schlein released his grip on the huge teddy bear's paw, both of them behaving as if the recent outburst had been purely accidental, the participants innocent bystanders.

"Yes, but—but you've already *got* those. At least let me have some of my Household escort you home," Schlein muttered. "All that to-do out there"—he nodded toward the door that gave on the Green deck corridor—"I think I remember what a rough time you had getting me back from The Emerald, checkpoints and all, never would've happened if I'd had the foresight to take Household along. Ex-Fleetledeets to a man, they are. To a woman. Thing. That's their whole job, after all, dealing with other military hoseheads. Why there's all this botheration going on in the halls and no hard info . . . hmph! Some silliness about searching for—I don't rightly know what." He shook his head. Gently.

"Ichtons, sir," said the Gerson with as much emotion as a human butler might say *socks*. "They're loose, you know."

"WHAT!" Too late, too late the netherbrained reminder that shrieking your head off in front of a Gerson is sure to be construed as Making a Scene. Peter Schlein's face went chalky enough to blend with the no-color of his platinum-blond hair. Had he owned a chin, it would have been trembling madly. "D'you mean to say the Ich—the Ich—the bloodthirsty fiends have *escaped*?" He cast his infantile blue eyes upward toward either Heaven or the Fleet installations on the *Hawking*'s upper decks.

"Only two of them, sir," Iorn replied. "If rumor is correct. There have been no official statements issued."

Schlein pressed a hand to his brow. It came away clammy. "And they—the Fleetledeets—they're searching this level for them?"

"All levels. Thoroughly. It will take much time." From the oven, a bell went *tling!* "Ah, good, it's done. I almost forgot." The Gerson showed his fangs in an Earth-approximate smile and headed for the kitchen as if Ichtons escaped strictest Fleet custody every day.

"Oh, don't bother, don't, I'll take care of my own dinner tonight," Schlein said hastily. His skinny form was far more agile than the Gerson's fearsome bulk and he nimbly darted past Iorn to reach the oven first. "It's the least I can do for you." He opened the hatch and reached in.

Later he couldn't recall whether his shriek of pain had been louder than Iorn's bulkhead-rattling roar. He remembered thinking that he did not recognize the cooking vessel he pulled from the oven, that ordinary pans were not supposed to retain heat that way, and that a sensible man would certainly let the offending dish drop, even it did mean that it shattered and splattered all over the floor. There were people to clean up the mess after. When you were Schlein there was always someone else to clean up after you.

He really didn't think Iorn was justified in batting him so hard across an already weakened skull that every light in the Peter Schlein private universe flickered out.

He woke up with Iorn's face looming over him, the Gerson's breath smelling like a bizarre combination of old meat and violets. Another memory came tippytoeing into his battered brain, one of an All Decks Alert stench wafting up from the cook pan he had so unceremoniously dropped.

He tried to sit up and found it remarkably easy. His head was clear, all vestiges of the *djroo* purged from his system by Iorn's magical blend. That was to the good: he would have hated to confront his present situation drunk, because it was hardly bearable cold sober.

"Where the—?" He turned his head this way and that, but it was too dark to make out any object farther than arm's length from his eyes. He could feel that the bed he rested on wasn't your standard *Hawking*-issue bideawee. It rustled too much, was loosely covered with a coarsely woven throw, and again, the *smell*—!

"Sir Schlein honors us," said Iorn to the dark.

"Us?" the family man could only repeat, at a loss.

"Honor is done," came the response, and the sound of large bodies with the tip-off Gerson gait of shamble-rock approaching. Two more of the huge ursinoids emerged from the blackness to stand beside Iorn, though one was considerably smaller than the other.

For the first time in a short life ill spent, Peter Schlein felt like the goldy-haired girlie in the nursery tale his *madonnamech* had played for him at bedtime in the fargones. The bears in the story had wound up tearing the juvie trespasser limb from limb, in the righteous vindication of the private property laws, but that was only a cautionary *fabula.*

Wasn't it?

"Welcome to my home, sir," said Iorn in a voice so neutral Peter was hard-pressed to divine whether his once-harmless servant had mayhem in mind. "Our thanks for your presence." He spoke his native tongue here.

"Think nothing of it," Schlein replied in kind, with only the slightest hesitation. In truth he was very good at what he did, linguistically, when he was functional enough to do it. If he sounded a bit dubious, it was more from wondering what Iorn had in store for him now.

We're all the way in down-below Violet, where these eetees have their home-from-homes, he thought. *Which explains this away-in-a-manger excuse for a bed. Violet Nineteen deck, maybe even Twenty, for all I know. Half the world away from home for me, and all the way to hell and gone from those top-crawling Fleetledeets for sure. Never did think I'd want to see one, but* autres temps, autres *temptations. Too easy to ask how he got me here. The sight of Peter Schlein being hauled unconscious around the* Hawking*'s so damn common the kiddies set their chronos by it. Anyway, once we hit Indigo levels, the quartermasters don't look twice at anything they can't check in or ship out, and here in Violet where there's just eetees and cold, cold storage, who's going to interfere with a full-grown Gerson on business bent? Mutation! Whatever the fuck I did to twist Iorn's tailypo, he's got me at his mercy for it now, in spite of all this finicky show of ceremonial hospitality. If things could get any worse than this for me, I'd bleeding like to know how!*

And somewhere the God that family Schlein had written off so long ago as a poor business partner laughed and complied.

"Sir Schlein will forgive us if the lighting of our humble home is less bright than what he is used to," Iorn went on. "It is an unfortunate necessity. Among the Gerson, guest-right is divine, and first-come guests must be accommodated in all things, even at the expense of later-come guests' preferences."

"Then . . . I'm not the only one you've—" *Careful, Peter, careful! A Gerson can rip your arm off single-pawed and absentminded.* "—invited?"

"Didn't I tell you he was wise, Mate?" In the dark, Iorn sounded cheery enough. "Perceptive. I always said how deeply I was indebted to the psychs for having granted me my employment as—what did they call it?"

"Therapy," came a second growly voice, a whit less throaty than Iorn's. "So that you would refrain from future outbursts of slaughter."

Iorn chuckled, Peter cringed. "All wisdom to the psychs," the Gerson said. The words unadorned were a simple, ritual statement of high regard for the brainpokers, but Peter Schlein picked up on the linguistic music of intonation that translated Iorn's remark to mean, *I took those fools to market and back and came home wearing their asses for a hat!*

Peter's eyes made adjustments. The Gerson whom Iorn called "Mate" plopped herself down beside him so that he could see her a little better. Her muzzle was somewhat blunter than Iorn's, though her fangs looked just as sharp. The smallest Gerson pressed itself close to her back. There was more glittering around its head than Schlein could put a reason to. In the warmth of Iorn's quarters he felt cold.

And then Iorn gave him cause to feel colder. "Sir Schlein is kind, as always, Mate. You will learn this as I have, the longer he honors us with his company. Certainly one who speaks our tongue so well—taking into account the Ten Degrees of Courtesy almost as well as a homeborn—will offer us his help in entertaining our first-come guests as they deserve."

Something chittered and whined in the dark. Something large rustled in a corner of the room that Schlein still couldn't see.

"Ah!" Iorn sounded pleased. "They are hungrier. They are almost always hungry." He lumbered off and the shadows swallowed him.

"They're here," Schlein said, half to himself. "Ichtons." There was no denying it, once he got past the mental obstacle of a flatly pronounced *It's impossible!* Peter Schlein had once been dragged along up-level to view some of the *Hawking*'s prized captives, in the empty Fleetledeet hopes that the Family man might be persuaded to enlist his considerable linguistic skills in the cause of in-depth decoding of Ichton communications. No one had to tell Schlein *or* the Fleetledeets that there's more to translate in a language than merely what is said.

He would never forget the skin-crawling sight of the captive Ichtons, and he would never forget their *smell*! Which was why he didn't need his eyes to confirm what his nose had just told him. Impossible or not, they were here. Looking back, Schlein believed it was the horrific thought of spending so much time near that god-awful Ickie stink that made him refuse to cooperate with the Fleet. He had declined the honor by pricing his services in a way to make the family back home proud, and gave the despised popgunners to know that if they coerced him, he'd be only too happy to translate . . . wrong. There were other, lesser linguists aboard the *Hawking,* some even Fleet personnel. None as good as Schlein, but good enough to make do. They let him off.

Who would do the same for him now? The chirring in the darkness grew louder, accompanied by a bone-shattering clashing sound. "How in the name of downtrade he managed to bring two full-grown Ickies—oh, God, they're really fucking *here*!"

"Yes, they really fucking are. And what we are to fucking do about it I do not fucking know," said Mate. Schlein hadn't expected a response at all, not from her, less so in his own tongue, least of all using that sort of language. What he could make out of her expression was proud and self-satisfied. "Iorn has been teaching me," she explained, pleased with herself. "To learn to address all guests in their own speech is my *ghruhn.* Oh! Apologies. It is my *fucking ghruhn.*"

Peter Schlein made a mental note to stand vigil over his own vocabulary around Iorn in future. If "future" was a word he could still use as more than a bad joke.

"Do you—do you suppose your *ghruhn* might include explaining why your hubby has turned your happy home into an illegal Ichton shelter?" he asked. "Or why he decided to invite me to join this little exercise in getting us all deep-spaced when the Fleetledeets finally get their search parties all the way downball to this level?" Sotto voce he added: "If there's any shred of my nerves left after finding out I'm in the same room with the fuzzybuggies."

"You have no ease, honored sir? You fear our first-come?" Her voice was richer and deeper than Iorn's. Courtesy served, she had returned to speaking Gerson. The little one at her back—little only beside herself and Iorn—slipped around to insinuate itself into her lap. It was pretty big for such babyish snuggling, but Schlein reflected that he really didn't know enough about how fast Gersons matured to be a critic.

"Well, my dear hostess, to tell you the truth—"

It was then he saw it. Total dark would have been a blessing, even if it left Schlein blind, but there was light enough to let his eyes suck more and more sight from the blackness—the pattern if not the color of Mate's tunic, the shimmer of moisture at the tip of her snout, the gentle curve of the paws cradling the smaller Gerson to her chest. Now through the pounding waves of sickness in his gut he could not keep himself from staring even while he prayed not to see.

Half the child's head was torn away, replaced by a silvery shell that glittered with a compact array of multicolored lenses and telltales. The bearish snout was gone, and the lower jaw; a simple, flexible tube ran from the convex metal muzzle cup-shaped like a surgeon's mask down into the throat incision. Idle clasps and fasteners dangled from the gap where the small Gerson should in a rational universe still have a right upper limb.

"He will not wear it," Mate said softly. Eyes fully used to the dark, she had seen where Schlein's gaze ultimately came to rest. "The medics have been very kind to us—our debt endures—but he refuses to wear the 'tronic arm that they have made him. It is too hard, he says. It reminds him too much of—"

How can he say anything? Schlein wondered, staring at the nearly faceless creature in Mate's arms. Aloud he said, "They did this to him? The Ichton?"

Mate's heavy head nodded. "Iorn fought with the rest of our city; no good. We were able to escape to the caverns, awaiting help, but it was so deep, so dark in there, so close and crowded—" Her paw tenderly stroked the metal face cup as if it were responsive flesh. "Nn'ror was always impetuous, like his father; a leader. He would not mind his elders. He stirred up the others of his year, brought them out of the caverns by a secret way—spying on the enemy, he said, to learn their weakness so that someday he and his followers could attack them, defeat them, drive them away."

"They caught him?" It really was a stupid question.

"All of them, his year-friends, Nn'ror, all. It was yet in the time before they made our world ash. They reaved the surface, then. As nearly as we could have any news, we heard they meant to use all they could find for the maintenance of their hatchlings." Her gaze fixed itself on the child's mangled face. "Ours was always a good world for raising children."

Hesitantly, as if acting on its own, Schlein's hand stretched out to touch the small Gerson's ravaged face. Mate saw, and nodded ever so slightly, allowing it. The child flinched away when Schlein's fingers came within brushing distance of its shell—sensors in place and functioning, top-of-the-line synthetic nerve replacement, nothing too good for these martyrs to the Ichton scourge. Every sentient on the *Hawking* knew what the Gersons had suffered; everyone was more than willing to make excuses and allowances for anything a Gerson survivor might do.

Which explained, perhaps, why Iorn had managed to spirit off the captive Ichtons unhindered, undetected. Folks tended to look the other way when a Gerson passed, going about his business. *If we give them what they need or want, maybe they'll go away,* Schlein thought. *And if they go away, we won't have to look at them, and remember what they went through, and live with the dead scary thought that such things can happen in this galaxy and maybe—not so big a maybe—maybe next time we'll be the ones it happens to.*

"Almost all the others were fully . . . taken by the hatcheries when Iorn and the others were able to learn where they were and stage a raid. It was easier than they hoped. They did not yet know that word had come to the invaders to move out, that the resistance elsewhere had made our home not worth the effort to subdue, that it would be burnt in retribution and example. There were so many other worlds to be had, so easily. Nn'ror and perhaps two others of his year-friends still lived, left behind with those few eggs that had not hatched. Those two—" Mate shuddered. "Those two Iorn himself had to kill."

Speechless, Schlein tried to force an unwilling mind to form a picture of towering, shaggy, benevolent-looking Iorn killing children of his own kind. What could bring any sane, feeling being to that point? Part of him didn't want to know, part would go mad if he stayed ignorant.

"Why—why did he kill—?"

"For kindness. They could not live long with what parts of them remained uneaten," said Mate, and Peter Schlein vomited noisily into the bedding.

Peter Schlein never dreamed he would turn out to be such an apt short-order cook.

"At least the recipe's simple," he said, taking the dish from the oven. "You're a good teacher, Iorn."

"It is my *ghruhn* to instruct you as you desired, sir Schlein," the Gerson rumbled. This time he sounded as if he had gotten some actual pleasure out of fulfilling *ghruhn.* "I ask your pardon for my unfortunate temper before, when you dropped the dish. It goes against our way to keep a guest hungry."

"To say nothing of wasting good food," Schlein replied. The smell wafting up from the cook pan was still rank enough to make him turn his head away. "Whew! How do you stand the stink of this?"

"With the philosophy, sir Schlein, that at least they do not smell quite so bad cooked as raw."

"So you feed Ickie A to Ickie B, in installments, and contrariwise?" Schlein set the steaming dish on the counter, picked up a spatula, and poked the bubbling contents. He could have sworn that something poked back. "And, uh, how long do you think it'll be before the two of them are all . . . done?"

"Not soon enough." Iorn's expression was stern. "Word comes that Fleet has redoubled search efforts. There may not be time enough left until they are discovered. Their deaths are not my cause."

"Aren't they, then? Because at the rate you're going—I mean, they do have mighty healthy appetites, these fuzzybuggies. Do they know who—what they're eating?"

"From the start. They are untroubled by it." It was no hard guess to make that Iorn wanted the Ichton to be *very* troubled before they died. "I do not understand their samespeech, as you do, but I would give my heart's self to know why this is so, why they can live unsorrowed by what is an abomination among my kind, yours, nearly all sentients I have known."

"Look, Iorn, I don't pretend to speak fluent Ickie, but I'm willing to hazard a could-be for you," Schlein volunteered.

"I would be obliged."

"As you were for kitchen privileges; I know." Schlein kept a lid on his esophagus, trying very hard *not* to think of what it was Iorn had been cooking in the same oven as the family man's food. "You see, though it's not a custom we Terrans are any too proud of, we have been known, in times past, to nibble the odd fellow man. Strictly ceremonial reasons. In the far-gone oldens, when you defeated an especially valiant enemy, you did him the honor of eating his heart, thereby gaining his valor for your own. Or if he'd been cunning, you munched his brain. D'you get the idea?"

"I do." Iorn nodded sagely. "And if he was admired for being the father of many young, then you—"

"Oh, no, no, no, no need to get carried away, is there? Ahahahaha." It almost sounded like laughter. "However, we don't do that anymore."

"No?" The ursinoid's brow furrowed. "We do not abandon our own customs so lightly. Meaning no offense, sir Schlein."

"Don't suppose it was *custom* that made you coldcock me so's you could drag me downball just to meet your—ah—first-come guests?"

"I admit it was the inspiration of the moment. I was rather put out by the loss of my so carefully prepared dish, through your mishap. It did mean I would have to procure more of the raw material, thus lessening the time I would have to entertain my honored Ichton guests according to their merits."

"Just so," said Schlein, turning greener by degrees as Iorn spoke of "raw" material, knowing what he did of Iorn's "entertainment" of the Ichtons. "Spur-of-the-moment forsooth. I mean, it was hardly the sort of invitation one reads about in all the best etiquette books."

Iorn showed teeth. "Would you have come had I invited you any other way?"

"Not this century."

"And it *is* our custom to take mortal offense when our offers of hospitality are declined. So you see . . ."

Indeed he did, especially the way in which Iorn pronounced "mortal" so that it almost rhymed with "fatal."

"Well, all that aside, I'm glad you—*asked* me to drop in." Schlein regarded the still-seething surface of the Ichton casserole grimly. "I only wish you'd done it earlier on. I'd've had a chunk of Ichton *au poivre* myself, just to get the ball rolling."

"You would devour them, sir Schlein?" Iorn looked puzzled. "But I believe you said that Terrans no longer—"

"We don't eat people. These are Ickies. And since you did say your goal wasn't to destroy their bodies so much as their minds—though there's a lot to be said for shredding the fuzzybuggies straightaway, Fleetledeet strategy be damned—maybe the sight of a mere human chowing down on their formerly private property might shake 'em up like they deserve to be shook."

The Gerson parsed all this slowly, then brightened. "An excellent idea!" he roared, and wasted no time in catching Peter Schlein upside the head with another most effective backhanded blow that removed all possibility of objection.

"Look," Peter Schlein said, trying to keep the shrill note of desperation out of his voice. "I was hungry."

Captain Conway stared at the skinny little family man before him and tried to link the pathetic picture he saw to the concept of "monster." No use. Though the evidence garnered by the search party was irrefutable—they'd burst in and caught him in flagrante, trying to floss a piece of carapace out from between his front teeth, for pity's sake!—some concepts still refused to merge in the human mind.

Fleet or not, Captain Conway was human, even if the *Hawking* was his first "real" assignment. He took a deep breath and got a stronger mental toehold on reality before saying, "Schlein, in the Fleet we don't eat our prisoners."

"Well, that's all right, then," Schlein replied, all sweet reason. "I'm not Fleet."

"But you are here on Fleet sufferance."

"So if I fuck up what happens? You send me home?"

Captain Conway passed a hand over his brow. This was just the way the interview had been going ever since the leader of Team Crater had returned to announce that the prisoners were found and in what condition they had been found and then threw up all over Conway's desk.

"Schlein, what do you think would happen if I let it slip out to our allied eetees that you'd been—reducing the chances of us learning more about how Ickie minds work?"

"I'd get a medal? A parade? All due respect, Captain, but Iorn's hunger for privacy to the contrary, I'm wagering word's already out about how your precious fuzzybuggies used their own captives. Children, sir! Fed piecemeal to their young. If we preserve them alive, we might someday learn all the wonderful, apparently rational-to-them reasons why they can take other beings' babies and use 'em as meat for their own. Apart from the great and marvelous contribution to sweet, holy Science, who gives a shit?"

Captain Conway pulled back involuntarily. Passion had transformed the wispy family man into something with backbone, something almost worthy of Fleet respect. What Schlein said about the Ickies was true, if you believed the Gerson survivors' reports. Iorn was not the only one to tell that tale, though he had been hardest hit by it. Records were clear: the futile rage within the huge ursinoid had triggered more than a few violent episodes aboard the *Hawking*—barroom brawls that ended just this side of needing a body count—until the psychs suggested placing Iorn in a position of service where Gerson *ghruhn* might siphon off the creature's wild anguish into productive channels.

Productive! There was a laugh. Unless you called adding a few truly arcane chapters to *Child's Guide to Intergalactic Cookery* productive.

"Don't start looking for a place to hang that medal quite yet, Schlein," Conway said. "Even if every eetee aboard agrees with what you did in practice, they're compelled to object to it on principle. If we show ourselves to be no better than the Ichtons, can their victims ever trust us?"

"Ah, the moral edge." Schlein sounded weary. "Once upon a time, I liked to believe it'd cut warm butter, but I learned better. I did what I did. Hand me over to the eetees and let's be done with it."

"But *why* did you do it, Schlein? And tell me 'I was hungry' one more time and you're going to have an unfortunate 'accident' on your way to confinement."

Conway's fist was truly impressive, particularly when held so close to Schlein's gently bred nose. Schlein swallowed the first upsurge of instinctive panic, then said, "Call it . . . a favor to a friend."

"No good." The fist lowered. "Your friend Iorn's in custody, too; him and his family."

"What?" Schlein sat up straighter. "Mate? Nn'ror? They've done nothing."

"The psychs thought it best to separate them. Unhealthy—family atmosphere cited."

"Separate . . . So Iorn's in solitary—"

"All three of them are. The psychs reported—"

"One psych can kill more poor suffering bastards with his triple-damned *reports* than all you Fleetledeets and your bum-blasters combined. Mate and Nn'ror did nothing, I tell you! Look, not even Iorn's guilty here. It was—it was all *my* idea! I can prove it, too. Iorn was my servant, his *ghruhn* wouldn't allow him to disobey anything I asked of him. He couldn't have done any of it without me, my kitchen, my fucking start-to-finish *complicity,* for the love of Chomsky!"

Schlein rose from his seat, his face contorted. "You march right out of here and tell your buddies to let Iorn's family go, or at least lock 'em up together. That kid of theirs needs his kin. He's teetering on the edge, and he'll take his parents with him if he goes over. Or haven't enough of the Gersons died to suit you? Try breaking *that* news to your supermoral do-the-civvie-thing eetees! See how happy they are with you Fleetledeets then!"

Conway had no trouble getting Schlein to sit down again. One firm shove to the breastbone did the trick, even if the little man took a wild swing at the Fleet captain before subsiding. Gasping for breath, Schlein managed to add a last verbal jab to his tirade: "Especially when they find out that all your precious Fleet intelligence you got from studying those captive Ickies wouldn't fill a thimble next to all I learned about 'em over one friendly little . . . *lunch*!"

It was Conway's turn to sit down. "Say what?"

Schlein grinned. "You'd be amazed to learn all the new Ickie words—nay, cultural-linguistic concepts, may they flourish—that I was able to pick up while chewing the fat with our *honored guests*." He used the Gerson term there and savored Conway's bewilderment until he offered the translation. "It looks like we—*I* guessed right. One Ickie getting the nibblies on another is socially acceptable. They're even got a whole catalog of courtesy terms to describe the gallant donor, beginning with the noble fuzzybug who sacrifices his substance for a battle comrade and rising in honor until you reach the noblest Ichton of 'em all, one willing to lay down his spare parts for the nourishment of the egglayers and the hatchlings. Not that he wants to; it's the least pretty of deaths. Those newborns are terrifying and *mean*."

"You actually learned those terms?"

"And many more." Schlein made a self-effacing bow, no easy task in a chair. "I was called the inverse of every one of them as soon as I told my dinner companions just what it was I was eating with such relish. There is something terribly, terribly irking to an Ickie when he realizes his sacred flesh is being devoured by a lesser being, one who cares Khalia-squat about the all-precious hatchery. Food means a lot to the fuzzybuggies. The only appetite they haven't been able to govern is appetite per se. Ol' metabolism's got 'em, and got 'em bad. Give 'em enough time and they come up with a slew of airtight rationalizations for why it's okay to eat Grandma. My sister was like that about chocolate. I perceive a *waste not, want not* subtext. Perhaps I'll do a monograph on it someday."

"You'll do it now and forward it to us immediately, if you know what's good for you. The more we know about the enemy—"

"Trade you," said Schlein.

"Trade?" Conway's fingers curled around the armrests of his chair.

" 'Course. Until someone tells me different, I'm Schlein. Trading's our life. Family ghosts would show up en masse to beat the ectoplasmic shit out of me if I didn't try to get something out of you in swap for what I know."

"There isn't much trading you can do in deep space without a suit," Conway said meaningfully.

"There isn't much Ickie interpretation you Fleetledeets can get out of my corpse," Schlein countered. "Come on, O captain mine, you know you want me on your side. You did before, if you'll check your own records, and you want me even more now, with what I've got to share."

"Our own methods will uncover everything you've learned."

"So they will, given time. How much of it can we waste? Be a sport, friend. All I'm asking is the release and reunion of Iorn and his family—no sense you holding on to innocent parties, anyhow—and in exchange I'll give you my full cooperation, professional services, and first dibs on the soon-to-be patented Schlein Method of Ickie Interrogation guaranteed to yield results undreamed of, swiftly and accurately."

Captain Conway steepled his fingers in thought. All that Schlein said was true. He was the best linguist the *Hawking* had to offer, and if his results did derive from less-than-conventional methods, at least they were *results*. Fleet could use results.

"Point One: We will release the Gerson family," Conway said at last. Schlein beamed. "In exchange for which consideration, you will serve Fleet interests—"

"Of course. I said I would."

"*—by becoming Fleet.* Point Two: Your enlistment buys their freedom. Got it, Cadet Schlein?"

Peter Schlein's face fell. "This is going to kill Father." Then he perked up. "This is going to *kill* Father!"

"Point Three: You will have to develop an equally successful alternative to your so-called Schlein Method at once. We will *not* eat Ickies. It isn't—it just isn't *Fleet.*"

Schlein smiled. "We won't have to."

The captive Ichton looked up at the scrawny Fleet cadet who came boldly into its cell, whistling. It was accompanied by a Gerson carrying a tray. The Ichton's interest flared unexpectedly when the uniformed Meat addressed him in an almost-fluent version of the Lesser Dialect, saying, "Breakfast!" The Gerson set down the tray and shoved it through the small, temporarily disrupted zone in the Ichton's confining forcewall.

"I know it's not much," said the Meat, brushing aside a lock of its pale blond headfur. "But we Fleeties do insist that all our guests belong to the Clean Plate Club. Oh, doesn't translate, does it? Simple: no more for you until *that's* all gone. Or until you choose to have a little chat with me about, oh, all sorts of things! Nearly anything you've got to tell me about you and yours will be fascinating, I know. And you'll like the food much better. You *are* hungry, aren't you? Born hungry, I hear. Well, don't waste time picking at your food. Before too long, it may be picking at you."

The prisoner stared at his plate; at the holy, the horrific shape of the Ichton egg that was just beginning to hatch.

Iorn tugged at Peter Schlein's arm. "Let us leave them alone, sir Schlein," he suggested. "Family reunions should be private affairs."

"For a while," Cadet Schlein agreed. "Though I'll bet not for long. Exit," he directed, "pursued by a bear."

NET PROFIT

THE DISTANT SOUND of cannon has always been hazardous to morality. As it began to look doubtful whether the Ichtons could be stopped before reaching Emry, or even afterward, many of the less reputable merchants and Indies turned to bottom-line philosophy first attributed to Earth's long discredited Harvard School of Business. If the *Hawking* was soon to be destroyed, then any action needed to ensure their own personal gain was justified. After all, at their current rate of expansion the Ichtons would take another two hundred years to reach the Aniance itself. Best they return a success or spend their remaining years in opulence, even if later generations had to fight a bit harder.

Too often this attitude meant profiteering at the expense of the war effort. As the running battle continued, a new concern came to dominate those of Omera and internal security. How to prevent their own people from thwarting the war effort in their rush for gain? Or more often simply how to keep the level of chaos acceptable on the civilian decks?

Even the news of the destruction of an Ichton mother ship in a six-destroyer ambush personally led by the son of Fleet Admiral of the Red, Auro Lebario, failed to slow the frenzied rush for a quick gain. New sources of profit were sought. Some of these were found among the growing population of allied races occupying the lowest levels of the *Hawking*. Since the *Hawking* carried enough weaponry to dominate any one of their worlds, most of these allies found it understandably difficult to fully trust the selflessness of the Alliance battlestation, even while recognizing the necessity of cooperating with it.

JOINT VENTURES

by Don John Dugas

IT WAS ALREADY hot when I stepped into the lift for Violet Eight. Not too bad. Like a slow oven. But when the door opened onto the corridor, it got really hot: thirty-two centigrade if it was ten. The air was misty, the humidity was so high that the ceilings dripped. Every time I came here it was like this: overpowering, like boiling alcohol, boiler rooms, and reptile cages. The violet walls looked nearly black after the brightness of the green decks where I spent most of my shifts working for Omera. I wondered how they justified the damage the unplanned humidity did to the station's life-support system. Maybe they figured the two hundred ships the aliens living here seconded to Fleet command balanced out the trouble.

I turned down another corridor. The violet walls reflecting off the grilled metal decking in the bad light made everything look dirty. I passed an exhaust blowing steam. It crawled lazily down the passageway. I followed it until I came to her door.

"You see your boyfriend today?" I said after I'd kissed her. As usual her cooling system was doing about half the job and I peeled off my shirt as I entered.

Viv, wearing only a clinging T-shirt, walked farther into the apartment. The invitation wasn't very subtle. But then I wasn't there for subtle. The Institute had gotten her a great place—two rooms all to herself. Not bad for a university sentiologist on a grant. Shame it was down here among the gators.

"You bet."

"Handsome as ever?" I asked.

"Beautiful," she said, clearing aside a scribe unit and some more junk so I could sit down. "He was in the caf for almost three hours today. Just sat there again, tapping his fingers."

Viv was an antiquarian that had turned out to have a talent for dealing with other races. She had silky blond hair, a most generous figure, just where it should be, and the biggest and deepest brown eyes I had ever gazed into. Said I was an antique of sorts, but never explained. With her legs, I never questioned what she saw in a low-paid, civilian security investigator. Every day Viv worked near the caf, talking with the gators, getting to know the way they thought. The Institute was paying her good money for the culture profile and she was earning it. I'd seen the pile of disks cluttering up her apartment. The gators were the most important of all the races that were supporting the Fleet against the Ichtons. Physically very different, but surprisingly like humans in their attitudes.

Last week Viv told me she had spotted him. She'd described her mystery man as between twenty and thirty, with the body of an unarmed-combat instructor and white-blond hair. His only flaw seemed to be that he wore glasses, but Viv said it made him look sensitive and intellectual. And he just sat there for hours, motionless, staring at some spot on the bulkhead. She'd guessed that he was another scientist working with any of the dozen alien races that had settled into the lower levels of the *Hawking* and asked me to look out for him, let me know more about what he did and where he went. I went to the caf, a dingy place at the upper end of the color that dealt with several races, but he had gone. Then we had that mess involving the Ichton attempt to bribe their way aboard the *Hawking* on an Indie so they could breed larvae and I'd had no time.

The next day, in bed, she'd informed me that at precisely the same time, he was there again. And the next.

"The guy's in a rut," I said. I had been on Violet Eight for less than a minute and was already sweating freely. She opened up the small galley freezer, pulled out an icy one, slid it through her auburn bob and down her neck for the cool, and threw it to me.

"I'm telling you, he isn't normal," she said. "There's something funny about the way he's been acting."

"I'm sure it's nothing," I said, opening it. "Probably got the hots for one of the caf workers. Or maybe he likes the smell of gators."

"Squams!" she said angrily.

"Sorry." The Squams were an allied race. They looked like a large, multicolored walrus that had been shoved into an alligator coat and weren't very comfortable with the result. They walked on all fours, thick hands at the bottom of each foot. For fine work they used a beard comprised of a dozen long, silky fingers just under a wide, smooth-toothed mouth. On the upper decks most people had never seen a real Earth gator, so the nickname had stuck.

Viv looked at me like I'd just given my kid sister a haircut with a steak knife, then flopped down on the bed beside me. "Today I watched him while I pretended to type. He sat there for nearly four hours without moving anything but his fingertips."

"Like this?"

She knocked my hand away. "I'm serious!"

"All right," I said. "Forget the caf workers. I think he's got the hots for you."

"Yeah. Right," she said.

"Why not? You said you always went for lean men."

She traced the old scar that ran across my left pectoral with her fingertips. "Almost always."

We fooled around for a while after that. Afterward, she said, "That woman was there again today, too. I've seen her at the Handi-Mart."

"Pretty?" I arched an eyebrow.

"Very. Distinguished-looking."

"Hmm. Sounds like my type." I watched her reaction and took another pull of beer from the bottle, now warm.

She shot me an amused look.

"Well, that's it," I said. "Mr. Handsome sits across from Ms. Beautiful."

"Or vice versa," she said.

"Who cares? Someone's leering at somebody."

"That's all you ever think about." But she smiled.

"I'm a cop in a small town with some big-town tastes," I said, trying to forget the big-city trouble that had forced me to volunteer for the *Hawking*. "Besides, since I haven't seen your mystery man yet, I don't have anything but your say-so to go on."

"Can I help it if he shows up while you're working?

"Go on, laugh if you want," she said. "Just the same, there's something about him. He scares me now." She looked at me and I believed her. "He doesn't even move his eyes behind those glasses."

"You sit close enough to see whether his eyes move?"

Viv knew I'd caught her out. "All right. I went over to have a closer look. I wanted to see if you were right about . . . perspectives. I thought the woman was alone at first, but one of the Squams I talked with told me she was there to watch two hatchlings!"

It was kind of unusual for a human to nanny aliens, but the *Hawking* was a human station. The richer aliens had figured out that a human could do a better job of keeping their offspring out of trouble on it. Most also figured an armed battlestation was a lot safer place to raise them than their own worlds with the Ichtons busily invading one about every two months.

"She stays all afternoon?"

"No," Viv said. "She arrives around 1200, an hour or so before he shows up. They leave almost at the same time, though—around 1730. She spends all her time talking to the Squamlings—teaches them English, I suppose—while she knits."

"Knits?"

"Scarves, I think."

I let that pass. "The parents of those kids must be pretty rich if they can afford a nanny," I said. "Have any of your gat . . . Squam friends told you who they are?"

"I haven't asked."

She was quiet for a minute. "I wonder if he's there to spy on someone."

"Why do you say that?"

"He's never in the caf at any other time. I asked one of the waitresses to keep an eye out for him. He always paces back and forth just outside the door before he goes in, like he's waiting for a signal."

"That's new."

"No. Jannie—that's the waitress—says he's done that since he first started coming in."

"What's the beautiful nanny doing while he's walking around?"

"I don't know. She lives near the caf on Violet Seven. When I've seen her at the Handi-Mart she's always buying a lot of stuff and usually she has the Squam kids with her."

I looked at her. "Maybe I should bring down an application form."

"For what?"

"Security. You could replace Kenvich—or Omera."

"Ha-ha. You'll see."

Around 2000 I made dinner. Afterward, we decided to leave the dishes and walk over to the caf for a drink. Viv rooted around in the junk for her sweatpants. She'd gotten about as much as she was going to get out from these gators and had already found a new place on another deck. Half her things were already packed. The other half were strewn all over the floor.

As for me, I had no choice but to put my shirt back on despite the heat. Walking around with your blaster showing is considered unprofessional in undercover cop circles.

The walk to the caf was quiet. Most of the residents in Violet kept to their own special environments. After eight hours walking through the rec areas, keeping the Indies from getting too rough, it was nice to be able to relax with your girlfriend. Even if you had to do it in a sauna.

We walked toward the lifts, then turned right. We came into a large open area, a kind of city square the amphibious aliens had put together themselves. Some of the condos connected up to Violet Seven, giving the place a split-level effect.

The most expensive places faced onto the long, shallow tanks in the center of the square. Squams, old and young, lay on their backs in the pools. They were happiest when they had plenty of humidity to keep everything going smoothly. The steam vents they had rigged up from the heat-dissipation system were okay, but there was nothing a Squam liked better than a nice soak in that green, reclaimed water.

Viv made some noises at a few of the Squams sitting on the curbing around the pools. I just smiled. We were always getting lectures by the Fleet sentiologists on how to deal effectively with all the Alliance races represented on the *Hawking*. The warm-fuzzies (as we usually referred to all the vaguely mammalian races) you could pretty much treat like everyone else. It was the hard-skinned, cold-blooded ones that I couldn't get used to. They were just so completely *different*.

As we made for the caf, a Squam male (Viv had taught me how to tell them apart) stopped her. They hissed at each other while I looked around. He was impressive. They all were. He measured a good two and a half meters from claws to crest. His horny skin was a dull gray-brown and there wasn't an ounce of fat on him. He looked like a giant swimming machine—all muscle and shoulder—wrapped in a boxy alligator bag.

But the thing that stayed with you was the eyes. Nothing lived in those faces except for them. Black. Deep-set. Shining. Unknowable. Never moving, never dilating. Once in a while, the greeny-white membranes would sort of roll up in something like a blink, but that was all you ever saw.

I took a last drag and threw the soggy cigarette into a can and looked into the crowded caf.

"Hey," I said.

Viv hissed something else to the Squam and turned around. "What?"

"Is that him?"

Her gaze followed mine through the big plastic-walled front with the frosted edges and the glitzy chromium fittings. Beyond the chairs and a couple dozen heads, I had seen a white-blond human.

"That's him!" she said.

It felt like I was meeting an in-law for the first time.

"What's he doing here so late?" I asked.

"I don't know!" She said it like it was indecent for him to be there. "Let's go."

She took my arm and we went into the caf.

It was dark inside and there was a steady flow of clientele. There were a couple of admin types getting stupid on the funny Squam beer. Some girls from the rec decks were helping them. The staff were mostly human, with one or two Khalians thrown in. Except for Romeo, the rest were pure gator.

There was an empty table next to his and we took it. While I sat with my back to him, Viv scoped him out from over my shoulder.

"Hey, Viv," a woman in a tight synthetic T-shirt asked. "The usual?"

"Hi, Jannie," Viv said. "Yeah."

"Soda water it is." The waitress looked at me.

"Whiskey," I said. It wasn't the real stuff, but it worked.

"Single malt or blended?"

"In a glass'll be fine."

She didn't smile.

"He been here long?" Viv whispered, nodding at the man.

"Since you left," Jannie said before walking away.

"Well?" I said quietly. "You going to ask him to the prom?"

"I don't know," she said. "He looks like he's asleep."

His eyes looked white in the reflection of the halogen light strips in his glasses.

"You said he doesn't move much."

She looked at him. "His fingers aren't even moving."

Jan reappeared with the drinks a few minutes later and Viv paid. We talked for a while about the profile she was working up and what she was planning to do after she got back from the Core.

"You want to teach?" I asked her. That's what most sentiologists I'd met wanted to do.

"I doubt it. I've got other interests."

"Yeah?"

She leaned forward. "You don't think I took this job just for the fun of talking with other races, do you?"

"I was under the impression that this was the kind of fieldwork some sentiologists wait a lifetime for," I said.

"I'm more interested in, shall we say, planetary resources."

I smiled. "You want to be an Indie instead of a sentiologist."

She laughed. "Indie? They're poor. I want it big time—merchant or nothing! How many people do you think have the cultural and linguistic background to trade with the Squams? Ten? Twenty? Three of us."

"Anybody can talk to them with a translator," I said. I had never seen her so animated.

"Anybody with a tie-in to a Fleet battlestation mainframe, you mean. Otherwise not enough to really do a deal."

I saw her point. "So you're going to get a job with the merchants cutting deals with the Squams." The Squams were one of the few expansive races we had found in the galactic center, they occupied almost seven worlds and were looking for more when the Ichtons arrived.

"That's it."

"What about the Institute?"

"They'll get their culture profile."

"And so will some merchant."

"Why not?" she asked. "They've already paid for it."

Double pay. No wonder she could afford a bigger place.

"He still there?" I asked a few minutes later.

She looked over my shoulder. "You . . ." Her face went pale and she stood up. Her eyes were fixed on the man behind me.

"What is it?" I said, turning as I followed her eyes. Under his chair a small pool of blackening blood congealed with some kind of transparent fluid. He was very dead. Viv screamed.

Almost an hour later the forensics team had finished with the scene. After that, it took only a minute for the med team to bag him up and haul the body out of the caf. I was just finishing with Jannie when Kenvich walked in. His Fleet uniform was perfect, right down to the freshly polished Military Intelligence pips on the collar.

"What's the situation here, Detective?" he said.

"What the hell are you doing here?" I asked.

He folded his arms together. "You know the drill, Bailan. Security is supposed to be informed on all felony calls. Informed immediately."

It had been like that ever since they'd declared martial law on all levels after Gerson and it stank like moisture-reclamation tanks under a whorehouse.

"Handsome over there got in the way of a needler," I said, pointing to the black body bag the medicos were carrying away.

"Boys said you were first on the scene. Notice anything?"

"I was less than a meter from him when the lady there"—I hooked my thumb at Viv—"spotted the blood. Prelim assessment puts the time of death around 1700, but we'll know for sure soon."

Kenvich looked hard at Viv, then back to me.

"How long were you here?"

"About a half an hour before she spotted the blood."

"You sat next to a stiff for half an hour and you didn't notice a damn thing?"

Kenvich was a weenie. I'd known officers like him in the Marines and I hadn't been impressed.

"Right, Kenvich."

"*Captain* Kenvich."

"Asshole," I said.

"What was that?!"

"I said 'Yes, sir,' *mon capitan.*"

He glared at me and looked at the plastic caf front. The frosted edging as well as the clear windows were unmarked. "Shot from outside while the door was open?"

"That'd be my guess," I said, "which means whoever offed him is one hell of a shot or had really good sights and a stable platform. Could've been someone passing by or from the condos across the square."

Kenvich grunted. "About the victim," he said. "Confine your investigation to the external elements of the case as much as possible."

"What?"

"You heard me."

"Trying to steal a little thunder, Kenvich?"

He moved in close. "Listen, mister. You do what I say, when I say it. In case you'd forgotten, you're under martial law. It's only out of courtesy to Chief Omera that we're letting you civilians handle this at all. And as for your wiseass remarks, this comes straight from Internal Security HQ: leave the victim out of it as much as you can."

"Great. How about the murderer?"

He gave me one last look and went over to talk with a couple of the uniforms who were questioning people.

I walked over to Viv. "When you're ready, I'll take your deposition."

"Me?"

"Absolutely. You're the only person who can give us something useful to go on."

"What about his ID? His room?"

I moved her into the corner. "He didn't have any ID on him. Nothing in his pockets except for a card key to a storage container, location unknown, and a *lot* of credits. No distinguishing features. So far we have nothing on the guy."

Viv looked at me.

"Don't say it," I said. "Either Fleet Intelligence is already in on this or they will be in about two hours. And I mean *in.* Security's already dicking around. It's only a matter of time before the big boys want to play, too. Let's hope we can get this thing rolling before they put a lid on it. You ready?"

"Sure."

I got a recorder from one of the uniforms and came back. "All right. Did you notice this man today?"

She smiled. "Yes. When I arrived here this afternoon he was in his usual place."

"And the blond nanny?"

"Yes. She was over there, as usual."

"And in the last eleven days you never once saw them speaking. Is that correct?"

"Yes. From where they sat, they couldn't have without shouting. They were about eight meters apart."

"And they'd sit there, motionless, all afternoon?"

"Except for her knitting and talking to the young Squams."

"Always knitting? For nearly two weeks?"

"Yes."

"You didn't notice what type of knitting it was, did you?"

"No."

"When did this woman leave this afternoon?"

"Around 1700."

"1700. Just about the time the forensics boys think he bought it. Did the woman leave before or after 1700?"

"I don't know. I left around 1615 and she was still there. Why? Do you think she . . ."

"I don't know. We won't know anything beyond what you've told me until the lab finishes. You don't know where she lives, do you?"

"Yes. Liz at the Handi-Mart said she lives on Violet Seven, just above the caf."

"And how about the Squams she works for?"

"Across the square in that condo."

"That's all you've learned?" I said.

"Is it enough?"

I laughed. "If you hadn't taken an interest in your boyfriend, I'd be in a real jam now. You've given me something to go on."

"The blonde?"

"The blonde. That reminds me . . ."

I walked over to a com and called HQ. "This is Bailan. Cal, pull the file on Violet 7.135.280."

"You got it, Detective," the kid said on the other end. As com operators went he was a good one, no silly questions and backed up about ten of us and occasionally came to our rescue with a squad of uniforms if things got rough. I heard the sound of a keyboard.

"Rugh Hass, Squam Indie. Nonresident landlord."

That meant he paid the bills but didn't live there. "Any other listings for Hass?"

More keys being punched. "Yeah. Violet 8.135.310. Big place on Violet Eight."

I figured that put him in the condoplex across the square. "Put a plainclothes on the first address. If a blonde comes out, stay on her and call me right away."

"You got it."

I hung up. "I've got to get going," I said to Viv. "Why don't you turn in?"

"No way. This is too interesting. Where are you going?"

"I've got to go up to Med Green. The body boys should be finished pretty soon and I want to get the report in person."

"Why?"

"Transmissions and files can be intercepted. I know we're under martial law, but I'll be damned if I'm going to let Internal Security or Military Intelligence screw this up."

"Okay. Will you be back down later?"

"I don't know. I'll try."

"If you are, I could use some consolation."

Twenty minutes later I was warming my heels outside Dr. Obor's lab on Green Five. She saw me through the window and came out in her operation greens. Behind her I could see him on the slab. His white hair made the victim look like a statue waiting to be posed and placed. Not human anymore, no one that loved or hurt.

"Hey, Bailan."

"Doc."

"Do I get to wash up first or are you going to grill me right here?"

"We'll compromise," I said. "How about you tell me in the scrub room?"

We walked in. She took off her gloves and started to clean up. "Death was almost instantaneous. The victim was shot from between twenty meters and eighty meters away. The projectile was a six-centimeter ceramic dart with a triangular cross-section. Standard round."

"Where was he hit?"

"In the skull," she said. "One point seven centimeters above and behind the right ear—that's why there was so little external bleeding."

"Any idea how fast the dart was moving?" I asked.

"I'd say that based on the penetration about 270m/second."

"Pretty low velocity," I said. Whoever did it could have used a silencer. "Okay. What about the victim?"

"Human. Mainstream. White male. Caucasian. Twenty-eight years old. Evidence of extensive physical training, probably tank swimming and unarmed combat. And get this. Implants."

"Where?"

"In the fingertips. Very simple mobile keyboard linkup with squirt-transmission capability."

"I better check how many of those we have aboard."

"Eighteen," she said, smiling as she pulled off her booties. She was a pro. "None of them match up. This guy isn't on any *Hawking* files."

Or maybe he wasn't on the kind of files normal people had access to. "Anything else?"

"Excellent health. Remarkable physique . . ."

"Yeah, I heard that from Viv."

She raised an eyebrow but didn't say anything. "Scar on left shoulder indicates reconstructive surgery," she continued, "probably from a blaster deflection or laser wound, about three years ago."

"How about the clothes?"

"No labels. Very used and shabby, except for the underwear and socks."

"How so?"

"They're practically new. The pants are pure silk."

I didn't know what to make of that so I kept my mouth shut.

"The shirt and pants were permeated with very fine hybrid flour—not pure, but mixed with traces of rice. His glasses are hard-tempered acrylic with a slight amber tint."

"Shooting glasses?" I asked.

"Shooting glasses," she confirmed.

"Fingerprint matching came up with a big zero," she said. "Like I said, no one on the data base has heard of this guy."

She looked at me. I didn't say anything.

"That's it," she said finally.

"All right, Doc," I said, going for the doors. "You've been a lot of help. Really."

She smiled. "Tell me about it sometime."

Back on the lift, I tried to imagine him. Not as the corpse on the table, but as a living man, twenty-eight years old. Handsome, fit, putting on the cheap old clothes over the expensive underwear before heading off to a little caf on Violet Eight.

Where did he go? What did he do until 1300? Did he always dress like a bum or did he change somewhere? How was it possible for him to sit there for hours every afternoon, staring at a point in space, while quietly typing? And where was the computer he had been typing into?

How long had it been going on?

Where did he go at night? Did he have a private life? Who did he see? Why the flour and traces of rice in his clothes?

All these questions kicked around inside my head as the lift dropped me back to Violet Eight. I retraced my steps back to the square and walked into the condo. A human guard—more of a doorman really—stood inside the lobby.

He wasn't terribly impressed by my badge. He kept his knees from knocking together long enough to say, "What the hell do you want?"

"Which of your tenants employs a nanny?" I asked him. "Beautiful. Blond."

"Agnes Wunderlei?"

"Could be. Every afternoon she takes two Squam kids across the square to the caf."

"That's Agnes," he said. "She works for Mr. and Mrs. Hass, resident aliens. Squams."

"Which is theirs?"

He pointed down the hall. "Second door on the left, pal."

"What do they do?"

"Mr. Hass is listed as being in speculation and arbitrage. The missus is a tech aboard one of those fancy destroyers the Squams brought into the Fleet."

"Either of them here now?"

"Mr. Hass just went out, but she's still here I think."

"And Agnes?"

"She doesn't live here."

"Thanks," I said, making for the hall. I clipped on my translator and rang the bell. I could hear it ringing inside, but nobody answered. I rang again. At last the door opened.

She was well over two meters tall and she knew it. Her scales were smooth, tapering to frosty edges of near-transparent tissue. The skin on her neck lightened evenly into a pale powder-green and her eyes were true jet, not the charcoal color that a lot of the females had. From what Viv had told me about their aesthetic, she would be considered a real knockout. She was wearing a silk floral-print dressing gown.

"Yes?" she said. The translator turned her hiss to a flat monotone.

"My name is Bailan," I said. "I'd like to speak with Mr. or Mrs. Hass. I'm from the police."

"May I see your badge?"

I showed it to her.

"Very well."

She opened the door reluctantly, holding the gown closed tight in front of her. I walked in.

It was a magnificent apartment. The walls were tiled all the way up to the intricate moldings of the high ceiling. The furnishings were tasteful, the ornaments expensive.

"I'm sorry if I seem rude," she said, "but I'm alone with the children. How did you get here so quickly? It can't be fifteen minutes since my husband left."

"You were expecting me?" I said, hoping the translator would disguise the surprise in my voice.

"You or somebody. I didn't know the police were so quick. I suppose my husband is on his way back?"

"I don't know."

"You didn't see him?"

"No."

"But then how . . . ?"

I wasn't going to help her.

"Do you mind waiting for just a minute?" she stammered. "The children are in the kitchen and I'm always concerned little Rugh will try to put his sister in the oven and dry her out."

She walked away, her claws remarkably quiet on the tiled floors.

I heard her saying something in the next room. When she came back there was a faint smile on her snout. She showed me her teeth.

"Please excuse my manners," she said, "I never asked you to sit down. I do wish my husband were here. He's the only one who really knows the value of the jewels. After all, he bought them."

Jewels? And why was she so impatient for hubby to get home? She seemed almost afraid to speak.

I kept my face as neutral as I could.

"We've heard of so few robberies here," she said, still stalling. "I guess it must come from living in such an enclosed community."

"When did you get home tonight?" I asked.

She gave a start. "How did you know I went out?"

"I know you work and where."

"You work fast."

"I was already in the neighborhood."

She was wondering what I had meant by that. I let her wonder.

"Have you checked her room? I'm the only other one who ever goes up there. Besides, it's a real mess . . ." She hardly suppressed a sigh of relief as footsteps pounded outside the door and paused. A card key slid through the lock. "My husband. Dear? In here!"

This one was getting his vitamins. He was closer to three meters than two, filling the room like a fist fills a boxing glove. His head barely cleared the ceiling and the disk case he carried looked like a cigarette lighter in his horny fist. He looked at me.

"Darling," she said. "The detective got here ahead of you," she said. "I was telling him you'd be right back."

He looked down at me with polite interest, but I could sense an air of defiance in him. "I beg your pardon," he said in English. Perfect accent—even too perfect—with just the slightest trace of hiss. "I'm afraid I do not understand, Mr. . . ."

"Bailan," I said. "Detective Bailan."

"Detective Bailan," he corrected himself. "But how odd. And you wanted to speak with me?"

"In your capacity as employer of the nanny, Agnes Wunderlei."

"Oh. But you cannot mean that you have already recovered the jewels? I know this all must seem peculiar, but the coincidence is so curious that I am still trying to understand it myself. You must realize that I have only returned from Security headquarters where I lodged a complaint against her. I come home and I find you here, and you tell me . . ."

It was hard to tell with something that couldn't sweat, but he seemed nervous. It was clear the wife had no intention of leaving the two of us alone.

"What was the nature of the complaint?" I asked him. His wife went stiff.

"The jewel robbery, of course," he said. "Agnes did not come for the children this morning, nor did she call. When I went to her room, she was gone. While she was at work, my wife realized it might be good to check our valuables. She called me. When I looked, it was clear why Agnes had gone."

"You went to her room?" I said. "The doorman said she didn't live here."

"She lives on a higher deck, directly above," he said. "Our building connects through a service passage."

"I see," I told him. "You went up and the box was empty."

"Exactly."

"What time did you check the box?"

"Around 1800."

"So you stayed with your children?"

"Yes," he said.

I turned to her. "And you returned . . ."

"About 1830," she said evenly.

"Why did you wait until nearly 2200 to lodge the complaint?" I asked him.

"I had left dinner cooking all day," she said, a little too fast. "We didn't think . . ."

"I should like to know what you were doing down here," Hass asked me. "Is it usual for Security to assign people in our residential area?"

It was apt to get racial pretty fast unless I could get out of it. "I'm not from Security. Like I said, I'm just the police. And I was off duty."

"But you were questioning my wife in your official capacity, were you not?"

"Yes."

"Regarding what?" he demanded. "I'm sure Alliance Relations would be very interested to hear that the police are invading people's homes. . . ."

"And listening to what people tell them?" I said. His righteous act was starting to bug me. "You can't say it's my fault. Since I got here, you've done nothing but talk about some jewel robbery that doesn't interest me in the least. If you want to get tough, we can do that, too. Right now I'm here investigating a much more serious crime."

"More serious?" she said. There was a lump in her throat.

I kept my eyes on the husband. "You didn't hear about the crime that was committed this evening in the caf across the square?"

"No," she said with some relief.

"I fail to see," he said, "what concern . . ."

"This could be of yours?" I said. "As far as I can tell, none. I'm just interviewing people who might have seen something."

"Murder?" the wife gasped.

"I don't recall I mentioned the nature of the crime," I said, "but as it happens, you're right."

The husband shot her a cold look through eyes that were half-lidded in warning.

"We have reason to believe your nanny was acquainted with the deceased. What time did she disappear?"

"Sometime between 1830 last night and 0800 this morning," Hass said without any hesitation.

"That would be logical," she chimed in.

"Okay. Can you show me her room?"

They looked at each other. "Very well," he said. "Let me get my key. I'll show you up."

He took me upstairs and through a converted utility shaft. He had a tight squeeze getting through. When we got to the other side, we were on Violet Seven. Through the grilled deck I could see the square below us.

We came to a door. The key was already in the lock. Hass pulled it through. The door opened.

I looked at him. "Your wife just said she was the only one who came up here."

"Of course. But sometimes I . . ."

The lights came on automatically. The room was bare and cluttered at the same time. Only one corner seemed clean. I walked over to the small dresser and opened it.

"She left without her clothes?" I wondered aloud.

"She's not very bright," he said. "After all, how far can you run on a battlestation? Of course, if she's sold the jewels she could easily buy a new face, new ID. As I told the man at headquarters, they're worth in excess of two hundred thousand credits."

"Free enterprise," I said. I walked over to the bare patch on the deck and went down on my knees. Two levels of the deck had been cut out with an oxyacetylene torch. About sixty-five meters down and across, I had a clear line of sight through the plastic front of the caf.

"How long has she been with you?" I said.

"We hired her when we arrived on the *Hawking*—about a hundred days ago."

"You found her through an ad?"

"Her references were impeccable," he said. "And she spoke perfect Squam within weeks."

I stood up and filed that one away.

"Mr. Hass," I said. This was going to be a tough one. "By any chance—and this is just a routine question, you understand—by any chance was your relationship with Agnes anything more than employer and staff?"

It was just a shot in the dark, but oddly enough, he paused. He looked more concerned than he had been. "Will my answer be a matter of record?"

"It'll never come up."

If he knew what the hole in the floor meant, he'd know I was lying. "Yes."

"Here or in your apartment?"

"Here, of course. She was of great help in my trading business, unofficially. She often entertained potential clients, or . . ." he hesitated. "Sometimes I would find it expedient to entertain certain clients of my own and she would absent herself. With so many of our men serving on ships many of my race are here alone, without the benefit of husband or family. It is almost my duty . . ."

"I can take it from there." Or could I? Jesus. "I asked because I noticed that a button of your tunic has fallen off. I just found one like it under the bed."

I held out the button. He took it with surprising speed.

"When was the last time?" I said.

"Two days ago."

"Did you see Agnes last?"

"When I was entertaining my last guest here. She waited until I arrived and then left. She often waits in a nearby caf for . . . me to leave."

"She didn't act unusual?"

"Not at all."

"Did you know if she had any visitors?"

"Visitors?"

"Any . . . males?"

His snout seemed to disappear into his long neck. The teeth came out. It wasn't comforting. "The question never came up," he said flatly. "However, had Agnes had a lover, I would in no way have known. That would have been her own business."

He almost seemed jealous. Hell, he weighed a ton and was a different species. Still, I had to ask. Maybe white hair was her lover and this hulk decided to play the jealous type.

"Can you tell me where you were today between 1700 and 1900 hours?"

"Of course"—I think the Squam actually smiled—"I was with my children, we spent the entire time by the pool. There were dozens of neighbors there that I spoke to. Such with their father outings are vital to the younger ones' development. I am totally dedicated to my mate and our hatchlings."

"I see. Well, thank you for your cooperation. It's late and I think that pretty much covers it."

"Fine. Shall we go back down?"

I wondered if a minute had gone by when he wasn't lying.

After Hass had taken me down and shown me out, I stopped back at the concierge's desk. He was reading one of those sleaze mags, the kind that came with the disposable vibrator gloves for three credits ninety-five.

"You get everything?" he asked.

"Were you here around 1800 last night?"

"Sure."

"Did you see Agnes bring in the Squam kids?"

"Like I see you here now, pal."

"Did she usually come out here or did she go up to her room after she finished?"

"She always came through here."

"Did she yesterday?"

"Yeah. Mrs. Hass got home late. It was nearly 1900 when Agnes left. She ran outta here in a big hurry."

"Thanks."

I lit a cigarette and walked over to the caf. It was almost 0100 now and the place was empty. I called in to HQ and got Cal at the desk to punch up a list of the employees at the Violet Eight Handi-Mart. Only one was named Elizabeth. With any luck she hadn't gone out.

The com rang five or six times before someone picked up on audio.

"Yes?" a bleary voice said.

"Ms. Taeder? I'm sorry to bother you so late, but it's police business."

That seemed to get some respect. She turned the visual on. A small woman with big collarbones stared back at me. Her kinky brown hair was dragged back all the way. It made her look like a greyhound. Behind her was a hole of a room, just a foldaway bed, a small video, a commode, a dry-shower, and a dresser. She looked like any checkout girl, only a little more so.

"What is it?"

"My name is Bailan. I'm investigating the disappearance of a woman named Agnes Wunderlei. I understand she did all her shopping at your Handi-Mart."

She looked surprised and worried. "I hope she's all right."

"She's just gone missing," I said. "We'll find her." That was me. Bailan of the Space Scouts. We find anything. "Can you tell me anything about her?"

"Umm . . ."

"Anything at all."

She worried her lower lip for a couple of seconds. Then something clicked. "She wasn't a domestic."

"What do you mean?"

She blushed. "Off the record?"

"It depends. Try me."

"Well, you know, we give sort of a rebate to servants so they'll do their shopping with us. One credit back for every ten of their employers' money they spend with us. It's good for business."

She looked at me like she expected me to call the fraud squad right there.

"Yeah?" I said.

"Well, the first time we gave her the money, she just stood there stupid."

"And after that?"

"Oh, she took it, but more to fit in than for the money."

"I see. So what do you make of that?"

"She acted like she was rich. Rich and well educated."

"How so?"

"We get all kinds down here. Herfets and Emry off Five. But especially Squams. Lots of different languages. Hell, I wear my translator all day."

"Sure."

"Well," she said, narrowing her eyes, "every time Agnes would come in, it seemed as if she was listening to them. Like she understood."

"How can you be sure?"

"She never wore a translator, but every time somebody would make a joke, she'd smile like she understood."

"Anything else?"

She shrugged. Her shoulders were bony and overworked. "Noth . . . Well . . . No. Forget it."

"What?"

"You'll think it's stupid."

"Tell me."

"She knitted."

"What about it?"

"Well, I saw what she was working on a couple of times when she was waiting at the register. It was junk."

"People have different tastes," I said.

"That's not what I mean. My mom used to knit. What Agnes was working on wasn't anything, just knots. Just one long web of knots."

It was nearly 0200 when I got back to my room. I grabbed a cup of rehydrated coffee from one of the machines down the hall and gulped it back. I stripped down and went for a shower. As the caffeine and the cold water started to splash together, I considered the options.

If Hass had caused Agnes's disappearance, the theft of the jewels was a good way of diverting suspicion. It was attractive, but it proved nothing. It was also, I had a hunch, not true. Then again, this Agnes might very well have boosted the jewels.

There was another possibility, and I would have to start giving it some thought.

I toweled off and walked back to my room. I grabbed the com and dialed headquarters.

"Police Headquarters, Carroll here . . . Jesus! Bailan, where you been?"

"I've been on Violet Eight since I called you. What's up?"

"All hell's broken loose up here. You got a priority/Umbra message—I think it's from Security—burning up the hard disk. Omera's got a copy, too," he added. We went way back.

"Great." It was just like Kenvich to go tattling. "I'm at my place now. Can you mail it, Cal?"

I saw him reach for the terminal off-screen. "Sure."

"Anything else?"

My terminal powered up automatically as the message came through. "You bet your ass," Cal said. "Some Squam Indie named Hass called Alliance Relations about you. Said you'd been rousting his family."

"They always do."

"Yeah, but they usually don't turn up dead a couple of hours later."

"What?!"

"The call came in a few minutes ago. Some maintenance guy found Kostas clogging up the drain in one of the pools they got set up down there. Security stepped in right away—we're out of it."

"How did he get it?"

"Somebody emptied a needler into him close-up. Very messy."

I pulled on my pants and checked to see my blaster was charged. "Hey, did the blonde ever come back to Violet 7.135.280?"

"No."

"Thanks, Cal. I'll take it from here."

He shook his head. "Don't be stupid, Bailan. Kenvich is already gunning for your ass. Says you've been exceeding your authority—been screaming about security risks. Don't make it any worse. Hit the sack and let the chief sort it out tomorrow."

I looked over at my rack. It was calling to me.

"Talk to you later, pal." I hung up and pulled open the memo-file with the mouse.

It wasn't from Security. It was from Fleet Intelligence. After quoting the regs at me for two pages, they finally cut to the chase. Hass and his wife were Squam agents. In fact, *the* Squam agents aboard the *Hawking*. Hubby collected data from various moles and sleaze-bags while wifey transmitted from the Squam ship she was a techie on. Very neat.

The thing was, Counterintelligence fed them almost everything they were getting. In a weird way, this kept everybody happy. The Squam government trusted us more because Fleet would confirm what they already knew to be the "truth." In turn, they trusted us more and so were more cooperative—essential if we were all going to eliminate the Ichtons.

I didn't read the cease and desist part of the letter—I headed for the lifts instead. As the elevator dropped I tried to figure out other ways for the pieces to fit together, but they kept coming up the same way.

I was sweating again when the door finally slid open on Violet Eight. I stepped into the passageway. A Squam with a needler in his fist walked toward me. I was going for my gun when somebody killed the lights.

The blaster coughed twice in my fist. His head and upper body broke apart with a flash as the plasma took him. I saw him twitch before it went black again. The deck shook as the big lizard hit hard. A hatchway hissed open close to where I stood and I heard more claws on the decking.

I dropped onto the wet deck and rolled. A heartbeat, then the whine of a needler spray ripped the air.

What sounded like hundreds of ceramic toothpicks zinged and ricocheted down the passage. The hair on the back of my neck stood up as the air whistled and tore over my head. I wanted to slip down between the slick grating, but all I could do was hold on.

One of them went into my calf. Maybe more than one. That was the way with needlers: it started to hurt only a few minutes after you'd been hit, unless they hit you somewhere important. Then it didn't hurt at all.

More scratching. Closer this time. I was in trouble. My blaster would light the passage—and me—up like a torch. Needlers had no flash. I heard their labored, reptilian breathing as they came down the hall. There were two, maybe three of them in all. I held my breath. They came on slowly, listening and sniff-ing.

I reached up, groping for a door or anything. We were all out of luck. They were only a meter away when I opened up.

I fired as fast as I could, shooting and shooting. They screamed and twisted and I kept firing, lighting the place up like a Dore illustration. A few droplets of the plasma spattered back onto me. I scrambled back on the steamy floor, wiping myself as best I could.

Every alarm in the place went off. I checked my blaster and looked back. There had been only two of them after all. Molten heaps bubbled where they had been. I looked away, staggered against one of the sickly violet walls, and lurched off toward Viv's.

I found a vidcom and called in. Carroll said they'd meet me there.

Her door was open. Back in her T-shirt again, she had almost finished packing. Three big plastic crates stood where the bed had been. The rest was bare.

Her hand was wrapped around the butt of a needler, a strip of cloth in between so she wouldn't leave prints. She knew who it was, but she didn't look at me right away. When she did it didn't mean anything much. She just lifted the mean little pistol a little and slid along the deck toward me, her lips tight-set.

But I had my blaster out myself. We looked at each other across our guns. Maybe she knew me, I hadn't any idea from her expression.

I said, "You killed them, huh?"

She shook her head a little. "Just Hass. He did Paolo."

"So that was his name."

"Yes. He worked for Counterintelligence. He was Hass's case agent."

Kenvich was going to go strategic.

"Put the gun down," I told her. "You're through with it."

She lowered it a little. She hadn't seemed to notice the blaster I was pushing through the air in her general direction. I lowered that, too.

"Why did you cap Hass?"

She looked up at me. "He got panicked after you went to his place. He came down here, convinced you were going to uncover the whole thing. He was going to blow it."

"He was renting you the information before passing it on to the wife."

"Right."

"And you sold it to the highest bidder via Paolo."

She nodded a little. "Most of the time our buyers would get the Fleet movements before the orders were even posted."

Profiteering. It was an old scam with a new twist. The merchants would come in and spread rumors that the Fleet was on the way and as the panic began to spread, they could buy up everything that wasn't nailed down at rock-bottom prices before moving on. Needless to say, it also compromised mission security with the enemy.

"You fed the info to Paolo . . ."

"But we couldn't be sure if Intelligence was onto him," she said.

The penny dropped. "The knitting."

"Just old-fashioned Morse code," she said. "I knew it would take a long time, but I couldn't risk being seen with him."

"The grain they found in his clothes. What was that about?"

"He had a transmitter set up in a container of long-storage grain on Twenty deck."

She didn't seem to mind telling me. It was almost all there.

"Why the elaborate setup?" I said. "What went wrong?"

"Two weeks ago, Paolo sends me a message. Says he wants more money."

"So pay him."

"I did. Three days later he says it's not enough. Says he's going to turn me in to Intelligence and take a big fat promotion unless he gets a lot more."

"So you told Hass Paolo was Intelligence. Hass sends over the hard-boys and it's *Adios, Paolo.*"

She didn't say anything after that. She just stood there, looking small.

"Who was it set me up?" I said finally. "You or Hass?"

She looked at my blood-soaked pants. She lowered the needler and took a step toward me.

I brought my blaster up.

"You're a bad horse, Viv. I'm not betting on you anymore."

I made a broad, disappointed gesture and moved a little closer. She backed up. I should have taken the chance when she gave it to me.

"So what's the plan now? Change apartments and find a new supplier?"

"Sure."

She said it like I'd asked her to go on a Ferris wheel. "Tell me," I said, "was it worth it?"

"What do you mean?"

"The money."

She looked at me like I was stupid. Maybe I was.

"Are you kidding?" She laughed. "Since Hass rolled over, I've cleared over 1.3 million credits. Tax-free and in the clear."

I didn't like what her definition of "in the clear" was. "The merchants pay pretty well."

"I would say the most valuable commodity going is knowledge, wouldn't you say?"

"Grace is given of God," I said, " 'but knowledge is born in the market.' "

"Dickens?"

I shook my head.

"Whatever. The point is, there's plenty of cash to go around. It's evident from tonight's fiasco that I need someone who can handle it when things go bad. Why don't you join me?"

I looked at her for the last time, really. There were a lot of things she might have said, that I maybe would have fallen for, but that wasn't one of them.

She saw it in my eyes.

Viv jerked up the needler and squeezed the trigger at me. She did it without moving a muscle of her face.

Nothing happened. It puzzled her in a vague, month-before-last way. She turned the gun around, still careful about the cloth wrapper around the grip, and peered into the muzzle. She shook it and then remembered I was there. I hadn't moved. I didn't have to, now.

"It's on full auto, but that yellow telltale means the clip is empty," I explained. "You left them all back in Hass."

She moved to go and I raised the blaster. The motion shifted my balance and the wounded leg almost gave way. A pain rose and my vision closed to only a narrow hole. I fought back and found myself nauseous, but leaning against the wall. Viv had moved a few steps, whether to help me or grab the blaster was a good question. She looked toward the door and took a few steps. The question in her expression was clear. I wasn't sure myself. Part of me knew I could simply let myself fall and no one could say I hadn't tried and passed out. The pool of blood at my foot was all the excuse I needed.

Two images fought each other in my mind. One was the memory of her soft body so desirous in my arms. The other was the cold, motionless slab of flesh in the morgue up on Green that had been her partner. For a long time neither of us moved.

When I heard the sound of the security overrides on the door and Cal telling the rookies to stay alert as he opened it, I knew what I decided no longer mattered. He'd read the report I'd filed after the fight in the hallway and figured out where, even wounded, I had to be going. Good police work. Though sometimes too efficient backup can be a pain.

I let go and let myself slide slowly down the wall as Cal came through. Viv gave me a look that hinted she somehow felt betrayed. It really didn't matter, but I was just too hot and too tired to care. Letting Viv go now would simply have delayed things. Hass had been right about one thing. There was nowhere to run on a battlestation.

STERN CHASE

A ROYAL NAVY adage is that a "stern chase is the longest one." There is also an old army saying, "Hurry up and wait." Perhaps the most draining part of any modern battle is that generally everyone is bored most of the time. Hours of mind-dulling tedium are interspersed with minutes, even seconds, of furious combat. Spacemen would arm, prepare, and then warp for hours to drop back and engage the Ichtons in a few minutes of carefully planned combat. Those lucky enough to survive then fled back to the relative safety of the main fleet or, farther back, to the *Hawking* itself.

In that sense the *Hawking* had proved a success in its appointed mission. The battlestation had more than proved itself capable of supporting large forces at an unimaginable distance from their home base. Further, it now had provided both a base and safe port serving a large fleet under combat conditions for almost three years.

To those Fleet personnel serving on the Battlestation *Stephen Hawking,* this record was a matter of pride. Unfortunately there was little time for satisfaction as a constant stream of broken men and ships returned and had to be made ready to return to the battle. This continuing grind of unbroken crises had to begin taking its toll. Fatigue alone became a major factor in Anton Brand's calculations. Also of concern to the *Hawking*'s commander was the tenuous morale of the allied races.

Brand attempted to break off the pursuit after nearly twenty days of constant small battles. As the Fleet ships pulled back, the Ichton warships followed. There could be no respite. Too many ships had warped back toward the *Hawking* and any lapse in the pressure would release major Ichton formations from guarding the mother ships. Freeing them to attack the *Stephen Hawking* itself or nearby allied worlds.

So they continued as best they could. Fighting without respite. The not so lucky returned their torn and shattered men and ships for repair. Everyone assisted in maintaining the faith of the allies. Sometimes this last was hard to accomplish. This was even more difficult when it appeared the ally's world might be the next Ichton target.

THE HANDMAIDEN

by Diane Duane

"DON'T JUST STAND there," Kashiwabara said. "Hold the retractor."

I'm not just standing here, Sal thought. But all the same she took hold of the J-shaped thing and pulled. "Not that way," Kash said irritably. "Welder, Junie. Thanks. More toward you, Sal. That's the way."

Kashiwabara was up to her elbows in the man, her eyes screwed half closed. To Sal she looked like a child at school, engaged in some particularly engrossing piece of work with modeling clay. It was not clay she was working with, though, but flesh, some poor man's intestine. At least Sal thought it might be intestine. She had a general impression of wet glistening rounded shapes, of squelchy wet noises: and she wanted nothing more definite than that. This was hardly her proper business, and she didn't intend for it to be so in the future, if she could help it.

O God—she started, and lost the thread again, her eyes widening in dismay as the air abruptly fizzed red around them all. "Didn't think it would spurt like *that,*" Kashiwabara said, her voice bemused, her hands suddenly moving very fast, perhaps three times as fast as before. "That one, right there, Junie. The one next to it. Thanks. Should be right under there— *There* it is. Jeez, look at the state of it—how is the boy still with us? Guts."

"A good anesthesiologist," said a mild voice from the head of the table, down past the glow of the sterifields.

"You shut up, Belle. Don't take the man's credit. You barely know where to put the tubes. Junie, where's the dish?"

"Here. Kash, is that going to be enough left?"

"You kidding? More than plenty. Twenty cells is enough to clone from in situ. In a week he'll have a nice new spleen. Get the one down to Path, Junie, the ghouls'll want it. Where's the dittosplen?"

O God, Who holds all lives from their beginnings to their ends, Sal thought, *keep this man in mind—* Man, though: it was hard to see him as a man, at the moment. More a collection of tubes and oozing liquid, with the fields shimmering over everything and making it look unreal, like something out of a vid. Sal shook her head, abruptly angry with herself. There was a hell of a way for a chaplain to see one of her charges, as a thing rather than a—

"Getting to you, Sal?" Kashiwabara was looking across the body—the *man*—at her, with an expression that had just a little malice about it. No more than usual, she consoled herself.

"No," Sal said. That was only partly true. When she had first seen the man brought in, only survivor of the Ichton attack on her little fleet, he had looked like someone much more in need of prayer than of the surgeons—burned, explosively decompressed when his suit gave: the debridement alone, before the surgery, had left Sal sure she was working with a corpse. People did not just lie and take the dreadful peeling off of burnt material and flesh fused to it that the man had undergone—not if they were alive. They woke up, and screamed. Sal's nightmares rang with those screams. But the man had simply lain there, in shock so profound that he had noticed nothing; and then he had gone into the OR. Kashiwabara had taken all of ten minutes over him now—a surprising amount of time for her.

"He'll live," Kashiwabara said, in the matter-of-fact tone of voice of someone announcing the score of a football game some light-years away. "Whether he'll like it—" She shrugged. "Fuser now, Junie. Thanks. Let go of that, Sal. Just take it out and throw it in the bucket. Junie, count the retractor out." Kash took the fuser and wielded it, closing the operative site with negligent skill. "It's not my table," Kash said, to Sal this time. "I just patch them up. After that, they're your business." Her eyes were direct, cool, almost merry. Sal's eyes burned. She looked away.

"Who's next?" said Kash.

"Khalian," said the circulating nurse, glancing at the wall screen. "Head trauma, enucleated eye, possible brain trouble. Contrecoup, they think."

"Poor Weasel," Kash said in that same cool voice. "Pull out a head tray and get him in here, and prepped. Him? Her?"

"Him."

"Your table?" Kash said to Sal.

It was her table, of course. But she said, "I'll pass on this one. Back in a while."

Kashiwabara nodded. "I need a new skin," she was saying as Sal shouldered out of the OR. "Try getting me one a size larger—"

She leaned against the wall of one of the many corridors up in the Blue and fought to slow her heartbeat down. People passed her, glanced at her, glanced away with expressions of pity or concern. With the battle going on over their heads, everyone was busy: but her uniform singled her out for their pity. It was standard Fleet uniform except for the dog collar, and the tabs with the Uniform Religious Insignia on it, the circle with the dot in the middle. "The Holy Ovum," Ricky Woods had called it while they were in the Fleet orientation course together, how many years ago now? . . . And there had been quite a few other names, most of them rife with innuendo. Where was Ricky now? Sal wondered. Was she even alive? . . . Or in the body, rather. Sometimes, of late, in the rush and fury of a war that could mean the end of whole civilizations, it was hard to remember that there were more important things, more meaningful things, than mere physical life.

So she had always believed, anyway.

And do I believe it now?

Sal pushed the thought away, straightened herself up, tried to look a little less doleful. There was nothing more depressing, to the onlooker, than a depressed minister. Her job, here and now at least, was to help people find their way to their strength; and if she chanced to be able to be useful in some other way as well—like holding a retractor—she did that. Though it was hardly her primary function.

Not that some people seemed to realize it. *Make yourself useful,* Kashiwabara had said, very casually. *Or is it just my own uncertainty showing? We all have these periods of not being sure what we're for—but this one has lasted longer than usual. What real good have I done anyone here? Sometimes I think I should just go out on combat duty and get killed like the rest of them—*

Her pager beeped. She sighed and pulled it out to look at its little screen. It said, MY OFFICE, PLEASE, IMMEDIATELY. F.

Sal took herself off along the corridor in a hurry. Frank Arnasson was no one to keep waiting, especially in the middle of a war: nor at any other time. He was coordinator for Inhabitant Resources aboard *Hawking,* and Sal's immediate superior. He did not take his own position seriously, since it involved coordinating things as disparate and low profile as Food Services and Janitorial; and Frank always growled about how his title and a few credits might get him a cup of soup on some benighted world where no one knew any better. But there were few people who could quicker get you in deep trouble than Frank if he suspected that you weren't doing your job.

She took the lift down two to Blue Three and trotted along the corridor to 270, where Frank's office was. Sal paused only long enough to get her breath back and yank her tunic into place, then buzzed.

The door snapped open for her. She stepped in and saw Frank hunched behind his desk as usual, eating something, a food bar of some kind. Nothing unusual there: Frank was the worst person she had ever seen for snacking at his desk—he never stopped. Standing across from him, though, watching him with an expression that at first glance seemed like mild interest, was an Emry.

Sal paused there as the door hissed closed behind her, and the Emry turned to look at her. It was in Fleet uniform, very dark and simple, but oddly decorated with something unusual—a silver chain, very massy, like the ceremonial chains that Sal had seen in pictures of mayors from some parts of Europe, back on Earth. The chain shifted as the Emry tilted its head to look at her, revealing a glint of gold on the low-cut collar of its uniform. It was the Holy Ovum.

Frank put aside his food bar and folded his hands, looking at Sal, too. His honest, ugly face, big and blunt, with its potato nose and little eyes, smiled slightly as if she were the solution to a particularly thorny problem.

"Fleet Chaplain Salvatora Arkas," Frank said, "Fleet Chaplain Ewa n'Vhuurih."

The Emry bowed, a graceful gesture, but his head did not bow, and his eyes never left Sal's. For a moment she was lost in those golden eyes, then she blinked, taking in the beauty of the dark pelt with its faint pattern of darker spots, and the long nose with the abrupt patch of pink at the end. This, fortunately, was one aspect of her chaplaincy that was easy for her. She had never had trouble seeing the Creator in species that were alien to her own. The problem, perhaps, was that she had sometimes been too good at it, and this could be impolitic, when all the energies of one's highest superiors were being vested in hating one of those species or, worse, manipulating it.

"Chaplain," Sal said, wondering how she looked to those golden eyes. And the question rose immediately to mind: What sort of religion do they have? No one had even mentioned the word in connection with them before.

"The chaplain," Frank said, "is the Emry's first member of your service. I want you to make him welcome, show him around, see that he's properly oriented. . . ."

The Emry made a gesture that looked like someone casting something to the ground in front of himself: plainly ceremonial, though what it might mean, there was no telling. A touch of excitement began somewhere down inside Sal. *How do they see You?* she said to the One Who listened. *What might we find out from them? Thank You for this opportunity—*

"I thank you for your help," the Emry said. "This means a great deal to us."

Sal shivered slightly. The translator might convey words, but the voice was more clearly that of an animal than any alien voice she had heard before: it was almost furry around the edges.

"You're very welcome," Sal said. "Have you been quartered?"

"Go on, go on," Frank growled, and picked up his food bar in one hand and a stylus in another. "Take care of the amenities elsewhere. You two have work to do, so do I—"

Sal glanced at the Emry and found what looked like the same expression of slight amusement there. They headed for the door together, and as it closed behind them, the Emry said, "A sudden sort of creature."

Sal laughed. "He is."

"I am up in Yellow," the Emry said. "A comfortable enough little den. It is diplomatic quarters, if I understand these things correctly. Perhaps better than I would normally be given, if those here understood my function. Or if I did." His jaw dropped in that amused look again.

Sal nodded. "We all spend a while trying to find out exactly what we're supposed to be doing here," she said. "For humans in our service, at least, there are certain basic duties. Rotation through the various kinds of religious service—there's never time to do them all in one day, so we take turns—"

"We," said the Emry. "There are more than one of you, then?"

"Normally there would be." It was surprising that Sal's eyes could still start stinging again over *this* issue: she had thought it was settled. "There were three of us on board—enough to cover, it was thought. We managed, just barely. But some of the ancillary craft needed coverage, those staff went off to take care of business there—" Sal shrugged. "One of them was killed during an Ichton attack while he was performing a wedding. The other—we have no idea what happened to the ship: it just never came back. Probably Ichton again."

So uncaring, said the raspy voice in Sal's memory, *what else should it be in this part of space?* That had been Larry's constant refrain, always a little sad, always with a slight edge to it, as if he held God personally responsible for the mismanagement of the whole galactic situation, and was daily expecting Him to do something about it. Larry had gone about all his work with that same slight impatience and irritation, but always unfailingly good-natured: he was one of the most simply loving people Sal had ever known. And now he was gone, with the captain and the first officer of the little ship to which he had traveled. Doubtless, though, he had gotten the job done. Sal was sure they had been married for at least several seconds before they were dead.

"And now you are alone here," the Emry said.

Sal raised her eyebrows. "Inasmuch as any of us are ever really alone," she said, "yes."

The Emry looked puzzled at this, and his tail thumped. It was a short one, making the gesture look peremptory, almost annoyed. *But there's no telling,* Sal reminded herself. *I must be careful not to anthropomorphize the gestures of a species we don't know very well as yet—*

"I should like to see what you do in a given day," said the Emry, "if there is no prohibition against it."

"I think that was the general idea," Sal said. "No, there's no prohibition. Come on, I'll show you the chapels."

They went up three levels and made their way about halfway around the curve of *Hawking*. "Here we are," Sal said, and touched the door panel. It slid open: they went in.

The Emry looked around, blinking solemnly. "But there is nothing here. Just a table."

Sal laughed. "The dangers of a nondenominational chapel. We can dress it as necessary. Shinto, Jewish, various flavors of Christian, Buddhist, you name it."

"Flavors," the Emry said thoughtfully as Sal went over to the holography panel. "This is a matter of taste, then."

Sal chuckled at the joke . . . then wondered if it was one, as she saw that puzzled-looking expression on the Emry's face again. She touched the panel and said, "Here's one of the standard Christian configurations."

The light on the bare walls shifted, and a radiance grew near the ceiling, as of stained glass somewhere above; the cross, very plain, appeared over the table, which was now made plain as an altar. "Solid artifacts we keep stored in the next room," Sal said. "Candles, canopies, and whatnot. The usual equipment." She looked curiously over at the Emry and said, "Do you use such things?"

He shook his head, looking up into the radiance. "No," he said.

Sal looked at him. "I'm sorry . . . I don't know what to call you."

"H'ewa," the Emry said.

"H'ewa . . . I'm very curious, but I don't want to break any prohibitions either, and I have no idea what sort of rules you might have about your worship—"

"Very few," H'ewa said, and blinked. "You mentioned—'Shinto'?"

Sal nodded and touched the panel again. The light shifted once more, falling into squarish patterns of brightness and dark, evoking a feeling of screens pulled across a source of light outside.

The sound system cut in and from somewhere off in the middle distance came the sound of bass voices intoning one of those scalp-raising triple-voiced chants to the Jewel in the Lotus. "I know a few of the chants myself," Sal said, "but they're hard on the throat. Not any of the serious ones, though, the healing chants: almost all the masters who knew them died a long time ago, and the recorded ones just don't seem to work the same. . . ."

H'ewa nodded—that gesture, at least, they seemed to have in common. "You would use this room fairly frequently for your—'worship,' then."

"Yes. You do it otherwise?"

"It is not a personal matter? One must have a special place to perform it?"

Sal shook her head. "Not necessarily. Some religions feel that worship works best in groups, that's all. Other say not: that each person makes his own choices, and needs no mediator between himself and the First Cause."

"What do you say?" H'ewa said, looking again at Sal. It was a direct expression, a little challenging.

"Well—" Sal leaned against the wall. "I was trained first as Church of Mars, of course, and your first training tends to color your thinking somewhat. So I tend to believe, in common with other people of my sort, that God made the world, but the world became marred: so to redeem it, He descended into it Himself, first as man, and in other times, in other shapes, to draw the natures of those kinds of beings into His own."

H'ewa nodded, but his face was getting that perplexed look again. " 'Believe,' " he said. "You don't *know?*"

"Well, historical proof is an oxymoron half the time," Sal said. "Hard enough to tell what really happened ten minutes ago, or ten hours, as opposed to what a 'historian' would say. But—" Then she stopped, seeing the look of perplexity on H'ewa's face intensifying. "No," she said. "No, of course I don't *know*—that's the whole point of faith. No one can ever *know* for sure, or have Deity proven to them past all doubt. The mere physical nature of the universe won't permit it. Belief is all we've got."

"But other 'flavors' say differently?" H'ewa said. There was a sound of urgency creeping into his voice.

"Well, some say that knowing is possible, but unnecessary for the assured soul." Sal was beginning to sweat, not least because she had no idea where all this was going. "Some say that neither God, nor the universe symptomatic of Him, care whether you believe in them: that belief itself is unnecessary. Just as believing in the table is unnecessary, because it's there whether you believe in it or not. Even if you can't perceive it."

H'ewa turned away, looking troubled. "H'ewa," Sal said, "I want to help, truly I do. Tell me what the trouble is."

The Emry turned back to her. "Who knows?" he said. "Who knows what the truth is?"

What is truth? someone had said a long time ago, and washed his hands. Sal wished she could do the same. "None of us know," she said. "All we can do is go on as we've done in the past, and look for new answers. We thought—I hoped you might have some new answers for us."

H'ewa bared his teeth suddenly. It was an alarming expression, and Sal stepped back involuntarily, then stopped, seeing the desperation still in his eyes.

"I was sent to find out what I can," H'ewa said. "I must try to do so, even if you don't know. But we thought you did—about this First Cause: this God. It is a great disappointment."

He sighed. "Show me the rest," he said.

Sal opened the door and showed him out, her mind in an uproar too great even for prayer.

Several hours later Sal had shown him the hospital wards, and what a chaplain did there, visiting the sick. She had also done two or three counseling sessions that she really didn't need to do, but scheduled gladly enough, to give her some kind of routine to fall into while that golden-eyed regard was with her. With the counselees' permission, H'ewa had sat through the sessions, his handsome ears swiveling to follow the conversations, eyes blinking gently. Sal wondered if it was her imagination that her counselees were being a little more forthcoming about their own troubles than usual. Maybe it was the fascination of the stranger: or maybe that H'ewa was an uncommonly good listener, in the way of someone very uncertain of what they're hearing, who therefore concentrates on every passing word.

They broke for a meal after a while, H'ewa going off to his quarters—apparently the Emry preferred to eat in private. Sal, for her part, went straight off to Frank's office. He was eating, again, or still. He looked up at her as if she were excessively unwelcome, but that was par for the course with him.

"I don't think the Emry *have* a religion," Sal said before he could get started. "Who put that creature in a chaplain's uniform? Was it some kind of joke?!"

"If it was a joke," Frank said, putting down one of the eternal food bars, "it was a big one. Right from the top, that lad came. Some relative of one of the people who run the planet, sent here at their orders. And the orders specified chaplain—it was a six-sigma translation, so don't blame it on an error in syntax."

"But they don't have any religion," Sal said again, feeling helpless. "They don't know what God is, or gods, *any* gods, as far as I can tell! They don't know what religious services are, or priests or ministers of any kind!"

"Maybe they want to find out," Frank said heavily. "Possibly they think they're missing something, seeing that so many of the other species in the Alliance have such things. Who knows how they think of it. A weapon. An advantage."

Sal's eyebrows went up. That struck her as a very inappropriate way to consider religion.

"And don't you go getting judgmental," Frank said. "I know that look. Sal, all I'm sure of is that this situation is politically provocative. Apparently our lad has orders to go back to their high council, or whatever it is, and report to them after his visit—and I hear rumblings that what he says will make some kind of difference to their alliance with us and with the other Indies. This is too important a matter to screw up, so whatever you do, you'd better do a good job of it, Sal, or by whichever God's turn it is in the rotation today, I'll have your butt in a sling. Now get out of here and let me finish my dinner."

Sal smiled thinly, thinking (and tempted to say) that no one had ever seen Frank finish a meal before, and it was unlikely to start happening now. But she thought better of it—the remark was uncharitable, anyway: how he handled stress was his own business. She went away to see about the evening service.

• • •

There was no one there for it, which was a common enough variation when *Hawking* was in battle. The other main variation was that a given service was filled to overflowing, whether the people attending were of that denomination or not. The need for reassurance, for consolation, sometimes seemed to flow through the station like a wave. Other times, like now, people were just too busy. At such times, Sal particularly remembered the old prayer attributed to Cromwell before battle—though she herself doubted that that cold young man had ever said any such thing: "O God, Thou knowest how busy I must be today: if I forget Thee, yet do not Thou forget me." She made it her business on such days to remember God on behalf of all the people who didn't have time.

The rotation said that today should have been the Zoroastrian service, but plainly no one would care, and Sal was feeling shaken: so she went back to the old familiar, the C of M service, which would console her, if no one else. The holography installation had filled the chapel with the pale, cool, rose-tinged light of one of the old Martian underground sun temples, one shaft of light coming down from the pierced ceiling to fall on the altar, which now looked like a plain slab of sandstone. The cup and plate were of stone as well, not ornamented, not polished. Only the bread and wine had not changed. She was just in the act of lifting the cup up into the light and pronouncing the words celebrating the Change when the door opened.

Sal had long learned to ignore such things. She kept herself where she belonged, in the moment of miracle, until it was finished, paying no attention to the silhouette in the doorway. It vanished, the door closing. Only a short shadow, standing back there in the reddish darkness, watched her: she caught the gleam of golden eyes.

Sal finished the service as she had done for some time now, with the old optional prayer for use "in times of War and Tumults"—*not that most times aren't that, one way or another,* she thought. "King of Kings and Governor of all, whose power no creature can resist, to whom it belongs to justly punish wrongdoers, and to show mercy to the repentant: Save and deliver us, we beg You, from our enemies: abate their pride, assuage their malice, and confound their devices: that we, being armed with Your defense, may be preserved evermore from all perils, to glorify You, the only Giver of victory—"

"Does anyone truly have such power?" came the quiet voice from the shadows, the beast's voice. Sal shivered a little for the pain in it.

She finished what she was doing, took off her stole, and made her way back into the shadows herself. "So I believe," she said, folding the stole up, "but that won't be good enough, will it?"

There was a moment's silence. "We have need of certainties," H'ewa said. "Now more than ever."

"A lot of us have been looking for them, too," Sal said, "for a long time. Without much success."

Frank's words were much with her at the moment. She had been trying to figure out for the past little while exactly what she could do to be of help to H'ewa, to the allied species, to the Independents . . . and had found no answers. *Frank is on his own this time,* she thought.

"But some success," said H'ewa.

"It depends on who's judging it."

H'ewa sighed. "Our world," he said, "needs saving. All the ships, even this one—with all its power—seem able to do little. The Ichton fleets are all over this part of space, and all your might is only able to barely hold them away from us. What kind of civilization is it that can only survive with the help of aliens and strangers?"

Sal sighed, too. "Ours has been that, on occasion," she said. "If one thing that's been lost in the past years in our sense of ourselves as being competent to deal with the world . . . maybe that's not a terrible loss. Certainly those of us who believe that there is a Master of the universe also believe that our sense of ourselves as surrogate masters sometimes gets in the way of any real interaction with It. . . ."

"But you have not interacted with it," H'ewa said, "at least, not to any effect."

"We think we have," Sal said. "But our idea of effect, and Its idea of effect . . . are two very different things."

H'ewa shook his head again. "These are not the answers I came looking for," he said. "I need to know; where can help be found, if not in all these ships and armaments? We had hints, from other people like you, that help might be found in other ways. Spiritual ways."

"It depends on what you mean by help," Sal said. "Victory? Triumph over one's enemies? I have no guarantees of help from the First Cause, the Powers, whatever you prefer to call them—on that account."

"Nothing like that. Just peace," H'ewa said, and that terrible pain was in its voice again, like the voice of a beast caught in a trap. "Just to be left alone."

Sal shook her head. "As for the second, whether it's available in the universe anymore, if it ever was," she said, "is a good question. You can ask an all-powerful God for things, but even the omnipotent is helpless against simple nonsense. Like saying, 'Oh, God, please turn blue into yellow.' Were we ever, any of us, really alone—in a universe in which every part affects every other—to be left that way again? By each other, let alone by other species—however mindless or well intentioned?" Sal breathed out. "As for peace—we keep asking. We're told, in most religions, that someday we'll get it. Or it will get us. But rarely while we're breathing. Life seems to be mostly about problem-solving, the way most species see it—and the more problems you solve, the bigger and more complex they get."

They were quiet for a moment as the shaft of sunlight slid away from the altar. "You spoke just now, up there, of a coming again," H'ewa said. "One of these—Powers—saying it would come back. That evil would die."

"But not when," Sal said, shaking her head. "Never that: no data on the future. As for the rest of it . . . all the stories of the Powers coming into the world, actually into it, to intervene . . . are in the past, a long time ago. Very old. Increasingly, we seem to be the ones who do the intervening. The Powers may speak . . . but they don't *do* much. We seem to be the ones who do the doing."

"We are not doing it very well, it would seem," said H'ewa.

Sal laughed, not as bitterly as she might have. "We never have," she said, "but we do what we can with what we've got. You're quite right, about the weapons not being enough. It's hard to stop using them, though. Right now, we don't seem to have much choice. If we stop shooting at the Ichtons, they'll roll over us and dome us over in a matter of minutes."

H'ewa bared his teeth again. This time Sal felt no need to step back. "I think we will not let them do that," he said. "And in the meantime . . . we will not wait for the Powers, either."

"It's not recommended," Sal said. " 'The gods help those who help themselves'; that's a popular refrain in a lot of places. They may not help with hardware, or logistical support . . . but there are other ways."

H'ewa looked at her a moment, eyes glinting gold. Then he moved toward the door and went out.

Sal went to her prayers, distressed, and not knowing what else to do about it.

The next morning, when she went by the address H'ewa had given her for his quarters, she found the door standing open, and a cleaning robot working busily inside. "Where is the occupant, please?" she said to it.

"Vacated," the robot said, and kept dusting under a chair.

Sal put her eyebrows up and went off to Frank's office. He was eating at his desk and barely looked up at her. "What did you say to him?" he growled. "He was up all night in the library, ransacking the computers. Then left on the shuttle about half an hour ago, back to Emry."

"Nothing offensive, if that's what you're worried about," Sal said. "I gave him the truth—as much of it as I could find in such a short time, anyway. It seemed to be what he wanted."

"You'd better hope so," Frank said, looking, at least on the surface, relieved. "Well, go on, do you think I have all day to sit here jawing?"

Sal smiled at him and went off to the wards to visit some of the people she had missed yesterday—some of them missed on purpose, because they were a touch xenophobic and wouldn't have cared for the presence of an alien while Sal was ministering to them. She couldn't get rid of the memory of those golden eyes, blinking at her conversations, listening to the people she had been talking to; the comical swivel of the ears, but also the intensity. . . .

"Sal, they've got incoming in OR, a lot of it," said one of the nurses from the doorway as Sal got up from the last bedside. "You free? Some of them may need you."

"On my way." She pulled her stole out of her pocket and headed for the lift—OR was one level down. It was a madhouse when she got down there, but that was nothing new. The scorched-bacon smell was nothing new, either—she knew it of old, and hated it. More burn cases. *At least they'll be alive. But will they like it—*

As usual for large emergencies, Sal took herself into the prep room, where triage was taking place. There was already a sad row of plastic-sheeted shapes over on the side of the room; dead, or soon to be: too hurt to waste time with, in any case. The second group, those awaiting surgery but not critically enough wounded to need it right away, was fairly large. Sal deafened herself for the moment to their cries and stopped long enough to pronounce the general absolution over those already dead, then turned back to see to the cat-two people—trying to make out who was conscious, who needed a hand to hold, who was dealing with their pain sufficiently to notice someone with them.

She was almost past him before she saw the sheen of the dark pelt, the darker spots, and the flesh under it, startlingly pale, except where the burns blistered it. His jaw worked, but no sound came out.

Stricken, Sal dropped to her knees beside him. For some time he didn't notice she was there, just worked his jaw. A slight, slight moaning came from him: not the sound of the beast, now, not at all, but that of a child in pain too great to otherwise express. After a while, this stopped, and one eye opened. The other was burned closed, or burned away entirely—there was no telling, nothing but a mass of blistered, furless flesh all down that side of his face.

It took a while for the eye to see her, for the sight to register. She was already speaking the words softly, whether he would understand them or not; in the middle of the prayer he said, rough-voiced, halting: "Who are you talking to?"

"You and God," she said. "Now shut up!" She was horrified at her own tears as she went on with it. " 'Lord, visit and relieve Your servant here, for whom we pray. Restore him, if it be Your pleasure, to his former health—' "

"One of us at least is here," H'ewa said, his jaw dropping briefly. "Not for long, perhaps. They caught us—halfway—"

He coughed bloody froth, could not go on for a moment. "No matter," he said. "I had made my report: last night."

Sal stopped praying and stared at him. "On what? The existence of God?" She was tempted to laugh through the tears.

H'ewa hissed—maybe it was laughter, too, or pain. "Just so."

"And what conclusions did you come to?"

"Noncombatant," H'ewa said. "But possibly available for discussions."

She shook her head, in amusement and bitter rue. "What will this mean for your people?"

"In the war? Nothing. But after we have all survived it—we will have one more thing to talk about, perhaps. For a long time. We have been looking— We thought we were the only ones—"

There was more blood, this time, and less froth. Sal knew this sign. It meant lungs that had had more vacuum than was good for them: many vessels ruptured, maybe a big one. "I need a reassessment here!" she cried, but all the staff were busy, running around like mad people: and those golden eyes met hers, stilled her.

"Now that I have done some of the doing—" said the voice of the beast, calm, as if speaking to a child. "Talk to these Powers for me, so that I can—see how it is done. It is practice. You will have to—do the same again, for others will come looking, in a while. You will have—quite a few visitors."

Sal swallowed, and on the impulse of the moment changed prayers. " 'God, giver of all good gifts, who has made varying Orders in Your scheme of things, give Your grace to those called today to Your service, replenish them with the truth, so that they can faithfully serve You—' "

Much too much blood, this time. "Junie!" she shouted, trying to get the attention of the only nurse she knew well, but no one came. H'ewa turned his head, and exhaled blood, and nothing else. His eyes did not close, but their gold began to tarnish.

Sal wiped her eyes and went on with it, even to the last line, for though breathing might stop, the nurses had always told her that hearing was the last thing to go. " 'You are a priest forever,' " she said, " 'even after the order of Melchisidech.' "

She stood up then, as one of the other nurses came along, knelt down by the body, touched the control on the stretcher, and steered it into the OR. Sal watched them take H'ewa's corpse away, and knew it was hopeless; but at the same time, could not lose an odd feeling of anticipation. *Apostle to the Emry? Not apostle, that's too high. Missionary?*

"I am the handmaiden of the Lord," it said in the documentation. Sal smiled a sad smile. " 'Let it be done to me as you say,' " she whispered.

Meantime—

She went off to kneel by a man whose arm had been blown off, checked the tourniquet, and began to pray.

IN DANGER'S WAY

AS THE TWO opposing fleets converged on Emry, the intensity of the battle grew. Enough Fleet ships had been eliminated to force lulls in their attack that allowed the Ichtons to regroup. The Ichtons had themselves suffered heavily enough that they were finding it difficult to protect the mother ships and the tens of thousands of soldiers and millions of eggs they carried. But no one could fight harder than an Ichton protecting those eggs.

The *Hawking* arrived at Emry to find the planet already under attack. Anton Brand held the battlestation in the system's Oort cloud, where it could hide among the cometary debris. Even so the constant parade of ships to and from the station would soon divulge its location. Nonetheless, Brand made every effort to disrupt the Ichton attack. Fierce battles erupted as the Fleet and their allies tried to tear their way through the more numerous Ichton attackers and destroy the mother ships. On the second attempt a sortie from the surface of Emry actually succeeded in tearing apart one of the massive Ichton vessels. This made the remaining Ichtons meet the next incursion in an almost suicidal frenzy. Two days later the siege of Emry continued unabated.

Reluctantly Anton Brand stripped the *Hawking*'s escort until every functioning warship had entered the battle. Soon even hastily commandered armed merchant ships joined the battle. Anton Brand had at this point committed every ship that carried a weapon except the *Hawking* itself. The station was simply too valuable as a base to risk in combat. But this meant that before the final stages of the conflict had been joined, Brand had committed all but his last reserve.

Under sublight drive the sheer bulk of the *Hawking* made the battlestation slow and hard to maneuver. This meant that the three hundred laser cannon and two hundred missile tubes that served as the station's final line of defense had to be manned constantly. All were needed to drive off the occasional Ichton sortie against the station itself. Already stretched to the limit, the Fleet personnel turned to the civilian levels for reinforcements. Considering the low level of morale, this was not an easy task.

SHOOTING STAR

by Jody Lynn Nye

"NEVER!" LYSEO ANNOUNCED with a look of horror. He glanced up in outrage from the image of his face in the makeup mirror to those of his two visitors.

"C'mon, Hammy, we need you to bang the drum. It's just a few little training films. So what?"

The scene: Lyseo's dressing room. The characters: Arend McKechnie Lyseo himself, Fleet Lieutenant Jill FarSeeker, and Kem Thoreson, Lyseo's personal manager. The time: perhaps badly chosen.

"So *what*?" demanded Lyseo. "I did training films before I took up performance art, me bucko. I even did a recruitment film for the Fleet." He drew himself up from his chair into a perfect attention stance, and forty years dropped from his mobile face as it formed into a look of terrified obedience. "Lyseo does not repeat himself."

Morale Officer FarSeeker sighed. She was a small, businesslike woman of twenty-nine, with a thick knot of straight black hair tied up at the back of her head. "What constitutes repetition, Lyseo?" she asked patiently. "You've done Old Earth classics a thousand times."

"But never the same way twice," the actor explained, his long hands describing the cone of a spotlight before him, obviously peopling it in his mind with actors. "Ah, the differences you can bring out, the nuances of emotion!" He regarded her sternly. "How many nuances can there be for 'slide bolt home, making certain the power supply is disengaged before disassembling'?"

Jill FarSeeker laughed, losing her composure. "All right, they are boring, but they're necessary. Be reasonable."

For her, Lyseo allowed a tiny smile to touch his eyes. He gathered up her hands in his and kissed them. "Lyseo is never reasonable either. Why me?"

"McCaul's idea, really. We're running out of trained gunners, and frankly, our only remaining pool of being power from which to draw is the civilian population of the *Hawking.* It's a frightening concept to most of them, so our demonstrator needs to be a civilian. The Fleet won this engagement, but casualties were higher than we expected. We've only got a few days to enlist some volunteers, while the *Hawking* cleans up in this system and we move on to the Emry's. Our scouts report we're going to face a massive force there, and we need backup techs. The Emry are already skirmishing with the enemy, so time is short. I could use someone from the theater company, but Kay wants the most visible, most impressive, most charismatic personality on board the ship to be the center of these videos. Your presence alone will make more people watch them."

With every erg of praise, Lyseo was visibly softening. "These monstrosities won't be beamed back to the Alliance, will they?" His daily performances interpreting his impressions of life on board the *Hawking* were broadcast toward the Alliance star cluster to be collected on museum-grade video cube as his legacy to Art. The Fleet concurred in the practice, seeing Lyseo's visible support of the *Hawking* and its allies as a way to help secure funding for domestic projects as well as keep interest alive in the battlestation project itself. The same charisma was vital to engender enthusiasm in the instruction program.

"Not if you don't want them to be," Jill promised him. "They're strictly for internal use. We need to be able to put trained personnel onto the warships, and we need them soonest. You can help greatly by cooperating."

"I am already helping. The first encounter is fixed for 11:35 exactly, the second eight hours and ten minutes after that. I think you'll be well satisfied."

"That's all for morale," Jill pointed out. "Once you've raised their spirits, we need to channel them for maximum effectiveness."

"Do not spout your military jargon at me," Lyseo said, holding his head between his hands. He smoothed back his mane of white hair and straightened up, every move as graceful as if it had been preplanned. "All right, I will do it—but under one condition: I get complete creative control."

"That's reasonable, Jill," Kem put in, seeing that his client was ready to give in. He put an arm around Lyseo's shoulders. "Ari's got a reputation to protect. He can't be seen doing bit-bite dialogue."

"Okay," Jill replied, allowing herself to seem beaten. "Can we start today after your performance?"

"That would be acceptable," Lyseo said grandly. He put a hand each on their shoulders and ushered them toward the door. "And now, if you'll excuse me, I have my regular job to think about. Heavens around us, a regular job! Poor old Hambone."

The dressing-room door slid shut behind them. Jill heard the lock engage.

"So much for the early lunch he invited me to," she complained, looking at her chronometer. "Well, that's all right. I have other things I can take care of."

"He's thinking about your videos," Kem assured her. "You know how he gets when he's got a new project to chew on."

"I suppose I do," Jill sighed. "At least we got him to agree. I thought it would be harder than that."

"You applied the soap just right, Lieutenant. McCaul owes you a raise, getting Hammy to agree without a week-long fuss."

Jill shrugged. "He's the best performer for the job. Otherwise, I wouldn't be bothering him. With his support behind the training program, which otherwise could look like enforced conscription, my job will be a lot easier. It's going to be tough enough to sell the idea to grocers and hairdressers that they need to learn how to run laser cannon. I refuse to give them 'Your Starship Needs You' pablum. These are all adults, and they deserve to know the truth about their situation, but I have to prepare them first."

Thoreson sucked in his breath over his lower lip. "You're right, sweetie. Sorry I made it sound like a video contract coup. There'd be riots if you don't handle this right."

"There may be riots anyhow, Kem," Jill sighed. "I simply hope I've set enough backfires to keep from having to fight an internal battle while we're engaging the Ichtons on the outside." She squeezed Kem on the forearm and headed toward the lift.

"Lieutenant!" Jill's office door slid open on a breathless woman she recognized as the day hostess of The Emerald, the fancy restaurant on Green deck. "Trouble!"

Jill was on her feet before she thought to ask. "What kind of trouble?"

The woman, about fifty standard years of age, wiped her round, pink face with her sateenoid sleeve. "Master Lyseo and a man are having a loud argument in the lounge. I tried to separate them, but they got around me. *He* told me not to interfere." Jill didn't have to ask which one "he" was. "They're *throwing* things. Can you do something before one of them gets hurt?"

Jill grabbed the hostess's arm and hustled her toward the lift. "What are they arguing about?"

"The other man—I don't know him—made some kind of disparaging remark about the last battle, you know, that we're losing by inches, and we'll be eaten alive by the Ichtons. Master Lyseo was just about down his throat in a millisecond."

Jill groaned. She pounded on the lift panel, as if hitting the buttons would make the transport come sooner. It wasn't like Lyseo to enter into an argument in public. If someone tried to drag him into a fight, he was more likely to zing his opponent and walk away.

The transit from Blue Fifteen to The Emerald took just a year and a half longer than forever. Jill was nearly bouncing up and down in impatience to get there and see what mischief Lyseo had managed to raise in the half hour since she had seen him.

To her relief, no one else had become involved in the altercation. Lyseo and a human male in an Indie's flight suit faced off across ten meters of cleared space in the restaurant lounge. There were broken dishes on the floor against the wall behind Lyseo, and an upside-down plant half out of its pot not far from the trader's feet.

The trader sneered at Lyseo, but did not close the distance between them. The impresario was looking uncommonly dangerous, and the Indie probably didn't dare to see what the older man was capable of. Jill eyed the man. He looked slightly familiar, reminding her of someone with whom she'd had recent contact. She wondered if he was one of the paladins, one whom she didn't know well; or one of her "problem children," a discontented civilian who had passed the psych tests showing that he was fit to join the *Hawking* but who couldn't resist stirring up trouble in a group. There was no time to check out her data base; tension was escalating right in front of her.

"It's a crock!" the man barked, his voice cracking with passionate fury. "The Fleet brass are feeding us a line of sewage that we can ever beat the Ichtons! We've lost too many ships, too many pilots. We might as well give up and go back—admit it!"

"Admit it?" Lyseo boomed, filling the room with his magnificent voice. "Never! The Fleet will not fail in its mission. Perhaps you're too young to remember it, sonny, but the odds were just as great in the Family war, which they won rather handily."

"Handily," the man mocked, striking himself under the chin with the edge of his hand. It was a gesture of insult. Lyseo glared. "After fifty years of war, pops, in case you've forgotten. We're finished. You people make me sick. I'm tired of being cooped up with people like you in this centimeter-square can prison. We're too vulnerable. We have to draw back."

"Retreat? In the name of all traditions, boy, how did you pass the psychological screening? Don't think of the *Hawking* as a soap bubble that could pop on the suntides. Think of it more as a leucocyte in the bloodstream of the galaxy, here to wipe out an intruding organism." The man snorted, and Lyseo raised his voice further. Jill stepped forward to intervene, but an upswept hand stayed her. "If you don't think we have a chance, then throw your strength into our effort, boy," Lyseo said. There was a ragged cheer of encouragement from the restaurant patrons at these words. He thrust out a hand toward them. "See? Your fellow *prisoners* agree. Stop telling us what can't be done, and help with what *can*."

His oration earned him a scattering of applause. Reddening, the young man realized that he was surrounded by an audience. Jill decided now was the perfect time to intervene and diffuse the situation, but she wasn't quick enough to stop the Indie from reacting. He cast about for something else to use as a weapon. His eye fell upon a huge flowered vase sitting on a shelf on the wall.

The hostess beside Jill moaned and clutched her hands together as the man seized it. He threw it at Lyseo, and she shrieked. Jill gasped.

With magnificent reflexes, Lyseo snagged the vase out of the air by its rim and tossed it to her. With her jaw agape, Jill caught the ceramic urn and wrapped both arms around it for safety. To her amazement, she noted that it was a lot lighter than expected, and much sturdier. Surreptitiously, she tapped one side with a knuckle. It gave off a dull *tank-tank* sound. It was a fake, made of extruded plastic. Then she noticed the time. On the fancy chrono on the wall, it was just past 11:45. So this was the morale-raising exhibition. The confrontation was a setup, engineered by Lyseo.

She was so involved with her discovery that she missed most of the parting shot the artist fired at the retreating trader, in which he declared that the Fleet was stronger, more enduring, more intelligently run, more adaptable than its opponent, however great its numbers, "And we shall be victorious!"

There was a round of frenzied applause. Lyseo affected then to notice that he, too, had an audience, and bowed, a little sheepishly, to his public. The restaurant patrons and a crowd who had gathered from surrounding levels at the rumor of a fight in The Emerald gave him a standing ovation. He waved jauntily to them and strode to greet Jill with a kiss. Gallantly, he took the vase from her hands and restored it to its pedestal.

"Next performance at 1900 hours," he whispered in her ear as the hostess hurried over to see that the expensive objet d'art was unharmed. "No autographs, please."

"Why, you fraud," Jill said admiringly. "Who was he?"

"One of your underrated and overworked theatrical company, my dear, only slightly disguised. He'll be master of his own repertory guild one day. Does a splendid burn and dudgeon. Shall we sit down, my dear? Did I not promise you lunch in this overpriced beanery?"

"Yes, but do I dare eat it with you?" Jill asked, shaking her head doubtfully. "You have shocking manners in public."

He threw back his head and laughed. "I promise you that all the crockery will remain on the table, and knives will be used for no other purpose than severing bites of food."

"It was a great performance," Jill admitted after they had ordered. "I was completely convinced. How do you do that so well? Your speech was perfect, it was so . . . so stirring."

"I believe in what I said," Lyseo replied simply, hands extended palms upward. "Otherwise I would not have risked my life, which I hold precious, in such a venture as this space station. You ought to know by now which things are the greasepaint and which things hold true throughout. Among those things that are true is that I love you, and you bring bright starlight to me in the midst of the void. There's little enough I can do to return this sublime, matchless favor."

He raised his glass to her, and Jill returned his toast. Even after nearly two years of daily contact, his words, his voice, had a way of making her quiver all over. While their love affair was hardly eternal bliss, Jill was happier than she had ever been. All her life, she had admired Lyseo's work. In the Alliance, it was hard to find many higher up in the entertainment pantheon than he. She was amazed to find herself hopelessly crazy about the man behind the public image, the sensitive, flamboyant, easily moved personality that relied on her, trusted her for her honesty. He didn't need fans; he had billions of them who loved everything he did, good or bad. Jill just loved the man himself.

Lyseo was in a good mood. The day's performance was a humorous pantomime that involved the master entertainer transforming his lean frame into semblances of each of the allied races, one after another. Soon, a catlike Emry was chasing a fluttering, birdlike Nedge all over the stage. The Nedge fled, in spite of the Emry's insistence that he was trying to be friendly, and that any suggestion of aggression was all a misunderstanding. Jill, sitting in the control room at Lyseo's insistence, howled along with the technicians. She dashed tears out of her eyes at the little Emry pouncing after the terrified Nedge, trying to make friends.

"Damn, he's good," the Khalian director said. "My cheek muscles hurt from grinning. You'd think we had a stageful of actors. How can he do it, day after day?"

"He never repeats himself," Jill said, watching the Emry herd the birdman into a corner, where he rubbed up against him, kitten style. "I love it, but I wonder how much it will do for interspecies relations."

"Are you joking, esteemed ma'am?" the director asked, hissing with laughter. "The Emry delegation already called asking for holocopies to use in their diplomatic training packets—for use in those very intersystem relations after we've saved their system." Jill noticed that the Khalian meant when, not if, and approved his optimism. "When Master Lyseo showed up and asked to observe them, they thought they'd soon be featuring in a show. They think Lyseo has a point."

Jill admitted that he did. With the appearance of new allies, members of the Alliance were having to adjust to the values and characteristics of each. Lyseo had found the one sure key to helping such diverse races understand one another: humor. Of all their new contacts, the Emry were the friendliest and least likely to need further exhortations to their emissaries to use tact. She wished the same could be said of others. In Jill's opinion, the Saurians, whose ravaged home planet definitely justified their grief, also demanded significant concessions based on their status as galactic orphans, making it impossible to feel much sympathy for them.

Besides, those aboard the *Hawking* were beginning to wonder if they themselves would survive much longer. The classified message from Commander Brand ordering training of any qualified civilian in station defense continued to distract her from enjoying her favorite entertainment. How long could they continue to supply manpower to run the ships and guns? In worst case, what if the battlestation itself had to participate in an attack? There would be nowhere safe for damaged ships to run to, no hospital facility free of enemy fire. Helpless isolation, in the midst of the galactic center, terrified Jill as much as it did any of the nervous civies or Indies on board. In the meantime, the *Hawking* made its way toward the Emry system with all speed. Brand must have liquid freon in his veins.

The thought of a last stand with all resources committed had already occurred to someone who phoned in to Jill's paladins, the audio jocks who kept the action going over the sixty broadcast channels circulating through the battle cruiser. It had been an uncomfortable rumor for the better part of the last month, undoubtedly since it became evident how difficult it was to wipe out an Ichton fleet. Independent traders plying the newly opened space lanes collected gossip and spread it among the civilian population of the *Hawking*. Jill had had to perform minor works of wonder to keep morale from plummeting each time more was discovered about the Ichton culture, or when the Ichtons staged surprise attacks on the Fleet. The fact that there hadn't been suicides was a miracle.

She couldn't take credit for the best of the spirit-raising. The morale laureate belonged jointly to Lyseo and Driscoll Strind, Jill's self-confessed knight in denim armor and the most popular audio jock in the ship. Strind, with his cool head and calming, deep baritone voice, maintained order and restored perspective on his daily show, and wasn't afraid to go all the way to the top brass to get answers his listeners needed to have. Strind had credibility shipwide. He was Jill's fervent supporter and unmentioned second choice for the instruction videos.

It might have been easier if she had simply approached the paladin first. Getting Lyseo to buckle down and recite the words in the simple script was a lot harder than she had even feared it might be.

"There are three hundred laser ports on the surface of this vessel," Lyseo complained, eyeing the minute gunnery chamber in the rear of the "south pole's" food service center. "Or so this uninspired missal tells me. Why choose this dreary outlet for me to do my piece?"

"Because it's well out of the way of daily operations, and ninety percent of the extant installations match the configuration or have elements in common with this one, including those aboard commissioned attack vessels," replied Gunnery Captain Thano Carrin, Jill's official consultant on the project. He was what she classified as "regular army," a specimen of the by-God, by-the-book military mind. "We want the information conveyed in this exercise to have the widest utility."

Lyseo winced, and Jill stepped in to translate. "You mean most of them look like this one," she said. Carrin nodded.

"Right. All the low-power gunports are identical. All that's needed when the alert sounds is for the person or persons closest to the port to strap in and connect the communicator to his, her, or its aural appendages, and fire away at the bugs—on command from the battle bridge, of course. They're really very simple to use. Anyone could do it."

"If anyone can," Lyseo said dangerously, "then *get* anyone. Anyone else."

Carrin turned red with impatience. Kem Thoreson leaped in to the rescue. "Yeah, but no one can show them how to do it better than you can, Ari. Go on."

Jill recognized Lyseo in a difficult mood, and stepped in. "Let's get the take done quickly, and get it over with, shall we?" she suggested.

With a calibration visor strapped around her head and resting firmly on her beak, the Nedge camerawoman set up holopoints around the inside of the gun turret, then placed a small, circular red light near the end of the sights and one to the side of the chamber next to the controls. "If you face the one that lights up, Master Lyseo, we'll be able to synch captioned credits in the edit."

Lyseo took his place in the gun emplacement and adjusted the seat to fit his frame. With a wink at Jill, he slipped on the communications gear and settled back. Captain Carrin pulled a headset from a wall niche and put it on.

"I'm taking the place of the battle bridge, citizen," he said. A tinny echo of his voice was audible from Lyseo's earphones. "I'll tell you what to do and give you target sightings to fire at. This is what you'd hear if this were an actual attack."

Lyseo nodded and tapped the earpiece with a long forefinger, the little gesture dynamic with focused energy. The actor's whole stance depicted fear, determination, and excitement all at once. Jill began to feel a sense of urgency, as if there were a real battle going on, and he was part of it. That was Lyseo's gift. He could make even a make-believe situation seem real and exciting.

Carrin ran him through the mechanics of operating the gun and how to read the screens. The actor was a quick study, picking up the mechanics accurately after one or two essays. "You are number 231. The Ichton ships fly slowly, but you have to take into account the fact that you're on a ship moving many times that of your opponent. Your own speed can ruin your aim, so unless you're an ace, let the targeting computer follow your mark. Once you've acquired your target and the computer locks on and verifies you have an enemy ship, not an ally, fire using the hand control."

Lyseo nodded, his eyes sweeping the skies and the tiny screen at eye level for imaginary enemy craft.

Carrin burst out suddenly, "Number 231, enemy at 245 degrees, 1500 klicks off center! Target and destroy!"

The gunner's head went up, eager eyes sweeping the darkness to the left of center. His laser's muzzle followed as he moved the hand controls, tracking the enemy craft. There was a muffled beeping as the computer locked on to a piece of space debris. Carrin glanced at the heads-up display to make certain that Lyseo's target wasn't live, then shouted, "Fire!"

The red tracer beam lanced out of the gun, striking the fragment of rock and ice, which exploded in a glorious display of white and hot yellow. "Well done, 231," Carrin congratulated him. Lyseo's shoulders relaxed.

The cinematographer signaled him to begin his lines. "To insure the continued defense of this space station and our newfound allies, the civilian and military administrations of the *Hawking* want you to know how to operate the defensive emplacements aboard the station and its attendant vessels when our commissioned comrades are wounded or disabled."

He swung around toward the second camera spot, raising a hand for a sweeping gesture. "Our numbers are few, but our spirit is great. *You* are a vital—OW!" The hand had whisked up past his chest and smacked solidly into the edge of the bulkhead. Lyseo curled up over his hand, hissing.

"Cut," the Nedge squawked into her throat mike. "Are you all right, citizen?"

"Confound it!" he shouted, his voice echoing in the metal-walled corridor. Jill winced. "Why are we using such a miserably small cubbyhole as this?"

"It's a typical laser station," Carrin replied, a little bewildered.

"I can't work in here," the star declared. "There isn't room for me. Look at my hand!" There was a dark purple bruise like a whip mark coming up across the back of Lyseo's palm. His knuckles were white.

"It should be all right, citizen," the Nedge said imperturbably, "if you keep your gestures small. Do you want to start again?"

"Why in blazes should I? This isn't Shakespeare or Eerk Kraakknek."

"Perhaps another location, with more elbow room, would be the answer?" Jill offered. She smiled hopefully at Lyseo. Her hope of getting the filming over in just a few takes was fast becoming a forlorn one. The crew gathered up the equipment and followed Captain Carrin to the next laser port. A Khalian gunner recognized the great Lyseo first and the captain's bars on the officer consultant second, and scrambled out of his seat with whiskers a-twitch.

Lyseo climbed into the seat and looked around him. "No." He crossed his arms, refusing even to put on the headset. "The lighting in here is dismal. I want another one."

"What?" Captain Carrin demanded. "This one is fine. It's big enough to jump rope in."

"I have full creative control," Lyseo reminded him. "Take me to a suitable setting, or let me go back to my dressing room. I have other engagements."

The little Khalian looked disappointed until the actor patted him on the back. "It's not your fault, little friend. Fortunes of war, fortunes of war, that is all."

The Khalian brightened, but he was the only happy being in the corridor. Resigned, the camera crew loaded up and trudged down the beltway, stopping at each laser port. Lyseo found something to complain of in each one, and rejected them in turn.

"I swear that if you're marching us around the perimeter just to get a rise out of us, I'll make the camera tech save all the takes and beam them straight back to the Alliance," Jill said warningly.

"I am quite serious about finding just the right place to make your dull little video," Lyseo replied. "It could only be your charms, raven-winged maiden, that led me to agree to such a tedious proposal. It will waste all the rest of my day and most of my night."

"Only if you don't cooperate," Jill observed. "We're only days out of Emry space. We don't have a lot of time to waste on theatrics, not especially yours."

"You wound me," Lyseo said plaintively. "I serve Art. Wouldn't you prefer that these videos be of the highest caliber that may be achieved? I promise the next setting we choose will be the last."

"All right." Jill allowed herself to be mollified.

"Yellow alert," the loudspeaker said as they emerged from the lift on the next level. "Yellow alert. Ion trails from Ichton-type ships have been detected in this area. Please stand by for any further instructions. That is all."

Well, that wasn't terribly surprising. The system had to be full of Ichton spoor, from the ships that had retreated from the battle with the Fleet. The indicators ran on automatic, sending the alarm directly to the computer without relaying it first through a living operator. The announcement repeated in several languages and on screens at the lift stations. Jill mentally crossed her fingers that the shrinks and the paladins were ready for another panic attack. The passengers waiting for the lift immediately looked nervous. One of them abandoned the queue and hurried down the aisle toward a cross-corridor. The others muttered among themselves as they boarded.

"Everyone's nervous," Jill commented. "There shouldn't be another Ichton for light-years around us."

"Every moment, it becomes more vital to strengthen our defense," observed Lyseo, carefully watching the faces of the people who passed him. The crew stopped a robot transport vehicle going toward the nearest laser ports and loaded the equipment aboard. Lyseo shook his head at the first few, all occupied by gunnery staff on alert, then, to Jill's surprise, nodded thoughtfully at the fourth. She signaled the robot brain to stop and let them off.

"What do you think, citizen?" asked the Nedge. "Will it do?"

"Plenty of room to swing about in," the actor said, surveying the alcove more closely, "even for my overblown posturing. Well lit, clean, almost ideal."

"I'll settle for almost," Jill said, and turned to the crew. "Set up, please. I'll clear things with the gunners."

Like the Khalian on the upper level, the two human female officers were delighted to make way for the great Lyseo.

"Will anyone be able to tell it was our port he sat in?" one asked. "Maybe if you let me leave the picture of my mother in it? She runs the arcade on Blue Fourteen. She'd be so proud."

"Certainly," the actor replied, glancing at the small holo of a middle-aged woman in a smock. "Her image will act as a reminder of those for whom we are fighting, and why we must succeed."

Both sergeants giggled and sighed while he clambered into the cockpit and strapped in. The emplacement was twice as wide as most of the others to make room for a second laser and operator.

Carrin hooked himself up to the corridor-side headset and ran Lyseo through the operations once again. Lyseo checked the mechanism of the new weapon, getting used to the differences between its action and the one with which he had worked before. When the actor nodded that he was ready, Carrin started him off with mock targets. The Nedge muttered quiet directions to her crew. She made quiet clicking sounds of approval to herself as Lyseo provided them with good action shots full of expression that also showed clearly how the hands were placed, and what use should be made of the monitors and computer.

"Gunner 198," Carrin barked, "target coming around to you at 90—that's three o'clock, mister—maximum range."

"I hear you, sir," Lyseo responded, swiveling the laser to meet it.

"Red alert," the computerized voice announced over the tannoy. "Red alert. All crew to battlestations. All civilians to secured areas. Ichton fighters approaching. Red alert."

Jill slammed her palm against a wall-mounted communicator. "Battle bridge, this is Lieutenant FarSeeker. What's going on out there?"

The reply crackled through the speaker. "A bunch of orphan fighters without a mother ship, Lieutenant. Looks like they're on a suicide mission to do what damage they can because they can't get away. Secure to quarters or battlestation. Out."

"Out," she replied.

Jill's eyes widened. A sneak attack! The Ichtons must have set up an ambush inside the Oort cloud surrounding the system. People and vehicles hurried in all directions through the wide hall, rushing toward their stations. An alarm went off, and there was shouting and the squeal of straining machinery.

"Target destroyed, sir," Lyseo told the headset microphone crisply, and Carrin nodded in response, as lost in playacting as the dramatist himself.

On the small amber screen under Lyseo's nose, the unmistakable formation of Ichton fighters moved into target range The first sign of them that was visible to the naked eye was the gleam of the small lights at the extremes of each small ship.

"Multiple targets approaching at 135 degrees, 10,000 klicks from center," Carrin recited automatically, and stopped, surprised, as he realized that this enemy was real. One of the gunners sprang into her seat and strapped in. "Get him out of there," she barked, gesturing at the actor.

"Sir, may I take over for you now?" the other gunner asked, holding out her hand to the actor.

"I have it!" Lyseo announced, tracking it with his laser and paying no attention to the young woman. The chair swiveled around and downward.

Startled, the officer glanced at Carrin for orders. Carrin looked at Jill. Jill shrugged. There were 256 laser emplacements arrayed about the *Hawking*. Sixty or more were covering this quadrant of the space station's defenses. If one was manned by a neophyte, it shouldn't hurt anything. Carrin nodded once, sharply, giving approval. The camera crew, who had started to take down their equipment, hastily reconnected everything.

"Steady . . . steady," Lyseo admonished his targeting computer. "Hold it right there, you! Yes! Permission to fire?"

"Given," Carrin said, hearing the word echoed a second later on the headset from the battle bridge. Lyseo squeezed the trigger, causing the red beam to lance out into the darkness. Other red needles joined it, converging on a target a long way off. There was a tiny explosion of white that bloomed and winked out.

"He got one," the Nedge said excitedly. "Well done, citizen!" The crew cheered.

Lyseo wasn't listening. With the single-mindedness for which he was famous, he had immersed himself in what he was doing, and doing it incredibly well for having had only one lesson, Jill thought.

The *Hawking*'s fighters scrambled within seconds, and green dots joined the white ones on the small amber screen. Lyseo's chair swung first one way and another as he lined up on targets. He shot at several more, but the computer confirmed no other kills besides the first one. Dozens of red tracer lights lanced out alongside his, searching for the touch of Ichton craft. The Fleet fighters were also getting kills several seconds before the gunners' eyes registered that their targets weren't out there anymore. White fire bloomed occasionally from above or below them as a plasma torpedo launched from the larger cannon at the *Hawking*'s poles.

There were fewer than sixty Ichton fighters. In minutes, the battle was at an end. The loudspeaker announced that the enemy had been destroyed, and the siren emitted two blasts for all clear. The corridor was filled with cheers and hoots of relief. Jill was relieved, too. The *Hawking* could defend herself, in an emergency. She hoped she never had to live through it again.

Lyseo fell back in the chair with a gasp, as if he had been swimming underwater. He glanced up at the camera at his shoulder, which was still recording.

"There," he said, drawing himself up with dignity. "Now, if *I* can do it, *anyone* can do it."

"Wonderful," crowed the Nedge.

"That was really well done, sir," one of the gunners said. He turned to look at her. "You've got a natural eye for it."

Surprised eyebrows arched into his hairline, Lyseo glanced over at Jill, who raised her hands and began to applaud. She was joined by Carrin, the film crew, and the two gunners.

"Encore!" Jill called, her eyes filled with mischief. "Encore!"

"My dear young lady," he said, grinning at her affectionately, "Lyseo *never* repeats himself." Unbuckling the straps, he eased himself out of the seat and stretched. "That was a fascinating experience, citizens, but I have no wish to repeat it. Besides, I have an appointment." He took Jill's arm and steered her away toward the nearest lift.

"Where are we going?" Jill asked, looking over her shoulder at the crew. The Nedge cocked her head, asking for permission. Helplessly, Jill nodded back. The crew began to put away the equipment. There was plenty of good footage, and it would make a dynamic training video. There was the ring of truth in every single frame. The first chance she got, she'd call up Driscoll Strind and leak news of the video to him. People would be clamoring to see it before they thought about the fact it was meant to drag them out to do active duty. There might be a number of volunteer gunners, all Lyseo fans who wanted to emulate their idol.

As for Lyseo himself? "Come, my dear," he urged her, escorting her into the lift. "If we hurry, you can catch my next surprise performance. I'm planning to have a duel in the video library. Data cubes at thirty paces. My opponent takes a dive on the fourth toss." He grinned, the lazy, magnificent smile that Jill loved. "I always prefer to fight battles that I know I'm going to win."

THE LAST RESERVE

NAPOLEON IS OFTEN quoted as saying that the army with the last reserve wins the battle. After three days orbiting the Emry system, it was apparent to Anton Brand that without his introducing some new factor they would be unable to drive the Ichtons away from the already-battered Emry home world.

In an attempt to give the Emry some relief Brand ordered a complete withdrawal. He had hoped the Ichtons would follow his ships outward, as they had during the earlier parts of the month-long battle. Instead they used the pause to redouble their attack on Emry. It was apparent that the Ichtons were continuing their new policy of destroying all opposition at any cost. He would have to recommit quickly or lose the planet.

Six hours after the withdrawal a squadron of the largest of the Fleet ships made a near light-speed run through the Emry system. Streaking past the Ichton screen they managed to destroy two more of the ten remaining mother ships. But the Ichtons responded quickly by throwing up a barrage ahead of the fast-moving ships. Moving too rapidly to avoid the missiles and mines, the Fleet force lost three of their eight heavy cruisers. This was too high a price and Commander Brand forbid any repeat of the maneuver.

Two days after the loss of the cruisers the battle had degenerated into a series of strikes on the Ichtons who had formed a widespread globe around their mother ships. This globe then settled into a distant orbit around Emry and anytime they were not directly engaged by the Fleet ships the Ichtons returned to the merciless bombardment of the planet. Anton Brand had not left the battle bridge since ordering the withdrawal four days earlier. He had slept only in short naps, unable to pull himself away from the battle. Finally Dr. Althea Morgan appeared and threatened to declare him medically incompetent unless he slept.

As it turned out, Commander Brand only got three hours rest before the dramatic conclusion of the battle.

BATTLE OFFERING

by Katherine Kurtz

THE CATASTROPHIC FATE of the Gerson world left scant reason to suppose that the enemy was anything other than pitiless and brutal. More than an hour of visual recording brought along by the last of the Gersons to escape told of planetary devastation almost beyond imagining, and on a scale hitherto unknown in Alliance memory except as a result of natural disaster.

For the gentle, bearlike Gersons had resisted invasion all too well. Before the coming of the Ichtons, the Gerson planet had been blanketed by rich farmlands and lush forests almost primeval by most worlds' standards, its land masses girdled by wide seas teeming with life. Modest technological achievement had given the Gersons reasonable commerce with their nearest neighbors in the galactic core, but had also made their world ripe for exploitation by a race whose imperative was to expand, whatever the cost to other life-forms.

Now the Gerson world was a smoldering cinder. The Ichtons destroyed what would not submit. Impersonal and efficient, the Ichtons simply overwhelmed whatever stood in their path, no matter the level of indigenous civilization. This was not mere policy; it was a fact of existence. They had been hurt too much to sacrifice any warriors or ships to preserving resources while subduing a new planet. Any resistance by cities or military installations provoked immediate neutralization by antimatter and other bombing, followed by occupation of egg colony sites and the beginning of the stripping and exploitation of all the planet's resources.

The unvarying pattern of Ichton expansion then became a cold, methodical extermination of all higher life-forms. The dead were eaten, whatever their species; all plant life likewise became fodder for the expanding Ichton colonies. Like the legendary Terran locusts they somewhat resembled, the Ichtons left nothing living where their swarms had passed. Forbearance and compassion were not terms within the Ichton comprehension.

Shaking his head, Commander Anton Brand punched the Cancel button on the arm of his recliner and laid his head back, though he did not close his eyes. He had seen the recording too many times already, and the scenes he had cut short already haunted what little sleep he managed to steal between bouts of battle. The slagged Gerson cities and barren, windswept plains were bad enough. But the worst was the final scene—an aerial glimpse of a cowering Gerson female trying desperately to shield her cub from the notice of half a dozen Ichton soldiers advancing through a burning village. The first time Brand had watched the Ichtons dismember the pair and begin devouring them alive, he had been all but physically ill.

The twittering sound of his intercom broke the intensity of unwanted memory and recalled him to the present, where the Ichtons were threatening to add another world to the string of stripped and lifeless husks already left in their wake. The little ready room adjacent to the command bridge was his personal hideaway for snatching a few minutes' respite from the tension of command, but it was also conveniently close enough that he could never really escape.

Thumbing the response plate, he said, "Brand here."

"Tashi here, Commander," said his second-in-command. "Ah—we have an incident developing down on Yellow Two, in one of the destroyer bays. It seems a couple of dozen Gersons, all armed, are asking for one of the destroyers. I've already got a security team on the scene, and so far it hasn't gotten ugly, yet. Now the Gersons are demanding to speak to you specifically. The leader's name is Hooth. He was the commander of that last ship that came in with the Gerson survivors. Shall I have security gas the lot and then clear the bay, or do you want to talk to them?"

"Let me talk to them," Brand said, sitting upright and swinging his feet to the floor. "The Gersons have been through enough, without their own allies turning on them. Who's the security officer in charge?"

"Tucker, sir. He's a level head, and he likes the Gersons, as you know, but it's getting really touchy."

"On my way," Brand said.

Shaking his head, he buckled on his side arm and headed out the door. This move by the Gersons did not really surprise him. He supposed it was only natural to want to strike back at least one small blow for Gerson pride. Out of a onetime population of close to three billion, something less than one hundred Gersons remained. The sheer scale of the genocide carried out by the Ichtons was simply beyond the comprehension of most sentient beings. The Gersons were a noble race, and had seemed to accept their situation with more stoic resignation than one might have expected, but Brand knew how easily anger and helplessness could shift into heroic but futile gesture.

The grav-lift doors were just closing as he approached, and he jogged a few steps to touch the call plate before the lift could leave. The doors immediately retracted to the turning form of a medical officer, who grinned and nodded as she saw him. Anton Brand was, had been, one of the Fleet's rising stars. Tall, and always thin, he had crossed into the painfully thin category months earlier. He had retained the sparkle in his bright blue eyes, but it was surrounded with the wrinkles and dark spots you can only gain from too much repsonsibility and too little sleep.

" 'Lo, Anton," she said. "That bad?"

"I hope not," he muttered as he ducked in beside her and added, in the direction of the lift's computer, "Deck Yellow Two, command override."

"Right," she said, she and Brand both steadying themselves on grab handles as the lift began to drop with stomach-wrenching speed. "Forget I asked."

Brand gave her a sidelong look and a mirthless smile. Before the war, Maggie Conroy had been a medical planning specialist—no minor function on a ship the size of the *Stephen Hawking*. Of late, however, emergency trauma management had become the specialty of no choice for nearly all Fleet medical personnel. She was wearing a tan lab coat over blue surgical scrubs, with a medical field kit slung over one shoulder.

"Sorry, Maggie. Busy in your section?"

"When is it anything else, these days?" she replied. "I've just been up to the command bridge to make certain everybody's still alert. How're you doing?"

"Ask me in about an hour," he said. "Sheer adrenaline cancels out a lot of ordinary fatigue."

She cocked her head at him. "Sounds serious. Can I help?"

"Depends on how much you know about Gersons. They're asking for a destroyer. What do you want to bet they're considering a suicide run?"

The lift came to a halt with another queasing of stomachs, and the doors sighed open on an impatient-looking security lieutenant and a sergeant at arms.

"Too late, Commander," the lieutenant said, gesturing down a right-angle corridor and already heading out. "Tucker just gave the order to flood the bay with knockout gas. They were trying to take the ship."

"Tell him to belay that order, *now*!" Brand retorted, breaking into a run.

He could hear the lieutenant relaying the message, was aware of the sergeant at arms and Maggie following close behind him as he ran. There were several more security officers in the little control module outside the series of airlocks that led into the docking bay in question, and Brand could hear the whine of large turbo fans starting up as he reached the module.

"Sorry, Commander, but everybody's down," one of the men said. "They started throwing riggers off the boarding ramp. They'd also captured a couple of access keys. If they'd gotten aboard, there wouldn't have been anything we could do to stop them taking the ship."

On one of the viewscreens of the bay's interior, Brand could see dozens of green-clothed Gersons sprawled across the decks just outside the ship, security men in gas filter masks moving among them to remove weapons. The boarding ramp was choked with unconscious tech personnel, and security men were beginning to carry them off and lay them out in neat rows.

Brand took it all in and sighed. Sometimes, despite the best of intentions, things just didn't work out the way they should. The knockout gas would leave no permanent effects, but it was hardly conducive to leaving the Gersons in any positive frame of mind, when they came around.

"How much of a dose did they get?" Brand asked. "Has Med been called?"

"Yes to the last, sir, and I'd say everybody will be down for half an hour or so," the man said. "For the Gersons, it might be a little more or less. The gas is safe for a broad band of species, but I'm not sure exactly how the dosage works for them."

Brand glanced at Maggie. "What about it, Mags?"

She shook her head. "No problem. Larger body mass, smaller proportional dose. If anything, they'll recover more quickly than the humans, barring unusual reactions of individuals. Do you want me to start checking them, while we wait for the Meds?"

"Let's do that," he said. They headed for the set of airlocks that led into the docking bay in question. Because the bays were routinely opened to hard space, inside entrance and egress to them was protected by not one but two airlocks set in serial. As they entered the first lock and its safety doors sighed closed behind them, the doors ahead parted on a tall, sandy-haired security captain with a gas filter mask pushed up on top of his head.

"Tuck, I'm disappointed," Brand said, already moving forward. "Didn't they tell you I was on my way down?"

"Aye, sir, they did," Tucker replied, turning to accompany them back into the intermediate lock he had just left. "Unfortunately, the Gersons had already decided to take matters into their own hands by then. I stopped the gas as soon as I got your counter-order, but it was too late. Everybody should be up and about in a little while, though."

"Were they really trying to take the ship?" Maggie asked as they came through the last of the doors and into the bay, heading for the downed Gersons sprawled all around the ship.

"Sure looks that way," Tucker said. As Maggie knelt to check the nearest Gerson, he returned his attention to Brand. "Apparently they came in just as the tech crew had finished rearming it, and wanted to know how to rig the warp engines to overload."

Maggie glanced up sharply at that, but Brand only shook his head.

"Can't say I blame them," he said. "But I haven't got destroyers to spare. You think they were serious?"

"Sure sounds that way," Tucker replied. "They talked most with one of the tech crew, before we got called in. He's over there." He gestured toward the sprawled figure of a balding little man whose sleeve patches proclaimed him a spec-5 armorer. "Name's Max Faber. His argument was actually making a lot of sense, before we had to gas everybody."

Brand cast his eyes over the clutter of sleeping humans and Gersons and shook his head.

"All right. I've got to get back up to the command bridge. Tuck, when they're awake again, I want to see the ringleaders in the ward room. Give me Hooth and a couple or three of his head honchos. Include Mr. Faber, too. I'd like to hear his arguments to justify a suicide run by the last of a race. And, Maggie, can you bird-dog this for me, make certain everybody's recovered before I start chewing ass?"

"I'll take care of everything," she said. "Give us a couple of hours, though. You've heard of people who wake up as grumpy as a bear that's been woken out of hibernation? Well, the Gersons bear more than a physical resemblance to their ursine forbears—if you'll pardon the multiple plays on words."

Brand grimaced and made a gesture of dismissal, then headed back out of the docking bay.

Captain Tashi did not glance back as Brand stepped out of the darkened passage that was the transition from the bright-lit outside corridor to the dim lighting of the command bridge, but Brand knew his arrival had been noted. Command staff wore personal coders that not only admitted them to the bridge but broadcast a short sequence of pips in the earphones of duty personnel, so that visual attention need not be diverted from what could be vital continuity in a battle situation.

It was always far quieter than Brand expected it to be, for the virtual nerve center of the *Hawking*. The bridge was mostly dark, lit primarily by the several dozen numbered status screens ranged to either side of the central command plinth and the enormous holotank set close to the far wall. Command staff manned five workstations in the pit between the tank and the command plinth. Two of them were battle tacticians when the *Hawking* was on alert, each provided with computer links to the ship's battle bridge and her gun decks; the other three were technicians who oversaw nondefense aspects of the ship's operation.

Alert status also meant that the command bridge duplicated many of the functions of fire control, over on the battle bridge, necessary for overall coordination when the *Hawking* was under periodic attack. Colored dots floated in the tank to mark the location of the ships engaged in the battle: white for Fleet ships, blue for allies, and red for the Ichton forces. The images in the tank kept changing as Tashi shifted first one screen and then another into the tank to get a fresh perspective, occasionally speaking softly into a tiny microphone attached to an earpiece in one ear.

Not speaking, Brand mounted the three steps of the command plinth and crouched beside the command chair, glancing at the information display screen embedded in the left chair arm and then letting his gaze range quickly over the large status screens and then on to the huge three-dimensional tank that showed the battle under active consideration. Near the center of the tank, not to scale, floated a small, semitransparent greenish sphere meant to represent the besieged Emry planet, closely surrounded by moving red dots, some of them far larger than others and pulsing. The latter were Ichton mother ships, most desirous of all targets because they carried the precious Ichton eggs, whose protection was the sole focus of the Ichton support fleet.

Once the mother ships landed on a planet and began setting up egg colonies, and especially once they became entrenched, they were much more difficult to destroy. Most desirable was to destroy such ships while still in space, since this also eliminated thousands of future Ichton soldiers. But even heavy damage to one would draw off Ichton escort vessels in an attempt to save the eggs—which lessened the number of ships available to resist Alliance forces as they swept in on desultory raids.

Such a raid was in progress now. From far on the right of the tank, a cluster of perhaps eight small blue dots was crawling toward one of the Ichton mother ships, small red dots beginning to swarm outward from it toward the blue ones.

"Emry?" Brand asked quietly.

"Yes," Tashi murmured, not taking his eyes from the tank. "They aren't going to make it, though." He hit a switch in his right armrest. "Abort. Break off."

At first nothing seemed to happen, but then the last four blue dots veered off in an oblique line, away from the advancing red dots. But the other four continued on.

"Call them off, damn it! They aren't going to get through," Tashi said into his mike.

But the blue dots kept going, now engaging with the Ichton ships. Where red and blue dots touched, a tiny flash always left only one dot lit. The blue dots lost three, but the red dots lost five. The remaining blue dot continued on, now heading directly toward the closet mother ship, its former escort blue dots now swarming in behind it to weave erratically among the defending red dots—and far more of the red dots went out than blue ones.

"God, they're brave little suckers, but it isn't going to work," Tashi whispered, now clenching his left fist to his mouth, trying to will the blue dots to hold on. The blue dot heading for the Ichton mother ship was still on course, two more red dots flicking out as Brand and Tashi watched. But when the blue dot finally touched the mother ship, it was the blue dot that disappeared.

"Damn!" Tashi whispered.

But even as he shook his head in denial, Brand was touching his sleeve and gesturing toward the tank, where one of the tacticians had changed the scene to a closer perspective of the Ichton mother ship. Actual visual contact was not possible at this distance, but from the movements of the many red dots now converging on the mother ship, it soon became clear that the last Emry ship had not been the only casualty of the ultimate engagement.

"I think they may just have holed her," Brand said, calling up a display on the chair-arm screen and scanning the readout. "By God, they did. And that's almost better than a kill, because they have to swarm in and try to save as many eggs as possible. Dirty fighting, but it may be all we've got."

They watched the display for another few seconds; then one of the tacticians had shifted to another perspective, another battle in progress, and Tashi regained his objectivity. After another little while, Brand took over, figuring he might as well give his second a break until it was time to go and deal with the Gersons.

He knew what the Gersons probably had in mind; just like what the Emry had just done, but on a larger scale. A destroyer rigged to overload its warp engines in the middle of an Ichton battle formation could wreak unbelievable havoc. The firepower of a destroyer, in and of itself, was formidable; but the energy contained in a destroyer's warp drive could be made to explode almost like a small star, if it was all released at once. It was not something that could be done by remote control; but it could be done by a willing crew, determined to settle at least a small part of the debt incurred by the enemy on a world many light-years away. But the Gersons were the last of their race. Not only that, destroyers were in short supply.

He ran battles for another three hours, by which time he was ready to let Tashi take over again. He was beginning to be concerned as to why he had not yet heard from Tucker about the Gersons. He hoped Maggie had not underestimated the effect of the knockout gas; the Gersons were aliens, after all. He had retreated to his ready room and was just preparing to call Security and get an update when the speaker twittered on his intercom. The sound startled him, for he had been just about to press his thumb to the button. He pushed the Receive button instead.

"Brand here."

"Anton, it's Maggie," said a familiar voice. "Would you like to come down to the ward room? I think we may have worked out a compromise solution to your problem."

"What compromise?" he replied. "What problem? They're the last of their race, Maggie. I can't let them go on a suicide mission, even if I could spare a ship."

"Just come to the ward room," she said. "They've gotten over their mad about the gas. But they've got some interesting arguments. Out."

He did up the collar of his tunic to reinforce an appearance of authority, told Tashi where he would be, and headed for the ward room. Two of Tucker's security men were standing guard outside, and came to attention as he approached.

"No one's armed except you, Commander," one of the men said, just before he activated the control that made the door retract.

They were standing around a small conference table over to one side of the room, Tucker and Maggie flanking the chair reserved for him. A slight, balding man in Fleet uniform sat to Tucker's left, his head resting on one hand, and four of the bearlike Gersons occupied the other end of the table, one of them a female. Gerson males towered over most humans by nearly a head, but the females were more delicately boned and rarely came past Brand's shoulder. Brand thought he recognized this particular one: Joli, Hooth's mate. It was certainly Hooth at the other end of the table: a glossy, black-furred Gerson obviously in his prime, proud and impressive.

All eyes turned in Brand's direction as he entered the room. Tucker looked very grim, Maggie more wistfully expectant. The human tech raised his head but did not stand, probably nursing the grandfather of all hangovers from the knockout gas, though all of the Gersons seemed fine. As Brand sat between Tucker and Maggie and everyone else also sat, he touched the Translator button on his collar to activate it.

"Hoidah, Hooth, Gersonu," he said, which totally exhausted his command of the Gersons' language.

Hooth lifted his sleek muzzle in what might have been an expression of disbelief in a human. Brand suspected it had something to do with his accent, but the other Gersons' great bear-jaws parted in what he imagined were grins, or at least small smiles, pleased that he had made the effort. His translator's flat, uninflected voice whispered, *Greetings, Hooth, People of Gerson.* The Gersons were adjusting little speaker buttons in their rounded, furry ears, their black shoe-button eyes darting back and forth among themselves.

"Commander Brand," Hooth said. "I offer friendship." What he actually said sounded like a series of growls and whines, but the translator gave him an electronic basso voice with a trace of a Germanic accent.

"And I offer friendship to the Gersons," Brand acknowledged as he turned his attention to the human specialist. "And you are?"

"Spec-5 Max Faber, Commander," the little man said. "Ah—sorry about the little contretemps down on Green deck. The—ah—Gersons wanted me to turn over the *Prince Buthelezi* and destruct-rig it."

"So I understand." Brand turned his attention back to Hooth. "Would you mind telling me exactly what you proposed to do with a destruct-rigged destroyer, Hooth?"

"We want to take it into the center of the Ichton fleet," Hooth's translated voice said. "Since we would not be planning to come out again, we can divert all energy to the shields until we are very close to a mother ship, using the ship's missiles and lasers to keep the enemy at bay as we go. When we overload the warp engines, the explosion will destroy many Ichton ships."

Brand leaned back in his chair. "I can't let you do it, Hooth. Aside from the fact that I haven't got any extra destroyers to intentionally blow up, you're the last of your race. I won't be a party to genocide."

Hooth looked away for a moment, exchanging a poignant glance with his mate, then back at Brand.

"Commander, we Gersons have loved life as well as any other sentient creature. But the Ichtons have destroyed our world. They have destroyed our race. Now they will destroy the Emry and perhaps many other races, if they are not stopped. If we can prevent the destruction of even one other race, then perhaps our own obliteration will not have been for nothing."

Brand glanced at the other three Gersons, especially at the female, with one pawlike hand laid protectively over her stomach, then back at Hooth.

"Hooth, this is a noble thing you ask to do, but I can't allow it. If you go like this, you finish what the Ichtons started."

"If we stay, the same thing is accomplished," Hooth replied. "And yet—" He glanced at Maggie. "Commander, we are but eighty-four individuals remaining. Only twenty-six are females. Three of those are past breeding age. But—" He glanced uneasily at Maggie again. "I cannot explain, Doctor."

Maggie nodded, turning back to Brand. "Theoretically, we have the medical technology to possibly reestablish the Gerson race, Commander. With a pool of only twenty-three breeding females, it won't be easy or fast—but it won't happen at all, if we lose this war.

"So what I'm proposing is a way to give the Gerson race their best chance of survival, and still allow Hooth and some of his people to make a more direct contribution to the war effort. If we can preserve the full gene pool from all the remaining Gersons, a future in vitro fertilization program might be possible. To even have a chance of starting it, we'd need to collect and freeze sperm donations from all the males who elect to go on the mission Hooth is proposing. Needless to say, none of the females could go. Even then, there's no guarantee that we'll ever be given the opportunity to try the in vitro project. But at least it's a chance."

Brand was shaking his head by the time she finished. "Maggie, this is crazy," he said. "Oh, I know enough about in vitro fertilization to know that it should be theoretically possible to reestablish a race from such a small sample, but—" He shook his head again. "It still doesn't justify sending a shipload of Gerson males to their deaths. I've got enough to worry about without that on my conscience. I may have to commit the *Hawking* to battle—and that *still* might not be enough to win."

"Defeatist talk, Anton," Maggie said.

And Hooth said, "If the allies lost the Battle of Emry, and the Gersons had not given fully of their efforts, we would always hold ourselves partially responsible for the annihilation of another race besides our own. And if the Alliance does lose this battle, and eventually the war, it will not matter what any of us do today. You have seen the swath of destruction the Ichtons leave in their wake. If the Ichtons are not stopped, they will eventually reach the home worlds of the Alliance itself."

Brand sighed, knowing that in this last, at least, the Gerson was right; and knowing that he had no choice but to grant the request of these gallant beings who were willing to put everything on the line to stop an enemy that annihilated whole races. Even if he couldn't spare a destroyer. He glanced at Faber.

"What about it, Mr. Faber? If I did allow what the Gersons ask, could it really make that much difference?"

Faber nodded. "Oh, yes. Depending on how deeply they were able to penetrate the Ichton fleet, they could do an enormous amount of damage. They might take out two, maybe three mother ships, and who knows how many escorts and even light cruisers. Furthermore, they could open a breach in the Ichton line to give us the opportunity for follow through. It could be the best bet we've got to break the impasse."

"*Could,* Mr. Faber?" Brand asked. "Or *would*?"

Faber shrugged and shook his head. "It's just too close to call, Commander."

Brand pursed his lips and let out a low whistle, then glanced uncomfortably at the waiting Hooth.

"All right," he said quietly. "I can't say I'm happy about this. But if you're determined to do it, I can't deny the possible value to the Alliance. I shall miss your courage, Hooth—yours and all your people."

Hooth inclined his shaggy bear-head.

"It is easy enough to be brave going into battle, knowing you will die," he said, slowly reaching across to take his mate's hand. "I think perhaps it is harder to live, to stay behind and one day become the mother of the race."

"No!" Joli said fiercely. "I will not let you go without me. This right I claim, who have borne you eight healthy cubs but have not the will to live without you."

"Hush, we will speak of this later," Hooth said. "Commander Brand, I apologize for my mate's impetuous words. I ask that you make all necessary arrangements as soon as possible, for I know that this battle weighs heavily upon you, and wondering whether the *Hawking* itself must eventually be called into battle. Dr. Conroy, we will go to my people now, to explain what is required."

"She'll join you in a few minutes," Brand said, staying Maggie with a gesture as Hooth and his companions rose. "Mr. Tucker, why don't you show them where to go?"

"Med Blue, Tuck," Maggie said, sitting back down.

When they had gone, Brand glanced at Faber.

"How long will it take to rig the ship?"

"Four to six hours. You really want me to do it?"

Brand nodded. "I have to let them try it. It really could make the difference in the war. Do we have a choice of destroyers?"

Faber shook his head. "The others are out on patrol. I'd have picked the *General Schwartzkopf*—she's already taken a lot of battle damage—but the *Prince Buthelezi* is what's available. A pity, because she's the best of the lot."

"Well, perhaps that's what they need, to give them the best chance to make their sacrifice count for something. Make sure they have a full complement of missiles, everything they can possibly throw at the Ichtons on their way in. Do the Gersons have the technical ability to operate the ship at full efficiency?"

"Well, it isn't what they're used to, but I can jury-rig something, simplify some of the controls. That's part of what will take a while. She's already armed, though. It's mainly a matter of disengaging the fail-safes and rigging so that the warp drive will blow when Hooth is ready, and not before. When it does blow, we'd better be farther out than we are now, and warn any other of our vessels likely to be in close."

"You'd better get on it, then."

When Faber had gone, Brand glanced at Maggie.

"I might have known you'd come up with something like this," he said. "Will it really work?"

She shrugged. "Given ideal conditions and some peace, it might," she said. "Meanwhile, if Hooth and his crew are determined to make this gesture—which could well make the major difference we've been praying for—they've also done everything they could to ensure the survival of their race. Their genetic heritage survives, even if the individuals don't—at least so long as the *Hawking* survives. And if they *are* to end here—well, I think it means a lot to them to be able to do *something*, as a final statement of their race. It isn't a terrible memorial, you know. *Here died the last of the Gerson race, who offered up their lives to buy the survival of the Emry and all other races who otherwise might have fallen to Ichton oppression.*"

"Yeah," Brand whispered. *"Dulce et decorum est, pro patria mori."*

"No, 'Greater love hath no man than this: that he lay down his life for his friends,' " Maggie said. "That's a lot closer to the Gerson philosophy, regardless of the fact that they'd never heard of Christianity until the Ichtons had nearly wiped them out."

"What about Hooth's mate—Joli, is it?"

"What about her?"

"Will he let her go? I should think she's still of breeding age."

"Oh, she is. We've already taken specimens from her and from Hooth. We had to make certain that the in vitro procedure would work as well for Gersons as it does for humans."

"Does it?"

She grinned. "I'm happy to report that we have several dozen Hooth and Joli zygotes tucked away in our freezers, and we'll hit him up for another donation for the Gerson sperm bank after we've done everybody else who's going. We decided to go ahead and take all of Joli's eggs while we were at it, but she can still be a surrogate mother when the time comes."

"Not if she goes with Hooth."

"Oh, she isn't going."

"She thinks she is."

Maggie smiled. "Hooth says she isn't. I had to promise him that I'd make certain she didn't, or he wouldn't agree to any of the rest."

"God, what a tangled web, Maggie."

"Survival, Anton. It's the strongest instinct there is, no matter what the species." She patted his arm and rose. "But I'd better get back to the lab and supervise. I have to say that the thought of a room full of giant teddy bears—well, let's just say that it isn't exactly the kind of family practice I used to have. Still, it beats emergency trauma."

Brand managed to restrain a grin until she had left the room, but his mirth had totally died away by the time he called Tashi and two of the gunnery officers to the ward room to brief them on the plan that was taking shape in his mind.

"I'm trying to avoid committing the *Hawking,* as you know, but we may not have that option," he said when he had finished telling them what the Gersons wanted to do. "Sacrificing the *Buthelezi* may give us the edge we need. It isn't the sort of thing I could *ask* anyone to do, but since the Gersons have not only volunteered but practically insisted, it behooves us to make the most of what it will cost them."

The mood was sober in the little ward room, and one of the gunnery officers tapped a finger on the tabletop in agitation.

"It's a big gamble," she said. "If Hooth can get the *Buthelezi* in close enough to waste a mother ship or two, that's only to the good, but it's hard to predict how the Ichtons would react to destruction on that scale. Their usual pattern is to swarm to the rescue of wounded egg ships, and not pay much attention to anything else. I'm not sure they really understand the idea of vengeance. But if we wreak enough destruction among the mother ships—"

"Yeah," said the other gunnery officer. "They might just pull out, flatten what's left of the planet, and move out for their next destination—cut their losses. That gets them out of here, but bad luck for the Emry."

"How close could we get, if I wanted to piggyback the *Buthelezi* in, give it a head start?" Brand asked.

The two gunners exchanged dubious looks.

"Big risk, Commander," said the woman. "Emerging from warp in occupied space could be disaster for us and them. On the other hand, a mere close encounter could simply disrupt the drives of nearby smaller Ichton escorts. I presume you'd warp in and out as quickly as possible—unless you're thinking to do with the *Hawking* what the Gersons intend with the *Buthelezi*."

"I didn't have it in mind to take us on a suicide run," Brand said sourly. "But if the ship didn't have to carry anything but missiles and could overcharge all the turrets because they didn't need to conserve fuel, one ship might make a difference. How long would we have to be in close, to safely disgorge the *Buthelezi,* give it time to make distance, and get us out of there?"

The male gunner cocked his head. "Five minutes? Eight, at the outside. Our shields will hold for that long against anything short of a dreadnought, and surprise will be on our side. The last thing they'll be expecting is to have the *Hawking* suddenly pop into normal space right in the middle of their fleet. But even if our shields protect us from most of what they could throw at us, they could do a lot of damage. As we have already seen, they wouldn't hesitate to ram us. The cost could be high."

They continued discussing options for another quarter hour, after which Brand gave them his decision and then retired to get some sleep. The Gersons' farewell appearance was nothing he intended to entrust to anyone else aboard the *Hawking*. It was a privilege as well as a burden of command. He slept badly, and woke to the sight of Maggie perching on the foot of his recliner, inspecting him with a physician's eye.

"Howdy, Skipper," she said quietly. "The Gersons tell me it's a good day for a battle."

He let out a sigh and closed his eyes briefly, massaging the bridge of his nose to clear the cobwebs from his brain.

"Is it time?" he asked.

"Just about," she said. "The Meds have done their part. The ship is rigged, and the tech staff are briefing the Gerson crew." For just an instant her professional demeanor slipped. "Oh, Anton, they're so personable, so quick and eager to learn. I hate to see us lose them."

"Yeah," Brand said, "war's a bitch." He sat up, rubbing both hands across his face. "How are the remaining Gersons handling it?"

Maggie shrugged, back in control. "They're not happy, as you can imagine. I've had to sedate a few, including Joli. I took the liberty of commandeering one of the staff lounges and having a direct feed piped in from battle ops, so that at least they can watch the battle sequence. I wasn't going to do it, but one of the old-timers said she wanted to be able to tell cubs of later generations how their ancestors died for a good cause."

Brand buried his face momentarily in one hand. "Are there going to be later generations, Mags?" he asked.

"If we don't fight this battle and win it, there certainly won't be," she replied. "Are you okay?"

"Yeah," he said, getting to his feet. "Just not in a hurry to send that ship out. Is Tashi on the bridge?"

"He is." She set a hypospray against his wrist and triggered it before he could object. "That's just a bit of stimulant. You should feel it in a few seconds."

He could feel it already, a pleasant coolness spreading up his arm and through his body, clearing his brain like a wave of ice water. He drew a deep breath and let it out with a whoosh. His body was ready to cope, even if the task ahead was one of the most difficult he had ever had thrust his way.

"Okay," he said. "Let's go."

Up on the bridge, Tashi gave way immediately as Brand and Maggie came out of the transit passage, though he crouched down beside the command chair as Brand took his seat.

"Mind if I stay?" Tashi asked. "I've done the setup. I'd like to be here for the resolution."

For answer, Brand gestured for him to open one of the pull-out seats that allowed someone to sit on either side of the command chair. He opened the other one for Maggie. The tech support crew were glancing up from the command pit as Brand put on a headset and settled in, running his fingers over the control pad under his right hand and already calling up a readout under his left.

"All right, ladies and gentlemen, this is not a drill," Brand said, flashing through a sequence of battle perspectives in the tank ahead and then narrowing on a red-lit view of the command cabin of the *Buthelezi.* "Hooth, this is Brand. Is everything to your satisfaction?"

The Gerson leader swiveled in his command chair and looked directly into the camera pickup. The red lighting softened the ursine lines of his muzzle and rounded ears and made him look far less alien than he did in person.

"We are well pleased, Commander," Hooth's translated voice said. "We cannot thank you enough for this opportunity to save both our race and our pride. May Harsha of the Battles smile on all our endeavors today."

"A bit of Gerson theology," Maggie murmured, close by Brand's ear. "The first time it's come out. God, we had so much to learn from them. And now there's no time."

With a gesture to desist, Brand made the camera pan around the *Buthelezi*'s control room. The other Gersons in sight were all mature males as well, some of them almost white-muzzled. As the camera panned back to Hooth, Brand raised a hand open-palmed in the universal gesture of friendship and farewell.

"Hail and farewell, Hooth," he said, keeping his voice steady with an effort. "There may not be time when we enter normal space and launch you. You're sure you want to go through with this?"

Hooth only nodded slowly, then touched a button that put the destroyer's ID number on the screen instead of the view of the control room. Respecting their wish for privacy, Brand shifted his perspective to a view outside the *Buthelezi,* from near the security lock.

"How many?" he asked Maggie as he memorized every line of the doomed destroyer.

"Thirty-one, down from the usual forty," she replied. "Faber was able to eliminate some of the normal crew positions. Other than Hooth, they're the older ones, as you saw."

"Does that leave you enough to work with?" he asked.

She shrugged. "It's what I've got. It will have to be enough. We have the crew's donations on ice, though. There isn't a whole lot more we can do, for now."

"Right." He slapped his controls and put up a view of a perspective from the *Hawking* toward the beleaguered Emry planet. Out beyond the white-glowing horizon that was the *Hawking*'s reference point, scores of white and blue dots were scattered like diamonds against a field of void. And far beyond, the faintly green-glowing pip that was the Emry planet, surrounded by a reddish glow.

"Helm, do we have that course plotted in?"

"Aye, sir," one of the stations replied as a new schematic came up in the holotank with a white-flashing light in the midst of red and blue ones. "Insertion at the point indicated should give us very close to three minutes to get the *Buthelezi* away and even launch some SBs that have just returned to rearm to provide a diversion, if everything goes according to plan."

"What is the chance we will drop back in an acceptable location?" the station's commander demanded of his chief navigation officer. If they dropped back too close, there was a chance of the *Hawking*'s warp drive interacting with one of the Ichton ships. The result would be a spectacular explosion and total disaster.

"There is no way to tell, sir," the Khalian replied honestly. "We've never done anything like this before. But my instincts say we will."

"What's the risk to the *Hawking*?" Brand then asked the gunnery chief.

"Less than losing Emry, sir," the tall Perdidan lieutenant answered with the typical bluntness of his culture. "We can pretarget the plasma cannons and missile tubes in a general way, and even let loose with the laser belts, once we're there. Give cover fire, until the *Buthelezi*'s far enough away for us to warp out again."

"Fleet standing by?"

"Aye, sir," came another voice. "We've got both battle plans ready to go, depending on your orders."

"Very well." Brand keyed a switch on his console. "All sections, rig for battlestations. Sound general quarters. This is not a drill. Emergency services, stand by. All sections, report."

His words produced action that set off alarm signals all over the ship. The winking lights on a tote board up on his left told of stations securing, section by section. The civilians aboard were not going to be happy, but it couldn't be helped.

"Stand by, Helm," he said as the last of the lights lit to green. "Prepare to go hyperspace on my mark—now!"

He felt the ship leap to his command, the jarring shudder of megatons of matter being wrenched into another dimension, the accompanying surge of vertigo that was the body's way of acknowledging that shift of existence. All the exterior screens had gone to white, for a ship in hyperspace jump was blind and deaf.

He found himself almost holding his breath as he counted out the mere seconds that the jump would last, for the battle zone he had selected was only light-seconds from where they had begun.

The ship wrenched again, and they were back in normal space. Instantly the screens lit back to life, reading out new data. Not more than a few hundred kilometers away, three of the oak leaf–shaped Ichton mother ships were hanging in formation amid a cloud of lesser escort ships, the disk of the Emry planet huge behind them. A tally to his right told of the destroyer bay already opening to let the *Buthelezi* into space.

The *Hawking* shuddered as the two massive plasma cannons at either pole began firing toward the Ichton ships, dozens of small, swift fighters now streaming out of the *Hawking*'s fighter bays to engage the enemy. As the missile tubes laid down covering fire, the belts of laser cannons also opened up, picking off Ichton escort vessels and splashing harmlessly off the strong shields of the three mother ships, now turning ponderously to head away from the growing battle.

Soon the *Buthelezi* was physically clear, though not yet clear of the *Hawking*'s mag fields if the latter attempted to warp out. Brand ceased fire in the *Buthelezi*'s direction as she moved out, already heading straight for the mother ships, picking up speed as she launched her own covering screen of missiles to clear a path before her. Other Ichton ships were being drawn to the mother ships' defense, several light cruisers and a dreadnought, which suddenly diverted when it noticed the *Hawking* and began closing fast.

"How long until we can warp?" Brand demanded, watching the dreadnought close. "Get that guy."

The *Hawking* adjusted attitude and the massive spinal-mounted plasma cannons spoke, sending bolt after bolt against the dreadnought's shields. Brand could see its shields starting to overload, but would it be in time? More Ichton ships were aware of the *Hawking*'s presence now, turning increasing firepower upon her. Beyond, the *Buthelezi* was almost clear of the *Hawking*'s shields. Any second now—

"Helm, go hyperspace at will," he said. "Helm, you're cutting this awfully close—"

The wrench of the hyperdrive kicking in coincided almost exactly with the shield overload on the approaching dreadnought. As the ship steadied into hyperspace, Brand was sure they must have taken some damage. Alarm lights blinking on several of his tote boards confirmed it.

"Damage Control, give me status reports," he demanded. "Can you sustain return warp?"

Mercifully, the responses coming in confirmed that damage thus far was slight. But meanwhile, they were deaf and blind to the fate of the *Buthelezi*. He glanced again at the helmsman, aware that this was a slightly longer jump, calculated to bring them out almost directly opposite from where they had first departed. The ship wrenched again, and they were back in normal space.

Frantically he searched for the display that would show the *Buthelezi* going after the mother ships. An automatic touch of the correct button transferred it to the holotank.

Even as he watched, two red dots flared and disappeared. The screens on one of the mother ships were glowing brighter, edging into blue—

"Go, Hooth!" Brand found himself whispering, one clenched fist pounding gently on the display screen in his chair arm. "Get the bastards!"

As if in answer to his prayer, the screens flared into violet and then white incandescence. A cheer went up among the bridge staff as the screen cleared and the mother ship was gone. Already the *Buthelezi* was forging on toward the next mother ship—and hordes of smaller Ichton escorts were converging on the attacker.

"No," Brand whispered. "Let him get another one. Helm, stand by to reengage."

"Commander?"

"Pick me a spot nearby, and be ready to engage!" Brand snapped. "Prepare to redirect every ship we've got, to follow through. Hooth is opening us a window. Let's use the chance he's buying us at such a cost."

He could see the screens on the *Buthelezi* starting to overload now. The red dots were converging on the beleaguered Fleet destroyer. Soon it would be too late to turn it into a miniature sun. If Hooth waited too long—

Suddenly the entire screen lit up in a gigantic wash of brilliant white light. The tank sensors stopped down immediately to damp the glare, but for just a few seconds circuits overloaded and the entire tank went dark. As a murmur of consternation whispered among the bridge staff, emergency circuits kicked in and the tank relit. It took a second to reorient.

As the image steadied, one thing became immediately clear. The *Buthelezi* was gone, but so were both the remaining mother ships and nearly every Ichton escort that had been on the screen.

"Well done, Hooth!" Brand whispered, almost in awe of what the Gerson had accomplished. "All right, Helm. Let's make it count for something. Is the Fleet ready to shift?"

"Aye, sir."

"Then go FTL—now."

In the weeks and months to come, the battle for Emry would be cited as one of the greatest Fleet victories in the war against the Ichtons. Commander Anton Brand's bold move in taking the *Stephen Hawking* directly into battle was questioned in command circles, but no one could question the result. The *Hawking* sustained heavy damage, especially in the civilian sectors, but the back of the Ichton fleet was broken. Of the five remaining mother ships either on the surface or in orbit around the Emry planet, only one escaped, with a ragtag escort of less than a dozen small ships. Losses in the rest of the Alliance fleet were minimal: one destroyer and perhaps a score of fighters.

But that this had been made possible by the bravery and self-sacrifice of the Gerson crew of the *Buthelezi,* no one could deny. Later that evening, when the battle was over and the worst of the emergencies were under control, deep in space, where the *Hawking* had withdrawn to lick her wounds, Brand went down to the room where the rest of the Gersons were waiting. Maggie Conroy came with him, still blood-spattered from dealing with the injured.

Utter silence settled over the room as Brand came in. The last fifty-three Gersons in the universe slowly stood as Brand moved among them, the low mutters of their comments unintelligible by Brand's translator. They quieted as he turned to survey them, fifty-three pairs of black shoe-button eyes fixed on him in hope and fear.

"You—saw what happened today," Brand said quietly, gesturing toward the large viewscreen across one wall, now blank. "I'm not certain you understood what you saw, but the Emry planet has been saved. Not only that, but the Ichton fleet was routed and mostly destroyed. We know of only one mother ship that got away, along with a very small number of escorts."

He paused to glance at his feet and draw a fortifying breath.

"Unfortunately, a lot of other good people died in today's battle. But I can tell you that the bravest of them all were your Gerson loved ones who went out of here to avenge the death of your planet and put their lives on the line to save another race from a like fate. I stand in awe of what Hooth and the others did today. I want you to know that the Alliance appreciates the sacrifice they made. We will not forget."

He could not go on at that point, but one of the Gerson females came closer with a cub in tow, ducking her head in commiseration. Through the dull numbness of his grief, Brand realized that it was Joli, Hooth's mate.

"We will not forget either, Commander Brand," she said, the nasal growl of her actual voice coming through the translator as a pleasant alto. "And we will not forget what you and the Healer Maggie have made possible. We came to the Alliance convinced that our race was doomed to extinction, but you have given us hope that the Gerson might become a people once again."

Maggie pursed her lips. "It's a long shot, Joli. I told you that when we started."

Joli's bear-jaws trembled, the shoe-button eyes moist with tears. "It was a 'long shot,' what Hooth and the others attempted to do," she said. "But they succeeded. And we shall succeed. We shall do it in their memory. You will see, when peace is restored."

She turned away at that, heavy shoulders shuddering in the ursine equivalent of weeping, and Brand had never felt so helpless. He was turning too when the Gerson cub came close enough to put its furry paw in his hand, turning liquid black eyes to his. It said nothing, but no words were needed.

This was why the Alliance had fought today. Not for this particular Gerson cub, but for all the young of all the races under threat of annihilation by the Ichton. Brand supposed that the Ichtons might offer the same argument—that their expansion had to do with the young of their race. But the Ichtons must be taught moderation. There was room in the universe for all beings, if each race learned to respect the right of others to exist.

There would be more mere battles to see which side could kill the most of their opponents, but ultimately communication must be established to make the Ichtons understand. As Brand stroked a hand gently across the Gerson cub's head, he decided that perhaps all of today's sacrifices had been worthwhile, if that message eventually got through.

BEQUEST

THE BATTLE OF EMRY was a tactical success. The Ichton fleet was shattered and the Emry home world saved. On another level it had been a painfully Pyrrhic victory. The Fleet had suffered losses that more than balanced out all the reinforcements they had received so far. Further, many of the surviving warships were far from combat worthy. The *Hawking* itself had suffered major damage on virtually all levels. Over three hundred crewmen and civilians had died when a force of thirty Ichton fighters had made suicidal plunges at the battlestation. Six had broken through the defenses and smashed through the hull. Worse yet, one of the massive plasma cannon was disabled and couldn't be repaired without parts only available in the Alliance.

Two weeks later Commander Brand called a meeting of the Squam, Emry, and other allied commanders. Anton Brand had to admit that what remained of their combined forces could not win another such battle. He also presented new intelligence showing that the Ichtons were massing another fleet off the ruins of the Gerson home world. This new fleet was already half again larger than the one they had just defeated. Brand had requested more reinforcements, but there was a limit to what the Alliance, surrounded by potentially hostile neighbors, could spare. Nor was he sure the Senate would much longer support a losing cause.

Intelligence was still erratic. They had no idea how many worlds the Ichtons controlled. Nor if they were even facing the bulk of the invader's forces. The insectoids could well have a dozen more fleets farther up the spiral arm than these had disgorged from. Emry was now too devastated to supply any of the parts or metals needed for repairs. They would have to move the *Hawking* and her fleet close to another intact world and hope the Ichtons did not return to Emry before they had accumulated sufficient strength to meet them.

The *Hawking* had arrived three years earlier hoping to create a military solution to the threat. The idea had then been to make it too costly for the Ichtons to continue their rampage. They had since achieved, at best, mixed results. Of the three races the battlestation had come to assist, two had virtually ceased to exist and the home world of the third lay in ruins.

Although they had completely destroyed one Ichton armada at great cost, the only visible result was that another larger fleet was forming as they spoke. The conclusion was painfully obvious. Any purely military solution was impossible. They could hurt the Ichtons, but were losing a war of attrition. Another approach was needed.

The obvious solution was to convince the Ichtons it was to their advantage to cease pillaging the galaxy. Something no other race had demonstrably ever achieved. And something they certainly had just failed to do militarily. After more hours of debate the diplomats were called in. They too were forced to admit there seemed no way to get the Ichtons to talk, much less of moderating their instinct-driven behavior. All that could be suggested was a holding action. Holding until another way presented itself. If it ever did.

Fortunately the needed solution presented itself only a few months later.

FAILURE MODE

by David Drake

IN THE MIRROR-FINISHED door to the admiral's office, Sergeant Dresser saw the expression on his own face: worn, angry, and—if you looked deep in the eyes—as dangerous as a grenade with the pin pulled.

"You may go in, sir," repeated Admiral Horwarth's human receptionist in a tart voice.

Dresser was angry.

Because he'd gone through normal mission debriefing and he should have been off duty. Instead he'd been summoned to meet the head of Bureau 8, Special Projects.

Because it had been a tough mission, and he'd failed.

And because he'd just watched a planet pay the price *all* life would pay for the mission's failure. Even the Ichtons would die, when they'd engulfed everything in the universe beyond themselves.

"The admiral is *waiting,* Sergeant," said the receptionist, a blond hunk who could have broken Dresser in half with his bare hands; but that wouldn't matter, because bare hands were for when you were out of ammo, your cutting bar had fried, and somebody'd nailed your boots to the ground . . .

Dresser tried to stiff-arm the feral gray face before him. The door panel slid open before he touched it. He strode into the office of Admiral Horwarth, a stocky, middle-aged woman facing him from behind a desk.

On the wall behind Horwarth was an Ichton.

If Dresser had had a weapon, he'd have shot the creature by reflex, even though his conscious mind knew he was seeing a holographic window into the Ichton's cell somewhere else on the *Stephen Hawking*. The prisoner must be fairly close by, because formic acid from its exoskeletal body tinged the air throughout Special Projects' discrete section of the vessel.

People like Dresser weren't allowed weapons aboard the *Hawking*. Especially not when they'd just returned from a mission and the Psych readout said they were ten-tenths stressed—besides having to be crazy to pilot a scout boat to begin with.

"Sit down, Sergeant," Admiral Horwarth said. She didn't sound concerned about what she must have seen on Dresser's face. "I'm sorry to delay your downtime like this, but—"

She smiled humorlessly.

"—this is important enough that I want to hear it directly from you."

Dresser grimaced as he took the offered chair. "Yeah, I understand," he said. "Sir."

And the hell of it was, he did. Even tired and angry—and as scared as he was—Dresser was too disciplined not to do his duty. Scouts without rigid self-discipline didn't last long enough for anybody else to notice their passing.

"I suppose it was a considerable strain," Horwarth prodded gently, "having to nursemaid two scientists and not having a normal crew who could stand watches?"

Dresser had been staring at the Ichton. He jerked his gaze downward at the sound of the admiral's voice. "Sorry, sir," he muttered. "No, that wasn't much of a problem. For me. The trip, that's the AI's job. There's nothing for human crews to do. I—"

Dresser looked at his hands. He waggled them close in front of his chest. He'd been told you could identify scouts because they almost never met the eyes of other human beings when talking to them. "Scouts, you know, anybody who's willing to do it more than once. Scouts keep to themselves. The boat isn't big enough to, to interact."

He raised his eyes to the Ichton again. It was walking slowly about its cell on its two lower pairs of limbs. The top pair and their gripping appendages were drawn in tight against the creature's gray carapace.

"The scientists," Dresser continued flatly, "Bailey and Kaehler . . . they weren't used to it. I think they were pretty glad when we got to the landing point, even though it didn't look like the right place . . ."

"You've done something wrong, Dresser!" snarled Captain Bailey as *Scout Boat 781*'s braking orbit brought the vessel closer to the surface of the ruined planet. "This place hasn't beaten off an Ichton attack. It's been stripped!"

"At this point, sir," Dresser said, "I haven't done anything at all except initiate landing sequence. The artificial intelligence took us through sponge space to the star that the—source—provided. There's only one life-capable planet circling that star, and we're landing on it."

He couldn't argue with Bailey's assessment, though. Mantra—properly, the name of the project file rather than the nameless planet itself—was utterly barren. Only the human-breathable atmosphere indicated that the planet's lifelessness resulted from an outside agency rather than incapacity to support life.

The agency had almost certainly been a swarm of Ichtons. The chitinous monsters had devoured the surface of the planet, to feed themselves and to build a fleet of colony ships with which to infect additional worlds. The Ichtons were a cancer attacking all life . . .

Mantra was gray rubble, waterless and sterile. Before they left, the invaders had reduced the planet to fist-sized pellets of slag, waste from their gigantic processing mills. The landscape over which the scout boat sizzled contained no hills, valleys, or hope.

"Chance wouldn't have brought us to a solar system, Captain," Kaehler said. She was small for a woman, even as Bailey was large for a man; and unlike her companion, she was a civilian without military rank. "It must be the correct location."

When Dresser thought about Kaehler, it appeared to him that she'd been stamped through a mold of a particular shape rather than grown to adulthood in the normal fashion. Events streamed through the slight woman without being colored by a personality.

Dresser thought about other people only when they impinged on his mission.

Dresser remembered that he wasn't dealing with scout crewmen. "Hang tight," he said. Even so, he spoke in a soft voice.

The AI pulsed red light across the cabin an instant after Dresser's warning. A heartbeat later, the landing motors fired with a harsh certainty that flung the three humans against their restraints.

Approach thresholds for scout boats were much higher than the norm for naval vessels, and enormously higher than those of commercial ships. The little boats might have to drop into a box canyon at a significant fraction of orbital velocity in order to survive. The hardware was stressed to take the punishment, and the crews got used to the experience—or transferred out of the service.

SB 781 crunched down at the point Dresser had chosen almost at random. They were in the mid-latitudes of Mantra's northern hemisphere. That was as good as any other place on the featureless globe.

"Well, sirs . . ." Dresser said. The restraints didn't release automatically. Scout boats were liable to come to rest at any angle, including inverted. The pilot touched the manual switch, freeing himself and the two scientists. "Welcome to Mantra."

"Was there a problem with the equipment?" Admiral Horwarth asked. "The Mantra Project was the first field trial, as I suppose you know."

She gave the scout a perfunctory smile. "I don't imagine that information stays compartmented within a three-man unit."

The Ichton turned to face the pickups. It seemed to be staring into the admiral's office, but that was an illusion. The link with the prisoner's cell was certainly not two-way; and in any case, the Ichton's multiple eyes provided a virtually spherical field of view, though at low definition by human standards.

"The equipment?" Dresser said. "No, there wasn't any difficulty with the equipment."

He laughed. He sounded on the verge of hysteria.

"There," Kaehler called as the pole set a precise hundred meters from the imaging heads locked into focus on her display. "We have it."

"I'll decide that!" Captain Bailey replied from the support module twenty meters away. He shouted instead of using the hard-wired intercom linking the two units.

The breeze blew softly, tickling Dresser's nose with the smell of death more ancient than memory. He watched over Kaehler's shoulder as the image of the pole quivered and the operator's color-graduated console displays bounded up and down the spectrum—

Before settling again into the center of the green, where they had been before Bailey made his last set of adjustments.

"There!" Captain Bailey announced with satisfaction.

They'd placed the imaging module twenty meters from *SB 781*'s side hatch. The support module containing the fusion power supply and the recording equipment was a similar distance beyond. A red light on top of the fusion bottle warned that it was pressurized to operating levels.

Though there was a monitor in the support module, Bailey had decreed that in the present climate they needn't deploy the shelters that would have blocked his direct view of the imaging module's three-meter display. If Kaehler had an opinion, the captain didn't bother to consult it.

Kaehler folded her hands neatly on her lap. "What has this proved?" Dresser asked, softly enough that he wouldn't intrude if the scientist was really concentrating instead of being at rest as she appeared to be.

Kaehler turned. "We've calibrated the equipment," she said. "We've achieved a lock on the target post, one second in the past. We'll be able to range as far back as we need to go when the artificial intelligence harmonizes the setting with the actual output of the power supply."

"That's what the captain's doing?" Dresser asked with a nod.

"The artificial intelligence is making the calculation," Kaehler said. "Captain Bailey is watching the AI while it works. I presume."

Dresser looked from Kaehler to the pole, then to the horizon beyond. "I don't see how it could work," he said to emptiness. "A second ago—the planet rotates on its axis, it circles the sun, the *sun* moves with its galaxy. Time is distance. Time isn't—"

He gestured toward the distant target.

"—the same place on a gravel plain."

Kaehler shrugged. "In this universe, perhaps not," she said. "We're accessing the past through the Dirac Sea. The normal universe is only a film on the—"

She shrugged again. It was the closest to a display of emotion Dresser had seen from her.

"—surface. Time isn't a dimension outside the normal universe."

"Kaehler!" Captain Bailey shouted. "Stop talking to that taxi driver and begin the search sequence. We've got a job to do, woman!"

The target pole hazed slightly in Dresser's vision, though the holographic image remained as sharp as the diamond-edged cutting bar on the scout's harness.

"I wanted to learn what it did," Dresser said in the direction of the image on the admiral's wall display. "I don't like to be around hardware and not know what it does. That's dangerous."

Admiral Horwarth glanced over her shoulder to see if anything in particular was holding the scout's attention. The Ichton rubbed its upper limbs across its wedge-shaped head as though cleaning its eyes. It raised one of its middle pair of legs and scrubbed with it also.

Horwarth looked around again. "Captain Bailey was able to find the correct time horizon, then?" she prompted.

"Not at first," Dresser said in his husky, emotionless voice. "You said five thousand years."

"The source believed the event occurred five thousand standard years ago," the admiral corrected. "But there were many variables."

"Kaehler went back more than ten thousand," Dresser said, "before she found anything but a gravel wasteland . . ."

"There," Kaehler said. Bailey, watching the monitor in the support module, bellowed, "Stop! I've got it!"

Dresser was watching the display when it happened. He might not have been. The search had gone on for three watches without a break, and Mantra's own long twilight was beginning to fall.

The pulsing, colored static of the huge hologram shrank suddenly into outlines as the equipment came into focus with another time. The score of previous attempts displayed a landscape that differed from that of the present only because the target pole was not yet a part of it. This time—this Time—the view was of smooth, synthetic walls in swirls of orange and yellow.

Kaehler rocked a vernier. The images blurred, then dollied back to provide a panorama instead of the initial extreme close-up. Slimly conical buildings stood kilometers high. They were decorated with all the hues of the rainbow as well as grays that might be shades beyond those of the human optical spectrum. Roadways linked the structures to one another and to the ground, like the rigging of sailing ships. Moving vehicles glinted in the sunlight.

"Not that!" Bailey shouted. "Bring it in close so that we can see what they look like."

Kaehler manipulated controls with either index finger simultaneously. She rolled them—balls inset into the surface of her console—off the tips and down the shafts of her fingers. The scale of the image shrank while the apparent point of view slid groundward again.

Dresser, proud of the way he could grease a scout boat in manually if he had to, marveled at the scientist's smooth skill.

"Get me a close-up, damn it!" Bailey ordered.

The huge image quivered under Kaehler's control before it resumed its slant downward. "We're calibrating the equipment," she said in little more than a whisper. "We're not in a race . . ."

Pedestrians walked in long lines on the ground among the buildings. Vehicles zipped around them like balls caroming from billiard cushions instead of curving as they would have done if guided by humans.

The locals, the Mantrans, were low-slung and exoskeletal. They had at least a dozen body segments with two pairs of legs on each. They carried the upper several segments off the ground. A battery of simple eyes was set directly into the chitin of the head.

Kaehler manually panned her point of view, then touched a switch so that the AI would continue following the Mantran she had chosen. The alien was about two meters long. Its chitinous body was gray, except for a segment striped with blue and green paint.

"They have hard shells, too," Kaehler commented. "You'd think the Ichtons might treat them better."

"The Ichtons don't spare anything," Dresser said softly. He had once landed on a planet while an Ichton attack was still going on. Then he added, "On our bad days, humans haven't been notably kind toward other mammaliforms."

"Kaehler, for God's sake, start bringing the image forward in time!" Captain Bailey shouted. "We aren't here as tourists. We won't see the locals' superweapon until after the Ichtons land. Get with the program, woman!"

Kaehler began resetting the controls on her console. Her face was expressionless, as usual.

"Humans," Dresser said, looking over the stark landscape, "haven't always done real well toward other humans."

Dresser glanced at Admiral Horwarth, then shifted his gaze to the captive again. He continued to watch the admiral out of the corners of his eyes.

"They had a high tech level, the Mantrans," Dresser said. "I made myself believe that they could have built something to defeat the Ichtons. But I knew they hadn't, because—"

Dresser swept both hands out in a fierce gesture, palms down.

"—I could *see* they hadn't," he snarled. "There was nothing. The Ichtons had processed the whole planet down to waste. There was nothing! Nothing for us to find, no reason for us to be there."

"Our source was very precise," Horwarth said gently. "The Ichtons have genetic memory, which our source is able to tap. Mantra was a disaster for them, which has remained imprinted for, you say *ten,* thousands of years."

The "source" was an Ichton clone, controlled by a human psyche. Dresser knew that, because the psyche was Dresser's own.

The scout began to shiver. He clasped his hands together to control them. With his eyes closed, he continued, "It took Kaehler an hour to get dialed in on the moment of the Ichton assault. Bailey badgered her the whole time . . ."

"I think—" Kaehler said.

A bead of blue fire appeared at the top of the image area. The terrain beneath was broken. The Ichton mother ship had appeared in the southern hemisphere. *SB 781*'s navigational computer told Dresser that the vector was probably chance. The Ichtons didn't appear to care where they made their approach.

The display turned white.

"Kaehler!" Bailey shouted. "You've lost the—"

"No!" Dresser said. "They follow an antimatter bomb in. That's how they clear their landing zones."

The white glare mottled into a fire storm, roaring to engulf a landscape pulverized by the initial shock wave. For an instant, rarefaction from an aftershock cleared the atmosphere enough to provide a glimpse of the crater, kilometers across and a mass of glowing rock at the bottom.

The Ichton mother ship continued to descend in stately majesty. A magnetic shield wrapped the enormous hull. Its flux gradient was so sharp that it severed the bonds of air molecules and made the vessel gleam in the blue and ultraviolet range of the spectrum.

Kaehler's right hand moved to a set of controls discrete from those that determined the imaging viewpoint in the physical dimensions. As her finger touched a roller, Captain Bailey ordered, "Come on, come on, Kaehler. Advance it so that we can see the response! It's—"

The display began to blur forward, if Time had direction. Bailey continued to speak, though it must have been obvious that Kaehler had anticipated his command.

"—the response that's important, not some explosion."

The glowing mother ship remained steady. The Mantran reaction to being invaded was violent and sustained. War swirled around the huge vessel like sparks showering from a bonfire.

Kaehler advanced the temporal vernier at an increasing rate, letting the ball roll off her finger and onto the palm of her hand. She reached across her body with the other hand and switched a dial that increased the log of the rate.

A convoy of Ichton ground vehicles left the mother ship while the rock of the crater still shimmered from the antimatter explosion. The twenty vehicles had not escaped the frame of the display when the Mantrans engaged them from air and ground.

Ichton weapons fired flux generators like those that served the creatures as armor. The shearing effect of their magnetic gradients—particularly those of the heavy weapons mounted on the mother ship—wreaked havoc with the defenders, but the quickly mounted Mantran counterattack nonetheless overwhelmed the convoy vehicle by vehicle. The last to disintegrate in a fluorescent fireball was a gigantic cylinder carrying the eggs that were to be the basis of a new colony.

The Ichtons didn't send out further convoys. Instead, they ripped at the defenders with their flux generators. At intervals, the mother ship lofted missiles that exploded with the flash and actinics of antimatter when the Mantrans blew them up. Very rarely, a missile disappeared from Kaehler's display without being destroyed.

Mantran earthworks grew around the mother ship like mosaic virus expanding across a tobacco leaf. The defenders' weapons bombarded the vessel ceaselessly, but the Ichton armor absorbed even fusion bombs without damage.

"This isn't where they'll develop it," Bailey said abruptly. "We need to check their arsenals, their laboratories."

Kaehler didn't react. She continued to move the image in time without changing the spatial point of focus.

"This is where they'll deploy any weapon," Dresser snapped. "This is where we need to be for now."

Bailey was in command of the expedition and the scout's superior by six grades. Dresser didn't care. The command had been foolish. One of the reasons Dresser was a scout was his inability to suffer fools in silence, whatever the fools' rank.

On the display, seasons blurred between snow and baked, barren earth. All life but that armored within the mother ship and the defenders' lines was blasted away by the mutual hellfire. The sky above *SB 781* darkened, but the huge hologram lighted the boat and the watching humans.

"Stop playing with the scale, Kaehler," Captain Bailey ordered. "I'll tell you if I want a close-up."

Kaehler looked startled. Her hands were slowly working the temporal controls, but she hadn't touched the spatial unit since she initially focused on the mother ship.

"It's not the scale that's changing," Dresser said. "It's the ship. It's expanding the volume covered by its shields, despite anything the Mantrans can do."

The innermost ring of Mantran defenses crumbled as the blue glare swelled, meter by meter. Seasons washed across the landscape like a dirty river . . .

• • •

Dresser unclenched his hands. He looked at Admiral Horwarth in embarrassment for being so close to the edge. "It was like gangrene, sir," he said. "Have you seen somebody with gangrene?"

She shook her head tautly. "No," she said. "I can imagine."

"You can't cure it," the scout said, speaking toward the Ichton again. The creature was huddled in a corner of its cell. "They just keep cutting pieces off and hope they got it all. Which they probably didn't."

"But the Mantrans *were* able to hold?" Horwarth prompted.

The scout shrugged. "For years," he said, "but it didn't matter. The fighting was poisoning the whole planet. The atmosphere, the seas . . . The land for hundreds of kilometers from the mother ship was as dead as the floor of Hell. The Ichtons didn't care. The whole Mantran infrastructure was beginning to break down."

Dresser laced his fingers again. "Then the Ichtons sent out another convoy . . ."

Dresser looked from Kaehler to Bailey. Both scientists were glassy-eyed with fatigue.

"Ah, Captain Bailey?" Dresser said.

Bailey didn't reply. He may not even have heard.

The display was a fierce blue glare that sparkled but never significantly changed. It was like watching the play of light across the facets of a diamond, mesmerizing but empty.

"Cap—"

Thousand-meter fireballs rippled suddenly at the north side of the mother ship's shields. Through them, as inexorable as a spear cleaving a rib cage, rocked a column of Ichton vehicles.

The leading tank spewed a stream of flux projectiles that gnawed deep into the Mantran defenses until a white-hot concentration of power focused down on the vehicle. The tank ripped apart in an explosion greater than any of those that destroyed it, widening the gap in the Mantran defensive wall.

The convoy's second vehicle was also a tank. It continued the work of destruction as it shuddered onward. The defenders' fire quivered on the Ichton shield, but the Mantrans couldn't repeat the concentration that had overwhelmed the leader.

"They can't stop it," Dresser whispered. "It's over."

The image volume went red/orange/white. The dense jewel of the mother ship blazed through a fog that warped and almost hid its outlines. The blur of seasons was lost in the greater distortion.

"Kaehler, what have you done, you idiot?" Bailey shouted. He stepped out of his module; hands clenched, face distorted in the light of the hologram. Except for the blue core, the image could almost be that of the display's standby mode—points of light in a random pattern, visual white noise.

Except for the Ichton mother ship at the blue heart of it.

"It wasn't . . ." Kaehler said as her hands played across her controls with a brain surgeon's delicacy, freezing the image and then reversing it in minute increments.

" . . . me!" The last word was a shout, the first time Dresser had heard Kaehler raise her voice.

The image froze again in time. A disk of the planet's surface, hundreds of kilometers in diameter, slumped and went molten. Its center was the Ichton vessel. Vaporized rock, atmospheric gases fused into long chains, and plasma bursting upward from subterranean thermonuclear blasts turned the whole viewing area into a hellbroth in which the states of matter were inextricably blended.

The scout understood what had happened before either of the scientists did. "They blew it down to the mantle," Dresser said. "The Mantrans did. Their weapons couldn't destroy the Ichtons, so they used the planet to do it."

And failed, but he didn't say that aloud.

Kaehler let the image scroll forward again, though at a slower rate of advance than that at which she had proceeded before. The Ichton convoy vanished, sucked into liquescent rock surging from the planet's core. Plates of magma cooled, cracked, and up-ended to sink again into the bubbling inferno.

Sulfur compounds from the molten rock spewed into the stratosphere and formed a reflective haze. The sky darkened to night, not only at the target site but over the entire planet. Years and decades went by as the crater slowly cooled. Night continued to cloak the chaos.

"Bring it back to the point of the explosion, Kaehler," the captain said. Bailey spoke in what was a restrained tone, for him.

For the first time during the operation he used the intercom instead of shouting his directions from the support module. "Freeze it at the instant the shock wave hit them. That must have been what destroyed the ship."

"It didn't destroy the ship," Kaehler said. Her voice had even less effect than usual. The image continued to advance.

The magnetic shields of the Ichton vessel provided the only certain light. The ship floated on a sea of magma, spherical and unchanged.

"They're dead inside it!" Bailey shouted. "Focus on the microsecond of the first shock wave!"

"You damned fool!" Kaehler shouted back. "I don't have that degree of control. We've got a hundred-millimeter aperture, or have you forgotten?"

Dresser watched Kaehler's profile as she spoke. She didn't look angry. Her face could have been a death mask.

The display continued to crawl forward. Lava crusted to stone. Cracks between solid blocks opened less frequently to cast their orange light across the wasteland. Century-long storms washed the atmosphere cleaner if not clean.

Bailey blinked and sat down in his module. Kaehler turned back to her controls.

"Their own people," she said in a voice that might not have been intended even for Dresser. "There were thousands of them in the defenses. They all died."

There had been millions of Mantrans in the defense lines.

"They couldn't pull them out," the scout said softly. "The defenses had to hold until the last instant, so that the mantle rupture would get all the Ichtons."

"Did they know they were going to die?" Kaehler whispered.

"They knew they'd all die anyway," Dresser said.

Everything in the universe would die.

The mother ship released a sheaf of missiles, bright streaks across the roiling sky. Their antimatter warheads exploded in the far distance, flickers of false dawn.

Three convoys set out from the mother ship simultaneously. Mantran forces engaged one convoy while it was still within the display area, but the vain attempt lighted the hummocks of lava as briefly as a lightning flash . . .

• • •

"I knew it was over then," Dresser said to his hands in the admiral's office. "I'd *known* it before. They don't quit. The Ichtons don't quit."

He looked at the captive again. It now lay on its back. Its six limbs moved slowly, as though they were separate creatures drifting in the currents of the sea.

"It may have been the failure of conventional techniques that forced the Mantrans to develop their superweapon," Horwarth suggested. She wasn't so much arguing with the scout as soothing him.

Dresser shook his head. "There was never a superweapon on Mantra, Admiral," he said. "Just death."

"Move us forward faster, Kaehler," Captain Bailey ordered over the intercom. "And—change the spatial viewpoint, I think. Follow a moving column."

For once, Dresser thought the captain had a point. There was nothing useful to be seen in the neighborhood of the mother ship.

Three more convoys set out across the cooling lava. These met no resistance.

Kaehler remained fixed, as though she were a wax dummy at her console.

There was nothing useful to be seen anywhere on the planet.

"Kaehler?"

The female scientist began to change settings with the cool precision of a machine that had just been switched on again. She did not speak.

The images on the display flip-flopped through abrupt changes in time and place. An image of all Mantra hung above the console. Half the planet was in sunlight. Yellow-lit cities of the indigenes and the blue speckles of Ichton colonies studded the remaining hemisphere.

For the moment, the colonies were small and there were only a few of them visible. For the moment.

Kaehler's fingers searched discrete blocks of time and space like an expert shuffling cards, throwing up images for a second or less before shifting to the next:

A barren landscape with neither Ichtons nor Mantrans present.

A distant nighttime battle, plasma weapons slamming out bolts of sulfurous yellow that made Ichton shields pulse at the edge of the ultraviolet. Just as Kaehler switched away, an antimatter warhead obliterated the whole scene.

Ichton machinery with maws a kilometer wide, harvesting not only a field of broad-leafed vegetation but the soil a meter down. Enclosed conveyors snaked out of the image area, carrying the organic material toward an Ichton colony. The invaders' tanks oversaw the process, but their waiting guns found no targets.

A Mantran city looming on the horizon—

"There!" Bailey called. "There, hold on that one!"

Kaehler gave no sign that she heard her superior, but she locked the controls back to a slow crawl again. Perhaps she'd intended to do that in any case.

Mantran resistance had devolved to the local level. This city was ringed with fortifications similar to those that the planet as a whole had thrown up around the Ichton mother ship. Though the defenses were kilometers deep, they were only a shadow of those that the invaders had breached around their landing zone.

The Ichton force approaching the city was a dedicated combat unit, not a colonizing endeavor. Turreted tanks guarded the flanks and rear of the invaders' column, but the leading vehicles were featureless tubes several hundred meters long. They looked like battering rams, and their purpose was similar.

The city's defenders met the column with plasma bolts and volleys of missiles. A tank, caught by several bolts and a thermonuclear warhead simultaneously, exploded. The failure of its magnetic shields was cataclysmic, rocking nearby vehicles as the Mantran bombardment had not been able to do.

For the most part, Ichton counterfire detonated the missiles before they struck. Plasma bolts could at best stall an Ichton target for a few moments while the vehicle directed the whole output of its power supply to the protective shields.

The tubular Ichton vehicles were built around flux generators as large as those of the mother ship's main armament. Three of them fired together. A section of the Mantran defenses vanished in a sun-bright dazzle. It shimmered with all the hues of a fire opal.

The gun vehicles crawled closer to the city. The height of the flux gradient of their projectiles was proportional to the cube of the distance from the launcher's muzzle. Even at a range of several hundred meters, the weapons sheared the intra-atomic bonds of the collapsed metal armoring the defenses.

All the available Mantran weaponry concentrated on the gun vehicles. The ground before their treads bubbled and seethed, and the nearest of the indigenes' fortifications began to slump from the fury of the defensive fire.

The Ichtons fired again; shifted their concentrated aim and fired again; shifted and fired. The gap before them was wide enough to pass the attacking column abreast. Counterfire ceased, save for a vain handful of missiles from launchers that hadn't quite emptied their magazines.

The column advanced. An inner line of plasma weapons opened up—uselessly.

In the ruins of the outer defenses, a few Mantrans thrashed. Muscles, broiled within their shells by heat released when nearby matter ionized, made the Mantrans' segmented bodies coil and knot.

Sergeant Dresser turned his head. He was a scout. He was trained to observe and report information.

There was nothing new to observe here.

"Kaehler!" Captain Bailey shouted from the edge of Dresser's conscious awareness. "Bring us forward by longer steps, woman! This isn't any good to us."

When Dresser faced away from the holographic display, he could see stars in the sky of Mantra. He wondered if any of them had planets that had escaped being stripped by the Ichton ravagers . . .

"Bailey figured," Dresser said in a voice too flat to hold emotion, "that we'd be able to tell when the superweapon was developed by its effect on the Ichtons. When we saw signs of the Ichtons retreating, of their colonies vanishing, then we'd know something had happened and work back to learn what."

Admiral Horwarth nodded. "That sounds reasonable," she said.

"They should've taken a break, Bailey and Kaehler," the scout added in a non sequitur. His mind, trapped in the past, bounced from one regret to another. "Going straight on, I knew it was a mistake, but I wasn't in charge."

Horwarth looked over her shoulder at the captive Ichton. The movement was a way of gaining time for her to decide how to respond. The Ichton still lay full length on the floor of its cell. Its limbs wrapped its torso tightly.

Horwarth turned again. "Should we have sent more than one team?" she asked. "Was that the problem?"

"No," Dresser said sharply. The harshness of his own voice surprised him.

"No, sir," he said, meeting the admiral's eyes in apology. "I don't think so. Time wasn't that crucial. Bailey got focused on finding the superweapon. The more clear it was that no such weapon existed—"

Dresser's anger blazed out unexpectedly. "The planet was a wasteland!" he snarled. "We knew that from the prelanding survey!"

"The Mantrans could have developed their weapon when it was too late to save their planet, you know," Horwarth suggested mildly. "What we have is evidence that the Ichtons were traumatized by the contact—not that the Mantrans survived it."

Dresser sighed. "Yeah," he said to his hands, "I told myself that. But Bailey—and I think maybe Kaehler, too, though it didn't hit her in the same way. They weren't focused on the long-term result anymore."

He shook his head at the memory. "They were too tired, and it was getting toward dawn . . ."

Captain Bailey walked toward them from the support module. For a moment, Dresser saw his head silhouetted against the telltale on top of the fusion bottle. The red glow licked around the captain's features like hellfire.

Bailey didn't speak. Kaehler had ignored the last several of his commands anyway.

On the display, two Mantrans huddled together on a plateau as invaders approached from all sides. There were probably fewer than a thousand indigenes surviving at this time horizon.

Kaehler waited like a statue. Her fingers poised above the controls. The apparatus scrolled forward at one second/second.

"How long has it been since the Ichtons landed?" Dresser asked quietly. He wasn't sure she would answer him either.

"Six hundred standard years," Kaehler replied without moving more than her lips. "At the time we're observing, the Mantran year was at two-eighty-one standard. The Ichtons took so much mass with them that the planet shifted to an orbit longer by forty days."

The atmosphere on the holographic display was so foul that the sun shone wanly even at noon. Nevertheless the image area was lighted vividly by the six Ichton colonies visible from this point. Each colony had grown as large as the mother ship was when it landed.

When the time was right—when everything useful on Mantra had been processed into Ichton equipment or Ichton flesh—the myriad colonies would blast off from the stripped planet. Each would be the mother ship of a fresh brood, capable of destroying a further world in logarithmic progression.

"What sort of equipment do the defenders have?" Captain Bailey asked. He was looking at Kaehler.

"They don't have anything, sir," Dresser replied. He knew—all three of them knew—that Kaehler wasn't going to speak. "I thought they were dead, but a few minutes again, they moved a little."

Military operations on Mantra had ceased generations before. The Ichton columns grinding away the rock on which the pair of indigenes sheltered were miners, not troops.

"Pan back a little ways, Kaehler," Bailey said. "I want to get a view of the enemy."

Kaehler didn't respond.

The Mantrans were life-size images above the purring console. One of them coiled more tightly. Bright yellow blotches of fungus were the only color on either body. Illumination from the Ichton colonies turned the hue to sickly green.

Bailey cursed under his breath. He stamped back toward the support module.

When her superior was halfway to his proper position, Kaehler adjusted her controls. The apparent viewpoint lifted, giving Dresser a view of the approaching Ichtons.

The plateau on which the pair of Mantrans lay was artificial. Mining equipment ground away the rock from six directions, lowering the surface of the plain—of the planet—by twenty meters. A snake of tubing connected each of the grinding machines to one of the Ichton colonies that squatted on the horizon. There the material would be sorted, processed, and built into the mother ship growing at the heart of each colony.

The closed conveyors gleamed with magnetic shields. Such protection was now unnecessary. Not even rain fell. Separate conveyor lines carried tailings, the waste that not even Ichton efficiency could use, into the ocean basins already drained by the invaders' requirements.

Cutting heads snuffled up and down the face rock, then moved in a shallow arc to either side with the close of each stroke. An Ichton in shimmering body armor rode each machine, but there was no obvious need for such oversight. The cutters moved like hounds casting, missing nothing in a slow inexorability that was far more chilling than a cat's lithe pounce.

Bits of the upper edge of the plateau dribbled into the maw of a cutter rising to the top of its stroke. One of the Mantrans coiled because the ground was shifting beneath its segmented body. Dresser wasn't sure that the movement was conscious. Certainly the indigene made no concerted effort to escape.

Not that escape was possible.

Kaehler touched her controls, focusing down on the two Mantrans. The images swelled to larger than life size. Edges lost definition.

One of the creatures was chewing on a piece of cloth. Its chitinous jaws opened and closed with a sideways motion. The fabric, a tough synthetic, remained unaffected by the attempt to devour it.

"The left one has a weapon!" Captain Bailey suddenly cried. "Increase the resolution, Kaehler! This must be it!"

Dresser could see that the Mantran, writhing as the plateau disintegrated beneath it, didn't have a weapon. The yellow fungus had eaten away much of the creature's underside. Most of its walking legs were withered, and one had fallen off at the root. That, hard-shelled and kinked at an angle, was what Bailey's desperation had mistaken for a weapon.

Kaehler turned toward her superior. "I can't increase the resolution with a hundred-millimeter aperture," she said in a voice as empty as the breeze.

Bailey stood at the edge of his module. His head was silhouetted by the telltale behind him. "You could if you were any good at your job!" he shouted. "I'm tired of your excuses!"

The cutting head rose into sight on the display. The Ichton riding it pointed his weapon, a miniature version of the flux generators that had devoured armor denser than the heart of a star.

Kaehler stared at Bailey. Her left hand raised a panel on the front of her console. She didn't look down at it.

Dresser touched the woman's shoulder with his left hand. He was icy cold. "Ah, ma'am?" he said.

"All right, Captain," Kaehler said in a voice like hoarfrost. "I'll enlarge—"

"Wait!" Bailey shouted.

Dresser didn't know what was about to happen, but he wouldn't have lived as long as he had without being willing to act decisively on insufficient data. He gripped Kaehler and tried to lift her out of her seat.

Kaehler's hand yanked at the control that had been caged within the console. Dresser saw Captain Bailey's face lighted brilliantly in the instant before another reality enveloped the imaging module and the two humans within it.

The Ichton fired, knocking the head off the nearer indigene with the easy nonchalance of a diner opening a soft-boiled egg. Rock beyond the Mantran disintegrated also, spraying grit into Dresser's face as his right hand snatched his cutting bar.

The air was foul with poisons not yet reabsorbed by ten thousand years of wind blowing through a filter of porous waste. The sky was black, and the horizon gleamed with Ichton colonies gravid with all-destroying life.

Kaehler had opened the viewing aperture to the point that it enveloped herself, her equipment—

And Sergeant Dresser, who hadn't carried a gun on a lifeless *desert,* for God's sake, only a cutting bar that wouldn't be enough to overload Ichton body armor. Dresser lunged for the monster anyway as it turned in surprise.

A stream of flux projectiles blew divots out of stone as the Ichton brought its weapon around. Kaehler didn't move.

Dresser's powered, diamond-toothed blade screamed and stalled in the magnetic shielding. He tried to grab the Ichton weapon but caught the limb holding it instead. The scout's fingers couldn't reach a material surface. Though he knew his arm was stronger than the exoskeletal monster's, his hand slipped as though he were trying to hold hot butter.

Dresser looked down the muzzle of the Ichton weapon.

He thought, when he hit the ground an instant later, that he was dead. Instead, he was sprawled beside *SB 781*. Plasma spewing from the fusion bottle formed a plume that melted the upper surfaces of the support module. It was brighter than the rising sun . . .

Dresser met Admiral Horwarth's eyes. "He'd vented the containment vessel," the scout said. "Bailey had. He knew it'd kill him, but it was the only way to shut the apparatus off fast enough from where he was."

"I've recommended Captain Bailey for a Fleet Cross on the basis of your report, Sergeant," Horwarth said quietly. "The—cause of your transition through the aperture will be given as equipment failure, though."

Dresser shrugged. His eyes were wide and empty, with a thousand-meter stare that took in neither the admiral nor the image of the motionless Ichton on the wall behind her.

"It wasn't Kaehler's fault," the scout said. His voice sank to a hoarse whisper. "She cracked, people do that. It wasn't a fault."

He blinked and focused on Horwarth again. "Is she going to be all right?" he asked. "She wouldn't talk, wouldn't even move on the trip back."

"I'll have a report soon," Horwarth said, a bland placeholder instead of an answer.

Dresser wrapped his arms tightly around his torso. "Maybe it wasn't Bailey's fault either," he said. "I figure he cracked, too. Even me, I'm used to the Ichtons, but it bothered me a bit. He wasn't ready to see the things he saw on Mantra."

"A bit" was a lie obvious to anyone but the man who said it.

Dresser's smile was as slight and humorless as the point of a dagger. "I brought his feet back in cold storage. Everything above the ankles, that the plasma got when he dumped the bottle."

"There doesn't appear to have been any flaw in the equipment itself, though," Horwarth said. "Until the damage incurred in the final accident."

"I was the one who screwed up," Dresser said to his past. "I should've grabbed her quicker. *I* was supposed to be the scout, the professional."

"When the equipment can be rebuilt," Admiral Horwarth said, clamping the scout with the intensity of her gaze, "there'll have to be a follow-up mission to complete the reconnaissance."

"No," said Dresser.

Horwarth ignored the word. "I'd appreciate it if you would consent to pilot the mission, Sergeant," she said. "You know better than almost anyone else how impor—"

"No!" Dresser shouted as he lurched to his feet. "*No,* you don't need a follow-up mission! We'd completed the mission, and we'd *failed.* That's why it happened, don't you see?"

"What I see is that the incident aborted Captain Bailey's mission before it reached closure," the admiral said.

She rose also and leaned forward on her desk, resting on her knuckles. Her voice rose as either her facade cracked or she let some of her real anger and frustration out as a means of controlling the scout. "What I see is that we *have* to find the weapon the Ichtons fear, because you've proved that no conventional weapon can defeat them in the long term."

"Admiral," Dresser begged.

He turned to the closed door behind him, then turned again. He didn't realize that he was crying until a falling tear splashed the back of his hand. "Sir. The coordinates were wrong, something was wrong. The only thing left to learn on Mantra was whether the last of the indigenes died of disease or starvation before the Ichtons got them."

Horwarth softened. She'd skimmed the recordings the expedition brought back. She didn't need Psych's evaluation of the two survivors to understand how the images would affect those who'd actually gathered them.

"Sergeant," she said, "something happened to the Ichtons before they spread from Mantra. It made memory of the place a hell for them ten thousand years later. We have to learn what."

"Sir . . ." Dresser whispered. He rubbed his eyes angrily, but he was still blind with memory. "Sir, I'll go back, I'll do whatever you want. But we failed, sir, because there was nothing there to succeed with. And since I watched Mantra eaten, I know just how bad we failed."

"We've got to try, Ser—" Admiral Horwarth began.

The electronic chime of an alarm interrupted her. Horwarth reached for a control on her desk.

Dresser's gaze focused on the holographic scene behind the admiral. Three humans wearing protective garments had entered the Ichton's cell. They stumbled into one another in their haste.

"Duty officer!" Admiral Horwarth snarled into her intercom. "What the hell is going on?"

Two of the attendants managed to raise the Ichton from the floor of the cell. The creature was leaking fluid from every joint. It was obviously dead.

The chitinous exoskeleton of the Ichton's torso was blotched yellow by patches of the fungus whose spores had traveled with Sergeant Dresser from the surface of a dying planet.